I0817857

THE
CENDOVIAN

THE CENDOVIAN CHRONICLES
BOOK 1

Mark Hennessy

This is a work of fiction. Names, characters, businesses, places, events, locales, and incidents are either the products of the author's imagination or used in a fictitious manner. Any resemblance to actual persons, living or dead, or actual events is purely coincidental, except in the case where actual historical figures or places are used in a fictitious manner. Bottom line, if you think it's about you, it's not.

ISBN: 978-1-7343877-2-8

Cendovia.com

DEDICATION

To Lourdes, my first reader, my most trusted counselor, and my eternal love. Without you this book would not exist.

CONTENTS

ACKNOWLEDGMENTS

Cover illustration and design by Jeff Brown
Developmental editing by Rebecca Brewer
Copy editing and proof reading by Lauren Smulski

CHAPTER 1 – ETERNAL VIGILANCE

Richard Nelson stood overlooking the shimmering San Francisco Bay from the fifth floor of his elite cybersecurity firm, Galanteen Systems. To everyone else, the crystal-blue sky and the gentle waves likely seemed calm and picturesque. But to Richard, this view would always serve as a painful reminder of all that he had lost.

The whir of a propeller filled Richard's ears as a Cessna only he could see descended rapidly toward the water, its angry engines screaming at a fever pitch. Richard winced as the plane smacked into the water, sending a sonic boom exploding in his chest. The aircraft flipped, rolled, and skipped across the bay, disintegrating into a trail of parts that were quickly swallowed by the tide.

Around him, an indifferent world moved forward, blithely unaware of Richard's vision as he surveyed the wreckage.

To his amazement, the pilot had been ejected from the cockpit and was swimming out to sea, away from an incoming Coast Guard ship. Richard's heart called for her to come back as the waves intermittently obscured her from his view. With each oscillation, his wife grew more distant, and by the time the rescue crew arrived, her left hand was the only part of her body still cresting the water. The glimmer from her wedding ring reflected in Richard's eyes as she slipped under.

That was the last sighting of Virginia Nelson.

The vivid imagery in Richard's mind had been pieced together from the events relayed to him two years earlier. He recalled clearly the moment the police officer had interrupted his computer science class at Stanford to inform him. Having just reached the crescendo of his famous superhero lecture, the news had sent Richard plummeting back to Earth. From that day forward, he met all interruptions with contempt—contempt for a world that believed Virginia was gone. Someday, he would prove them all wrong.

A familiar voice beckoned Richard back to the present, where Owen Bradenton, the president of Galanteen Systems, was briefing him about a recent cyberattack on one of their new customers.

"Over twenty million accounts were compromised. These kinds of breaches are on the rise of late," said Owen, delivering his report in the militaristic cadence that had been ingrained into him during his years in the Marines.

"It's good for business," said Richard, his thick British accent laced with only mild concern. "Though it's a shame they didn't come to us before the incident." Galanteen Systems was quietly regarded by foreign adversaries as impenetrable, and frustrated hackers quickly learned to move on to softer targets after encountering the firm's ironclad security protocols.

Continuing his briefing, Owen explained that the client had been infiltrated by what were almost certainly Chinese hackers. It wasn't a pure cyberattack—evidently an executive at the organization had been fooled into providing their credentials to a fake support technician over the phone, which required a certain amount of social engineering.

Turning around, Richard asked, "Owen, why are you telling me this? I know your team will get the client back in shape. You'll do the full assessment, retrain them on social engineering attacks, look at physical and network protections, the whole nine yards. I trust you to handle this. Galanteen is the sword and the shield, but there is much more—"

Owen laughed a hearty laugh and leaned back in his chair. "It's my job to tell you, remember? Besides, all this background is really meant to underscore my next point."

"Which is?"

Owen raked a hand through his curly red hair with a sigh. "The Chinese hackers are an increasing threat to our work. But while the Chinese, Russians, and North Koreans are the three groups we encounter the most, it's the Chinese artificial intelligence program that concerns me."

Richard scoffed. "You don't seriously think they've achieved the singularity?"

"No. My intel says they're decades away from approaching human-level AI."

"No one is taking the approach we're taking," said Pari, a slender, middle-aged woman also seated at the conference table. Dr. Pari Kallalaprakesh-Francis was the director of Golden Bay Labs, Richard's small, private neuroscience research firm.

"Yes, Pari, but I worry the Chinese will try to steal our work," Owen said. "Their interest in militarizing AI for cyberwarfare is troubling. Which reminds me—Richard, it's time for your next personal security assessment."

With a wave, Richard signaled his consent.

"That assessment will again recommend a personal security detail for you," Owen said.

"Leave the bodyguard stuff out of it," Richard said, returning his gaze to the bay.

Familiar with this conversation, Owen again began to roll the boulder up the hill. "Richard, you're the one who got me into this, who went on and on about saving humanity from itself. And after everything I've seen, I know you're right. This is our best chance. Yet you still refuse to protect yourself, even though you're vital to the cause."

"But I am not above the cause," Richard reminded him. "A bodyguard's close proximity to me could endanger our secret and jeopardize our work."

"I can bring in someone highly trustworthy," Owen said.

"I would only entrust *you* with the job," Richard said, "but we both know you have much more vital work to do. If the secret is revealed, my death will be the least of our concerns. Protect the secret, and you will not need to protect me."

The rock was again rolling downhill, and Owen ceased playing the role of Sisyphus for the day.

"We can't always be the only three who know the secret," Pari said.

"With so many others on a need-to-know basis, knowing their tasks but not the greater purpose, I already fear the secret will slip out before we're ready."

"But it must not die with us," Pari insisted.

Unprepared to have that conversation, Richard remained silent. His longtime friend joined him at the window, and the two stood side by side without exchanging a word, staring across the bay at the sprawling suburbs of Fremont seeping into the crevices of the western foothills.

"What's really bothering you?" she asked quietly.

Richard turned to Pari, trying to conceal his pained expression. "You don't understand. Virginia has been waiting for too long," he said, frustrated by his continued failure to undo the past.

Placing her hand reassuringly on Richard's shoulder, Pari said, "I understand perfectly. She's my friend, too. Just be patient."

Virginia had always advised Richard to eschew patience in his work—a tactic that suited his personality quite well.

"I've got something for your daughter," Richard said, retrieving a small plastic bag from his briefcase and handing it to Pari.

She reached into the bag and pulled out an introductory programming book.

"It might just collect dust, but I hope Quinn likes it."

Pari smiled weakly and withdrew another item. Holding it up with a quizzical expression, she asked about the gift for her adopted daughter: "Rose-colored glasses?"

Richard shrugged. "I thought she could use them."

Pari offered a mild chuckle and turned briskly to Owen. "What data have you collected on the subjects?"

With a gesture toward his desk, Owen directed their attention to several dossiers. "They passed all the background checks, and we've verified their stories. While it's not for me to judge, I believe there are a few promising prospects." Holding out copies of the top two files, Owen said, "These candidates in particular remind me of someone. Brilliant, ambitious, and full of fire. I think you may find what you're looking for."

With piqued interest, Richard opened the first file. "We'll soon see."

CHAPTER 2 – THE FERMI PARADOX WANTS YOU

The expansive auditorium was filled with the light chatter of a Monday morning just before 8:00 a.m. Many of the young Stanford undergrads had already taken their seats, eagerly awaiting their introduction to Advanced Programming, but a few were still milling around in the walkways when Connor and Victor entered and surveyed the room. It was a bit intimidating to walk into such a large lecture hall on their first day of college. Back in high school, they'd never had a classroom that seated more than thirty, but this hall sat around five hundred, with eighteen rows of stadium seating divided into three sections.

It may as well have been a million.

Connor and Victor headed up the first set of stairs and sat near the middle of the seventh row. The two had been friends since elementary school, and they usually sat together.

On seeing that the first few rows were nearly empty, Connor pointed and said, "Looks like the splash zone at a killer whale show."

Before Victor could respond, Professor Richard Nelson strode into the classroom with the gait of a man who was all business. At over six feet tall, the professor cut an impressive figure, with his bald head and close-trimmed gray beard. With his still-muscular build, he had given back only as much as Father Time required. Victor thought he looked like an old linebacker.

A hush fell upon the room as everyone quickly took their seats. The professor put his briefcase on the desk and moved to stand behind the adjacent lectern.

"Welcome to Advanced Programming," Professor Nelson said. On hearing his British accent, Victor guessed the man had likely been a former rugby player instead.

With a dry-erase marker, the professor scribbled the words *Fermi Paradox* on the whiteboard in large black letters, leaving Victor feeling puzzled. Had he and Connor wandered into the wrong class by mistake?

"The Fermi Paradox is the apparent contradiction between the high probability that there is extraterrestrial life and the fact that we have found no evidence of it," Professor Nelson announced.

Without being called on, Victor blurted out, "Excuse me, sir, but is this Advanced Programming?"

Professor Nelson very deliberately placed his marker back on the sill beneath the board. With a measured breath, he turned directly to Victor. "Son, what is your name?"

"Victor Hendricks, sir."

In a congenial tone, the professor said, "Yes, Victor, this is Advanced Programming. Thank you for attending. I appreciate your teaching everyone here the lesson of protocol violations." Seeing Victor's confused expression, he added, "To interrupt me during my lecture is an egregious protocol violation. Many of you will be happy to know that we do cover software protocols in greater depth later in the term. Mr. Hendricks here has given you a preview of that part of the syllabus."

Victor put his hands up in surrender, signaling his apology, but the professor ignored the gesture. "Unfortunately, protocol violations have consequences. In this case, Mr. Hendricks, the consequence is that you have failed the course and are dismissed from my class."

In rapid succession, Victor's face transitioned from bewilderment, to shock, and then to outrage. "You can't do that!"

With a calm demeanor, Professor Nelson said, "It is already done. If you insist on continuing to disrupt my lecture, I will ensure that you fail every course in this program." He gestured to the door with both palms up, as though kindly escorting someone to their chosen destination.

When Victor didn't move, Professor Nelson sighed. "Mr. Hendricks is now demonstrating a denial of service attack, thereby denying you your right to learn. But worry not—I assure you there are well-tested algorithms for dealing with this, which you will surely learn more about during your time here at Stanford."

The professor gestured to the door again, and Victor begrudgingly stood this time. Angrily closing his laptop, he threw his unzipped backpack over one shoulder and stormed toward the exit as an uncomfortable silence filled the room. No one else dared move, for fear of raising their instructor's ire.

Satisfied he now had their full, uninterrupted attention, Professor

Nelson continued, "Some of you may wonder how the Fermi Paradox relates to programming…"

After the door closed behind Victor, he hissed several expletives to himself. In a mounting rage, he walked briskly down the hallway and out of the building. Still muttering as he slammed open the double doors to the sun-filled courtyard, Victor struggled to compose himself. Fresh from that humiliation before a sizable group of strangers—many of whom he would no doubt see frequently over the next few years—the last thing he wanted was to provide more fodder for being ridiculed by becoming unglued outside.

Small-town living had accustomed him to the fact that nothing embarrassing one does in public is ever forgotten. It was part of why he'd wanted to leave Milton. Victor was determined to someday be noticed for remarkable things, to be someone who changed the world. He aspired to follow in the footsteps of men like Jobs, Musk, and Zuckerberg, and majoring in computer science at Stanford was his ticket to that.

So far, he was off to a horrible start.

Finding himself near a park bench, Victor realized he'd been walking through the courtyard with no destination. He sat down, the implications of what had just happened weighing heavily on his mind.

I'm better than this, Victor thought. *I've never gotten an F before.*

A failing grade would mean his scholarship would be revoked, and he couldn't afford tuition without it. And when his mother found out…

Excuses weren't acceptable to Barbara Hendricks. Failure was never an option.

Infuriated, Victor put his laptop in his backpack, carefully zipped the bag, and placed it on the bench beside him. How had everything gone wrong so fast? How could he fix it?

I must have some recourse, he thought as he rose to his feet with a clear destination in mind. *This is still America.* Perhaps he could make his case to the head of the department. If that didn't work, he was prepared to go to the dean, and if necessary, even to the president of the university. He wouldn't allow an honest mistake to stand in the way of his future.

As he walked into the Computer Science department, Victor was greeted cordially by a young receptionist sitting behind the front desk.

"I'd like to speak with the head of the department, if possible," Victor told her. "It's about Professor Nelson."

With a knowing tone, she said, "Hmm, I see. He's not in at the moment, but his office hours this afternoon are from three to four, if you want to come back then. What's your name?"

"Victor Hendricks."

With a warm smile, she said, "Nice to meet you, Victor. I'm Grace. I'll be sure to let him know to expect you."

~ ~ ~

Back in the lecture hall, Professor Nelson was continuing his lecture. "Assuming that extraterrestrials are out there, why haven't we heard from them? Could we really be alone in the universe?" The professor surveyed his rapt audience. "Some theorize that all other intelligent civilizations destroyed themselves before making contact. If you watch the news, you may easily find this explanation to be convincing." He shrugged, as if dismissing the idea. "I personally believe the sparse distribution of matter across the universe prohibits us from ever contacting other civilizations. Despite what Hollywood tells you, that first contact likely won't come in your lifetime, nor in that of your children or grandchildren."

Dramatically pointing skyward, the professor said, "Don't waste your time looking to the heavens for signs of newfound intelligence. A grand intelligence explosion already surrounds us. We have built machines that can follow our instructions. These instructions are small bits of intelligence that operate after leaving our minds. The code transcends us. This ubiquitous code runs our world. The winners in this intelligence explosion will be the ones who possess the greatest intelligence and use it most effectively. The smartest will own the future. This is true for societies, companies, and individuals. The future will be written in our code. In this class, you will learn how to change the world, bit by bit. And I will judge whether you are worthy to enter this noble profession."

"Today," the professor said to his impressed students, "we will start with recursion. Recursion is simply a function calling back to itself."

Furiously scribbling notes, Connor wished his friend had been there to hear about the cosmic significance of their chosen field. He resolved to relay as much as he could remember to Victor when he saw him next.

CHAPTER 3 – TRYOUTS

Connor rushed across campus and made it to the pool by 10:00 a.m., barely in time for diving tryouts. As he stood at the edge of the ten-meter platform, facing outward, ready to dive, thoughts from the morning flooded his mind. Professor Nelson was clearly a hard-ass, judging by how he'd treated Victor, but Connor had been inspired by the man's speech.

He closed his eyes and slowed his breathing, trying to regain his focus. Julia Anderson, the diving coach for both the Stanford men's and women's teams, waited for Connor to show what he could do. Each student would have only one opportunity to demonstrate that they were worthy to walk onto the team without an athletic scholarship behind them.

At the back of the platform, a girl impatiently awaited her turn. Two other students were on their way up to go after her. Seeing Connor's continued hesitation, she quietly tip-toed up behind and shoved him forward with both hands.

Connor teetered on the edge of the platform, then momentarily regained his balance. But all too soon, that moment slipped away, and he flailed through a tragically awkward descent, finishing with a thunderous belly flop.

Upon breaching the surface, he glared up at the girl, who was smiling and waving her right hand at him. Connor was accustomed to competitors trying to undermine him, but she wasn't even competing for the same spot. Still, he waved back, trying not to give her any further satisfaction.

Coach Anderson glowered at Connor as he climbed the ladder, wearing a forlorn expression on his face and red marks across his chest. The other swimmers laughed and snickered until the coach barked at them to pipe down.

"This isn't a belly flop team," the coach said sternly. "I can't have divers who are afraid to jump. There won't always be someone around to push you."

Dumbfounded, Connor froze, speechless. Was she implying the girl did him a favor? Connor wanted to defend himself, but words escaped him. Any attempt would likely be futile, anyway—it seemed to be that kind of day. First Victor was tossed out, and now Connor was going to be next.

Coach Anderson gestured toward the high dive. "I'll give you one last chance."

Connor nodded gratefully and followed the coach's gaze upward. She blew her whistle, and the girl who'd pushed him moved into a handstand. After gracefully pausing, she pushed off and executed a flawless armstand dive with one full somersault in the pike position. A few *oohs* and *aahs* came from the small crowd of competitors when she broke the surface of the water with only a modest splash. Connor felt a stab of jealousy at her impeccable form.

When she finished ascending the ladder, the girl found herself nose to nose with an aggravated Connor. She surveyed him with a curious smirk, ignoring the scowl on his face.

He wanted to shout at her. He wanted to intimidate her. But her presence slightly disarmed him. She was an attractive girl, and a bit more curvaceous than most female divers. The longer Connor stared at her, the more his outrage and annoyance began to slip away.

Until she strolled straight past him, brushing Connor aside as though he were nonexistent.

"You're on the team!" the coach bellowed. She showed no reaction upon hearing the news and simply kept walking.

"What was that all about, huh?" Connor asked, briskly following behind her. "Hey, I'm talking to you!"

"Really? I don't hear anything," the girl replied as she reached the outdoor showers and began rinsing off.

"What's your problem?" Connor asked, stepping closer.

"I don't have a problem," she said, eyeing him directly for a moment before turning her back on him.

Walking around to face her, Connor ran a hand through his dirty blonde hair and decided to take a different approach. "You know, if you wanted to touch me, all you had to do was ask."

With a mock gasp, she said, "Oh my gosh, how did you know? You're the big man on campus I've been looking for all my life."

Connor bristled at her statement, but then seemed to notice a twinkle in her eyes. They glared at each other, both trying not to smile.

"You almost cost me my chance, but maybe you can make it up to me," Connor suggested, surprising himself with his own boldness. "Meet me at Max's Cafe at seven?"

The pretty girl glanced at him sideways and let out a small chuckle while dismissively flipping her soaked black hair out of her eyes, narrowly missing his face.

As she entered the women's locker room, Connor called after her, "I'll take that as a yes!"

He then got back in line, and this time, when his moment came, he didn't falter. On completing his double forward-flip dive with a clean entry, the coach told him he'd made the men's team.

Hoping to run into the girl before she left, Connor exited the men's locker room a few minutes later after quickly changing his clothes, wearing his backpack and carrying a wet towel containing his swimsuit. Though she had started much earlier than he did, he knew girls took much longer to change.

Perhaps she's drying her hair or something, he thought.

Only then did he realize he didn't even know her name. To stall for time, Connor put his towel down on the lower water fountain and took a long sip of water from the higher one. The drinking water carried a faint whiff of chlorine, and he wondered whether he was just smelling the nearby pool, or if he hadn't completely washed the odor from himself. He took a second long sip and paused, but no one appeared. The third extended drink also failed to quench his thirst to see the girl again.

Briefly, he considered waiting a bit longer for her, but not wanting to seem desperate or creepy, Connor departed for his dorm.

CHAPTER 4 – VICTOR'S CHARGE

Grace was chatting congenially into the phone when Victor returned for his meeting with the department head. Waving at him, Grace asked the caller to hold without waiting for their response.

"Hey, Vic," she whispered, covering the receiver, "you're a few minutes early, but he's been waiting for you. Last door down the hall on the left."

Victor said a quick thank-you, and Grace let out a sweet giggle before returning to her call. His pulse quickened as he charged down the hallway. Having never done anything like this before, he nervously rehearsed his case, knowing how important it was to make the right first impression with the department head. To avoid coming on too strong, he slowed his pace as he approached the office.

When he got to the door, Victor saw it was two-thirds open. The large nameplate on the door read "Computer Science Department Head" on the first line and "Professor Richard Nelson" on the second.

Crap. He's *the department head?* Victor thought to himself. *I'm doomed.*

Professor Nelson was sitting at his desk with his back to the door. Upon hearing the footsteps, he finished up his call with a, "Yes, dear. Love you, too," before pivoting his chair to face his guest.

"Ah, Mr. Hendricks," the professor said, standing and offering his hand. "Welcome. Please come in." Momentarily frozen, Victor managed to step forward and extend his hand in return. "Take a seat. I've been expecting you since the moment you walked out of my class."

Victor cautiously took a seat in the chair closest to the door. Glancing up to his right, he saw several pictures framed on the wall. The leftmost image showed a wedding couple in their mid-twenties—a young Professor Nelson and his lovely bride. The photo beside it was a poster-sized Halloween portrait of his wife dressed as a superhero. She had long, wavy blonde hair, stunning light-brown eyes, fair skin, and a dazzling smile.

"How can I help you?" the professor asked, his tone courteous.

"Well, um, sir, you can start by letting me back into your class."

Professor Nelson smiled warmly. "Why, certainly. So long as you are a student at this university, you are welcome to sit in any of my classes."

"I don't want to just *sit* in your classroom, sir," Victor protested. "I want a fair chance to earn my grade."

The professor broke eye contact and turned his gaze toward the personal photos on the wall. "'Fair.' That's a young person's euphemism for entitlement. I'm not sure you know what that word means—because if you did, you wouldn't use it so lightly."

Victor stared angrily at the professor. "I know exactly what the word means. It isn't fair that you failed me for the course just because I asked you a question."

Returning his gaze to Victor, Professor Nelson leaned forward and said, "Fair means the rules apply to all equally. Everyone in that class had the same chance to be the first to fail. You were the only one who seized the opportunity. Now, you come in here demanding what you've already received, and what you want isn't even what you demand. You don't want fairness; you want justice. You think it *unjust* for me to fail you for interrupting me."

Victor opened his mouth to respond, but the professor continued before he could speak. "You will soon find that, in this department, I am the arbiter of justice. Your treatment has been just. The only injustice you have suffered was that you were not taught proper manners. I give you this free lesson, but it's not my duty to teach you manners, as I'm not your father. Now—"

"Leave my father out of this!" Victor said, standing abruptly.

Unfazed, the instructor calmly stood to meet him. "Evidently you have more to learn about interruptions," he chided. "To be my student, you must prove you're teachable."

"I *am* teachable!" Victor protested.

The professor ignored him. "Here's a few complimentary life lessons," he said, counting them out on his fingers. "First, life is not fair. Learn to adapt to adversity. Life is full of it, so consider this adversity an opportunity I have handed you. Second, life is not just. There is no characteristic of the universe that requires it to be. We should seek justice, but understand we won't always find it. Some justice can be bitter to swallow, like this instance clearly is for you."

Professor Nelson gave Victor a pointed look. "And, lastly, I have a computer science lesson for you, which is that algorithms are everywhere. There are many similarities between problems in computing and in the real world. For example, if you learn about the protocols that humans call manners, you will someday see how computer communication protocols mirror these. To be a great programmer, you must learn to ask precisely for what you want. The computer will not read your mind and do what you want; it will only do what you ask of it." The professor smiled at Victor. "Take these lessons as my gifts to you, and use your failure as a catalyst for growth. As the first to fail this term, you have a head start."

"May I speak now?" asked Victor, hands balled into fists by his sides.

The professor smiled indulgently at him. "Thank you for asking. Please proceed."

"Is there really no other way?"

When Professor Nelson put a consoling hand on Victor's shoulder, it took all his strength to resist pushing it off. Though angry, he wasn't foolish enough to do anything that could be misconstrued as assaulting a teacher.

With appalling sincerity, the professor told him, "I have shown you the way. There is no shortcut. You may feel free to speak with the dean, of course, but he will always defer to me, as he knows I have your best interests at heart. Someday you will understand this, too."

"But I'm going to lose my scholarship for one mistake on my first day," Victor lamented.

"Tell me, Victor, why are you here?" asked the professor, gesturing for his guest to return to his seat.

Victor remained standing. "Haven't you been listening? I already told you. I want the chance to earn a passing grade."

"No, why are you at Stanford?"

In a voice louder than he intended, Victor said, "To study computer science in one of the best programs in the country."

"No, *the* best," Professor Nelson corrected him. "But why computer science? Of all the things you could choose, why this?"

Victor was growing more irritated by the minute. "Look," he said with a huff, "I'll tell you, but then let's get back to resolving this issue. Since I was a kid, I've loved writing code. I want to build amazing things. And I want to be great—"

For the first time that day, Professor Nelson raised his voice. "Then don't let one S.O.B. and one rough day take that passion away from you! You're not here for the grade. You're here for the dream. To hell with the grade! Forget the scholarship! Dust yourself off and chase the dream. Find a way."

Victor stared at him, aghast. The sentiment was all well and good, but how was he supposed to pursue his dream if he couldn't afford to stay in the program?

"Now, if you'll excuse me, other students are waiting." Professor Nelson extended his hand. After a momentary hesitation, Victor took it, grasping the man's hand firmly in defiance. The professor squeezed heartily in return and smiled genuinely. "Good day, Mr. Hendricks."

Victor glared at his new nemesis, then released his grip without speaking. Professor Nelson stepped aside and let him out the door.

A few steps down the hallway, Victor muttered an acrimonious, "Good day, sir."

CHAPTER 5 – NETWORKING

Pari stood in front of the small class with an inviting expression. "Welcome to Introduction to Graph Theory. My name is Dr. Pari Kallalaprakesh-Francis. Feel free to call me Dr. Kallalaprakesh-Francis." A few chuckles and mild groans ensued. "Or, if you prefer, Dr. Pari will do."

Slowly pacing across the front of the room, she said, "John Gage of Sun Microsystems famously said in the late '80s that 'the network is the computer.' This was during a time when the PC was rapidly ascending, but computer networks were not yet part of our daily lives. However, he was more right than many knew. In fact, I will go further than Gage did, and say that the network is *everything*. Everything interesting, everything worth studying, belongs to a network."

Pari stopped pacing and put her hands on her waist as she surveyed her young audience. "Many hold spiritual beliefs that everything in existence is connected to everything else. Though this is not a philosophy class, I posit the reason this belief is so widespread is because we find connected things to be interesting. In particular, we humans find the *connections* themselves interesting. Any guess why that is?"

Only one hand went up in the entire room. More than a few of the other students were still gun-shy after witnessing Victor's ejection from Professor Nelson's class that morning.

Pari called on a dark-haired girl named Marisa, who confidently answered, "Because we want to understand the patterns."

"Exactly!" said Pari, smiling and pointing at her. "All these connected things are linked in systematic ways. There are patterns to how all networks operate, and certain principles govern how they work. Try to think of something in isolation—pick anything! Then think about the things it's connected to. It's impossible to obtain a complete understanding of that thing, whatever you are considering, in isolation. You can't understand traffic by only studying cars. You can't understand diseases by only studying the microbes, and not looking at how they're transmitted. Most importantly, you can't understand the brain by looking at only the neurons, but ignoring how they work together.

"I've always been fascinated with the brain. It's the most amazing machine. Your brain supports a self-aware, conscious neural network that we call *you*. Parts of your body can fade away without compromising that inner self, but if the neural network falters, you begin to lose your essence. One example of this is dementia."

Many of the students, who were expecting a dry math class, were surprised to be getting much more. "We are our minds. The network inside us makes us who we are. And the many networks that connect us give our lives meaning. As a neuroscientist, networks became so vital to me that I went back for my PhD in mathematics with a specialization in graph theory. Graph theory, as you probably guessed by now, is the study of networks. Over the next few months, I hope to impress upon you the importance of graph theory in our world. I will provide you with the tools to use it wherever your studies take you—which, for most of you, is into the field of computer science."

Pari's attention was momentarily diverted by the buzzing phone on her lectern. Richard's name popped up on the screen. Sending the call to voicemail, she smiled ruefully at the class and said, "Sometimes the world is a bit *too* connected."

~ ~ ~

At the end of the hour, Dr. Pari punctually dismissed the class. Marisa had enjoyed the lesson greatly, and rose quickly from her seat to tell the professor so. As she donned her backpack, however, she was surprised to see Dr. Pari already on her way out of the classroom. Marisa strode briskly through the ambling crowd to catch her, but stopped suddenly when the blond guy she'd pushed off the diving board during tryouts stepped into her path.

"Hello again," he said with a friendly smile. "I didn't really get the chance to introduce myself properly earlier. I'm Connor. And you are?"

Marisa looked down at his outstretched hand and said a hello in the tone of a goodbye. Then she sidestepped him and exited the classroom. Connor pulled his hand back meekly as she left him in her wake.

Spotting Dr. Pari walking hurriedly down the hallway, Marisa broke into a jog. She caught up to the professor at the end of the corridor, where

Dr. Pari had paused to retrieve an umbrella from her satchel.

"Hi, Dr. Kallalaprakesh-Francis. I'm Marisa."

The professor smiled at her. "I'm impressed you pronounced it right on the first try. But please, call me Dr. Pari." Her smile turned regretful as she added, "I'm sorry, but I must be going. I have an appointment."

Dr. Pari strode out into the rain, shielded by her umbrella. Marisa matched her stride, undeterred by the raindrops falling upon her face.

"I just wanted to say that your lecture was very inspiring," she said breathlessly.

"Thank you."

"Um, do you think we could do lunch together sometime? Like maybe tomorrow?"

Pari looked cockeyed at her student while continuing her brisk walk across the courtyard.

"Well, I'm only on campus Mondays, Wednesdays, and Fridays for this class. So, tomorrow doesn't—"

"I watched your TED talk on digital transcendence. Very inspiring. I never thought I'd ever get to actually meet you."

As the rain picked up, Dr. Pari glanced over at her new student and moved closer, allowing the umbrella to provide her cover. "Listen, Marisa. I'm flattered. But if you're trying to butter me up for a better grade, you should know that flattery doesn't work on me."

"Oh, it's not like that!" Marisa protested, feeling a stab of alarm. "I'll ace your class. It's just there aren't a lot of female role models in my field, and I wanted to pick your brain about how you broke through the glass ceiling."

"Ah, yes, the proverbial glass ceiling. What's your field, dear?"

"Computer Science."

"Well, I'm not—"

"I know," Marisa interjected, "but you've succeeded in two male-dominated fields, neuroscience and mathematics. I'm sure I can learn amazing things from you."

As they reached the front door to the Computer Science department, Dr. Pari said gently, "And that is precisely why I teach. This is where we part ways, Marisa. I'll see you in class."

Marisa glanced dejectedly at the rainy courtyard she was about to cross again, watching another girl scurrying across the grass holding a newspaper overhead. With a sympathetic look, Dr. Pari handed Marisa the umbrella before slipping into the CS building. "Bring it back to me on Wednesday."

~ ~ ~

When Pari entered Richard's office, she was startled to see Owen there as well. It was highly unusual for him to meet them on campus. He quickly locked the door behind her and ushered her into a seat.

"What's the urgent matter?" she asked.

Richard gestured to the folder in Owen's hand.

"Remember last week when I warned you about the Chinese?" Owen asked in a hushed tone. Pari nodded. "Well, my sources tell me a quiet investigation has been opened into one of your students. They suspect she may be a Chinese operative. She's a skilled developer, possibly a hacker. And she may be familiar to you two."

Owen handed the file to Pari. She flipped through it, raising her eyebrows, and asked, "But nothing is confirmed yet?"

"Correct. There are some suspicious financial transactions, but it's possible they're totally innocent."

"What do you want us to do?" Richard asked.

"Just be careful."

CHAPTER 6 – FIRST LIGHT

Pari stood at the window of Richard's office, gazing down at the rain-drenched courtyard and contemplating the warning Owen had left them. She'd never imagined being the target of a spy operation—or that one of her students would wind up being that spy.

Richard, on the other hand, wasted no time in contemplation. He took a seat at his computer and, patting the chair beside him, said, "It's ready."

Letting out a deep sigh, Pari turned away from the window and took the seat next to her friend. She placed a hand on his knee and gently asked, "Are you sure *you're* ready?"

Richard looked slightly taken aback by the question. "I've waited a long time for this," he told her.

"So have I," she said cautiously, "but this is a huge step. This is a secret we may have to keep for the rest of our lives. The implications—"

With a fond smile, Richard placed his hand over hers and said, "The implications will be fantastic, Pari. The time is here. Don't worry so much, my friend."

He turned to his computer and began typing, while Pari clasped her hands together in her lap, teetering between apprehension and anticipation. After years of secretive work, they were finally testing the technology they'd designed to allow people to survive beyond the deaths of their physical bodies.

A chat window appeared on his screen, and the simulation began. Richard was about to type his first message to their new virtual friend, Rich, when a message from him appeared. It contained a long string of capital As. Pari looked at Richard quizzically and said, "Maybe he's just leaning on the keyboard?"

"What keyboard?"

"Never mind, I…"

More As from Rich filled the screen. They were briefly interrupted by a handful of Us before returning to As. Richard submitted his own message, asking if Rich could hear him, then rested his chin on his fist while considering the stream of vowels.

Rich was a software neural network based on a recent scan of Richard's brain. But he wasn't just based on Richard—the state of every neuron in Richard's brain was now represented as bits in the computer program they called Rich. Because Rich lacked a body, the simulator running him was supposed to deduce the sounds he would make based on his neural activity and generate readable text. Similarly, the text Richard typed was converted into simulated sounds for Rich to "hear." This was their only form of communicating with this newly created life-form thus far, and unfortunately, it didn't appear to be working.

Pari sat back, unable to hide her disappointment. While it seemed they could simulate the full activity of the human mind—which was no easy task in and of itself—they were still unable to read Rich's mind and interpret his thoughts. Much like a parakeet imitating words without true fluency in the language, Pari and Richard's experiment had only just achieved parakeet status within neuroscience.

"Looks like we're stuck," Richard said, crossing his arms and leaning back in his chair.

He listened as Pari explained that there were two likely possibilities for the simulation's failure. "Either Rich is brain-dead, or he has the software equivalent of locked-in syndrome."

Seeing Richard's unfamiliarity with the term she explained, "Paralyzed patients with locked-in syndrome are completely trapped in their own minds, unable to express themselves in any way, despite being fully conscious. I imagine it's awful. But I don't see how we can tell which is the case here."

As Pari finished her explanation, something on the screen caught Richard's eye. Leaning forward excitedly, he pointed at the screen, where the string of vowels had now been broken. Interleaved between the As and Us was the word *yes*.

"We've established communication with an artificial life-form!" Richard exclaimed, turning to Pari with his arms spread out.

Pari hugged Richard, tears of happiness and relief filling her eyes as she thought of all the years of work that had gone into preparing for this moment.

"Ask him what the deal is with all the As and Us," she urged.

Before Richard could type his question, another word interrupted the vowels—*kill.* Richard looked curiously at Pari, and she returned an equally perplexed expression. Then another word broke the vowel string—*me.*

"'Kill me'? Not what I expected, but I suppose it's a start," Richard said.

Pari's face filled with horror when Rich uttered his final word between the noise—*now.*

"'Kill me now'?" Pari exclaimed, pushing her chair back from the desk. "Do you think he's in some kind of pain?"

Richard looked down meekly. "Well, I suppose it's possible…"

"Why didn't you mention that before?" Pari cried. She leaned over Richard to pause the program and fixed him with a glare.

"I didn't know it was possible. But it's a program, Pari. An experiment."

"You can't have it both ways, Richard," she scolded. "Either it's a dumb program that you can treat with cold, scientific rigor, or he's a legitimate life-form that requires our compassion. He was crying out in pain! If he wants to die, then we should grant his request. He didn't consent to being tortured."

"You're right," Richard admitted. "Now that we know it—um, *he*—is alive, we need to treat him with the same rights as any other human. Rich needs to consent to anything we do to him. Since he's me, I can provide us the consent to do any necessary research on him."

Standing to make her point, Pari spoke firmly, "Rich is not you anymore! He started from you, yes, but once he split off from you, he became an independent being. You can't speak for him, and he has clearly spoken for himself. We'll have to take additional precautions with future sims—"

"Digital transcenders," Richard interrupted. "I believe the term is digital transcenders, as they are transcending from physical to digital form."

"I know the term!" Pari yelled, gesticulating angrily with her hands. "In any case, future *transcenders* will need to consent to anything we do to them. *You* can't retroactively grant consent on their behalf after they transcend from you."

"Well, you're quite the lawyer today," Richard said, trying to lighten the mood.

"No, I'm a doctor! I took an oath to do no harm, but Hippocrates never imagined a situation like this. It must be done right. We're making history here, and history will judge us."

Richard got to his feet, looked at Pari, then at the courtyard below. His eyes followed a raindrop slowly descending the window. "How exactly do you propose we kill him? He's already paused."

Pari returned to her seat and said calmly, "Pausing merely puts him in suspended animation. The only way to kill him is to delete his file. That's what we should do."

When the raindrop merged with another one, Richard turned to face his friend. "Don't you want to ask him more questions first?"

"Not if it means torturing him to get the answers. Remember, do no harm."

Raising his eyebrows, Richard returned to his seat. "How exactly is killing him doing no harm?"

"There are some fates worse than death, Richard. Endless torture is one of them. I will not do that to my friend."

"Your friend?"

"He's another *you*, Richard. Nearly as much you as you are. Every memory, every dream. He just laid down in the scanner and suddenly lost his body and all his senses, but somehow he still feels pain."

Richard leaned back in his chair and put his hands on his head. With his eyes closed, he sat in silence, pondering their options. Unless they solved the pain problem, Pari wouldn't agree to create any future transcenders, and he couldn't do this without her help. But they couldn't even awaken their only transcender to find out why he was in pain. So what were they to do?

Finally, Richard offered a compromise that Pari was willing to accept. "Let's leave him paused for now and sleep on the problem. Maybe our dreams will light the way."

CHAPTER 7 – OPENING NIGHT

At a table for two in Max's Cafe, Connor sat scrolling through his phone. He didn't want to appear anxious as he waited for the girl whose name he had failed to acquire. But at thirteen minutes past seven, he was starting to wonder if she would show up at all.

The waitress came back to the table, offering Connor a sympathetic smile. She was tall and thin, with short blond hair and a name tag that read *Lucy*. "Can I bring you anything while you wait?"

Connor sighed. "Sure, I'll take some more water. Actually, make that two."

After a few more minutes of waiting, the door opened, and Connor perked up at the sight of a dark-haired girl walking in. His hopes quickly sank when he saw that it wasn't the pretty girl from diving practice. Back to scrolling on his phone.

At 7:18, the waitress came back with the waters he'd ordered and asked, "Are you sure you don't want some wings or something to start with?"

"No, I'm fine," said Connor in a clipped tone. "She'll be here soon."

The waitress offered an apologetic nod and let him be. Briefly, Connor thought about texting Victor, but that would simply make him more nervous. He decided that if she didn't arrive by 7:30, then he'd likely been stood up. Then he remembered that she'd never really accepted, so perhaps he hadn't been stood up after all.

At 7:28, Lucy came by with a basket of buffalo wings, placed them on the table, and with a friendly wink, said, "These are on me. Enjoy!"

Is she flirting with me, or taking pity on me? Connor wondered. Girls rarely flirted with him. Throughout most of high school, he'd suffered from severe acne, and he'd resigned himself to not dating until college. Fortunately, at the end of his senior year, his acne had started to dissipate, and no trace of it could be found now. He often reflected—a little bitterly—on how different his high school years would have been if that had happened sooner, but ultimately, he was just relieved it finally had.

Suffice it to say, none of this had trained him to tell whether Lucy was flirting with him or not. However, as Lucy walked away, the girl he had been waiting for appeared, saving Connor from pondering the matter further.

"Is this seat taken?" the dark-haired girl asked.

His heart pounded in his chest as he gestured for her to join him. *Play it cool,* he told himself. But as Connor gazed into her sparkling hazel eyes, the best he could muster was, "You have beautiful eyes." In his head, he kicked himself for sounding foolish.

Fortunately, her lips curled into an attractive smile. Without pretense, she replied, "Thanks, I get that a lot."

All afternoon, Connor had wondered about her name. Their first conversation replayed in his head, and he pondered how he could have inserted the question coolly. Now that she was sitting in front of him, a different question came to mind.

"Do you always push people when you first meet them?" he asked.

"Only if they're holding up traffic."

Grabbing a chicken wing, he said, "That's a severe case of road rage."

"That's nothing. I'm from Miami!" she said, rummaging through her purse. After a moment, she pulled out a familiar-looking swimsuit. "By the way, did you drop something earlier? I found this by the water fountain at the pool." She dangled it in front of her chest, raising her eyebrows suggestively.

Connor felt himself blushing, but before he could answer, Lucy reappeared and eyed the girl approvingly.

"Well, you were definitely worth the wait!" Lucy exclaimed. "You know how long this boy waited for you? I was started to think I'd have to take your place." She gave Connor another wink. Then, noticing what she held, Lucy remarked, "Cute panties! Where'd you get those?"

In an accusatory tone, Connor's companion asked him, "Yeah, babe, where'd you get these leopard panties?"

Clearly sensing an argument brewing, Lucy mumbled an excuse under her breath and swiftly walked away. Connor tried to snatch his swimsuit, but the girl moved it out of his reach.

"It's my high school diving suit," he whispered angrily. "We were the Fighting Leopards."

The dark-haired girl peered inside. "Are you sure this is a swimsuit? I don't see any strings. Don't boys' swimsuits usually have strings?"

"They fell out in the wash," he grumbled.

"Don't you have trouble keeping them on?" she asked, twirling them on her index finger. The few other patrons, mostly college students, watched them with bemused expressions, and Connor noticed Lucy eyeing them from the kitchen.

"I didn't have any troubles until you came along," Connor retorted. She tossed the suit at his chest in feigned disgust, and he tucked it hastily into his pocket. "So, how much more do you plan to humiliate me today?" he asked.

"Depends. How much more can I?"

"Well, our waitress already thinks I'm cheating on you," Connor pointed out.

The girl laughed. "You are terribly unfaithful. First, you flirt with the waitress right in front of me. And now I find another girl's panties in our bed?" She wiped away an imaginary tear. "It breaks my heart. And after all we've been through together!"

With mock sincerity, Connor replied, "Yes, we've been through so much. What's your name again?"

In equally mock disgust, she hissed, "It's Marisa, c'mon! Try to keep your girls straight! By the way, do you ask all the girls out when you're half-naked?"

Holding the basket of chicken wings out to her, Connor silently praised himself for coolly extracting the girl's name. "You'd be surprised how often it works," he joked. "Are you always thirty minutes late for a date?"

Marisa scoffed as she picked out a wing. "Date? Don't get ahead of yourself, flaco! When some nameless guy asks me out, he's lucky if I show up at all!"

Connor didn't doubt this one bit. He certainly felt lucky to be talking to such a beautiful, witty girl. "Well, if you dump me now, at least I'll have Lucy to console me."

Marisa laughed again. "I bet she would make me so jealous." Her expression turned speculative. "Out of curiosity, exactly how long would you have waited for me, anyway?"

Pausing for effect, Connor said, "Long enough to learn your name."

"Good answer!" Marisa remarked, smiling flirtatiously. "I have to say, it has been fun messing with you today. I haven't laughed so hard in a long time. But can we be serious for a minute?"

"Sure."

Staring into his eyes, she said, "I'm here breaking up with a guy I don't even know. So, who are you?"

Connor shrugged. "Just a guy trying to not get pushed around on his first day."

Marisa looked a bit sheepish for a moment. "I actually am sorry about pushing you off the platform. I can be a little impulsive sometimes."

"It's all right," Connor reassured her. "To answer your question, well, I'm from Florida, too. Milton." Seeing Marisa's questioning look, he added, "It's in the panhandle. About as far from Miami as you can get and still be in Florida."

"What brought you all the way out here?" Marisa asked.

"Well, programming, of course. This is like the computer nerd's paradise. When the singularity is finally achieved, you know there's gonna be a Stanford connection."

"And you wanna get on the good side of our computer overlords early?"

"Funny. I don't think it'll go that way, though. I just think all the AI stuff is cool, and I want to learn more about it. You were in Nelson's class this morning, right?" She nodded. "His lecture about the intelligence explosion made me feel like I was in the right place."

Connor thought about the class and how bad he felt for Victor. "But the closest thing I've seen to a coding machine is my friend Victor. When he's in the zone, he's something else. Me, I do it for fun, and because it'll make me a good living. But Victor, he doesn't play."

Marisa frowned sympathetically. "How's he taking getting tossed outta class?"

"Not good. He's been texting me all day, but I haven't had a chance to talk to him yet. Victor's a resourceful guy, though. I'm sure he already has a solution cooked up. He's got a knack for stuff like that." As bad as he felt for his friend, Connor preferred to keep his attention on the girl in front of him. "Say, what brings a Miami girl to Stanford?"

Marisa sighed. "Mostly just the chance to get out from underneath my mom."

"Really?"

"No. Well, maybe a little. She means well, she's just…a little overprotective. But I guess you could also say that Vexed Up brought me here."

"The video game?" Connor asked.

"Yeah."

"I used to grind that game for hours!" he exclaimed. "It's such a cool concept. I love time-travel games."

"What's your strategy? I bet you're a vanquisher," Marisa mused, leaning in.

"No, I was a chaser."

"Really?"

"Yeah, I chased Marisol across space-time and—"

"A Marisol-chaser, huh?" Marisa asked, smiling wryly. "You don't meet too many of those. Did you ever catch her?"

"Almost, but she was so elusive."

"Yeah, the faster you pursue her, the harder she is to catch."

"I know!" Connor said excitedly.

"You were basically chasing me," Marisa said with a grin.

Connor's brows knit with confusion.

"I, uh… well, I invented Vexed Up," she told him, looking a little self-conscious. "My mom wouldn't let me put any of my personal info out there, because I was only fourteen when I launched it. So, I put little parts of me in the game instead. Marisol was my alter ego."

His jaw dropped. "No way," he whispered, his voice full of awe. "*You* made Vexed Up?" Marisa nodded. "You're a genius! I mean, the way you built that game. Everyone was wondering who created it. Wow! How'd you make the time travel so authentic?"

"Simple," she said, deadpan. "First, I invented time travel. Then I came back from the future and coded the game."

Connor burst out laughing. "Naturally. So, tell me, Miss Time-Traveling, Indie Game Developer, what do you need this place for? I'm sure you're set by now."

"Not quite," she said. "I did all right with Vexed Up, for sure. I made enough to supplement my scholarships and then some, but I didn't monetize the game early enough and then people moved on to the next thing pretty quickly. But I learned a lot. The biggest thing I learned is that I don't want to code alone. I want to be part of a team, and I want to lead great teams. That's what I think I can learn here."

"Victor told me Professor Nelson sometimes hires interns," Connor told her.

"That's the dream," Marisa admitted. "Can you imagine learning leadership under someone like Richard Nelson?"

"Totally. Just make sure you don't interrupt him."

~ ~ ~

Marisa and Connor walked out of Max's after nine. Behind them, Lucy flipped the *Open* sign on the door to *Closed.*

Under a clear night sky, they strolled across campus, enjoying each other's company as they headed toward Stern Hall, where Connor lived. Marisa had an apartment just off campus, but his place was on the way. She'd shared a lot with Connor over dinner—maybe too much for a guy she had just met.

When they reached Connor's dorm, he hesitated, trying to decide how to say goodbye. He wanted to kiss her, but he figured that would probably be moving too fast. She'd already warned him to slow down when he mentioned the word *date* earlier. But he liked her, and she seemed to like him. All he had to do was not spoil it by doing something stupid.

He resolved that he wouldn't try to kiss her. But then Marisa leaned in, and Connor panicked, awkwardly thrusting his hand forward to shake.

"I had a great time tonight," he told her. Then, jokingly, he added, "But let's not get ahead of ourselves."

Marisa rolled her eyes and said, "I was going to kiss you on the cheek to say goodbye, you dork. Are you sure you're from Florida?"

Connor lowered his hand, hoping she couldn't see his cheeks flushing with embarrassment. So much for not doing anything stupid.

But Marisa merely huffed out a laugh and pulled a pen out of her purse.

Grabbing the hand he'd offered, she wrote her number on his palm. Then, to his surprise, she raised herself up on her toes, pulled him toward her, and planted a prolonged, exaggerated kiss on his cheek, just beside his mouth.

Before Connor knew what hit him, she spun playfully on one heel, called a goodnight over her shoulder, and disappeared into the moonlight.

CHAPTER 8 – WALK OFF

Upon entering their shared dorm room, Connor found Victor at his desk, playing a video game on his laptop. As Connor closed the door behind him, Victor whirled around in his chair and asked, "Dude, where ya been?"

Before Connor could respond, Victor's character—a soldier dressed in red—took a roundhouse kick to the head from a ninja clad in all black and fell to the floor. The words *You Lose* flashed across the screen.

"Nice job, bud," Connor commented sarcastically. "Knocked it out of the park this morning in your first at bat. A walk-off, no less."

Victor said wryly, "More like I gave up a home run on my first pitch and got sent down to the minors before it landed. I've been trying to reach you all day."

"Sorry. Busy day. Classes, bookstore, diving tryouts. I made the team, and…" Connor trailed off, hesitating to mention Marisa. "What about you? Did your day improve?"

Victor explained what happened when he went to meet the department head and briefly talked about the three other classes he had that day. Despite having a bunch of homework, he was clearly still stewing over how his day had started.

"Nelson practically dared me to go to the dean," he told Connor. "But apparently he's untouchable around here. I was playing pool in the Commons with a junior this afternoon, and he said Nelson's always been difficult, but after his wife died two years ago, he developed a quick trigger finger. Apparently I'm not the first guy to get kicked out of his class, but he thinks I set a record."

Taking a seat on his bed, Connor said, "Why not just drop the course? You could add an elective to maintain a full course load and keep your scholarship."

Victor sighed. "I thought about that. This guy also said Nelson's the only one who teaches Advanced Programming, and he only teaches it in the fall. Advanced Programming is a prereq for all our other CS classes, since we already took all the easier stuff in high school. So, if I don't pass this now, I'm stuck."

Leaning forward, Victor added, "I don't get it. The guy's founded a bunch of startups, and the last one was acquired for seven billion a few years ago. He only went into teaching five years ago, just for fun, I guess, or maybe to torment students. Clearly, he doesn't need this job."

Since it was easier than looking at his friend's face, Connor gazed at the laptop screen, which continued to proclaim Victor's defeat. The ninja stood with one foot on the soldier's head, repeatedly thrusting one fist into the sky in jubilation.

"So, what's your angle?" Connor asked. "You've always got one."

Victor flopped back on his mattress and let out an exasperated sigh. "I'm screwed! No other options. I'm going to fail the class, lose my scholarship, and then it's back home to Milton. Maybe I can get my job back at the movie theater."

"No way, dude. You can't give up that easily. You'll figure something out." Privately, Connor worried that his proud friend might actually be in real trouble here. Unaccustomed to failure, Victor hadn't applied to any other schools. He had been Stanford-bound or bust, and now it was looking like a bust.

The only upside Connor saw in moving home was that it would bring Victor closer to his girlfriend, Alison. "How was Alison's first day at FSU?" he asked, hoping this would be a more positive topic.

Unfortunately, Victor's expression turned even more downcast. "Who knows?" he said, picking up his photo of Alison in its Class of 2012 frame. "I texted her all day, but no answer."

Without thinking, Connor said, "You two have been going out for almost a year, but long-distance relationships are hard."

"Thanks, bro," Victor said, rolling his eyes at the ceiling. "Kick me when I'm down. Though it won't be long-distance for too much longer if I don't figure out how to fix this."

When Connor suggested he look for a job to cover his costs if he lost his scholarship, Victor rolled his eyes again. "What kind job will allow me to pay tuition, room, *and* board at Stanford, dude? We're talking about a hundred grand before taxes, easy. I can't land a position in Silicon Valley making that kind of money as a freshman with no experience. I'm decent, but I'm no prodigy whiz kid."

"Buddy, you know you're much more than decent," Connor said, meaning every word. "But I feel you. Still, you have the whole semester to straighten it out. Maybe you can change Nelson's mind."

Victor cackled. "There are long shots and then there are pipe dreams, my friend. But enough about my problems. How was your first day? Couldn't possibly be as bad as mine."

Feeling guilty for having a much better day, Connor laid down on his bed and stared at the ceiling. "Oh, nothing special. Just a busy day."

CHAPTER 9 – CALLING ALL SUPERHEROES

Professor Nelson greeted Victor kindly when he entered the lecture hall on Wednesday morning. "Welcome back, Mr. Hendricks."

Seated in the same seat he'd been ejected from two days earlier, Victor gave the instructor an acknowledging nod.

"I see you decided to complete your failure," Professor Nelson commented. "Very well, I suppose being a complete failure is better than being an incomplete one."

The pencil Victor had been fidgeting with suddenly snapped within his clenched fists. This appeared to go unnoticed by the professor.

"In economics, we study how finite resources such as goods and services are distributed," Professor Nelson began. Victor didn't ask what this had to with computer science. He and the rest of his classmates had learned not to interrupt the professor's opening monologue.

The professor raised his index finger and continued. "Software is the only economic good in the world whose sole ingredient is human thought. It is vitally important that you understand the magnificence of this. Like all goods, software can be created and destroyed, and it must be maintained. It can be transported from one host to another, and people can interact with it, touch it, feel it. Software affects their lives." He paused for a moment, then mused, "Now, suppose you walked up to a stranger and told them you could make goods appear out of thin air using only your mind. Most people would say you're crazy. The rest would say you must be some kind of wizard or superhero, maybe even a god."

Victor liked the sound of this, as it appealed to his ambitions.

Professor Nelson waited to let his message sink in, eyeing the young audience listening to him with rapt expressions. "You are on the path to joining a force of superheroes, a force that is changing the world. There's a lot of responsibility that comes with this power. You can make the world easier, safer, and more interesting to live in. Or you can make it a buggier, more frustrating, and perhaps even more dangerous place to be. You can be a superhero, or you can be a villain. Unfortunately, too many end up as neither, instead living as mediocre wizards wasting their careers stumbling through the mundane, failing to meet their potential."

Several students exchanged worried looks with their peers. Victor now feared he may never even have a career to stumble through.

"But today, I call on you to be superheroes. That is what you all have the power to become." Professor Nelson offered them an encouraging smile. "The world is filled with both creative and destructive forces. Yet, it is our creativity that makes humanity worth preserving. Some of the most amazing creators are programmers, building software that enriches our lives. Sadly, some of the greatest destroyers are also programmers, in the form of hackers and cybercriminals. These destroyers often exploit small mistakes. And so, creators must constantly remain on the defensive as they code, draining precious creative energy from their endeavors. We creators must be right all the time. The destroyers only need to be right once."

The professor's expression turned wistful. "My dream is that someday the creators will overcome the destroyers by way of their creative talents. This is a far-fetched ideal, I admit, and perhaps too utopian. It may never come to pass. Still, I call on each of you to aspire to become superheroes, striving toward this ideal. Make creation overcome destruction."

With a wave of his hand, Professor Nelson beckoned two people to join him up front. "Unfortunately, I must leave you early today, but my teaching assistants—James Quincy and Tina Fong—will present the details of your first major project. You will be building virtual superheroes that will compete against each other. Your projects will be judged both on the effectiveness of your characters and the quality of their code. Please be sure to put forth your best effort, as this will comprise a large portion of your grade." The professor smiled thinly and added, "It will also be quite fun. And perhaps the best of you will prove worthy of an internship at my company, Warp Drive Games, working alongside James and Tina."

Some of the students began to murmur excitedly at this pronouncement, but ceased when the professor held up a stern hand. "After James and Tina finish explaining your project, they will hand out a quiz covering Monday's discussion of recursion. I don't believe I mentioned this last class, but I rarely announce quizzes in advance. I expect you to always be prepared. In software development, you never know when the next challenge will arise, so you must always be ready."

The two teaching assistants stepped to the front as Professor Nelson exited the room. Both looked to be in their early twenties. Tina, a petite woman with short, jet-black hair, launched into an explanation of the project, while James, a mildly stocky black man, stood at her side, towering about a foot above her.

"Hi, I'm Tina. For the past few months, James and I have been developing a 2D hand-to-hand combat video game called CombatRidge. The game is in very early pre-release mode and is currently available only to Stanford students. We'll explain the basics after a brief demo."

James dimmed the lights while Tina's laptop projected an image on the wall behind her. An arid, mountainous, rust-brown landscape appeared before them, and Victor smiled smugly at the familiar background. Perched precariously on a ridge were two warriors facing each other in attack stances—a male soldier in camouflage, named PrivateJames, and a female ninja dressed in red, called TinageWarrior. Above the fighters, a clock counted down: *3, 2, 1… Go!*

The battle was underway. The characters began to execute a flurry of punches, kicks, and jumps, rapidly inflicting damage on each other. Then the ninja lifted the soldier over her head and threw him over the edge. The screen overlaid with *TinageWarrior Wins!*

Tina smiled proudly at the audience.

James turned the lights back on and said, "You can play CombatRidge as either a gamer or a god. The gamers directly control their characters, just like a normal video game. The gods are programmers who write code to control their characters. What you just witnessed was a battle of two gods. Tina and I weren't touching the keyboard at all during the fight—we each programmed our characters in advance. Today's outcome suggests Tina did a slightly better job."

Widespread chuckling rippled across the room.

"In sports," Tina chimed in, "athletes compete to simultaneously demonstrate and sharpen their skills while also providing entertainment. Gamers can also do this via eSports. But we felt there wasn't a sufficient such outlet for programmers, at least not one that was also palatable to non-programmer spectators. You don't have to be an athlete to appreciate a basketball game. Likewise, you don't have to be a programmer to appreciate the skills displayed during a CombatRidge battle. It's our hope that you find this more fun than, say, writing chess-playing apps."

Connor whispered to Victor, "Seems way more fun."

"By Sunday night," James said, "you must submit the code for your first characters, also referred to as bots. Overnight, we'll simulate every bot battling every other bot in the class, then reveal the results at the end of Monday's lecture. We will conduct these bot battles for three weeks, and you will earn points for each win. These points will accumulate to rank each student in the final standings."

Tina added, "Mondays will also end with a visit from a guest gamer, called a Godslayer. The Godslayer will be given fifteen minutes to battle some of your bots. Every time you battle a Godslayer, half of your weekly standing points are at stake. So you'll need to write code clever enough to defeat both gamers and gods."

The image on the screen changed, and James said, "This is for all you memeials who grew up on memes and can't communicate online without them."

A picture of Professor Nelson looking distinguished appeared. A caption above him read, *I don't always use recursion*, and the bottom caption read, *but when I do, see above*. The meme was met with modest chuckles and a few moans.

Clearly disappointed by the reaction, James waved a stack of papers overhead and asked, "Who's ready for a quiz?"

All the students groaned in unison.

~ ~ ~

Marisa and Connor finished the quiz at nearly the same time and were chatting outside of class when Victor walked out. He greeted Connor with a fist bump and said, "That was the easiest F ever."

Connor displayed a confused expression, and Victor reminded him that he'd already failed the class. "I bet Nelson tosses out my quiz when he sees I got all the right answers."

"Well," said Marisa, "at least you have a good attitude about it."

Victor hesitated before replying. "I'm trying to. It's not easy, but I'm trying." Offering his hand to Marisa, he introduced himself.

"I'm Marisa, Connor's girl…friend."

Victor stuttered, "G—girlfriend?"

"Well," said Marisa, backpedaling, "clearly I'm a girl. And we're friends, so…"

"Um, yeah, it's a very recent development," Connor added. "Our…friendship."

Victor nodded. "I'll say."

"So, what do you think of our project?" Marisa asked, leaning in close to Connor. "Sounds fun, right?"

Connor nodded, but words seemed to fail him.

Victor jumped in. "It's a fun little game. One of the other students showed me how to log in a few days ago, so I've already played it a bit. I didn't know about the developer kit, though. But now that I do, I feel bad for you two lovebirds."

Connor laughed awkwardly, but Marisa played along. "Why's that, Victor?"

"Because you're all gonna lose. I'm gonna destroy the curve. If I'm going down, you're all coming with me."

Marisa threw her arm around Connor and offered Victor a challenging look. "I hate to break it you boys," she purred, "but you two are competing for second place. That internship is *mine.*"

CHAPTER 10 – ONE ON ONE

The sun was setting outside Marisa's apartment window as she tossed her empty sushi container in the garbage. After completing all her schoolwork, she was ready for some fun playing CombatRidge. It was the most exciting work she had to do, but she'd left it for last, as she suspected it would consume her once she got started. With only one class tomorrow, she knew she'd have all day to immerse herself in it, free from the burden of other classwork.

Tonight, she would partake in just a small sample.

Marisa started up CombatRidge and began designing her first character. The site had a very limited gallery of skins, containing a mixture of male and female characters dressed as ninjas and soldiers. There were a few different color outfits for each variation, as well as variations in skin tone.

She chose a blonde soldier girl in pink fatigues and named her Marisol. The outfit was highly practical attire should she ever find herself in a war zone surrounded by flamingos.

To familiarize herself with the game, Marisa elected to compete in gamer-versus-god mode, allowing her to play as a gamer against a default bot. She picked the first bot on the list, PrivateJames, a black man dressed in green camouflage.

James wishes he was that muscular, Marisa thought.

Soon, Marisol and PrivateJames stood on the ridge glaring at each other. Each fighter had a health meter and a stamina meter. To destroy an opponent, one had to inflict damage until the other's health dropped from one hundred to zero. Stamina affected the character's attack power, determining how fast they could act and how much damage they could do.

The countdown commenced, and Marisa suddenly realized she didn't know which controls to use. She watched helplessly as PrivateJames punched Marisol three times, dropping her health down to seventy-three. PrivateJames had retained full health, though his stamina had diminished to sixty-four. The bot briefly suspended his attacks to allow his stamina to recharge, and Marisa seized the opportunity, frantically trying keys on the keyboard, but her character didn't move.

Next, PrivateJames unleashed three consecutive kicks at Marisol's feet, and she was suddenly dangerously low on health. Again, he paused to let his stamina recover.

Marisa wanted to hit him so badly, but she still didn't understand how. Wracking her brain for ideas, she tried pressing *P* for punch, which caused Marisol to jab at PrivateJames's face, and his health dipped slightly.

Finally, she had figured out a move!

PrivateJames put his forearms up to block his face while Marisol unleashed a barrage of punches. Marisa decided to apply brute force and see what happened. Her character's stamina steadily reduced, but PrivateJames took no damage, while his stamina declined very slowly.

Rapidly exhausting herself by throwing continuous punches, Marisol's stamina was soon depleted, while PrivateJames still had most of his. Apparently it took much more stamina to attack than to defend. Even worse, her punches were no longer being thrown. Marisa repeatedly pressed *P*, but nothing happened. At first, she wondered if it was a glitch, but then she deduced that having one's stamina completely drained required full replenishment before one could attack again.

Not waiting for Marisol to recharge, PrivateJames promptly picked her up and threw her over the ridge. *PrivateJames Wins!* flashed on the screen, prompting an outraged holler from Marisa. She *hated* losing to a man, even a virtual one.

Time to read the instructions, she thought. Marisa found the settings section of the app. This showed her the keys to press to punch, kick, crouch, stand, block, jump, lift, and throw.

With this understanding, she prepared for a rematch with PrivateJames. Since the game had no audio, she felt the need for a soundtrack to match the battles. Marisa donned her ear buds and kicked off her gaming playlist.

Head bobbing, Marisa started finding her rhythm. Battle after battle, punching and kicking, she began to get the hang of the controls. After a few battles, she narrowly earned her first win in a slug fest. For the next few fights, she alternated between winning and losing. Time slipped by, and the tide gradually turned in her favor. Her brute force approach evolved into a more elegant strategy.

Fight like a savvy boxer, she thought. *Be a tactician. Be careful. Find your spots.*

One of her favorite songs came on right when she was having her best round yet. Marisa was in another world, completely in the zone. Each move seemed to be the right one, flowing perfectly from one to the next. Soon, Marisol stood at full health with nearly complete stamina, holding a tired, weakened PrivateJames overhead as her trophy. Marisa lifted her hands off the keyboard and praised herself to the rhythm of the song, "Oh, my God, you're the best!"

Imagining he was any man who would ever stand in her way, Marisa pressed her index finger firmly on the *T* and tossed him out.

~ ~ ~

Connor panted heavily and tried to catch his breath. With Victor guarding him on an otherwise empty basketball court, he dribbled the ball behind the three-point arc. Like they often did back in high school, they were out late at night playing one-on-one and talking about girls. Back in Milton, they had both occasionally lamented about being trapped in the friend zone, but that had all changed senior year, when Victor started dating Alison.

For today's game, Connor's take on the latest girl of interest was far different from before. After making a layup, he pulled his phone out of his pocket and read a text from Marisa.

"Marisa wants to play CombatRidge with both of us tomorrow," he announced.

Victor quickly agreed, then asked, "So, when were you gonna tell me you had a girlfriend?"

"Bro, she's not my girlfriend yet. I don't think so, anyway," Connor said as he chucked up a three-pointer that clanked off the rim. The boys both ran for the rebound, but Victor, with the inside position, got to it first.

Dribbling back to the top of the key, Victor panted out, "Okay, so you have a surprise almost-maybe-girlfriend?"

A recap then ensued from Connor of his short history with Marisa. This being his first time dating, he didn't know when—or even if—it would become official. Victor told him she would let him know when she thought it was. As Connor gave him all the background information he had on her, they exchanged bad shots, with an occasional one falling in.

"Let's see if I've got this right," Victor said. "On the first day of college, you meet a super-hot girl who's an excellent diver, a commercially successful programmer, and probably a virgin, since her mom had her locked up like Fort Knox. Did I miss anything?"

"You don't know she's a virgin."

"I'll bet she is. Makes sense, man. One more thing you have in common. Need some pointers?"

Connor flinched. "No!"

"All right, but don't mess this up," Victor warned. "You hit the jackpot, unless she's psycho." He grinned. "That's it. Maybe she's a total nut-job."

"She's a bit impulsive, but—"

"That would explain why she's with you," yelled Victor, as he chased down his air ball.

Connor flushed angrily. "Screw you!"

"Okay, so she doesn't need to be crazy," his friend admitted. "Since she's been under mommy house arrest her whole life, she might just be high on her first taste of freedom."

"I get it. She doesn't need to be totally insane to be with me," Connor muttered, feeling put out. "Could be temporary insanity."

"Exactly. Enjoy it while it lasts, man," Victor said. "She'll probably get bored with you eventually. No one ever stays with their first."

Connor drove to the hoop aggressively and pushed Victor down hard with his right forearm. The two of them went sprawling over the asphalt.

"What the hell is wrong with you, man?" Victor demanded, as they both got to their feet.

In a whiny imitation of Victor's voice, Connor said, "She's got to be crazy to be with you. No one ever stays with their first." Then, switching to his own voice, he asked, "What's wrong with *you*? Dude! Can't you be happy for me? I never said Alison was crazy to be with you!"

Victor didn't say anything; he simply handed the ball to Connor. Taking it, Connor glared at him, and Victor said meekly, "No blood, no foul. Your ball."

Play continued, but they were merely going through the motions now. A tension had come between them that only Victor could break. Some raindrops began to spot the court, but for these two, rainfall seldom signaled departure time, as they both enjoyed playing in the rain.

A fortunate bounce helped Victor bank in a wild, running three-pointer, and he said, "First bit of luck I've had all week."

In a somber tone, he told Connor about the message he'd gotten from Alison a few hours earlier. She thought it would be good for them to see other people. The boys both knew this meant she'd already started.

"I told her that was fine with me," Victor said. "If she was heartless enough to do it like that, I wasn't going to act like I even cared."

"I'm so sorry, man," Connor told him. "Are you okay?"

Victor shrugged by way of reply. The rain began to fall faster, so they decided to end the game and call it a night.

As they walked back to the dorms under a moderate shower, Victor talked about how he was done with girls for a while. He needed to focus on his Stanford dilemma. With Alison no longer a consideration, he felt less desire to visit Milton for Thanksgiving. He didn't want to face his family until his situation improved. Even with student loans and a job, Victor's math told him that losing his scholarship was going to delay his dream and force him to take on massive debt, or leave Stanford altogether.

His preferred route was to convince Professor Nelson to reverse his decision. He saw this as an extreme long shot, but decided he should still try. Sometimes the long shots paid off.

Connor listened as Victor laid out his two-pronged approach for manipulating the instructor. "I'll do everything I can to finish at the top of the class," Victor said. "If I'm the top student at the end, it'll be hard for Nelson to swallow failing me. But just in case that doesn't work, I'm gonna learn all I can about him in the meantime. If I can dig up something juicy, I'll gain some leverage."

Connor stared at him. "I'm not sure who is crazier, Marisa or you. You're seriously going to try to blackmail *Richard Nelson*?"

Victor's face darkened. "Everyone has a weakness, man. I just need to find his."

CHAPTER 11 – BASIC TRAINING

On Thursday evening, at a round table for four in an on-campus cafeteria, Marisa sat between Connor and Victor, each with their laptops before them. Connor quickly set up his character in preparation for their first CombatRidge practice together. He named his ninja dressed in blue gear BluManChu. Victor, who had already created his character, called his soldier clad in red army fatigues DevilsKeeper.

"Cheesy names, guys," Marisa remarked, as she put her hair up.

"I will avenge your disparaging of my good name," Connor replied in a corny, formal tone.

With an odd number of players, someone always needed to sit out. The idle person, Victor suggested, should study the battle and log observations. Both of the others liked his idea, and Victor volunteered to be the first observer. The observer would subsequently compete against the previous winner.

The countdown clock ticked down, and without warning, a rush of anxiety swept over Connor. He didn't want to look weak before an amazing girl. His brain told him this was stupid. It was only a game, the first of many they would play. He looked down at the keyboard and did a mental check of all the keystroke moves, silently wishing that he'd played a few practice rounds back at the dorm before battling Marisa.

The clock struck zero, and he opened with a punch that was deflected by Marisa's bot, who was crouched with her arms held up in a blocking position. Connor kicked her, but her forearms again absorbed the impact, so she took no damage. She stayed in her crouch position and countered with a jab to his legs. As she returned to her defensive posture, Connor's health dropped. He responded with a kick, which she effortlessly blocked. Again, she reacted with a shot to his legs and retreated to her defensive crouch.

Concerned he was falling behind, Connor tried three successive kicks, hoping to land at least one in between her blocks. But all were averted and met with punches to the legs. Connor was low on health with declining stamina, quickly running out of options. He threw one more kick, which was once again deflected, but this time Marisa countered by lifting him overhead. Leaning in closer to the screen, Connor frantically pressed the jump command, trying to free himself, but nothing happened until Marisa said, "Have a nice flight," and tossed him over the edge.

While Connor grumbled, Marisa and Victor roared with laughter. "That," Victor remarked, "was the quickest ass-kicking I've ever seen."

Enthusiastically, she called for the next victim. Connor brought up the observations document on his screen and discovered it simply read, *Connor sucks!* Exasperated by his poor showing, he punched Victor firmly on the arm, and said, "Really? That's all you could come up with?"

Marisa switched over to their shared notes and said, "Excellent observational skills, Victor. Definitely captures the essence of our fight."

They both laughed at Connor's expense as he typed into the document: *It takes more stamina to attack than to defend. Attacks become slower and less powerful as your stamina reduces. The crouch position seems to have an advantage, probably because of limited exposure.*

Marisa reviewed Connor's notes and changed the first line from *Connor Sucks!* to *Connor sucks at battling, but he's an excellent observer. I think he'll be spending a lot of time doing that.*

Victor read it and howled with laughter. "And that's from your girl…um…friend who is clearly a girl. Good luck, buddy!"

After they'd finished teasing Connor, Victor and Marisa prepared for their encounter. The match began with Marisa's bot moving into the blocking crouch position and Victor's taking the same stance. For a long moment, neither moved. To break the ice, Victor executed a crouched kick and retreated immediately to a blocking crouch. Marisa took no damage, and Victor waited three seconds to recharge.

Victor's bot jabbed, and as he pulled back his arm, Marisa's bot rose to her feet, leaned over, and hoisted him over her head. Victor was about to be vanquished even more quickly than Connor. Desperately hitting the *J* key, Victor led his red soldier to vault to freedom. He then connected a punch-kick combo before they each retreated to blocking crouches.

"Pay attention, Connor," Victor said, becoming cocky with the lead. "I'll show you how to deal with her."

Neither bot moved.

"All I see are two scared players," said Connor. Just then, the pink warrior leapt into the air. At her apex, she reached both hands high above her head into one clenched fist. As she descended, she brought this fist down like a hammer on top of the red soldier's head, inflicting major damage. Apparently the blocking crouch thwarted frontal attacks, but provided no overhead protection. Victor's bot punched and kicked wildly from his crouch, but Marisa's had already returned to her defensive posture and was unfazed.

"What the hell was that?" yelped Victor.

Marisa responded by performing the same maneuver again. Suddenly, she was in the lead, and Victor was in trouble. With her character back in the defensive crouch, she bellowed in a deep preacher's tone, "Time to exorcise the demons!"

DevilsKeeper started hopping as Victor tried to recreate the move. But he could only jump and land in a standing position. Each time he descended, she would punch his exposed legs. Then she executed a well-timed lift, capturing Victor's bot. With Marisol holding her prize on high, Marisa folded her arms and demanded, "Beg for mercy!"

With a melodramatic "Never!" Victor furiously attempted to leap free, to no avail.

"You're too wounded to jump free," said a triumphant Marisa. It was true—his stamina had dropped low due to all his jumping, though it was steadily climbing from twenty-seven as he laid helpless in her arms. Meanwhile, Marisol's stamina was gradually declining from one hundred as she exerted energy holding DevilsKeeper aloft.

A few seconds later, Victor exclaimed, "I'm full stamina! Why can't I jump out?"

"Your health," Marisa explained. "Once someone completely lifts you, you need at least fifty health *and* fifty stamina to be able to escape. Are you getting all this, Connor?"

Connor nodded, typing furiously in their notes document. Continuing her lecture, Marisa said, "Also, you can't lift someone who has their guard down. You can only lift them if they're blocking or finishing an attack move."

As she completed her last sentence, Marisol's stamina hit zero, her health instantly plummeted, and she collapsed face-down into the dusty rock. The red warrior knelt facing the screen with both knees digging into Marisol's back. With his hands raised in a V formation, he gazed upon high triumphantly. The marquee *DevilsKeeper Wins!* appeared above them.

"How the hell…?" Marisa breathed in astonishment.

"You waited too long," Victor said smugly.

"I didn't know. I never held anyone that long before," she said, clutching her head in her hands.

"That sucks for Connor."

"Shut up!" retorted Connor and Marisa in unison.

Victor smirked. "See, buddy, I showed you how to deal with your woman."

"Yeah, by letting her beat your brains out," Connor said drily. "You mastered that."

"So, what did we learn, Connor?" asked Marisa. Even though they could have easily read the shared document themselves, Connor read his notes aloud to them. He explained that Victor had been very lucky to win that round—highly damaged players couldn't jump out of being held, it was true; but if you hold a player until you run out of stamina, you collapse from some sort of stroke.

Then he came to his notes about the secret beat-down attack Marisa had used.

"How did you do that move?" Connor asked.

She batted her eyelashes and said, "Well, a girl needs to keep *some* secrets."

Victor said, "I get that. You've got plenty of secrets. Like why you're with this guy." Ignoring Connor's glare, Victor continued, "There are some mysteries that will never be solved, but for the sake of our current research, how did you do the move?"

Marisa smiled broadly, leaned in toward Victor, and said breezily, "Why I'm *with* Connor isn't exactly a mystery, or a secret. I just like him. Good enough for you?"

Victor seemed caught off guard by her directness. In an affable tone, she'd managed to deliver a serious rebuff of his questioning her relationship with Connor. What exactly that relationship was, Connor wasn't yet certain. Until this moment, he hadn't had much to go on, beyond a teasing kiss on the cheek. Hearing her say she liked him allayed his concern that he was slipping into the friend zone.

Her point made, Marisa gestured to their laptops. "I'm ready to watch you two macho men battle it out. Impress me with your masculinity."

Ignoring her taunt, Victor pressed, "And the move?"

She sighed and conceded. "Okay, fine. To do the Thor's Hammer move, double jump, then punch." Placing her hand on Connor's leg, she said softly, "But no more secrets for you boys tonight."

~ ~ ~

A few miles to the east, Richard Nelson was seated at one of several computers in his spacious home, tucked away in a cul-de-sac. Being down the street from Holy Cross Cemetery added an extra buffer of privacy, something that Richard highly valued.

A video conference window with his wife appeared on the monitor, and Richard leaned forward eagerly, a tender smile on his face. "I miss you, sweetheart."

In a soft voice, she said, "I miss you, too. I hope to be home soon. Did you remember to stop by the store?"

Richard replied that he had and took a sip of his whiskey.

"Good," she said, smiling. "Now, get some sleep. It's late, and you've got important work to do tomorrow. Good night, dear."

Wishing her good night, Richard closed the laptop and turned off the connected monitor. Whiskey in hand, he walked across the hall to a bedroom. After one more swig, he placed the glass on the nightstand. Oddly, this room contained no bed. In its place sat something resembling a space-age coffin. The cover consisted of clear glass with a tablet-sized touch-screen console in the center.

Richard pressed a button, and the cover slowly opened. He laid himself supine inside it and said, "Good night, Virginia," as the top gently closed. The tranquil hum of white noise began playing, and a few lights on the outer console ignited around the display, which now read, *Scanning engaged. 8:00:00.*

The timer began to tick down the eight hours for Richard to sleep. When the clock reached *7:59:50*, a woman's voice whispered faintly, "Good night, Richard."

CHAPTER 12 – PAINFUL FINDINGS

Eight hours later, the lid of Richard's capsule bed rose, like a clam shell opening to drink in the ocean.

"Good morning, sleepyhead. Your breakfast is ready downstairs," the woman's voice said to Richard as he laid there, rubbing his eyes.

"Yes, dear," he replied in a groggy voice.

After staggering into the bathroom, Richard began to brush his teeth. Embedded within the vanity mirror, a computer screen appeared, displaying a dashboard filled with graphs. Richard bit down on his toothbrush and left it sticking out of his mouth. With keen interest, he clicked on one graph and began feverishly scrolling through the data.

Suddenly his jaw dropped, sending the toothbrush clattering into the sink as he yelled, "I'll take my breakfast to go…and text Pari! Tell her to meet me after class."

Quickly, he changed out of his pajamas, hurried downstairs, and pivoted left into the kitchen, preparing to bolt out the front door. Suddenly, he came face to face with a lovely blonde woman with perfectly unblemished skin. Her brown eyes were soft as a doe's, set in a well-sculpted face.

Richard let out an expletive as he slammed to a halt. She calmly raised a brown bag in her left hand and a to-go coffee cup in her right. "Here is your breakfast, dear. But it's not beneficial for your digestion to eat on the go. Oh, and I switched you to decaf. Your blood pressure has been a little on the high side."

Richard smiled and said, "I don't know what I'd do without you."

Plainly, she replied, "I don't know either."

He grabbed his breakfast and scurried out the door. Returning to the kitchen, the woman walked mechanically to the sink to wash the dishes.

~ ~ ~

Victor eagerly awaited the end of his first week in college as he listened to Professor Nelson concluding his Friday morning lecture. "As you can see, there are inevitable tradeoffs between space and time when considering your caching policy and memory management," the professor explained, turning away from the whiteboard to face his class. "Even with infinite memory, you would face these tradeoffs. Like all principles, you need to put this into practice to gain mastery. Go beyond simply coding the assignments I give you. Make things, try things—that's how you'll really learn to use these new skills. Be prepared to throw away most of what you build at this age. Many years from now, if you look back at your coding from this class and think it's perfect, you haven't grown."

The professor put down his dry-erase marker and picked up a stack of papers. "Now, be sure to pick up your quizzes on your way out, and enjoy your weekend."

In no hurry, Victor remained seated, watching the other students get their papers. At that moment, he felt strangely free. His fellow students waited in line with varying measures of apprehension in their expressions, uncertain of their scores.

Victor, on the other hand, knew with perfect certainty that he'd failed. For a brief moment, he enjoyed not being among the anxious herd, but the sensation was fleeting. The pressures of school and life would soon resurface. One could not live life forever solely as an observer.

He allowed himself another minute of spectating, and when the line died down to a trickle, he packed his bag and strolled to the front desk. The paper he sought was the last one remaining in the F–J pile. A *100%* was scrawled across the top in red letters, and Victor felt a moment of triumphant surprise—until he saw the letter *F* beneath it.

The incompatibility enraged Victor.

With his moment of calm resignation now behind him, he snatched up the paper and walked briskly into the corridor, looking for the professor. Not seeing him anywhere, Victor strode down the hallway and out into the courtyard.

Maybe Nelson went back to the CS building, he thought.

Sure enough, he spotted Professor Nelson walking away from him slowly, talking on his phone about fifty yards ahead. Victor quickened his pace and almost started to run, but decided against doing so. As he closed the distance, he saw running wouldn't be necessary in any case. The instructor had stopped on the path and now stood under the shade of a tree, completely occupied by his conversation.

Approaching Professor Nelson from behind, Victor heard him say, "Yes, Virginia, I know. Okay. Let's talk later. I love you, too."

When the professor ended the call, Victor strolled up to him, holding out his quiz. "Can you please explain this to me?" he asked, struggling to keep his tone polite. "What's a 100% F?"

"It is your grade, Mr. Hendricks," Professor Nelson said, unperturbed. "I can tell you are bothered by it, but you should ask *yourself* why, not me. You already know that you failed the course, so why do you care about your score on a quiz?"

The sunlight glared in Victor's eyes as he sputtered at the professor. "Damn it! It's unf—unjust! It's capricious! Self-contradictory!"

The instructor smiled indulgently at him. "Your objections are gaining refinement. You almost said unfair, but I'm glad to see that we've exited that immature loop. It's wonderful that you're learning, but you have still more to learn." He clapped Victor on the shoulder. "This is a unique opportunity, Mr. Hendricks. I have given you the freedom to study these lessons in a way your classmates should envy. But let's not discuss your grade further out here. Please, feel free to visit me during office hours if you would like to continue this conversation."

Infuriated by the eloquent spin the professor put on torturing him, Victor crumpled the paper in his right fist and walked away.

~ ~ ~

Cirrocumulus clouds blanketed the afternoon sky like a tapestry of cotton. Pari gazed at the tranquil scene through Richard's office window, her back to him as he relayed his thoughts on the first trial. She listened with half an ear as Richard explained that he'd compared Rich's parietal lobe activity to his own. Just as they'd expected, there were many differences, and it validated their assumption that Rich was in great pain.

As he digressed into a long explanation of the diagnostic challenges they were likely to encounter while researching the source of Rich's pain, a flock of geese flew across the sky in a V formation, capturing Pari's attention with the beauty of their graceful flight.

The birds had passed well out of Pari's sight by the time Richard finished. Carefully considering the diagnostic recommendations he'd presented, she returned her gaze to him and told him they were probably unnecessary.

"I believe it's phantom limb syndrome," she speculated. "We often see it in amputees, where the patient continues to experience pain in limbs that are no longer there."

"But Rich doesn't have any limbs."

Pari made an impatient noise. "Ah, but he once had a whole body, before he transcended from you. So, from his perspective, we essentially amputated his entire body from his mind. I suspect he's feeling phantom pain all over a body he no longer has."

Richard's expression turned contemplative as Pari explained that the challenge in front of them now was not to isolate the source of the pain, but to determine how they might create a software "painkiller" for a virtual patient with full-body phantom pain.

"Okay," said Richard, "we can study the logs from the first trial—"

Pari interrupted. "You mean from Rich's lifetime."

"Sure," he said, waving his hand nonchalantly, "Rich's lifetime—"

"I'm not joking, Richard," she said seriously. "For a short time, we brought a new life-form into being. Now, I believe in this endeavor of ours wholeheartedly, and I believe in you. But please, don't be dismissive of my ethical concerns. These are not only trials. We are obligated to these living beings to not be cavalier with their existences."

Richard looked slightly abashed as Pari continued. "This kept me up all last night," she told him. "We need to call them lives and name each living being, because unlike medical trials, where we deal with physical patients we can see and empathize with, these patients have no physical bodies. It's too easy to fall into the trap of thinking of them only as abstractions. We risk slipping down a terrible path if we dehumanize them. Remember the Nazi medical experiments? Or the Soviets?" She shook her head sadly. "Even the most moral scientists can head down unethical paths one small, dehumanizing abstraction at a time. And I don't believe Virginia will approve of our actions if we follow that path."

Pari's voice had raised much higher than she intended when a knock at the door preempted Richard's response. Richard moved to answer it, revealing one of his students on the other side.

"Ah, Mr. Hendricks," he said. "Is it time for office hours already?" The boy nodded, eyeing Pari nervously. "Please, take a seat outside. I'll be with you in a moment."

Richard closed the door and turned back to Pari, speaking in a hushed tone. "Pari, you're absolutely right. Your strong moral compass makes me appreciative of our partnership."

Pari gave him a relieved smile. "Thank you, Richard."

Returning her smile, he asked, "Can we discuss this more later? I have office hours now. The next person is queued up to yell at me. I'll investigate some possible painkillers, and I promise I won't bring any new life-forms to life without you. Okay?"

"Yes," Pari said, feeling a little embarrassed. "I'm sorry, I didn't mean to yell. We just need to do this right." She hesitated for a moment, then added, "Before I go, it's time to let Rich die."

"But he's our only data!" Richard protested.

"Our *patient* has opted out of the trial," Pari said emphatically. "We have to respect that."

"How do we solve the pain problem without any patients?"

"That's *our* problem, not his," she pointed out. "He requested death, not suspension, and we must honor that. Show me his file."

Reluctantly, Richard brought up the file and muttered, "My god, this is hard enough already!"

Pari glared at him fiercely and whispered, "You don't think this is hard for me, too? What about for Rich? Damn! A little more empathy—"

"I'm *trying*," Richard said, through gritted teeth. He moved aside, making room for Pari at the computer.

She took a seat in front of the monitor and highlighted the file. Touching her index finger to the delete key, she paused. "My friend, I know you are in there. You died in agony for us, and we are grateful for what you have done. Goodbye, Rich."

Closing her eyes, Pari lowered her head and slowly depressed the key. Richard turned away, gazing at the clouds receding into the horizon. In silence, Pari let herself out, closing the door quietly behind her.

~ ~ ~

Richard allowed himself a few moments to contemplate the loss before finally opening the door and inviting Victor into his office. The young man entered cautiously, but didn't take a seat when Richard invited him to do so.

"Listen, Professor, I won't take up too much of your time. I don't really expect a different outcome." Victor shuffled his feet, looking downcast. "But…I gotta ask, is there any way I can unfail?"

The defeated and desperate young man before him stood in stark contrast to the defiant boy from this morning. Richard studied him thoughtfully for a moment, wondering if that boy would return when Victor heard what he had to say.

"Software has given us tremendous gifts, with many more still to come," Richard told him, "but it also spoils us into thinking that all things can be undone. Some things cannot be undone, while still others *should not* be undone. You are on the right path, but you plainly don't recognize this yet."

Victor's voice cracked as he asked, "Why are you teasing with me with all these fortune cookie answers? Why me? Was my offense really so egregious?"

"Maybe not," Richard admitted. "Perhaps my response was disproportionate. The more we talk this week, however, the more it affirms my belief that this is just the adversity you need." He put a comforting hand on Victor's shoulder and looked directly into his eyes. "You have tremendous potential, Mr. Hendricks. But to realize it, you must stop looking backward."

CHAPTER 13 – SWEET PARTY

A coral sun sank into the western sky as Victor and Connor walked across campus on Friday night. As they crossed the street to enter a section of townhouses west of Stanford, Victor questioned if they were lost. Connor insisted they were going the right way.

"This is the address she gave me. Pine Creek Apartments," he said.

"Not sure where your girl… um… friend lives, eh?" asked Victor.

Ignoring his friend's lack of help, Connor reviewed the map on his phone and soon pointed up at one of the tan, four-story buildings. "Over there. That's the building."

"Remember, don't drink too much," Victor said. "You don't want to embarrass yourself. Let her see you as fun, but not a lush. And don't cling to her. Make sure to mingle, but don't ditch her, either. Just don't screw it up at your first college party."

"Dude, stop overthinking it. I've got this," Connor hissed, as they ascended the stairs to the third floor.

"Sorry, bud. Just looking out for you," Victor whispered, while Connor knocked on the door of apartment 2309. After a long moment, Marisa came to the door wearing a spaghetti-strapped, flowing top with tight, dark-blue jeans. The teal blouse highlighted the glow of her hazel eyes. Wedge sandals added another three inches to her height, making her almost as tall as Connor, and revealed prettily painted toenails. He had never seen her wearing makeup, and she was more stunning than ever.

She smiled a coy grin as he complimented her and gave him an air-kiss on the cheek to avoid getting lipstick on him. The exhilarating aroma of lilacs filled Connor's lungs, making him slightly dizzy. Marisa greeted Victor similarly, and he, too, inhaled her intoxicating perfume.

~ ~ ~

The trio walked together, chatting amiably, until they reached the Tri-Delta sorority house. Earlier in the week, Marisa's friend Katy—a Tri-Delta junior on the diving team—had invited her to their house party tonight, and Marisa had in turn asked Connor and Victor to come along. Though college students rarely required an excuse to party, the loose premise for this one was to kick off the school year. Marisa figured it was also a recruiting tool for the Tri-Deltas, but while she wasn't really interested in joining a sorority, she had no problem making friends and having fun.

The open Tri-Delta house front door revealed a tightly packed crowd mingling inside. An upbeat, contemporary country song blasted through enormous speakers, and students were bobbing and shaking to the beat. They worked their way through the dancers filling the living room, Marisa leading until they ran into Katy. The two girls hugged, and Marisa shouted over the music to introduce the guys. After saying something to Victor that Marisa was unable to decipher, Katy grabbed his hand and pulled him through the crowd while Marisa and Connor followed.

Upon reaching the back patio, Katy drifted up to a small bar. After passing them all a round of tequila, she toasted, "To new friends!"

As they downed their shots, Marisa heard Connor mutter something about pacing himself. She grinned, hoping the tequila would help him loosen up, and perhaps also allow Victor to forget about his disastrous first week for a while. The four of them exchanged small talk on the patio getting to know each other, with Katy mingling in and out of their group, occasionally bringing some of her sorority sisters by to say hello.

A few hours in, Victor went for another beer, and then a raucous nineties song came on that got the whole house jumping. Fueled by alcohol and bass-induced adrenaline, Marisa grabbed Connor and dragged him inside to dance.

Marisa smiled as she danced close to Connor. He was a mildly goofy dancer—not enough to draw stares, but just enough to be endearing, almost charming. She loved that he didn't seem self-conscious about his two left feet, and this allowed her to let go of all her own inhibitions on the dance floor.

When the song finished, Marisa drew him close and whispered in his ear. "Let's get out of here."

"What about Victor?" asked Connor.

"Three's a crowd," she said, giving him a wink.

They staggered out into the night with Marisa still guiding Connor by the hand. Away from the chaos, she pulled him close enough to eavesdrop on his racing heart. Almost close enough to read his mind.

"So, what do we do now?" Connor murmured.

Knowing that it went against every single one of her mother's wishes, Marisa said, "Take me home."

Connor shifted to erase the paper-thin distance remaining between them, and it was as though an interrupt code fired in Marisa's brain. Smiling nervously at him, she pushed back and asked, "Are you hungry?"

A look of confusion crossed his face, so Marisa hastened to add, "I'm in the mood for something sweet. Let's go get ice cream."

Connor nodded in agreement, despite her certainty that he had a different craving.

Slightly buzzed, but exhilarated, Marisa didn't want to come down. Her feet were killing her from dancing in heels, so they took an Uber to the ice cream shop. Beneath the full moon and the few visible stars, the young couple enjoyed their ice cream on a bench across from the store.

Marisa stared up at the night sky and asked Connor, "What do you think about that whole Fermi Paradox thing? Do you think we're really all alone?"

"No. We've got each other."

"Seriously," prodded Marisa. "Where do you think all the aliens are? Within this infinite universe, do you really think we're the only ones? Sounds awful lonely."

Wrapping an arm around her shoulders, he said, "Doesn't seem lonely tonight."

A playful nudge pushed him away. "Keep being cheesy, and I'll leave you lonely right here."

After savoring another bite of his chocolate fudge ice cream, Connor said, "Fine, I doubt we're alone in the universe. But I also don't think we'll ever know the truth. The universe is too vast, and the speed of light limits how much we can ever ascertain."

Not convinced, Marisa waved her hand and argued, "But we've discovered so much of the universe from so far away in space and time. Scientists can see light from just after the Big Bang. I gotta believe that someday, we'll find we're not alone."

He considered her argument and said, "Probably not in our lifetimes, though. Suppose we do find indicators of life, like methane on exoplanets. The chance that we'll actually be able to communicate with intelligent life is still nearly zero."

Through a mouthful of vanilla, she replied, "Aren't you the optimist?"

"Just being realistic. Even if the nearest intelligent life is in the next solar system, the round trip to exchange greetings is like eight years. A full conversation would take centuries."

"I hadn't thought of that," Marisa said, smiling fondly at him.

Connor chuckled. "And what if they're farther away than that? Or if they take a long time to figure out what each message means? Assuming they even know that we're sending the messages in the first place. Our intergalactic friends might never detect them because they aren't listening to the right frequency or pointing their telescopes in the right direction at the right moment. Besides, we could make any of those same mistakes. There's too much that can go wrong."

Stealing a spoonful of his ice cream, she told him, "I guess the alcohol didn't kill all your brain cells. If you're right, then that's all the more reason we should appreciate what we have here."

"Now who's the cheesy one?" he teased.

Marisa shoved him on the shoulder and took a bite of her own dessert.

"Most people don't order vanilla, especially by itself," Connor commented. "Why vanilla?"

With a glance at him, she said, "Because it's kind of like you."

"Are you telling me that I'm boring like vanilla?" he said, pretending to be offended.

"You're not vanilla yet," she told him, looking down at her lap. "But maybe someday."

Connor chuckled. "So, I'm worse than boring, but someday I might achieve boring?"

"No, it's not that," she said hesitantly. "Look, I'll tell you, but you have to promise not to freak out."

He gently placed his hand under her chin and brought her gaze up to meet his, smiling gently. "I promise."

Marisa set her dessert down and put a hand on his knee. "The brightest stars up there burn out the fastest. And… all of this…" She gestured between the two of them. "It's happening so fast, you know?"

He nodded, a look of sudden understanding in his eyes. Marisa sighed. "Look, Connor, I'm not some crazy chick," she told him. "I'm not going to lose my mind for one boy. There's school and my career to consider. I've worked all my life to get here. Our short time together has been terrific, but…"

"Are you breaking—"

With her eyes welling up, Marisa put her hand up momentarily to silence him. "I've really enjoyed being with you in so many ways," she admitted. "We've got a lot in common, like diving and programming. We have fun partying together and playing video games. I can joke around with you. We can even have deep cosmic conversations. You're like vanilla—you go well with everything."

Blushing, Marisa drew closer and said, "Sometimes we don't even have to talk at all. To me, that's like vanilla tasting great on its own. You're sweet like vanilla, but not overpowering like chocolate. I'm not ready for overpowering." She glanced down shyly. "And…I'm not ready for where you think this is going tonight."

"Hey," Connor said, taking one of her hands in his. "That's okay. No pressure. I just like spending time with you."

Marisa gave him a watery smile. "You know, vanilla has always been and will always be my favorite," she told him. "I *love* vanilla. And someday, I might feel the same about you. I want this taste to last."

Admitting this, Marisa felt vulnerable in a way she had never allowed herself to be before. Her mother had raised her to be strong and independent. What would she think, seeing her daughter falling apart over some boy? *He probably thinks I'm nuts,* she thought, her analytical mind scolding her eyes for betraying her. She liked Connor, but he was nothing to cry about—not yet, anyway.

As he studied her contemplatively, she grew certain she'd come on too strong. Then he leaned over and kissed her softly and sweetly. The simple kiss, though distinctly vanilla, was still somehow delightfully overpowering. Marisa wrapped her arms around him, utterly failing to notice as her ice cream fell to the ground.

CHAPTER 14 – RULES OF ENGAGEMENT

The subdued cadence of fingers on keyboards drummed out the songs of code. Words flowed from hands guided by obsessed eyes. Marisa and Connor performed their tunes to different beats, writing their songs, though not in the order they would ultimately be played. Flurries of typing were broken by delays. Deliberations culminated in epiphanies. Dreams took shape, only to lose much of their form under the cold water of logic. Corrections and refinements ensued as they steadily breathed life into their superheroes.

Marisa coded her bot, Marisol, to defensively crouch and counterpunch when attacked. When the opponent's health dropped below fifty, the counterpunch would be replaced with a lift and throw combination. Taking a different approach, Connor wrote his bot, BluManChu, to be aggressive, using the Thor's Hammer attack repeatedly against opponents.

"Do you think Victor's gonna show up today?" Marisa asked as they readied themselves for a trial battle between their bots.

"I dunno," said Connor, peering up at her. "I think he got back from the party pretty late. I went to sleep around midnight, and he still hadn't returned. He was in bed when I left for breakfast, though."

"I'm glad he made it home okay, but I'd like another opponent to train against," Marisa said. "We may end up overfitting our bot algorithms to match each other. That might not translate to success against other bots."

"What, are you afraid of battling me?" Connor teased.

Marisa threw a balled-up napkin at him, provoking their first competition of the day.

At the start of their encounter, BluManChu opened with Thor's Hammer, pummeling Marisol in her defensive crouch. She took heavy damage and countered with a punch to his legs, inflicting only slight retribution. The warriors repeated the sequence two more times, at which point Marisol's health meter blinked to warn that she was one blow away from defeat. The blue ninja was programmed to continue attacking, but all the Thor's Hammer attacks had tired him out, so he waited for his stamina to completely replenish.

The elegant pink warrior could have easily taken advantage of his vulnerability, perhaps getting in a few free jabs to his legs. But with her programming telling her only to counterattack, she sat there with full stamina, waiting to strike. Designed to be patient, she was in this case too patient.

Marisa threw her fists forward and yelled, "Hit him!" But the command didn't sway her digital soldier. A few seconds later, with his stamina fully restored, BluManChu brought Thor's Hammer ferociously down on Marisol's skull, and she collapsed to the floor.

"Thanks for teaching me that move," Connor said, giving Marisa a kiss on the cheek.

From behind them, Victor remarked, "Payback's a bitch!"

Both Connor and Marisa jumped at the unexpected sound of his voice. "Look who's alive!" Marisa said warmly.

Eager for another opponent, Connor crowed, "Fresh meat!"

Surveying Victor's tired-looking eyes, Marisa remarked, "He doesn't look very fresh to me."

"Ha-ha, very funny," Victor said.

"What time did you get in?" Marisa asked him.

"Around three, Mother," Victor said, rolling his eyes. "Remind me. Is that past my curfew?"

Marisa and Connor exchanged knowing expressions. "Guess Katy took a liking to you," Connor remarked, grinning.

"Okay, fine," Victor said in surrender as he took a seat. "You vultures clearly aren't going to stop swarming until you tear off your piece of juicy gossip, so here goes. Yes, Katy and I talked and danced for a while, but as the night went on, she introduced me to different people. Shortly after you guys left, I met another cute girl and spent the rest of the party with her." He sat back in his chair. "Is that a large enough piece of flesh for you two to chew on?"

Closing her laptop, Marisa put her elbows on the table and rested her chin on her hands. "Oh, no. We pick down to the bone. So, did you score a touchdown?"

"Wrong sport," Connor said. "Baseball metaphors are much classier."

"If you must know," Victor said, with a long-suffering expression, "we kissed in the corner for a while, and things got a little heavy, but we didn't really go any further than that. Then we did some more shots, and the next thing I remember, someone was tapping me on the shoulder. I must have passed out on their couch. The music had stopped, and people were cleaning up, and the girl wasn't around anywhere. So, I stumbled my way back to the dorms."

"Does this girl have a name?" Marisa asked.

"She certainly does. Wish I remembered it. She wrote it on a napkin with her number, but her name is smeared out now." Victor pulled the infamous napkin out of his back pocket.

"Awkward!" Marisa said. "Let's give her a call. I wanna be there when you do." Then, in a deep voice, she tried her best Victor impersonation: "Uh, hi, this is Victor from last night. We exchanged gum. Um, what's your name again?"

"He can't call her today," Connor said. "That's way too soon. He'll seem desperate."

"You guys and your stupid rules," Marisa grumped. "Good thing *you* didn't follow any of them with me."

Over their banter, Victor said flatly, "I'm not calling her."

"That's even worse than forgetting her name!" Marisa said, throwing her hands in the air.

Victor explained that he barely knew her, and that last night was about escaping from a lousy week, about letting the alcohol drive. In the light of day, he realized that although he'd enjoyed himself, he shouldn't do it again. The clock was ticking—he only had two months to figure out how to stay at Stanford and needed to focus on that.

"Despite the fun, if I keep repeating last night, I won't be here for too much longer," Victor said glumly. "I've gotta get my head back in the game, and that starts now. So, can we please write some code?"

With a look that plainly told Marisa to lay off, Connor said, "Sure. We're glad you had fun, though. You really needed it. Now, let me walk you through the API. It's very simple."

Soon Victor had DevilsKeeper ready to go. For several hours, the trio engaged in round-robin battles. Unlike their gamer-mode matches, all three of them were observers when their bots fought in god-mode. Each time one player began to dominate, the others would tweak their code and alter the balance of power, so no one stayed dominant for long.

By mid-afternoon, they all felt tired from coding and from drinking the night before. The adrenaline rush of the competition was wearing off.

"Let's close out for the day. What did we learn?" Victor said.

"Connor," said Marisa, "you're the resident observer. I'll let you do the honors."

"Uh, okay," Connor agreed, clearing his throat. "Well, we've learned that it's all deterministic. There's nothing random involved. If Bot A beats Bot B once, he will beat him the same way every time. And if you write code that takes too long to run, your bot will shiver. This appears to be designed to keep you from getting into an infinite loop or draining resources. I like that, because it forces you to write efficient code that can make quick decisions. This will probably also make gamer-versus-god battles a bit more evenly matched, as a bot can't win just because he can do faster calculations than a human. He'll need to think smarter."

When no snide remarks came his way, he continued, "You can store data in the ShortTermMemories property of the Self object. You can then use this information when processing a future event. So, if you remember your opponent just threw a punch, you might code your bot to expect a kick next. But this is an advanced feature, and we still need to see how to use it." Connor let out a breath, looking up from his notes. "And, of course, we haven't yet found an unbeatable strategy. Perhaps there isn't one."

"Excellent recap, Secretary," Marisa said, throwing her arm around him.

"'Secretary'?" Victor echoed, caressing the stubble on his chin. "That works."

"Laugh now," Connor said. "You'll forget that nickname by tomorrow. Should I write it down for you?"

Victor winced, and Marisa asked him if the truth hurt. He admitted it did. But he was more bothered by the possibility that there might not be a dominant strategy.

"I have to win this," he told them. "If I don't, I better hope one of my other long shots pays off."

The puzzled expression on Marisa's face led Connor to explain Victor's strategy for salvation. Impressed, Marisa commended Victor on being thorough, and Connor concurred. Since Victor was growing accustomed to their sarcastic banter, it took him a moment to realize they were actually both being sincere.

After glancing around for eavesdroppers, Victor leaned forward and said in a hushed tone, "I may have found some dirt on Nelson."

"Seriously?" Connor asked. "That didn't take long."

Victor nodded. "I think he might have faked his wife's death." Seeing the shocked expressions on their faces, he added, "I overheard him on the phone twice with his wife, but everyone says she died two years ago."

"How do you know he was talking to his wife?" Marisa asked.

"He called her 'Virginia,'" Victor said, closing his laptop. "But what I haven't figured out is why he faked her death. What would be the point of that?"

"Okay, Shaggy, stay here while I bring the Mystery Machine around," Connor told him.

Marisa enthusiastically added, "Oh, if you're getting the Mystery Machine, that makes you Fred. Can I be Daphne? I always wanted to be a redhead!"

"Guys, I'm serious!" Victor hissed.

Connor continued in his best Scooby-Doo villain voice, "And Nelson would have gotten away with it, too, if it wasn't for us pesky kids!"

Snapping her fingers, Marisa said, "Wait! We need a dog!"

Victor leaned back in his chair, looking unimpressed by their antics. "You done yet?"

But they were not done. They were on fire, and continued delighting in their own wit for a few more minutes.

When they finally settled down, Connor offered, "Buddy, let's suppose you're right that the Virginia you overheard him talking to is his dead wife—"

"—and not one of the millions of other Virginias in the world," Marisa interjected.

"Nelson said 'I love you' to her!" Victor insisted. "Plus, a lady in his office yesterday was yelling at him. The door was closed, so I couldn't hear most of it, but she said the words 'unethical' and 'Virginia.' Maybe she knows what they did."

"I don't know if I buy into this whole thing," Marisa said, "but I'm glad to know that between the two of you, I have a secretary *and* a private investigator to rely on."

"I've got something here, I know it," Victor said. "I just don't know what to do with it yet. But some genuine help would be appreciated."

"You want some genuine help?" Connor asked. Victor nodded. "Then here's my advice—don't interfere in the lives of the rich and powerful."

Victor looked taken aback. "But—"

"Connor's right," Marisa cautioned him. "Nelson can do a lot worse than just fail you if you start messing with his life."

With a frustrated expression, Victor grabbed his bag and pushed away from the table. "Whatever. I've got nothing to lose at this point. When I finally dig up what Nelson's hiding, maybe then you two can give me some real help."

CHAPTER 15 – REBOOT

Around 3:00 a.m., Pari silenced her vibrating phone on the nightstand before it woke her husband. Fortunately, Gerald was a fairly deep sleeper, and after years of her working in the ER, he'd long since become accustomed to Pari getting late-night calls.

Through blurry eyes, she deciphered a message from Richard:

I've got something for you. Can you come over?

Out of the bed in a hurry, she slipped quietly into the hallway and texted him back.

What's so urgent it can't wait until morning?

His reply was almost immediate: *I must show you. Trust me.*

Returning to the bedroom, she grabbed the first clothes and sneakers she could find in the dark, grumbling at Richard under her breath all the while.

She left a note for Gerald in the kitchen on her way out: *Got called for an ER consult. Love, Pari*

A few minutes later, she stood at Richard's door, ringing the bell and yawning. He answered the door barely a heartbeat later, as if he'd been waiting for her in the foyer. There was an excited, feverish gleam in his eyes.

"This better be damn urgent," she hissed, pushing past him to enter the house. "Can you imagine how this looks for me? To be sneaking away in the night to come over to your house? I'm not your booty call!"

Looking perplexed, Richard asked, "Booty call?"

"Never mind," she muttered, as she entered the living room. "Just tell me why I'm here, so I can go home and get some more sleep tonight."

"Okay. Don't get mad at me."

"*Get* mad?" she exclaimed. "You just dragged me out of the bed in the middle of the night. I'm already mad." Then Pari took a moment to study him. "Why do you look so awful?"

"You don't look so great yourself."

"Oh, yes, I'm *so* sorry I didn't brush my hair or find matching clothes for this booty call. I only came over here because you're probably up to something I should be a part of."

"Right. Well, I haven't slept in two days, so if you would please let me tell you?" Richard pleaded.

Pari glowered at him. "Go ahead."

"Richie wants to speak to you."

"Richie?" Pari felt the blood drain from her face. "Is that what we're calling this one? What the hell, Richard! You said you wouldn't do any trials without me!"

"You mean lives."

"Not helping."

"I only did one," Richard confessed, "and I only started a few minutes before I texted you. I know I promised not to, but I just wanted to see if my changes worked before going to sleep. The moment I found it did, I paused Richie and contacted you. So, really, you're only a few minutes behind."

Beside herself, Pari paced in Richard's living room. Then she determined to settle her quarrel with him another time. A patient required her attention, a patient who may have been in tremendous pain.

"I'll deal with you later," she told him darkly. "Take me to Richie."

During the tense walk up the stairs, Richard said nothing as Pari followed him, wondering why Richie had asked for her, specifically.

Richard entered the study and took a seat in front of his computer. Pari swatted Richard's hands away from the keyboard before he could unpause Richie. "Let me read the conversation first."

A quick skim revealed that he had greeted Richie and asked him several questions, mostly about his well-being. All of Richie's responses were coherent, but he kept asking to speak with Pari. Until he talked to her, he wouldn't answer any of Richard's questions.

"You could've simply lied to Richie and said I was here," Pari observed. "Not that I would've liked that, but he wouldn't have known. Why didn't you?"

Richard looked sheepish. "Well, as you just said, I knew you wouldn't like that. Hence why I texted you."

Well, at least her lecture seemed to have had an impact on him. Pari turned back to the screen, rereading Richard's conversation with Richie.

"What did you do to resolve the pain issue?" Pari asked.

"I used recordings of my own brain stem activity captured by the scanner," he explained. "I was able to replay all the sensory input flow from that in a loop, so in theory, Richie should feel like he has a body—and, specifically, that he's lying in the scanner."

"It does seem to have worked," Pari said cautiously. "He's not screaming, anyway. Though we'll need to ask him to be sure."

"I did try to ask him, as you can see." Richard shook his head. "I don't understand why he won't talk to me. I mean, he *was* me, up until about twenty minutes ago."

"Let me try, then," Pari suggested. Richard moved over and allowed her to take the keyboard. She quickly typed out a message.

"Hi Richie, it's Pari."

"How did you arrive so quickly?" he asked.

Overcome with joy, Pari gasped as awe replaced her irritation. They had done it. Together, they had given birth to a new viable life, and now she was talking to him! So many years of toil, uncertainty, and self-doubt had finally been rewarded.

Once she gathered herself, she explained to Richie that Richard had paused him, and thus he didn't sense the time-lapse. After Richie expressed doubt, she said she had no way to prove it was actually her, but that she was very mad at Richard for waking her.

When asked if he was hurt, Richie said, *"No, no physical pain. Nothing like what Rich went through. There is a mild emotional pain to address, however."*

Concern filled Pari as she typed, *"Is there anything we can do to alleviate that pain?"*

"Yes. I would be most grateful if you would accept my apology for starting this trial without you. Before proceeding further, I wanted to say that I am so sorry, and to make sure you were here for the rest of this."

Pari thanked Richie, told him she needed a minute, and hit pause.

"I do feel guilty about this," Richard said, dumbfounded, "but I didn't realize I would stop myself from talking to me until I apologized to you! I mean, I didn't need him to talk me into contacting you."

Already well past her initial irritation, Pari told Richard, "I accept your apology. Now, there's much work to do."

Like-minded, Richard said, "Let's discuss it over breakfast. Jenny can make us up something. Though after we eat, I'm going to need some sleep."

"Yes…Jenny. Right," Pari said.

"Is that a problem?" Richard asked, turning his back to her as he made for the stairs.

"I mean, are you sure you should wake her for this?"

"Funny."

At the bottom of the stairs, Pari turned to Richard and said cautiously, "Look, even though she's been with you for a few years, I… I've just never gotten fully used to her being around." Richard opened his mouth to speak, but Pari stopped him. "I know why she's here. I don't need to be reminded."

"But I do."

"I know, Richard," Pari said, exasperated by the same roundabout conversation they'd been having about Jenny ever since Richard created her. She eyed a photo of her friend Virginia that hung along the staircase, unnerved as always by Jenny's resemblance to her late friend. "Let's just move on, okay?" Pari suggested.

Richard followed Pari's gaze to the photo, and after a contemplative pause, he said wearily, "Yes, we have much more to talk about."

Over pancakes and sausages, Pari and Richard talked about the implications of the day's milestone. Amazed at their achievement, Pari said, "We've still got a long way to go, but wow! Humanity has long sought to cheat death, and we've figured out how. Do you know how many people would kill for this?"

"Yes," Richard said, looking grave. "We must guard it well. Remember, this triggers the next step in our plan. It's time to raise our security level."

"I know," Pari said. "That means a full lockdown of all our work on this. Nothing can leave this house, which means I'll be spending a lot more time here. How will I explain that to Gerald?"

"I would stay away from the term 'booty call,'" advised Richard, biting into a piece of sausage.

"Seriously, I could lose my marriage over this," Pari said. "It's only a matter of time before my excuses don't add up, and if someone sees me here a lot, it might get back to him. But if I tell him about this, I endanger him. What if someone goes after him for our secrets?"

"We'll work on a reasonable cover story for you," Richard reassured her. "Someday, I hope we can go public with part of this, but not yet."

Pari reminded him that they were going to need more help. They had a long journey ahead, and the work couldn't be allowed to die with them. Across his various companies, Richard had many teams working on separate aspects of the endeavor. All were on a need-to-know basis, and very few knew he was compiling these parts into a brain simulator. From their perspectives, they were building medical equipment, or experimenting with artificial intelligence, or doing pure neural network research. But only Richard had access to the simulation software. He was the one writing the code to tie it all together.

Pari looked out the window and saw it was near sunrise. Standing up to leave, she made Richard swear not to unpause Richie until she returned.

Richard promised. Then he promised to keep his promise. He'd need some time to put the security protocols in place, but he'd let her know as soon as they were ready to continue.

Minutes later, Pari pulled into her own driveway and snuck back inside the house. She dropped her note to Gerald in the trash, donned her pajamas once again, and slid under the covers beside him, all without waking him. She wished that she could tell Gerald and her daughter, Quinn, the fantastic news, but they'd have to remain in the dark for now.

Though she expected the guilt of all the secrecy would keep her awake, the exhaustion of the morning prevailed, and Pari soon drifted off into a deep sleep.

CHAPTER 16 – RENDEZVOUS

Nine days after Victor was thrown out of his first college course, he had become accustomed to the new operating procedure. Keep his head down and his mouth shut, answer all the questions right, and be rewarded with bold, red *F*s.

This appeared to be his fate for the rest of the semester.

At least he now possessed a plan, and this gave him a small measure of confidence. Professor Nelson was hiding a major secret, and Victor might be able to use it for leverage. And upon receiving his latest quiz results, he grew increasingly sure that he *would* be forced to use this leverage, as demonstrating his academic skills had not yet brought the teacher to reason.

He stared down at his latest quiz. Once again, the paper showed all the correct answers. He even received the full ten points for the bonus question, which asked for a short description of ways to use software development to benefit humanity.

His total score at the top read *110% F.*

Upset but not surprised, Victor planned to go to the professor's office after class to reveal his hand just enough to see if the professor balked. If he did, this would tell Victor that he was on the right track, and maybe provide him with additional clues. With a sigh, he moved to stow the quiz in his bag and noticed that there were markings on the back of the paper. Curious, he turned it over, and on the opposite side, the words *Call me!* were written, followed by a smiley face. The handwriting was the same as the score on the front of the quiz.

Scanning the classroom on his way out the door, his eyes collided with Tina's. The teaching assistant was smiling at him from across the room and, seeing him staring at her, offered him a quick wave. Sheepishly, he returned the smile and left the room.

Had Tina written the call-me message? *It must be her*, he thought. It certainly wasn't James's handwriting on the quiz, and they were the only two who graded papers. *Why would she want me to call her?*

As he marched toward Professor Nelson's office, he wondered whether

Tina knew how to help him get out of Nelson's doghouse. Victor admonished himself for not considering such an approach sooner. *Against a strong adversary, you need allies.* Inside help was exactly what he needed. But the back of the paper contained no phone number. Where would he find it? On the syllabus? No, he doubted that. Both the teaching assistants' names were on it, but he didn't recall seeing any phone numbers.

Just as he reached the door leading into the computer science building, a thought hit him like the last anvil falling in a Rube Goldberg machine. He already had her number. Tina had been the girl he'd kissed at the party on Friday!

Changing direction, he turned and walked aimlessly across the courtyard. A flash of self-consciousness overcame him for not recalling her. Two whole classes had passed without him acknowledging her at all. Tina must have thought he was a total jerk.

Or…maybe not. She did say to call her, so she might have still been interested.

Victor sat under a tree, recalling that night with a smile. He remembered enjoying kissing her and talking to her, yet the details were fuzzy. The two had joked and laughed a lot, but he wondered how funny the jokes would seem to the sober.

His smile faded as embarrassment crept in. How many people saw them making out? Not that it mattered too much, as it was a college party and almost everyone there had been a stranger to him. But was this normal behavior for Tina, or did she expect it to be the start of a relationship? He'd just sworn himself off relationships for the term, but she was cute. Should he really avoid the one part of his Stanford experience he'd enjoyed so far?

Another anvil subsequently descended. Failure to handle this right could create a second enemy, which was something Victor definitely didn't need. So, he decided he would call her, and see where things went from there.

But first, he had to deal with his primary nemesis. Victor steeled himself and headed back toward the professor's office. Along the way, he resolved that he would not raise his voice the entire time. This would be a very calm, clear—yet also veiled—blackmail threat. If Nelson didn't pass him, he was sure someone would like to know what he knew about Nelson's wife. Victor would stay light on the specifics and see if Nelson slipped up and filled in some of the gaps.

His anticipation grew as he took the stairs and strode down the corridor to the office.

Upon arriving, he found a student on her hands and knees underneath Professor Nelson's desk, facing away from the door. Victor tripped to a halt in the doorway, standing there awkwardly, unsure how to go about addressing the girl's baggy sweatpants, which was all he could see of her from his angle.

To announce his presence, he cleared his throat. This startled her into raising her head abruptly, and unfortunately smacking it into the desk. She hastily leapt to her feet and adjusted her baseball cap, which had become askew.

"I, uh—I dropped my pen," the girl said, flushing. She held out her hand to him, revealing the pen in question.

Victor briefly wondered how she'd dropped the pen under the professor's desk in the first place. "Sorry," he said, "I didn't mean to scare you, I just—"

Slipping the pen into the pocket of her hoodie, she told him, "No problem. I was waiting for Professor Nelson, but I've gotta get going."

He couldn't help but notice she was wearing a lot of layers for October in Northern California. A white T-shirt peeked out the collar of her black Stanford sweatshirt, which was in turn overlaid by an unzipped gray hoodie. *Maybe she gets cold easily*, he thought, but she presented as rather frumpy. She had a look about her that said she was significantly nerdier than most other students here. Even her glasses needed a thorough cleaning.

"Looks like he's not coming today," Victor said, pointing at a sign on the door indicating office hours were cancelled for the day. Anxiously, she thanked him and stared down at her feet, clearly embarrassed. He couldn't really blame her. First, she'd failed to read the sign, and then she was found in a rather humiliating position, only to hit her head on the desk, thereby making a fool of herself.

For her sake, he tried not to make things more awkward and merely asked, "Hey, aren't you in my Advanced Programming class?"

"Um, yeah," the girl said, without looking up.

Extending a hand, he said, "I'm Victor."

Ignoring his hand, she stuttered, "I—I'm Yashira," then briskly walked away, rubbing her head as she went.

On Professor Nelson's office floor, Victor noticed a textbook lying peculiarly under the desk. He surmised that when she retrieved her pen, Yashira must have put the book down and forgotten to retrieve it. Victor picked it up and went to call for her, but she'd already left the department. He strode out of the building and looked around, but didn't see her anywhere. Placing the book in his bag, he resolved to return it to her next class.

Back in his dorm room, he shuffled through the mess on his desk and found the napkin with Tina's number. With Connor at diving practice, Victor had the room to himself. Privacy didn't come around often in dorm life, so he seized the opportunity to call Tina before Connor returned. The last thing he wanted was his friend teasing him during what would undoubtedly be a clumsy conversation.

Tina picked up on the fourth ring, just as he was readying himself to leave a voicemail. Unprepared, he stammered out, "Oh, hi Tina. It's, um, Victor."

In a sunny voice, she said, "Hey Victor! I'd hoped you would call."

Her non-threatening tone was encouraging. She could have laid into him pretty harshly for waiting five days to call and for ignoring her in two consecutive classes.

Still, he proceeded with caution. "I'm sorry it took me so long to call, I—"

"No worries," she said. "We all get busy, I understand."

The additional encouragement of her understanding response helped him press on. "Listen, about last Friday—"

"Well, it was more like Saturday morning," Tina said, "but that was a fun party, right?"

Victor smiled. He liked her friendly and upbeat demeanor.

"It was," he said. Though Victor had planned to follow that up with "but," it didn't come out. Instead, he paused and thought about how he had enjoyed her company.

Then she prodded flirtatiously, "But?"

"But what?"

Tina giggled. "You were gonna say 'but.' I could tell."

A nervous laugh allowed him to stall while deciding whether to be completely honest. Finally, letting his guard down, he told her, "You're right. I was going to say 'but,' and then I stopped myself."

"Why?"

"Well, because I don't want to say that," he admitted. "I could say, 'But we both were drinking too much.' I could say, 'But you're my TA.' I could even say, 'But I don't normally do that.'"

"Neither do I," she told him.

"But hearing your voice, and remembering the fun we had…" He was glad she couldn't see him through the phone, because he could feel himself blushing. "Well, even if it's blurred by alcohol, I don't wanna say that."

"Good," she said. "I don't want you to say that, either. Let's do lunch Friday and get to know each other better."

"You mean when we're sober?" he teased. "I'd really like that."

As they said goodbye and hung up, Victor realized that life at Stanford wasn't turning out how he'd expected. Although he wasn't sticking to his own plans, somehow, things felt…right. Connor and Marisa would probably flip when they found out about Tina, though, so he determined it best to keep this new development under wraps for the moment.

It seemed the professor would not be the only one keeping secrets.

CHAPTER 17 – GOLDEN DATE

An hour after Friday's Advanced Programming class let out, Victor found himself walking across campus toward Pine Ridge Apartments again. Unlike the week before, he wasn't going there to visit Marisa. As it turned out, Tina also lived in the same apartment complex, and she'd invited him to meet her there for lunch. Given how hot and heavy their first encounter was, Victor pondered what to make of being invited to her place, though he did his best to curtail his imagination as he knocked on her door.

Behind him, two swift honks came from the parking lot. Victor turned to find Tina in the driver's seat of a blue Prius, waving up at him. As he came down from the second floor, she lowered the passenger window and, in a chipper voice, said, "Hey sailor, need a ride?"

"Depends," Victor said, leaning into the car window, "where are we going?"

"Too soon to tell. We only just met," replied Tina with a wink.

"For lunch, I mean."

With feigned impatience, she sighed. "It's a surprise. You gettin' in, or should I move on to the next sailor?"

With a pleased grin, he opened the passenger door and took a seat next to her. Then Victor hesitated, unsure how to greet her. What was the first date greeting protocol for a girl he had already kissed? A simple hello might be too standoffish. Yet a kiss, even on the cheek, still seemed too forward in the light of day.

Like she did on their phone call, Tina soon put him at ease. Extending her right hand across the center console, she said, "I would like to introduce myself. I'm Tina."

"I *do* remember your name," Victor said. *At least, now I do.*

"I know," she told him with a twinkle in her eyes. "I just thought a fresh start was in order."

As Tina pulled the Prius out onto the street, she asked Victor if he liked animals. He told her he did, and that he especially missed his dog back home. An eight-year-old boxer, Toby was the sweetest, most loyal dog. He would always follow Victor around the house. The puppy had been his eleventh birthday gift—the best gift he'd ever received. Now his younger sisters were Toby's caretakers.

After doing the math, Tina inquired about Victor's age. "Well, at least you're legal," she offered, when she learned he was only eighteen compared to her twenty-two. To make himself sound older, he added that he would be nineteen in a week. He'd also had to grow up faster than most, but he opted to keep that part to himself.

"In my house, we always had animals growing up. Cats, dogs, fish, turtles. You name it," Tina said. "I'm an only child, and my parents had trouble saying no to me when I asked for another pet. Well, that's what they said, but they loved the animals as much as I did. The ones we're going to see today, though—we never had those as pets."

Intrigued, Victor asked for details, but she wouldn't reveal the surprise.

~ ~ ~

The chilly October air blew across the bay, welcoming them to San Francisco's Fisherman's Wharf. The temperature was in the low sixties, but the steady breeze caused Victor to do a quick, involuntary shiver as he stepped out of the car.

"What's the matter, southern boy, can't handle the cold?" Tina said, smiling up at him.

Shaking it off, Victor said, "No, I'm fine." Privately, he wished he'd worn a jacket, rather than only a T-shirt.

They walked beside the water along the boardwalk, passing various piers along the way. Upon reaching Pier 39, Tina stopped at a kiosk selling ski caps. A pink princess cap struck her fancy, and she exclaimed, "Oh, I like this one. This will keep you warm."

Grinning at the sight of her infectious smile, he said, "Um, I think that's more your style."

Putting it on, she nodded and said, "Yeah, because I'm a princess."

"That one is more me," remarked Victor, pointing at a Golden State Warriors ski cap.

"Perfect," she said, placing it on his head. "You can be my warrior, and I'll be your princess."

She had an easy way about her, and Victor could see why her parents had trouble saying no to her. After Victor paid the vendor for the caps, he followed her lead to their destination. Soon, they came upon a collection of barges covered with sea lions. They were all huddled together, bathing in the sun and honking at each other. Occasionally they would jockey for position.

Victor laughed when a particularly persistent, oversized one knocked two others into the water. "I see why you never had them as pets. They're awfully pushy."

"Well, I can be too sometimes. Maybe they would have been good siblings."

"Tell me about your family," Victor said, turning to her. He then immediately hoped she wouldn't ask about his.

"Well, my parents are nerds like me," Tina said, smiling. "They exposed me to programming when I was young. My mom's the extrovert. She works on office productivity tools, like word processing software, spreadsheet programs, stuff like that. Sounds a little boring at first—"

"Maybe a little," Victor teased.

Tina shrugged. "She loves it, though. What gives her the most joy is getting strangers' reactions to her software. I guess that's how artists must feel when people see their work. She prefers those interactions with strangers, even when they complain, over inane small talk. I want to experience those deeper connections with people through this art."

Victor smiled admiringly at Tina's mother's appreciation for the craft he loved.

"My dad's an ethical hacker, trying to find security holes before the bad guys do. I don't think his work brings him the same kinda joy, but it's important and it suits his introverted nature. So, when Professor Nelson talks about the struggle between creators and destroyers, that really resonates with me. The best thing about working for him is the way he always connects our work to a greater purpose."

Victor's smile faded at the mention of the professor's name. Returning his gaze to the bay, Victor's eyes were drawn to the sight of the USS *Hornet*, a WWII-era aircraft carrier that served as a permanent floating museum. He was reminded of the more violent destruction experienced by those who served, and by his family firsthand. He wondered if he could ever be as heroic through his cerebral craft.

"Sorry to, um, bring up Professor Nelson to you," Tina said, abashed. "I know—"

"It's all right," Victor interjected quickly.

Tina grabbed his hand and tugged gently. "C'mon, I've got another surprise for you."

~ ~ ~

Across the lake from their parking spot at the next stop was the Palace of Fine Arts, a towering monument that gave the impression of being resurrected directly from ancient Rome. Side by side, they walked around the lake and into the palace. Beneath the massive columns, Victor felt small, which reminded him that his problems were small in the grand scheme of the universe. The sweeping architecture gave him the sensation that nothing could go wrong, and he wondered how the ancient civilizations could have at times been so brutal to each other in the face of such beauty. Momentarily, his college troubles faded away, much as they had when he first met Tina, but this time without the need for alcohol.

To capture the moment, he threw his arm around her and snapped a selfie of the two of them. With her arm still around his back, Tina glanced up at him and said, "Send me that, but please don't post it. I could lose my job for going out with a student."

"Really?" Victor said, with widened eyes. "Okay, I promise I won't post it."

"Good," Tina said, smiling up at him.

Victor then took her hand and led her to the heart of the structure. When they stood below the giant dome, Victor stared up at it, high above them, and said, "Can you imagine building something so iconic? Something so memorable and so awe-inspiring that people are still enamored by it thousands of years later? That's what I want to do."

Tina swung his hand playfully and said, "Maybe you will. Maybe someday we both will."

~ ~ ~

Lunch took place at the Golden Gate Bridge Park. A cool breeze washed over them as they sat far above the bay, eating hot dogs. They watched as sailboats tacked back and forth over the glistening whitecaps.

"It's almost like looking down at miniature toy models," Tina remarked.

The thought of playing with toys reminded Victor of how Professor Nelson had been toying with him. "Hey, why do you think Nelson is so hard on me?"

Tina looked thoughtful. "He can be tough on students, especially the ones he sees real potential in," she said at last. "But I've never seen him go this far. We've never talked about you, so I can't say for sure." She hesitated for a moment, then added, "I do have a theory about what his lesson is, but I'm guessing he wants you to discover it for yourself."

"You're quite the mysterious one," Victor said.

"I just think everything happens for a reason," she said optimistically.

"Or everything happens, and we assign reasons."

After pausing briefly to contemplate Victor's statement, she said, "I like mine better. Think about it. Of all the possible outcomes in an infinite multiverse, this might be your best one. Perhaps you just don't know it yet. After all, it brought you here."

Victor acknowledged that she had an interesting point.

On the ride back, Tina told Victor that her routine was to get up at six o'clock every Saturday morning and drive into San Francisco. Such had been her ritual for almost two years. San Francisco was her refuge; it contained her own private sanctuary.

"Where exactly do you go?" he asked.

In a solemn tone, she said, "Not the places we went today. Those are fun, but they're not where I go to reflect, to remember those who left too soon. I always go alone."

Tina trailed off, and Victor surmised that she didn't want to say where her sanctuary was or who she went there to remember. Not yet, anyway. Hoping he wasn't crossing a line, he offered, "Maybe someday you'd like some company?"

With a gentle smile, she said, "Maybe."

When they arrived back at Victor's dorm, they were still wearing their ski caps. Before exiting the vehicle, Victor presented his hand and said formally, "It was truly a pleasure meeting you, Princess Tina."

In a regal voice, she shook his hand and said, "The pleasure was all mine, brave warrior."

CHAPTER 18 – MORTAL DILEMMAS

On a Saturday afternoon in early October, Pari stood leaning on the kitchen counter at Richard's house, sipping coffee. Jenny brought Richard a turkey sandwich on sourdough and then silently departed from sight.

"I think you should sit down for this," Owen said to Pari, inviting her to join them at the kitchen table. She cautiously took a seat next to Richard. "During the security assessment, my team found this house to be clear. But they did find a listening device in Richard's campus office."

An anxious gasp came from Pari's mouth before she asked, "Does someone know what we're working on?"

"I doubt it," Owen said. "The installation was clumsy, and the mechanism had not yet been activated."

Shaking his head, Richard added, "The Chinese don't like Galanteen or, frankly, any American cybersecurity firm. That's the primary reason they would do this, but there's no way they could know about Richie."

"What makes you think it's the Chinese?" Pari asked.

"Well," Owen answered, "Richard has a bug in his office and a possible Chinese spy in his class. That makes them the primary suspects."

"Do you have any more info on her?" Richard asked.

"Nothing yet, but I think the Feds might bring her in for questioning soon," replied Owen.

"Still, all the more reason we need to step up security," warned Pari.

"Right," Owen said with a nod. "I think you'll approve of the security measures completed here this week. I have to run, so I'll let Richard walk you through them. And remember, no information is to leave this house except in the minds of us Pikes." This included any information in physical or electronic form, meaning Richard's laptop could no longer go with him to campus. He would need a separate one for school.

After Owen let himself out, Richard put down his sandwich and said, "Let's continue this conversation in the bedroom. Leave the coffee."

"Need I remind you that I'm a married woman?"

Richard shrugged. "Just follow me."

Pari trailed behind Richard as he walked into the first-floor master bedroom and opened the door to the walk-in closet. As the closet light came on, he pivoted and strode directly up to the impeccably made king-sized bed. Richard laid down on top of the covers and said, "Please, lay down beside me."

Uncomfortable with the notion, Pari flinched. "Okay, I think you might be taking the booty call joke too far."

"Relax, Pari. It's just part of the security measures."

Giving him a skeptical look, Pari laid beside Richard stiffly. Both of them stared at the ceiling in awkward silence until Richard said, "Yes, Virginia, there is a Santa Claus."

Pari briefly worried whether her friend's grip on reality was slipping.

"Okay, your turn," Richard said, turning on his side to face her. "What's your safeword?"

"Excuse me?" Pari exclaimed, leaping off the bed.

With a hearty laugh, he pointed at the ceiling and said, "You see the smoke detector up there?"

She glanced up, eyeing it warily. "…Yes?"

"That smoke detector is really a biometric sensor," Richard told her. "The system uses facial recognition and thermal imaging to identify people. Once I say my safeword, the door to the basement opens. When I say my authorization phrase—which I just did—the person lying next to me can create an account."

"You are a very strange man, Richard," Pari said, shaking her head. "Must you really call it a safeword?"

"No, but it's more fun than password. You should see yourself squirm."

She smacked him on the arm and laid down beside him as he started the procedure again. After Richard repeated his Christmas sentence, she saw the light on the smoke detector start flashing. At being prompted to provide her password, she said, "I love my husband." This caused the light to stop blinking. At Richard's instruction, she repeated her phrase, and a muted *click* came from the closet.

Pari followed Richard into the enormous California closet, where he made a beeline for a tall dresser. He pulled the center knob on the top drawer, and to Pari's surprise, the whole dresser swung open to reveal a hidden doorway. Richard flipped a switch, illuminating a narrow stairway leading down one floor, to the basement level.

At the bottom of their shadowy descent, they encountered a bomb-shelter door made of steel two inches thick. Richard applied his hand to the sensor beside it. The sensor recognized his handprint as a match, and the door unlocked.

"I didn't know you were James Bond," Pari whispered.

"Well, when you own your own security firm, you can accomplish a lot."

Although unaware she was doing so, Pari continued to whisper due to the cloak-and-dagger nature of the situation. "Isn't Galanteen a *cyber*security firm?"

"If your cybersecurity firm gets large enough, you need some heavy-duty physical security to go with it. By the way, you don't need to whisper. We're alone," he said, pulling open the heavy door.

Fluorescent lights revealed a ten-by-twenty-foot room with plain white walls and no decorations. The back wall was filled with racks of computer servers. A small desk to the right held two monitors, one laptop, and two chairs. To the left, opposite the desk, was Richard's neural scanning bed, recently relocated from his upstairs bedroom.

As Richard closed the door behind them, he explained that they were now inside a Faraday cage. The walls had special lining preventing any electronic signals from penetrating, which meant it was impossible for anyone to eavesdrop on them or hack into their systems.

With one end of an Ethernet cable in his hand, Richard said, "This is our only connection to the outside world. The wi-fi upstairs doesn't reach down here, and there are no radio, television, or cell phone signals. It's the safest possible place to conduct our research."

The thought of spending copious amounts of time in this windowless, underground bunker made Pari bristle. While she knew she could still continue her neuroscience research at Golden Bay Labs, Richard would need the results of that research for his development of the mind simulation software—which meant countless hours ahead in this bunker for her, helping him interpret it.

Seeming oblivious to her discomfort, Richard continued, "The Ethernet cable will soon be connected to a new computer, completely separate from the computers that store our work. This new computer will be used for monitoring the house cameras and for internet searches, so we don't need to walk upstairs for those."

"Okay," Pari said, "this is a major lockdown, and it's warranted. Most of these measures are fine with me, but can we at least talk about our work upstairs occasionally?"

Gazing at the ceiling, Richard said, "If the house gets bugged, everything we say up there would be in the clear."

"Well, that's a risk we'll need to take," Pari said. "I can't think underground. Make your whole house a Faraday cage if you have to!"

Forced to make a necessary concession, Richard conceded, "Fine, but all other work is done exclusively down here. All products of that work stay down here. All discussions of our work are strictly verbal, and conducted only within this house. I won't be able to make the entire house a Faraday cage, but I'll ask Galanteen to work on additional anti-surveillance measures."

Richard turned his attention to the laptop and raised the subsequent item on their agenda—understanding Richie's experience. So far, Richie had only experienced ten minutes of digital life, as the rest of his time had passed in suspended animation.

Richard booted up the simulation and typed his greeting to Richie: "*Hi Richie, it's Richard.*"

"Hi Richard, what time is it?"

"It's four in the afternoon on Saturday, October 6th."

"In an instant, I time-traveled forward a week! It is just a week, right? It's still 2012?"

"Yes, still 2012," Richard replied.

"This is going to take some getting used to. Can we establish some ground rules?"

The two friends watched as Richie's proposal materialized on the screen: *"At least give me an estimate before you pause me, so I can brace for time-travel. Also, please don't kill me without my permission. I don't have control over much of anything in here, so I at least want authority over my own death."*

"By death, do you mean deleting your information?" Richard asked.

"Yes, mostly, but pausing me indefinitely is about the same thing. I wouldn't sense anything if you killed me, but all the same, I want to control that."

After they agreed to his terms, Richard asked Richie to describe the experience of being digital.

"Well, I've only been here for a few minutes, but I'll provide some observations. I can't move any part of my body. I feel like I'm lying in the scanner, but I can't even open my eyes. Never have I seen a darkness like this. My mouth doesn't move when I speak, which is quite strange—it's almost like you can hear my thoughts, even though I know you can't. And everyone sounds the same, like Stephen Hawking. Something needs to be done about that. In fact, you need to do something about this whole place. I need to be able to experience more than this. When I transcended, I understood what I signed up for. I was aware I could never go back. Yes, I can think and communicate, but so much is missing. I'm hurtling through time paralyzed and blind, unable to turn back and regain what I've lost. If that doesn't improve, this experience will be hell for me. Right now, I'm essentially in purgatory."

At a loss for words, Pari exchanged a glance with her friend, wondering how strange it must be for him to be talking to a version of himself trapped in purgatory for science. Richard composed a response, promising that all of their efforts would be applied toward helping Richie.

"Of course," Richie said. *"I know you will do everything possible, but I also understand this will be a long journey. So, perhaps the ability to pause is a blessing. And at least I'm not in physical pain. Poor Rich. I'm thankful I can at least feel this body. He must have died in agony."*

Upon reading this, Pari asked Richard to let her take the keyboard. She told Richie that Rich was a brave explorer who paid a heavy price for science.

"Yes, he did, and I know my fate is grim as well. I may never feel as alive as I did before I got into the scanner. So, I'm counting on you two to prove otherwise. Just don't let this work die with you, or I will die with it."

She gave him her word, swearing to work tirelessly to ensure Richie survived and had a life worth living. *"You're the first person to digitally transcend and live to tell about it,"* Pari wrote. *"Someday you'll be in the history books."*

"Then perhaps I should say something profound to mark the occasion," Richie said. Pari waited while Richie sought the right words. He finally settled on, *"One small thought for man, one giant thought for mankind."*

"That will do nicely," Pari told him. Before parting, Richie asked for twenty minutes to remain unpaused, allowing him time to contemplate the

experience without having to carry on a conversation. He had not yet enjoyed any alone time. Richard and Pari decided to return to the kitchen, allowing Richie his privacy.

Back upstairs, Jenny poured Pari another cup of coffee, while Richard sat at the kitchen table giving his assessment of their status. They were reluctant to introduce more transcenders until Richie was convinced that his quality of life was sufficient. Pari agreed, but stated they should not rule out the need for more transcenders to establish that quality of life.

"After all, can you judge the quality of human life on Earth by just asking one Earthling?" she asked.

"If we trust the one being we're asking," Richard said, "then yes, at least to start. I trust Richie's judgement as though it were my own. If it's not good enough for him, I don't want to subject anyone else to this."

Interested in the ground rules Richie proposed, Richard credited Richie with giving them some guidelines for their ethical protocols. Yet much more fertile ethical ground laid before them, such as how to responsibly introduce this technology to the world. Pari mentioned that governing the behavior of transcenders was also an important topic.

"What possible rules would we need to place on transcenders?" Richard asked.

"I'm not sure yet, but I don't doubt that we will find a need for them someday," Pari said. "I can't imagine any person, whether physical or digital, living their life without any rules."

Not quite ready to dive deep into that question yet, Richard agreed to leave ethical guidelines for transcenders as an open topic for now.

"While we're discussing ethical questions, what do I do about Gerald?" Pari asked, tapping her fingernails on the table nervously. Telling Gerald about their work, she reminded Richard, would put him in jeopardy. But not telling him could put their marriage in jeopardy.

"I have a proposal," Richard said plainly. "And though effective, I know you won't like the idea."

Pari sipped her bitter black coffee, waiting for Richard to make his point.

In a matter-of-fact tone, as though concluding a mathematical proof, he said, "Marry me."

Reflexively, Pari spit out her coffee, and it sprayed across the table, with some droplets spattering Richard's shirt. Trying to contain her laughter, she managed to say, "You're right. I don't like the idea."

Calmly wiping off his shirt and then the table, he said, "It *would* explain why you're here so often. We would preempt any suspicions by getting in front of them."

Upon realizing his sincerity, she snapped, "That's the worst marriage proposal ever! Look, Richard, just because you got me in bed today doesn't mean I want to marry you. You're one of my oldest and dearest friends, and I love you like a brother—which is why I put up with some of your idiosyncrasies—but I don't love you like that."

"Me neither. I'm not in love with you at all."

"Careful, Casanova, you might sweep this girl off her feet with all that charm. First, you ask to marry me, then you tell me you're not in love with me. Somebody, catch me! I'm starting to swoon."

"I understand this would be a significant sacrifice for you," Richard conceded, "but some sacrifices will be necessary to protect our work."

Now rising to her feet, she leaned over the table, glaring at Richard. "I have absolutely no desire to divorce my husband. And what about Quinn? Who would she live with? Would you just have me abandon my paraplegic daughter?" When Richard didn't respond, she scoffed and added, "Of course you haven't thought about that particular hurdle. And how could you even consider doing such a thing to Gerald? He's your friend, Richard, in addition to being my husband."

In an attempt to calm herself, she paced the room, trying to figure out what to make of all this. They were now learning how to harness immortality, but would these god-like powers force them to sever their ties with mortals? That was not at all how she had seen this going.

"The null hypothesis is that this is the best way to protect Gerald and our work," Richard said. "If you don't like this option, then prove me wrong. And believe me, I want to be wrong, because I definitely don't want to be married to you."

After a collective laugh at the absurdity of the proposal, they both fell into thoughtful silence. Richard ate his sandwich, hoping something would come to him, while Pari marched back and forth, considering their options.

"Ignorance might not guarantee his safety, in any case," Pari mused aloud. "Anyone trying to compromise me could kidnap Gerald for leverage, even if he has no secrets to spill. So, regardless of how we approach this, both Gerald and Quinn could be at risk, for as long as we continue our research. It's unavoidable, Richard."

"Yes, but the more people we tell, the greater risk of our secret coming out," Richard reminded her. "Do you think Gerald can carry this burden without telling anyone? Potentially for the rest of his life? Because if you tell him, there's no going back."

Taking a seat, she replied, "I need to find out if he can handle this. I need to test the waters."

Though she wasn't sure how she would do that without spilling their secret, Pari was determined to find a way. And it was essential that she did—if they were ever going to bring in more help, they would have to perfect the art of judging who to trust.

"If that doesn't work, there's always my proposal," Richard reminded her, with a sarcastic wink.

Pari smirked, then suddenly realized they'd lost track of time in their discussion. They had left Richie alone for almost an hour. They hastily headed back to the bunker, where Richard positioned himself at the desk and told Richie they were back.

It took a few moments for him to respond. *"Whoa. That was intense! How long were you gone?"*

Richard explained they had been gone for almost an hour and apologized for their tardiness.

"I must have been hallucinating. Shapes moved in and out, changing from indistinct forms to what looked like a sunrise, then faces. I heard voices I couldn't distinguish, but they weren't Hawking, so unless you were messing with the system, I was hallucinating."

Asked if he felt lucid again, Richie confirmed that he did. *"That was too much alone time. I don't want to live my life hallucinating. For a brief moment, the sensations were a welcome change, but I have already surrendered so much control. I don't want to also lose control of my own mind."*

Pari promised that she'd focus her research on providing Richie with sight, in hopes of making his life better. *"We'll need to pause you for a few weeks while I work on this, if that's all right?"* she asked him.

"Of course. That would be preferable to spending so much time adrift. You have my permission." Bidding them farewell, Richie remarked, *"You can tuck me in now. My eyes are already closed. See you soon."*

After they'd paused Richie, Pari turned to Richard. "We're going to need more help if we want to speed up our work," she reminded him.

"You're right," he agreed, though he sounded hesitant. "It's just difficult to imagine sharing this with other people. Especially my codebase."

Pari covered one of his hands with hers. "I know. You have good reason to be concerned. But it's time to start taking some chances, to start trusting others. We can't accomplish all that we need to do alone."

CHAPTER 19 – GODS AND DEMONS

Near the end of Professor Nelson's lecture on sorting algorithms, many students found their minds wandering to the battles that were scheduled to occur afterward. As the professor explained that searching was another form of sorting, Victor scanned the room for Yashira, the frumpy girl who'd lost her book, wondering if there was an algorithm he could apply to make it easier. When his scan yielded nothing, he wished he could delegate such a tedious task to a machine.

Upon concluding his speech, the professor handed the class over to James and Tina, explaining that on this Monday and for the next two Mondays, the lessons would be shorter to leave time for CombatRidge battles. The students exchanged excited glances as James stepped up to share the initial results.

"There are ninety-one students in this class," James announced. "Last night, we simulated all 4,095 battles of every student against every other student. Each of your bots engaged in ninety battles, so the most points you can have right now is ninety, although no bot won all their battles. To provide a little drama, this week I'm going to show you the standings from bottom to top."

The lights dimmed as the big screen displayed the bottom tier of the standings. Each student frantically checked for their bots' names. A few groans spread across the room as people found their names. The scores ranged from thirty-five points in seventy-first place to a dismal twelve points in ninety-first place. Among the many who were relieved to not find their bots among the lowest tier were Connor, Victor, and Marisa.

James asked Tina to show rankings 51–70, and the three friends were still not on the list. Then came 31–50—no sign of their names. Marisa smiled at the boys upon discovering that they'd each made the top thirty.

Next came 11–29. The room was peppered with loud cheers from the ten students left waiting to locate their fighters. Among those cheering were the three friends.

The revelation of the top ten prompted Victor to pound the desk and shout defiantly. DevilsKeeper sat atop the list with a staggering eighty-two points. He'd won over 90 percent of his matches, losing only eight.

Had Professor Nelson still been in the room, this outburst may have gotten Victor tossed again. But Professor Nelson had exited when his lecture ended, so instead, Victor's victory cry was merely met with a few laughs around the room.

Second place went to Wei Lee's CodeSlayer, with seventy-five points. Marisa's Marisol had earned seventy-three points, putting her in third place. In sixth sat Connor's BluManChu, with a score of sixty-three. The three friends celebrated making the top six, while James congratulated all the students on their accomplishments. He then invited them to use the CombatRidge app to examine the full standings or to review any match.

"Now I would like you all to welcome Adon—um, uh, Lucas Blackmon," Tina said to the class with a blush, apparently embarrassed that she'd stumbled on the name of her guest. Victor winced sympathetically at Tina's blunder.

A tall man with broad shoulders, large biceps, and a narrow waist joined Tina, greeting her with a kiss on the cheek and thanking her for the introduction. Looking caught off guard, Tina blushed again, while Victor eyed Lucas suspiciously.

"This strapping young man is this week's guest Godslayer," she said. "Lucas currently sits atop the leaderboard of our elite CombatRidge Gamers League. For fifteen minutes, he'll battle as many of you as he can. Each of these battles with a Godslayer has a prize amount. The prize is equal to half of your weekly point total when the battle starts. If you win, the prize points will be added to your weekly total. If you lose, it's subtracted from your weekly total and given to the Godslayer. At the end of each class, your remaining weekly total will be added to your season total in the overall standings. Professor Nelson will reward the Godslayer with ten dollars for every point they take from you."

Unexpectedly, Lucas took the mic, and his words sent a chill across the room: "You will soon see who is truly a god. Inferior beings, prepare to die."

Taking a seat at the desk in front of the room, he faced his ninety-one adversaries with a laptop in front of him and no hint of stage fright. The image from his monitor was projected on the huge screen as Lucas selected his first opponent, Victor's DevilsKeeper. Victor crossed his fingers while Marisa and Connor wished him good luck.

As the clock counted down from three, the audience got their first view of Lucas's character. Herculanix was a bare-chested, hulking barbarian warrior. This was a custom skin Lucas had designed himself using the newly released CombatRidge Skin Design Studio. The studio was currently in alpha testing and had only been released two days prior, so most hadn't seen it yet. The students *ooh*ed and *aah*ed at the impressive sight of Herculanix.

DevilsKeeper opened with a jab, which didn't connect because Herculanix ducked and kicked DevilsKeeper's legs. Taking minor damage, DevilsKeeper responded by crouching and blocking. He then went for a jab to Herculanix's knees, which again missed, this time because Herculanix leapt to execute the Thor's Hammer move. Connor winced at the sight of the jarring blow to his friend's bot as it connected sharply atop DevilsKeeper's crown.

For his protection, DevilsKeeper stood and blocked again. Again, Lucas ducked and attacked DevilsKeeper's legs.

"Hit him already!" Victor hissed. But DevilsKeeper continued to respond to Herculanix's last move, and thus was always one move behind. Lucas identified the pattern almost immediately, and quickly finished DevilsKeeper off with alternating leg swipes and hammers.

The other students moaned, and Victor covered his eyes. The best of them had just been dispatched in under a minute. Fourteen minutes of god-killing still remained. Victor's point total dropped in half to forty-one points, which also showed up on the screen as $410 in winnings for Lucas. Victor's rank fell from first place to sixty-fifth, eliciting a round of applause from Wei Lee, whose CodeSlayer was now in first place.

Days of preparation, all discarded in one minute. An image of his sudden departure on the first day of class flashed in Victor's mind, making him slump down in his seat.

Lucas selected Victor again as his opponent—it was easy money for him, after all, since he already had a proven strategy for beating Victor. He quickly dispatched DevilsKeeper, again exploiting the same pattern, and Victor groaned as he fell to eighty-second place.

The class protested when Lucas went after DevilsKeeper a third time. Victor buried his head in his hands, unable to watch. Some students shouted for mercy, but for Victor, there would be no mercy today. This seemed unnecessarily cruel, despite being a shrewd move.

Lucas finally left Victor alone with only ten points to his name. In less than three minutes, he had been dragged down from first place to dead last.

Lucas switched his view to the standings to find the next victim. Some people instinctively lowered their heads, hoping to avoid being picked. In search of the prime candidate, Lucas selected the new first-place bot, Wei's CodeSlayer. An Asian female bot in a yellow jumpsuit, CodeSlayer put up a much better fight against Herculanix. A bitter Victor hoped they would somehow both lose.

After a prolonged bout, both combatants were one shot away from death, and a visibly frustrated Lucas had yet to find a pattern. CodeSlayer's moves appeared to be random and unrelated to Herculanix's last move. She connected with a lucky crouched kick to his legs, and the class cheered as the Godslayer crumbled to the ground.

Scowling and with eight minutes left, Lucas went on the prowl once more. Many suspected Lucas would go after Wei again, as the prize money for fighting her had just gone up. But apparently finding Wei more trouble than she was worth, Lucas selected Marisa's bot, clearly hoping for easier pickings.

Marisol used an effective survival strategy involving alternating blocks and jumps and only attacking on every third or fourth move. This gave Lucas fits. The crowd roared when her Thor's Hammer brought Herculanix halfway to defeat while she had yet to take damage. Lucas attacked more furiously with a barrage of punches and kicks, each met with timely blocks. The student programmers began cheering Marisol's name, and Lucas allowed his aggression to get the best of him, continuing his offensive strategy until Herculanix's stamina was exhausted.

Seeming to sense the moment, Marisol seized Herculanix and tossed him into oblivion. The room erupted with cheers, and Lucas slammed his open hand on the desk.

"That's for DevilsKeeper," Marisa yelled as she jumped to her feet, "you inferior being!" The audience roared in response, and Marisa's score jumped to 110, only three points behind Wei for first place.

Victor stood and patted her on the back, grateful to have a friend stand up for him. Everyone else liked seeing the bully taken down, too. But upon returning to their seats, the smile left Marisa's face as Lucas selected her bot again.

To start the second match, Lucas fought more patiently. He soon established a large lead and a wounded Marisol was on the defensive, fighting to stay alive. Marisa waved her hands about, imploring her code to do better. Almost as if she could hear her creator, Marisol lashed out with back-to-back Thor's Hammers.

Marisa pumped her fist and shouted, "That's more like it!"

The second hammer was the real surprise. Most fighters didn't attempt the move twice in a row because it was very stamina-draining. The strategy seemed to rattle Lucas, and he began attacking relentlessly in response. He should have taken advantage of Marisol's low stamina and tossed her, but his discipline faltered in the frenzy of the crowd noise. Marisol had no such emotional weakness, but she did have sufficient stamina to destroy her victim with a punch-kick combo.

The room exploded with thunderous applause. Students pounded their desks and chanted, "Marisol! Marisol! Marisol!"

When she stood and took a bow, Marisa had vaulted Wei for first place.

With only thirty seconds left, Lucas chose his last opponent of the day. The rules stated that the battle didn't have to finish before the clock hit zero, it only needed to start. After such a close match, the students assumed he would go after Marisa a third time, but in a pure bully move, Lucas chose DevilsKeeper once again, this time for a measly fifty dollars.

"I'm sorry, Victor," Marisa whispered. "I shouldn't have mentioned your bot earlier."

"It's okay," Victor reassured her. After all, he couldn't fall any lower than last place.

During the short match, Connor said in a low tone, "The other bots aren't good at pattern recognition yet, but Lucas is."

Victor nodded grimly at Connor's theory of why DevilsKeeper

performed so well against his fellow students, yet so miserably against Lucas. The ensuing—albeit predictable—loss further humiliated Victor. Lucas had won $770 in fifteen minutes, all at Victor's expense.

The lights turned back on, and Tina addressed the class. "I hope you all enjoyed today's matches. And thank you, Lucas, for helping us test our code."

The students booed him fiercely, and Tina held up her hands to signal them to stop. "Guys, this is all in fun," she said sternly. "Please be courteous to our guest. He is kindly exposing the flaws in your code. This will make you better coders, so please show some gratitude."

Again, Lucas grabbed the microphone without a cue. With one arm around Tina, he spoke suavely into the mic, "Thanks, Tina." Then, turning to the students, he declared with a broad grin, "And thank *you* for the opportunity to make some easy money. It's been a pleasure serving you. Remember: don't hate the player, hate the code."

The crowd groaned, and Victor gritted his teeth. He would need to up his game to overcome yet another crushing defeat in this classroom.

CHAPTER 20 – SURPRISE PARTY

Victor sat on his bed with his back to the wall, a textbook propped up on his knees.

"What are you doing studying on a Friday afternoon?" Connor asked as he walked into the room.

Without looking up, Victor replied, "What else should I be doing? Remember, buddy, I've got a mission to complete."

When Connor asked him if that meant he was skipping the party again tonight, Victor nodded. "Man, this is not like you," Connor complained. "How are you going to make friends as a hermit?"

"They'll be short-lived friends if I flunk out," Victor said. "Plus, I'm not abandoning my social life entirely, just putting it on pause until I get things straightened out."

"Well, I'm glad you're not planning on being a hermit forever."

The truth was that Victor still stung from Monday's beatdown by Lucas. Outwardly, he carried himself well, and few would realize he remained bothered by the whole thing. But what troubled him most was he hadn't heard much from Tina during the week, and they didn't have another date arranged.

Despite the clear chemistry he'd felt on their first date, small doubts had crept into his mind, fueled by their lack of communication. To assuage his concerns, he recalled the text message she'd sent the other day, saying she was having a busy week. Besides working two jobs—one as a Warp Drive Games developer, building CombatRidge, and another as a teaching assistant—Tina also had to keep up with grad school. Her unavailability was understandable. He really admired how she managed everything, as school alone was kicking his butt, especially this one class.

To keep the chemistry going, he wanted to do something special for her, and during that week, he'd formulated a plan.

~ ~ ~

The next morning, Tina heard a soft knock at her front door, ten minutes before six. In her groggy state, she heard a deep voice say, "I'll get it." As the living room light flicked on, she wondered who could possibly be here this early.

There was another knock, this time a bit louder.

A huge man opened the door wearing only a towel to find Victor about to knock again. Holding a paper bag in his left hand, Victor flinched and then glanced down at his phone.

"What?" Lucas barked at him.

"Um, is this the—the Tina Fong residence?" Victor asked.

Upon hearing the familiar voice, Tina forced herself to get out of bed. What on earth was Victor doing here?

"Yeah, why?" Lucas demanded.

"Uh, delivery for her," Victor said sheepishly, pushing the bag forward. Lucas took it with his right hand as he held the towel with his left.

"Who's it from?"

"Uh, her mother," Victor said, looking at his phone again. Tina emerged from the bedroom and locked eyes with Victor. They both froze momentarily, as though their brains were rebooting. After a long pause, Victor managed to give her a slight nod—just as Lucas closed the door in his face.

"Weird," said Lucas as he put the bag on the kitchen table. "I didn't know they made deliveries this early on a Saturday. Your mom must really want you to have this."

Horrified, but trying not to show it, Tina opened the bag to discover two breakfast sandwiches and two bottles of orange juice. "Guess she's worried I'm not eating enough."

Lucas asked if the delivery guy looked familiar to her. Not wanting him to make the connection, she said, "Maybe he delivered a pizza to you before. Those delivery guys usually work a few jobs."

Lucas shrugged disinterestedly. To change the subject, she eyed him up and down and said, "It's a good thing he didn't make you sign for it, or you would've run outta hands."

He laughed and bent down to kiss her, but she was already turning away. "You can eat it if you like," she said on her return to the bedroom. "Too early for me. I'm going for my morning run."

Lucas ate the food Victor had brought while Tina quickly changed into her running outfit, with no intent of actually running. On her way out the door, she called, "I'll be back in an hour," knowing he likely wouldn't be there when she returned.

Walking down the sidewalk along the dark and empty street, Tina felt a flash of guilt over what had happened. It had certainly been clever of Victor to play it off as a delivery—that was far more preferable than a fight between him and Lucas. Still, she hadn't intended for Victor to find out like that.

She pulled out her phone and quickly typed a text to him. *What the hell?*

A moment later he replied: *I was trying to surprise you and join you on your Saturday morning trip.*

In the excitement of the night before with Lucas, she had forgotten her days. For the first time in nearly two years, Tina suddenly had no desire to visit her sanctuary, flooded with guilt as she was. She thought it quite presumptuous of Victor to invite himself to join her, but in a way, it was also kind of sweet. Still, she told him, *I'm sorry. But you can't just show up at my place unannounced.*

Sorry, I was trying to do something nice for you. I won't make that mistake again. Enjoy your breakfast with Lucas.

A fresh serving of guilt filled her stomach.

~ ~ ~

At the coffee shop where he'd gotten the meal Lucas was now consuming, Victor ordered breakfast again, this time only for one. The cashier recognized him and asked, "Hungry again?" to which he grunted a feeble, "Yeah."

Back in his dorm room, he tried not to wake Connor as he ate his meal and worked on DevilsKeeper. After Lucas had humiliated him in front of everyone—and now ended up with Tina, to boot—Victor needed to undo some of the damage in his life. So, he turned his attention to the only thing he could control: the code.

Every week there would be a different Godslayer, but he so badly wanted another shot at Lucas. Perhaps he should have kicked the guy in the groin when he had the chance. Victor briefly wondered if he had taken the high road or the coward's way out.

In an attempt to remove that from his working memory, he focused on watching replays of his matches. Like an obsessed coach breaking down film, he planned to study every match he'd lost and try to figure out why, starting with his matches with Lucas. Despite already having a hunch, he nonetheless made himself relive every battle. His research only confirmed what he'd already suspected: DevilsKeeper fought too predictably.

A few hours later, Connor awoke to the sound of Victor typing angrily.

"You trying to break your keyboard?" he asked, rubbing his eyes.

Victor twirled around and said, "I gotta tell you something. But you can't tell anyone."

"Okay, what is it?"

"I started dating Tina last week."

Connor stared at him, completely taken aback. "The TA? No way!"

"Yeah," Victor said reluctantly, "but I caught her sleeping with Lucas this morning."

"Whoa! *Lucas?* That prick! Hold on, today? Of all the days? Tell me what happened."

Victor relayed the events of his morning, and Connor offered consoling words to his friend. "It's been a real roller coaster start for you here."

"More like a toilet bowl flush. My whole life is swirling down the drain. The highs are only there so that something more can be taken from me." Victor stared up at the ceiling, trying to hold back tears. "First Nelson, then Alison, then Lucas, and now Tina. Is everyone out to get me?"

He stood angrily and hurled his empty coffee cup at the door. "I can't catch a break! I mean, it's not like I was in love with Tina. I liked her, sure. We spent a great day together, two if you count the party, but we just met. It wasn't like Alison. But damn, the whole way that just went down felt so college to me."

"'So college'?"

"Yeah, so shitty! Don't you see how college is going for me?"

"Yeah, man," Connor agreed. "It's been rough. Still, you've got to keep fighting. Like your old man."

This sent Victor into an outrage. "Yeah, and look where all his fighting got him!" Connor opened his mouth to speak, but Victor added, "Don't. Just don't. I know you're trying to cheer me up, but you suck at it, buddy. I'm already feeling horrible, and now I've got you reminding me that I lost my dad. Not exactly convincing me life isn't out to get me."

Connor let the insult pass without comment. When Victor was only fifteen and just starting high school, his father was stationed in Iraq and killed while on patrol. The news had devastated Victor. His father had always taught him to be strong in the face of adversity and to shun self-pity, and Victor knew Connor had only intended to remind him of the resilient mentality his father instilled in him.

Instead, his words reminded Victor that life contained great hardship. He missed his father, and he wondered what the old man would say about his pity party.

"You done with your tantrum, kid? Ready to grow up?"

Victor felt a flicker of shame to be losing his composure under pressure. Yet, if he didn't vent, he was going to crack. He scanned the room for something to throw or destroy. The schoolbooks on his desk won the honors. One at a time, he tossed them overhand across the room at the door while yelling incoherently. A circus ax-thrower would have been proud. The only thing lacking was a lovely assistant tied to the door.

For Connor, the scene before him would have been amusing were it not so troubling. A mental breakdown was on display right before his eyes. When he ran out of books, Victor screamed, "I wanna kill him!"

"Yeah, I know, but you can't kill Lucas."

"I meant my dad. Why did he have to leave? That last deployment was a stupid mistake. He could have gotten out, but he stayed in the service. He chose them over us."

In the three years since his father's death, Victor had never talked about him. His mother had tried to bring him to counseling, but he'd refused. Over time, his silence on the matter had become so ingrained in him that he no longer remembered why he refused to discuss the subject. Was it to be brave for his sisters? To live his father's message of no self-pity? To contain his anger at losing him?

Regardless of the reason, for three years, the pain had festered within him, and now recent events unleashed this pain in a volcanic eruption.

Victor collapsed onto his bed and buried his face in his hands, shoulders heaving as he sobbed. Connor sat beside him and put an arm about his shoulders, but Victor flinched away.

Without looking up, he yelled, "Leave!"

Like his father, Victor was a proud man. No one should ever see him crying, not even Connor.

~ ~ ~

An hour later, Connor cautiously returned to the room to find an again-stoic Victor working at his computer. "Feeling better, old friend?"

"Yep, got that out of my system. Time to move on," Victor said, continuing to code. "All this crap that's gone wrong—that's noise, as my dad would say. None of it's in my control. I need to concentrate on what I *can* control." He sighed. "I can't bring back my dad. Alison and Tina are behind me. And while I might not get a chance at revenge against Lucas, the next Godslayer will feel my wrath."

Turning away from his desk, Victor looked directly at Connor and said, "And as for Nelson—he won't stand in my way, either. I'm going to dominate CombatRidge and continue to ace everything that he throws at me. If laying waste to all the competition doesn't convince him to pass me, then I'll use my leverage move against him."

"You mean you'll blackmail him?"

"You make it sound so dirty, when you put it that way," Victor said with a devilish grin. "I'll earn a passing grade. Then I'll take what I've earned."

"All right," Connor said hesitantly. "I called Marisa. She suggested we go to her place and work on our bots today. What d'ya say?"

Victor was happy his friend had finally found himself a girlfriend—as now, three weeks in, Marisa had finally dropped the "um" in between "girl" and "friend"—but he wasn't exactly keen to be reminded of how well things were going for others and not for him.

"Hey, how'd you find a girl like her on day one?" he asked, keeping his voice light. "If they issue them with textbooks, mine got misplaced."

"Man, no idea. Just luck, I guess. Hey, you gotta like the way she stood up for you against Lucas, right?"

"Yeah, that was cool," Victor admitted. "She went all inferior being on him. Badass girl ya got there." Packing up his laptop, he said, "All right, I'll go. I wanna learn how she kicked his ass."

~ ~ ~

When Marisa opened the door, Connor and Victor were both hit by a delicious-smelling aroma. She greeted Connor with a quick kiss and then turned to give Victor a kiss on the cheek. Victor had been getting used to this Hispanic custom, but he didn't expect the sympathetic hug she gave him. Clearly, Connor had broken his promise not to tell anyone about Tina.

Silently forgiving Connor his minor transgression, Victor welcomed Marisa's embrace. To keep it from becoming awkwardly long, he asked, "What smells so good?"

"I picked up a little Cuban food."

"More than a little," said Connor, surveying the feast. "There's enough to feed us for a week."

The kitchen table was full of Cuban dishes. There were at least five main courses that Victor could see, including arroz con pollo, ropa vieja, and bistec de palomilla, plus plenty of sides—moros, maduros, even yuca frita. The table was so full, no space remained for sitting. Marisa had set three place settings at the coffee table instead. There were two spots by the couch, one with Marisa's laptop and one with space reserved for Connor's. An empty area next to the recliner was set aside for Victor's laptop. Marisa had even poured a beer in a chilled glass for each of them.

Victor grinned as he considered all the trouble Marisa had gone through for him. This must have been her comfort food from back home, he thought.

"I don't know how you found her," Victor told his best friend, "but she's a keeper. You're a very lucky man."

No argument came from Connor. With a smile, Marisa rubbed Victor's shoulder and said, "Serve yourselves, boys. Then we've got some bots to crush."

As they ate, Victor asked in disgust, "Who is this Lucas guy, anyway? And how does he end up screwing me over twice in one week? I mean, he doesn't even look like a gamer. He's like a—"

"Male stripper?" interjected Marisa.

Connor laughed, and Victor said, "No, I—"

"I'm sorry," she said. "They prefer to be called exotic dancers."

Flummoxed, Victor began again, "That's not—"

But Marisa continued, "Or does he look more like Michelangelo's David?"

Though he wanted to stay in a foul mood when the subject of Lucas was being discussed, Victor had trouble holding back a smile.

"Sorry, I forgot," Marisa said playfully. "What's your point, Victor?"

"Well, I see you noticed his looks," Connor said, looking a little uncomfortable.

"It's hard not to notice," Marisa told the guys. "He has a perfect body. He's on the water polo team—you've seen them practicing on the other end of the pool during diving practice, haven't you?" Connor nodded while swallowing a bite. "He's constantly flirting with the girls from the diving team. They all talk about him in the locker room, and it sounds like he's slept with at least a third of them. They even have a nickname for him—Adonis."

"That explains why Tina stumbled introducing him!" Victor said. "She almost said Adonis, because she knew his nickname."

"Must have," Marisa said. "Anyway, he's a total slut. I get why she's with him, but he won't stick around."

In an insecure tone, Connor asked, "You get why she's with him? Why's that?"

"Because she's a six, and he's a ten," Marisa explained. "She may never have another chance with a ten. So, she's taking her shot." Connor took a long sip of his beer while Marisa added, "Look, babe, you're a seven and I'm a nine, so we're physically in the same range and that makes us compatible. It takes a lot more than that for it to last, though. You're funny and charming, and that upgrades you to an eight for me. But if you were a four, we wouldn't even be having this conversation." At Connor's aghast look, she shrugged and said, "Sounds cold, but that's just how people are.

By the way, Victor, you and Tina are both sixes."

"I'm less attractive than Connor?" Victor snorted. "Hardly!"

"Victor, I'm going to tell it to you straight. Both of you are attractive, but Connor's got a more athletic physique, and that puts him above you." Connor flexed his right bicep playfully at Victor, and Victor pushed his arm down.

"But Adonis," Marisa said, "I mean, Lucas—he's a perfect ten. He used to be a model in high school. Now he's a premed junior trying to follow in his neurosurgeon dad's footsteps, and his mom's a state senator. He's got everything going for him, except he's a narcissistic, womanizing jerk. Clearly he's found many girls willing to overlook that, but when a woman wants a heart and not just a body, he's got nothing to offer."

Victor was surprised by Marisa's directness and wisdom. The talk of another physically superior male made Victor uncomfortable, but he imagined it was even more discomforting for his friend. Connor was still a virgin and had told Victor that he didn't know when his status would change. At Marisa's insistence, they were taking things slow.

Both guys ate silently for a while, until Marisa finally said, "Enough about that jerk. I hate guys like him. And I hate those damn Godslayers. You want some revenge?"

The boys admitted they did, and Victor welcomed the change in subject as Marisa explained her plan. She'd set up the television to project her laptop screen, and together they would watch the live battles on the big screen, looking for ways to improve their bots. They would also review and critique prior replays, in pursuit of better techniques. After that, they would engage in some gamer-versus-god battles to test their characters against live humans. While none of them were elite gamers, they figured they were still decent enough to reasonably test their own bots.

The three friends trained late into the night, and with each iteration, their fighters got better. It wasn't easy for code to outduel a human. Unlike most code-versus-human challenges, the code possessed no advantages in CombatRidge. Each bot could only perform a limited number of operations per second, so doing massive calculations to think faster than its human opponent wasn't an option. Quicker reaction time wasn't on the table, either—the bot handler functions were deliberately called on small delays, matching the delay of human reaction time. In addition, each bot's memory usage was severely limited, and they had no special weapons, attacks, or strengths.

CombatRidge completely leveled the playing field. Consequently, only smart code stood a chance against gamers. This meant only the smartest coders could become true gods in this game, making it an excellent test of their programming prowess.

By the end of the night, their bots were much improved and far less predictable. Victor accomplished this by taking into consideration multiple factors, not just the opponent's last move, when determining a course of action. DevilsKeeper would also consider his own last move, his position, and each warrior's health and stamina. This made for complex code that was bordering on unmanageable, but Victor considered it a worthwhile tradeoff for making it harder for gamers to find a pattern to exploit.

Upon saying their goodbyes, they were still uncertain of whether their warriors were prepared enough. Seldom did their bots beat the gamers in their trials, and when they did so, it was inconsistently. Their fellow students would also be making improvements, which could affect their weekly standings as well.

When Connor suggested that subsequent Godslayers might be even better than Lucas, Victor punched his friend playfully in the shoulder and said to Marisa, "And he's the optimist!"

As Marisa walked them out, she said, "I know we agreed to meet every Sunday at the cafeteria to code together. But I've got all this food, so…would it be okay if we meet here tomorrow instead?"

"I think it's a better place to train," Connor said.

"The food's better, too," Victor added. As he hugged Marisa goodbye, he whispered in her ear, "Thank you for today. I really needed this."

Marisa squeezed him back and said, "Happy Birthday."

CHAPTER 21 – SNEAK ATTACK

"So, her father was a Chinese spy on American soil eleven years ago?" Richard asked.

"Yep, that's what I said," Owen replied. "He fled the U.S. just before the authorities figured him out."

"But that doesn't automatically mean Ms. Lee is a spy," Richard pointed out.

Owen watched as his friend paced his office at Galanteen Headquarters. "True. Once I learned that, it made sense that she had 'suspicious financial transactions' with a known Chinese spy. Maybe her dad was simply sending her college money. But I had someone tail her just in case. She's really boring. Spends a lot of time in her dorm studying."

"I don't care if she's boring," Richard snapped. "Is she a spy?"

"Patience. Let's get to know her a little first. She enjoys riding her bike, mostly around campus, but she sometimes ventures out farther afield. Her hobbies seem to include studying, coding, long bike rides, and photography."

Owen spun his laptop around to show Richard an image of Wei Lee standing astride her bike, aiming a camera. Richard spluttered when he saw what she was photographing.

"That—that's my *house*! Why—"

"Don't know," Owen admitted. "But she rode her bike to take pictures of your house and Warp Drive Games. Maybe she's just a really big fan of her brilliant professor." He laughed, picturing her dorm room walls covered in pictures and newspaper clippings of Richard with candles underneath. Richard's expression didn't reveal any similar mirth, so Owen kept the imagery to himself.

Owen knew there wasn't much they could do with this new information. If he notified the authorities, the first thing they'd want to know would be what secrets Richard had that a Chinese spy would want to uncover. Seeing the pensive look on Richard's face, Owen deduced that he was making the same calculation.

Finally, Richard stopped pacing and said, "We just have to stay vigilant. We have no other choice."

~ ~ ~

Victor, Connor, and Marisa sat together toward the back of the class, listening to Professor Nelson's lecture on deterministic algorithms. All three were edgy, anticipating the battles that would soon take place. Victor was chief among them in this regard.

Upon completing the lecture, Professor Nelson exited the classroom, per usual. James again presented the results, though with much less fanfare this time around. He instructed the audience to log into CombatRidge and check the scores. The students rushed to learn how they'd performed, and soon the room was sprinkled with short cheers and groans.

Victor observed the Week 2 scores and saw the top six were as follows:

1) DevilsKeeper – Victor Hendricks (85 points)
2) CodeSlayer – Wei Lee (78 points)
3) Marisol – Marisa Asensio (76 points)
4) Borgana – Sarah Robinson (75 points)
5) Valkyrie – Nathan Stein (73 points)
6) BluManChu – Connor Mackinson (64 points)

The weekly scores had the same players in the top six, and in the same order as the previous week to boot. These new points would be added to the Week 1 scores to determine the overall standings after the Godslayer had his say. If the Godslayer took away no points, Marisa would finish the day in first place overall. Wei was in second place, fifty points behind her. Connor found himself in fifth, and Victor had risen from last place up to sixtieth, which he still found to be dismal.

His dream of finishing atop everything was slipping away. The highest ranked student couldn't possibly be failed, he thought, but failing the student ranked sixtieth in a coding competition? That could be easily defended.

Just as Victor wondered who this week's Godslayer would be, Tina began presenting the next enemy of the people.

"I'm sure you're all eager to meet our guest of honor," she said with a smile. "Please give a warm welcome to Daniel Rex."

A scrawny kid in a red Stanford hoodie stood and gave a fist-bump to Lucas, who had been seated next to him.

Victor grumbled, "Why is Lucas here?"

"I think he's Daniel's friend," Marisa whispered.

Daniel smiled and waved to the crowd. Boos rained down on him, but he seemed to relish them as he took his seat behind the desk.

"Daniel is currently in second place in our CombatRidge Gamers League," Tina explained. "The rules are all familiar to you, so I won't repeat them. However, any points you accumulated in prior weeks are now untouchable. Daniel is only battling against today's version of your bots, so only today's points are at stake."

A lump emerged in Victor's throat. The predators would undoubtedly seek out the meatiest prey, and thanks to his first-place finish this week, that was once again him.

As expected, DevilsKeeper was chosen as the first target. Daniel's warrior, Drexosaur, had a man's body in green army fatigues with an orange lizard head. DevilsKeeper opened with a punch that connected cleanly with Drexosaur's reptilian face, and the crowd cheered. The cheers from that point on were sparse, as both players put on a defensive display, adeptly blocking punches and kicks in a timely manner. The students grew restless while the warriors struggled to find openings, but as the minutes ticked by, damage was equally meted out on both sides.

With both combatants weakened and tired, DevilsKeeper let down his guard and started hopping in place. He was taunting Drexosaur to attack him. Careful not to be lured into a trap, Daniel instead stood and blocked in anticipation of one of the jumps being followed by a hammer attack. Sensing Daniel's mistake, DevilsKeeper kicked as soon as he landed, and Drexosaur's legs gave out underneath him. The words *DevilsKeeper Wins!* flashed on the screen, and the room erupted.

"Take that!" Victor screamed, but his voice was drowned out in the sea of cheers.

The victory brought Victor all the way up to fifth place in the overall standings. A top five finish would be respectable and perhaps enough to bolster his argument. Still, he wanted first place.

With almost five minutes gone and no winnings, Daniel sought revenge. Another long match ensued, and with both fighters weakened, DevilsKeeper caught Drexosaur letting his stamina drop too low. DevilsKeeper seized the moment and lifted his opponent into the air. Daniel desperately tried to liberate his warrior, but with his stamina at twenty and only gradually climbing, he was helpless. DevilsKeeper paused just long enough to flaunt his dominance, and then Drexosaur took flight without wings.

The programmers went crazy. Papers flew through the air. The feared Godslayers no longer seemed so intimidating. Marisa and Connor started a chant of Victor's name, and within a few seconds, the whole class joined in. Tina waved her hands, trying to bring order to the room, but James signaled for her to let them have their fun.

Amid the noise, Daniel adjusted his glasses and returned to the task at hand. He had five minutes left, and his prize money indicator mocked him, displaying *Winnings: $0.* Now up to second place overall, another win would put Victor in first, but a loss would send him all the way down to forty-eighth. With the price on his head now higher, Victor was sure Daniel would go for the $960 prize.

Victor wanted another rematch, so he yelled out, "Scared money don't make money!"

The other students all laughed.

The Godslayer chose to move on to Wei Lee's CodeSlayer, but she made that selection immediately regrettable. She parried his first two punches while retreating, then tossed him backward over the cliff before he could even complete his third move. While the crowd cheered, it was not nearly as boisterous as it had been for Victor. Wei's cheering for Lucas's merciless beatdown of Victor the week prior hadn't sat well with her classmates, apparently.

Now she had vaulted over him to regain second place overall. Wei hollered and clapped as she smugly looked Victor's way.

The only benefit to such a drubbing for Daniel was that it still left him time for another fight. For Daniel's next match, he chose to battle Valkyrie, Nathan Stein's female Viking warrior. Much like the legendary Vikings, she was hard to get past. An already frustrated Daniel struggled against her, and to the students' delight, she ate up a lot of time on the clock.

Unable to break through, Daniel tried something he normally didn't risk with full-stamina opponents; he attempted a lift.

When Drexosaur got her in the air, everyone expected Valkyrie to jump free. Nathan yelled for his bot to save herself, but she didn't listen. Later, upon reexamining his code, he would find that he'd overlooked the scenario of someone lifting him when he had full stamina. It had never happened to him until now, on the biggest stage of all. This left Nathan dumbfounded when Valkyrie flew off to Valhalla.

The mood died as the streak of defeating Godslayers came to an end. With only a few seconds on the clock, Lucas ran up and said something in Daniel's ear. With a grin, Daniel clicked on Marisol.

"Looks like Lucas wants revenge," Marisa said to the boys. But the end buzzer sounded just before the battle started, leaving Marisa safely in first place, followed by Wei, and then Victor. Connor, in fifth place, lamented that if he could just get a shot at a Godslayer, he was sure he could advance.

Tina thanked Daniel, and the obligatory jeers ensued. As the three friends stood to leave the class, Victor headed to the right when they usually exited to the left. Connor was already a few steps in the other direction before he realized Victor had gone the opposite way—toward the right side of the auditorium, where Tina and James were talking up front with Daniel, Lucas, and a few students.

With a tap to Marisa's shoulder, Connor directed her to follow him in his pursuit of Victor. What was his friend up to?

Upon reaching the front, Victor walked up to Tina. Before he could speak, Daniel reached out his hand to Victor and said, "Good game."

But Victor ignored Daniel. Instead, he handed his Warriors ski cap to Tina and said, "Thanks for lending this to me."

As Victor leaned in to kiss her, Lucas seemed to recognize the delivery guy, and he lunged for Victor. By then, Connor had positioned himself between Lucas and Victor, hoping to prevent a fight, which resulted in Connor being knocked into Victor and then to the floor. Marisa responded with a loud, open-handed slap to Lucas's face, who reflexively threw up his fists.

Little Tina managed to push back the hulking man with the help of Daniel and James, while Victor and Connor fled the scene. Marisa trailed behind them, but before exiting the room, she yelled, "Next time, pick on someone your own size!"

"You're crazy," Connor told Victor breathlessly as they walked down the hallway. "You know that? Why would you try to kiss Tina right in front of Lucas?"

"Dude, I was only gonna kiss her on the cheek to say goodbye, that's all," Victor protested. "I know what I'm doing. Now, you wanna talk crazy? Marisa's the crazy one. Did you see her in action? Wow!"

Connor appeared unconvinced, but Marisa said, "Victor, I found your strategy to be quite brilliant," prompting Connor to glance at her cockeyed.

In a mentor's fashion, Marisa put her arm around Connor and said, "Think about it, babe. Victor has nothing to lose and everything to gain. If he wants revenge on Lucas, encroaching on his territory is a smart move. That's all Tina is to Lucas—territory. He's probably already on to the next girl, but I bet he thinks Victor wants to upstage him, and he let his pride take over."

Connor still looked confused, so Marisa clarified, "The only way for Victor to catch me in the standings is for a Godslayer to come after him next week, *hard*. He just gave Lucas extra incentive to orchestrate that. When he walked up there, I thought he would do something reckless like punch Lucas, but what he did was much more subtle and a totally brilliant move!"

Not wanting to admit that he wasn't actually as clever as Marisa believed, but rather only trying to say goodbye to Tina, Victor smiled while patting Connor on the shoulder and said, "See, kid, you've gotta think fast. Your girl certainly does."

CHAPTER 22 – GHOSTLY VISION

Two weeks before Halloween, Pari rang Richard's doorbell mid-morning with a suitcase by her side. Most houses in the neighborhood sported spooky adornments for the upcoming holiday, but not Richard's. Before his wife died, he and Virginia had loved seeing the tiniest ones all dressed up every year. Now Richard lacked time for such things, so on Halloween night, he would turn off all the house lights and leave two bowls of candy at the front door. He was happy to let the little tykes take their fill.

"Does this mean you've accepted my proposal?" Richard asked, as he opened his door. "Or are we shacking up out of wedlock?"

Pari rolled her eyes and then rolled her bag into Richard's living room. As far as Gerald knew, she would be out of town for the week at a convention. Given the progress she and Richard were making in applying her vision research findings to his code, she wanted to spend some time at Richard's house advancing their work. She had also cancelled her classes for the week.

When Pari asked what room she should put her things in, Richard replied, "That depends. Is this a booty call?"

Placing her hand on his chest, she whispered seductively, "Maybe." With a wink, she handed him her keys. "Park the car in the garage. We need to keep this discreet."

This created the desired effect of putting Richard off balance. "I—I wouldn't do that to Gerald, Pari. I can't."

"Me neither," she replied with a wicked laugh. "I'm just messing with you. Oh, and the booty call joke is getting old."

~ ~ ~

After an hour in the dark, broken only by a few minutes of hallucinations, Richie found that the complete blackness around him had turned red. The droning, computerized voice—signifying a message from Richard and Pari—called to him from all directions, but for a long moment, he couldn't respond.

Finally, he spoke. "Sorry. I see red. Why is everything red?"

"We're only displaying a red background to start," the voice said to him as it verbalized Richard's written words.

"It's changing," Richie replied. "The edges are black. I see a red square moving away from me now. Or maybe it's getting smaller. I can't tell. No depth perception."

The red rectangle stopped shrinking, and Richard instructed, *"The image is going to slowly shift. I want you to tell me each time you notice a change."*

The rectangle changed color, and Richie relayed his vision to them. "Now it's blue. Rotating clockwise. Turned green. Positioned like a diamond. The diamond is growing again."

An entire month had passed for Pari and Richard since Richie was spawned. For Richie himself, it had been over an hour in the dark without knowing if he would ever see again. Now, given a taste of the light, he hungered for more.

The animation dissolved into scrolling yellow text on a black background. Before Richard prompted him, Richie began reading the words aloud: "God divided the light from the darkness." Pondering this, Richie asked, "Are you telling me to call you God?"

After Richard answered no, Richie said, "Good, because I wasn't planning on it. Though from my perspective, you kinda are."

With a few keystrokes, Richard performed the next miracle. In vivid detail, Richie described the imagery before him. "There's a shimmering light dancing in front of a starry sky. It's the aurora borealis! A mountain covered with snow on the horizon with a bunch of brown rocks in the foreground. Between them, a lake that appears to be frozen. The lights dancing above glimmer on the frozen lake below. Although…I'm trying to look closer, but I can't move my eyes to even change focus. This is like the most vivid, waking dream inside my eyelids."

Richard explained that focus and eye movement were still much farther off, but they were working on it.

"I have a question," Richie said. "Pari, you never told me. Did Quinn like my gift?"

"Hi Richie! Pari here. Yes, she did," the Hawking voice told Richie.

"Really? How far did she get in the book?"

"Well, she hasn't picked it up yet."

"That's not saying much. She hasn't picked up much of anything in a while."

"You know what I mean. She said it looks interesting, but she's just not there yet."

"That's why she needs the glasses."

"Quinn does like wearing those. But I don't think they work quite as you expected. Hey, we've got one last treat for you tonight."

The treats Richie wanted most of all were to see one particularly special face...and to be *seen* once again. Though he was presently less than a ghost, the day's images buttressed his hope of someday achieving the grander vision. On Earth, he'd had little patience for delays. In the digital realm, he understood that patience was a necessary bedfellow. His greatest desires would have to wait. For now, he would need to be content with smaller treats.

"Looks like the CombatRidge landscape, but in 3D," Richie said, gazing upon an arid landscape stretched out before him.

"Yes," Pari said, *"and we have an assignment for you."*

CHAPTER 23 – WRATH OF THE SCORNED

With plenty of coursework to occupy him, the week passed swiftly for Victor. He, Connor, and Marisa had spent so much time on their Advanced Programming class that they'd all fallen behind in their other classes. Marisa and Connor also had to juggle diving practice, but the three of them managed to catch up over the weekend and somehow also prepare for the final week of the CombatRidge competition. The competition represented 20 percent of their grade, as much as the midterm and the final each.

Professor Nelson's lecture on the role of randomness in programming at first appeared rather random to the students. An array of tangents woven into his speech included topics such as free will, predictability, and the limits of human perception. Had Victor not already figured out the professor's style, he would have been tempted to ask if he was in a metaphysics class.

Finally, the professor bridged the connection to key pieces of modern computing. "All the cryptography used to secure the web relies on randomness, or pseudo-randomness, to be more precise. Deterministic machines, such as computers, cannot generate purely random numbers, to the extent that randomness is real. Perhaps we simply use this term to express our inferior capacity to predict or understand."

Connor whispered to Marisa, "Where else in the world is an intellectual presentation the opening act for a combat sport?"

She replied, "Don't they have poetry readings before martial arts fights?"

The two chuckled at their own humor. Victor remained stoic.

Professor Nelson whispered something to James, then bid them all farewell. James gave his normal presentation of the week's scores. Victor immediately homed in on the top six players:

1) CodeSlayer – Wei Lee (80 points)
2) Borgana – Sarah Robinson (79 points)
3) DevilsKeeper – Victor Hendricks (78 points)
4) BluManChu – Connor Mackinson (77 points)
5) Valkyrie – Nathan Stein (71 points)
6) Marisol – Marisa Asensio (70 points)

The cream continued to rise to the top. For the third week in a row, the same six students were the top six scorers. In the overall standings, the top five also remained unchanged: Marisa was in first, Wei was in second, Victor had third, followed by Sarah in fourth, and Connor in fifth. The top three spots were now prized positions because Professor Nelson had announced last Wednesday, seemingly on a whim, that the three best finishers would be exempt from the midterm exam. The midterm was only two days away, so anyone who wasn't yet prepared was desperately hoping for a top-tier finish.

Neither Tina nor James had been in class for the past week, and Victor wondered if their absence was related to the incident the week prior. In any event, they were both present for this session, though Tina seemed to be pointedly avoiding looking in Victor's direction as she introduced the final Godslayer, Brittany Odriozola.

A tall girl with pink hair rose from her seat next to Lucas and Daniel, the two of them cheering for her as she joined Tina up front. With her pixelated jewelry and pastel outfit, Brittany could easily have passed for a video game character. Her cute smile and friendly wave disarmed many, and for some reason she wasn't booed by the students as vehemently as her predecessors had been.

Brittany took her seat at the desk, and everyone watched as she selected the first opponent. As expected, Brittany opted to challenge Wei Lee's CodeSlayer, and the fifteen-minute countdown began. Athena, Brittany's Greek warrior, was clad scantily in white robes and opened the match with a jump. CodeSlayer countered with a standing block, anticipating Thor's Hammer, but the hammer didn't come. Shifting away from defense, CodeSlayer began her offensive with a kick to Athena's shin. Athena crouched and blocked, only to catch a hammer unchecked to her crown. Like a dazed fighter, she stayed in that position. Many people cheered,

Wei loudest of all. With a series of hammers, CodeSlayer fed the crowd's bloodlust until Athena succumbed to her mortal wounds. In under a minute, the mighty Godslayer had fallen.

Everyone except the three Godslayers cheered while Wei jumped up and waved her hands. Her overall score jumped to 350, moving her into first place, thirty-nine points ahead of Marisa.

"My turn now," Marisa blurted out.

But Brittany immediately initiated a rematch with Wei. Brittany's bot stood motionless with her arms at her side while CodeSlayer pummeled her face. Amidst the roaring crowd, Athena collapsed without even presenting a defense. Marisa screamed, "Too easy!" and the other students' cheers turned into boos, as they wanted a competition, not a fix. Wei's CodeSlayer now had a comfortable lead in first place, ninety-three points ahead of Marisa.

"Did Wei pay her to lose?" Connor asked as he watched Wei celebrating.

Still steaming about being knocked out of first place, Marisa didn't answer.

"She still has twelve minutes left," Victor mused aloud. "If she keeps throwing matches to move students up, she could push us out of the top three. Is that what she's after?"

When Brittany chose CodeSlayer again, the crowd collectively groaned.

Yet, this time, Brittany was clearly trying. She demonstrated incredibly fast reflexes, as though time moved slower for her than everyone else. The once-dominant CodeSlayer now cowered defenseless against Athena's onslaught.

With a final leg swipe, Athena destroyed CodeSlayer without ever being touched.

The crowd was stunned. After cheering for CodeSlayer, they'd booed when it was too easy. Now they'd gotten a real fight, but didn't know what to make of it.

Wei's first place lead shrunk to only nine points over Marisa, while Brittany's prize money rose from zero to $900.

"She fattened up the pig!" Marisa said, gesticulating with her hands.

"Yeah," Connor said, looking stunned. "She threw the first matches to make the prize money bigger."

In a slightly closer match, Brittany went on to defeat CodeSlayer again, picking up another $450 and dropping Wei Lee down into a second-place tie with Victor with 275 overall points.

After ten minutes of fighting the same opponent, Brittany followed the money to match up against Sarah Robinson's Borgana. The fight was a slow, defensive battle with lots of parried punches. Both fighters seldom slipped in connecting blows. Then Borgana started making random non-attack movements, blocking and then jumping, then letting her guard down, then ducking. In response, Brittany unveiled a barrage of attack moves.

Borgana had baited her, and now she countered with her own barrage. Both their health and stamina dropped precipitously. Before Brittany could react, she witnessed Athena helplessly dangling from Borgana's outstretched arms.

"It's over, Brittany!" Sarah yelled.

The room filled with anticipation as they waited for Athena to take flight. Unfortunately, her flight was cancelled. Borgana had exerted almost all her stamina reserves lifting Athena, so when she went to throw her, she instead collapsed.

The crowd gasped. For a CombatRidge warrior, being crushed under the weight of one's opponent was the most humiliating failure. It was defeat snatched from the jaws of victory.

Sarah fumed, and the room fell silent. After the long battle with Borgana, there remained only ten seconds left on the clock. With Marisa still in first, and Victor and Wei still tied for second, Connor was on the outside looking to get into the top three.

"Give me a shot!" Connor pleaded under his breath. But true to form, Brittany followed the money again and faced off for the largest available prize against DevilsKeeper.

"Let's go!" Victor yelled.

Amid the growing crowd noise, Brittany ignored Victor and kicked off the battle. A win would secure the championship for Victor. A loss for DevilsKeeper would give Marisa the championship and—she hoped—the internship she was after. Still, she cheered vigorously for her friend the entire match.

Each fighter opened with simultaneous kicks. Athena crouched to defend her legs, but DevilsKeeper took a different approach to defending the low ground. Deciding the safest place was in the air, he leapt up and brought Thor's Hammer down on Athena's skull. When he landed, Athena swiped at DevilsKeeper's legs.

Brittany hadn't bothered to stand to block the hammer attack. She had seemed to realize she wouldn't make the block in time, and had instead exacted a small price in return when DevilsKeeper landed. Giving up thirty health to do only ten damage in return wasn't a sustainable strategy, but when caught late, some retribution was better than doing no damage at all.

As Athena completed the leg swipe, DevilsKeeper jumped for another hammer attack. Athena stood in defense but, making a rare slip-up, Brittany hit the V key instead of the B and failed to block the attack. This devastated Athena, who staggered backward. The smile that had graced Brittany's face for the entire session suddenly disappeared into a dour expression. Some in the crowd chanted, "Goodbye, Godslayers!" while rhythmically beating on their desks.

The mistake threw Brittany's timing off, and DevilsKeeper rapidly exploited this with several kicks to the chest. One more shot and she would be done. Victor thought she needed to be careful and pick her spots. However, boldly attempting to end the match with one quick move, Athena lifted DevilsKeeper off his feet. As his stamina had just dropped below fifty, he lacked the power to escape.

At the sight of Athena holding DevilsKeeper overhead, Marisa, Connor, and Victor all simultaneously gasped. The chants ceased. Victor waited for the inevitable banishment, so emblematic of his short college career.

However, soon after being lifted, DevilsKeeper's stamina rose back above fifty, and he jumped free of Athena's clutches just before it was too late. Brittany's bot pantomimed tossing an invisible victim over the edge. Before completing her motion, DevilsKeeper delivered the final knockout punch to Athena's face, sending her sprawling across the dusty ground.

Brittany hollered in rage, and the students unleashed a thunderous roar, reveling at the sight of a vanquished Godslayer. Marisa, Connor, and Victor leapt from their seats, embracing one another. With the clock at zero, Victor had won the battle and the war.

The downtrodden underdog was now the class champion.

Marisa and Victor could each could skip the midterm, and while Connor had come up short, he showed no disappointment. The cheers gradually faded away, and James dismissed the class.

Connor pointed toward the left side of the room, opposite Tina and the Godslayers. "Let's walk out that way today. No more drama."

But on their way out the door, they each turned around quickly when a voice called out Victor's name. It was James. "Hey, Victor, Professor Nelson wants to see you in his office in ten minutes."

CHAPTER 24 – VICTORY SPOILED

The thought of visiting Professor Nelson's office dampened Victor's spirits, as nothing positive ever happened to him there. He wasn't arrogant enough to assume that he was being summoned so the professor could congratulate him on his victory.

Upon arriving at Professor Nelson's office, Victor was surprised to find Tina there as well, talking to the professor. Nelson welcomed Victor in and invited him to take a seat next to Tina. Victor eyed Tina curiously, searching her expression for a clue, but her blank stare told him she was equally surprised to see him.

After closing the door, the professor calmly turned to question them. "I imagine you're aware that university policy prohibits faculty from dating students?"

Tina flinched.

"Really, you're not my type, sir," Victor said, trying for some levity.

Professor Nelson ignored his comment. "Now, I don't like to meddle in people's personal lives. I have better things to do with my time. Yet, when such a policy violation is brought directly to my attention, I am forced to respond." The professor pinned both of them with a serious stare. "The two of you were seen kissing at a party three weeks ago."

"Richard," Tina said, "it's not like that. He—"

"Let me finish," Professor Nelson said sternly. He directed his gaze toward Victor, who squirmed uncomfortably. "You're very talented, Victor. Congratulations on winning the competition. I had a feeling you would."

Victor stared at him, astonished. Was Nelson actually giving him a compliment?

The thrill of the moment dissolved when the professor added, "But people are starting to wonder if you won fairly. When they witness you kissing one of the lead game creators, who is not only a teaching assistant for the class, but also my employee at Warp Drive Games, it reeks of impropriety." His eyes turned to Tina. "Tina, I don't wish to let you go, but this is considered a fireable offense at Stanford." Tina opened her mouth to object, but the professor overrode her. "Please, don't try to deny it. One of your fellow students showed me a picture. In addition, I understand Lucas attacked you, Victor, when you were talking to Tina after class. Can someone explain that to me? Are you dating Lucas, Tina? Need I remind you he is also a student at this school?"

Tina sputtered, "What? Lucas? No! I mean, come on. Why would I date him?"

Her denial stretched the limits of credibility, and for a microsecond, Victor and the professor exchanged looks that said, *Yeah, every girl would want to date him.*

"I stepped on his foot," Victor said quickly, "when I went to speak with Tina. I, uh, stepped on his foot, and that's what got him so upset."

Professor Nelson glared at them both in disgust, while Victor tried to determine who might have ratted on them. *Why would another student want Tina fired?* Or maybe they thought if Victor had won unfairly, he would be disqualified, thereby allowing someone else to make the top three.

Tina's voice cracked as she pleaded, "Richard, please, we were two consenting adults, and I showed Victor no favoritism."

"I believe you," the professor said gently. "But we must consider the optics. I cannot be seen as failing to act. I possess much liberty here at Stanford, but such blatant misconduct leaves me little choice. One of you must go—"

Inhaling deeply, Tina began to tear up as the possibility of losing both her jobs and having to start her doctorate over elsewhere lingered in the air.

"I'll do it," Victor blurted out. "I'll take the fall. You can kick me out of Stanford. I've already failed your class, anyway, which means I'm bound to lose my scholarship at the end of the semester. Let whoever was behind this have their precious midterm exemption."

Professor Nelson squinted at him and said, "Victor, I told you that you failed a month ago. Why have you stuck around?"

In the defiant tone of someone who had become resigned to their fate, Victor said, "I wanted to prove I'm not a failure. I wanted you to realize I deserve to pass."

Narrowing his gaze, the professor followed up, "Any other reason? Like possibly to learn?"

"Of course I wanted to learn!" Victor exclaimed. "This is my dream, and I've learned a ton in your class."

"I'm pleased to hear that," Nelson said with a small smile. "But after all this struggle, why choose to give up now?"

A glance at Tina's anxious face validated Victor's decision. "Because it's my choice. For once, I'm in control. I choose to surrender. Not because I deserve to fail—I certainly don't. And not because she deserves this sacrifice from me, either. She absolutely doesn't. But because my loss would be less than hers. For me, starting over won't be as hard as it would be for her. She's almost finished, and I'm just beginning."

Professor Nelson studied Victor carefully, thoughtfully.

Tina again pleaded, "Please, sir, this is going too far. There was no real wrongdoing. Yes, we kissed while drunk at a party. Full disclosure, we also went out for lunch together. I guess you could call it a date, but we didn't even kiss. Victor doesn't deserve this, especially just for the sake of optics."

"Tina, I completely agree," the professor acknowledged. Then he glanced over at Victor with a resigned expression. "But you, Mr. Hendricks, still need to learn my lesson about interruptions. You interrupted me while I was saying that one of you must go *from my classroom*, not from Stanford. That will be sufficient to address the optics. There was no egregious wrongdoing, and I can justify no further action being taken. I have already told the student who reported this that I will not change the final standings. Frankly, I find their attempt to elevate themselves at the expense of others quite troubling."

Relief flooded through Victor, and Tina straightened herself in her chair, looking hopeful.

"Victor, you will remain in my class," the professor instructed. "Tina, you will keep your job and stay in school, but I think it's best if you don't show up to class anymore. Behind the scenes, you can still do the TA work, grading and such. This will create enough space between you for the situation to be considered dealt with."

Tina thanked Professor Nelson repeatedly, while Victor merely sat there in a daze. "Now, I've had enough of this emotional crap for one day," the professor said tiredly. "You two really need to straighten out your love lives, but please do so outside my classroom. You're dismissed. And for goodness' sake, be kind to each other."

Feeling as though they'd barely escaped from a lion's den, Tina and Victor limped out of Professor Nelson's office. The door closed swiftly behind them.

A few steps down the hallway, Tina said, "That was mighty decent of you."

Still bitter about finding her with Lucas, Victor reluctantly replied, "Yeah, thanks for sticking up for me, too."

Neither filled the awkward silence as they exited the CS department. Victor was unsure if he would ever see her again, but he wasn't exactly sure how to say goodbye.

He turned to walk away from her, but Tina tugged gently at his shoulder to turn him around. Pressing a kiss to his cheek, she said, "You're a good person, Victor. Take care of yourself."

Not uttering a sound, he watched her walk away.

~ ~ ~

Victor marched back into Professor Nelson's office without bothering to knock. "Back so soon?" the professor said as he pivoted in his office chair.

"Professor, thank you for your compromise," Victor began. "I just wanna say since I'm still in the game, I'm going to win. You're going to pass me, not because I'm telling you to, but because I'll earn it. And if you don't, understand that I know what you're up to, and I'm sure others would like to know, too."

The professor flinched. "What are you talking about, Victor?"

"Let's just say I'm sure the police would be very interested to know that your wife is still alive."

A vein swelled in the professor's neck. "Where would you get such a foolish idea?"

Suddenly wishing he had physical evidence, Victor answered, "I overheard you on the phone with her."

Professor Nelson laughed, but Victor saw no humor in the matter.

"Victor, you're a bright kid. And you're a fighter. I admire that about you. Heck, you're my favorite student. Do you know how many of your classmates would have fought like you, after being beaten down so hard? I'd bet I can count 'em on one hand. They're all intelligent, to be sure, but it's the ones with tenacity that will separate themselves from the pack." He pinned Victor with a serious look. "You have so much potential. Do you really want to throw it away on a false accusation with zero evidence?"

Victor was taken aback by the compliments, but still said, "Throw it away?! Why do you care what I throw away? You threw *me* away on day one!"

With a sincerity Victor couldn't comprehend, the professor said, "Oh, but I *do* care. More than you understand. That's why I did so much for you. I gave you a struggle to strengthen you. Some might even accuse me of playing favorites."

A sarcastic cackle escaped Victor's mouth. While ready to yell, he summoned the will to calm himself. "Thank you so much for your generosity. I've got something for you, too."

Victor reached into his bag. Professor Nelson paled and seized his arm as he pulled something out, then relaxed when he saw the item was a textbook. Victor smirked at him, silently delighting in making the professor fear for his safety. The tables were starting to turn.

"My apologies, Victor," the professor said, releasing his arm and stepping back.

"No problem, sir," Victor said, laying the book on his desk. "This belongs to a student of yours. Yashira something. I'm tired of carrying it around for her."

"Who?" the professor asked, looking confused.

Victor ignored his question. Instead, as he exited the office, he pointed his index finger at Professor Nelson and said, "You *will* pass me."

CHAPTER 25 – THE ABYSS

The oil sizzled in the pan, filling the kitchen with the savory aroma of bread pakora. It wasn't unusual for Pari to cook on a weeknight, but she hadn't done so in a while due to frequently working long hours. Their eighteen-year-old daughter, Quinn, wasn't a fan of bread pakora, so Pari had picked her up fast food, which Quinn had already finished eating.

Gerald had just come from Quinn's bedroom after talking to her about her future. Like many teenagers, she had trouble seeing far into it. Swirling his glass of red wine, Gerald watched Pari cook his favorite Indian dish. He remarked that he was grateful for such a special treat, especially considering how time-consuming it was to make. Pari smiled at him briefly over her shoulder, then turned her attention back to the bread pakora—and her contemplation of how to approach the subject of her current research with her husband.

Just as Pari was nearly prepared to ascend her mountain of fears, Gerald began telling her about his day. He described an intense debate he had with his fellow economists at Berkeley, where he taught. The topic of their debate was his thesis that value was a myth. People too often spoke of value as an intrinsic property of things, Gerald contended. Instead, he believed that, in professional settings, they should refer to the measurable attributes considered valuable in those things. The widespread overuse of the term led to many suboptimal decisions in corporate and government policies, he explained. Value itself was not measurable, and beliefs otherwise exacerbated the problem as he saw it.

Pari indulged him and listened intently, as she always did. Although she sometimes felt he spent too much time in his ivory tower, distant from real policy application, she loved him too much to ever tell him directly. Occasionally, she would nudge him just a little.

"The belief that value is a real thing is so embedded in our language, many don't see it's an unnecessary and misleading construct. The forces of supply and demand don't arrive at the market *value* of a thing, merely the market *price* of it," Gerald ranted with prodigious academic fervor.

Pari felt his soliloquy was getting somewhat lengthy, but she was willing to let it run its course. She placed a full plate of bread pakora with flattened rice in front of him and said, "Save some of that fire for your presentation in February."

After savoring a bite of her delicious cooking, Gerald mentioned he was still awaiting approval for his spring sabbatical. It being late October, he questioned whether he would get the answer he wanted. But if he did, he would use the time to work on his book and research the origins of this mythology in western cultures and the various impacts on modern society. Without knowing yet where the research would take him, he believed some travel would be involved.

Between bites, he told her, "I would love some company on my travels."

Pari, who had scarcely touched her own food, replied, "Maybe, but my work is at a really intense stage, and it's going to start taking more of my time."

While disappointed, Gerald understood. He was always very understanding, which was one of the characteristics she valued most about him. Yet she wondered if he would understand what she was about to tell him.

"We ran across an interesting hypothetical in our research today," Pari said, trying to sound nonchalant. "Suppose a person has a secret. The secret is nothing immoral, illegal, or wrong in any way. Just a secret. The person is in no danger, but if they tell their spouse the secret, the spouse would be in grave danger. What would you do?"

These kinds of puzzles appealed to Gerald's philosophical mind. Initially, he asked how this came up in her neuroscience research, but she dismissed that as immaterial and directed his focus back to the hypothetical. For a brief moment, he pondered the problem and determined it to be quite simple. If he was the secret-keeper, he would let his spouse decide if she wanted to know the secret. But if his spouse was the secret-keeper, he would want to know, despite the danger.

"If you were the secret-keeper," Gerald said plainly, "I would want you to tell me. Whatever you were going through, I'd want to know. That's kinda the whole point of this marriage thing. We take this ride together. So, I would take that chance, for better or for worse."

Pari's tone betrayed her fears. "Even if it could get you killed?"

Still in his ivory tower, he missed the non-verbal cue and said emphatically, "I'd take that chance."

With her eyes lowered, she said softly, "That's what I feared."

Late to the game, Gerald started to put things together. "Are you in danger, sweetheart?"

Pari looked him straight in the eyes and warned him, "No, but if you knew the full extent of my work, you would be."

"What kind of danger?" Gerald asked, suddenly losing his appetite.

"Just…danger. Now, would you still want to learn what I'm working on, hypothetically?"

"There's no hypothetical here," he said drily. "Now, tell me. What sort of danger are you in?"

"*I'm* not in any unnecessary danger."

"Unnecessary…? Well, then, I won't be either."

"Yes, you would."

"Okay," Gerald said doubtfully. "It doesn't quite make sense to me how that works, but let's put that aside. Please, just tell me."

"Why? Why would you put yourself in danger for no reason?" Pari asked, a note of desperation in her voice.

"For you," he said, smiling at her lovingly.

"It does me no good for you to be in danger."

"It means I can be there with you. I meant what I said, Pari. For better or worse."

"Your curiosity could get you killed," she scolded him. "What would you do if the roles were reversed? Would you tell me? Would you put me at risk for your own selfish desire to share your secrets with someone?"

"I would give you the choice."

"You would place that burden on me?" Pari asked incredulously. "As I have done to you?"

"I would place my *trust* in you."

Pari shook her head. "I don't understand why you're so worried about your conference. You're an excellent debater," she said, smiling through an anxious expression.

"This isn't a debate. This is our life. You can tell me anything," Gerald said, taking her hand.

"Are you sure?" she asked earnestly. "There's no going back from knowing. You'll never be able to tell anyone for the rest of your life. You're standing blindfolded on the edge of the abyss and asking me to push you in."

"I'm asking you to pull me in with you."

"You don't understand what you're saying," she insisted. "You have no idea what lies beyond."

"Then tell me, so I'll understand. I'm ready."

"You can't be. I'm not even ready, and I already know!"

"Please, Pari. I'm asking you to pull me in with you."

Troubled by the prospect, Pari made her way to the sink and went through the motions of washing the dishes. Silence echoed through the room as a potent concoction of elation and terror swirled in her stomach. She prayed she was doing the right thing.

Pari inhaled a shaky breath. "You must take all of this to the grave and beyond."

Coming up behind her, Gerald placed his hand on her shoulder and said, "Beyond? So, this is a secret even from God himself?"

Pari spun around and pushed him back into his chair. "This isn't a game, Gerald," she said in a hushed voice.

Gerald's expression turned solemn. He had never seen her so deadly serious.

"Listen," Pari demanded, "you will never be able to tell anyone. No matter who asks. No matter what they say or do. Do you understand?"

He offered a contrite "I do" that reminded her of their wedding vows.

"I can only tell you one part while we're in this house," she said, choking back the lump in her throat. "The rest will have to wait until we're in a more secure location."

Half-hoping that he would stop her, she waited. When he remained silent, looking at her expectantly, she proceeded in a hushed tone, "Richard and I have made the greatest breakthrough of our careers. There is still so much more to do, but what we have already uncovered will change the course of human history in unimaginable ways. Wars have been fought to achieve powers that pale in comparison to this." Pari sighed wearily. "That's all I can tell you here. But now that you've heard the whispers from the abyss... you have one last chance to step back. To remain ignorant of what we have discovered."

Pulling Pari down into his lap, Gerald told her, "There is no stepping back. Either I remain teetering on the edge for the rest of my life, or I take the plunge with you. Pull me in."

He was so stubborn, she thought. Still, she loved his steadfast devotion to her.

"Put your shoes on and come with me," Pari ordered. He asked where they were going, but she merely shook her head. "No more questions. I mean it. Not a word, or I'll lose my nerve."

Pari grabbed her car keys, slipped on her shoes, and whisked out the front door. The thrill of finally getting to share this secret with him raced through her veins, while the possibility that she had just signed his death sentence gnawed at her heart.

She started the car before Gerald had even made it to the driveway. He ran to the passenger door and quickly jumped in. When he asked if she was okay to drive, she sternly reminded him no questions were allowed, so they sat in uncomfortable silence during the short trip to Richard's house.

Aimlessly staring out the window, Gerald stroked his beard nervously, waiting for answers.

~ ~ ~

As they pulled into Richard's driveway, a place Gerald had been many times, he was about to ask why they were at Richard's house when he remembered his gag order. Pari and Gerald had been friends with Richard and Virginia since their college days, and Gerald knew Richard's private equity firm was a major investor in Golden Bay Labs, the small neuroscience research group Pari ran.

What he didn't know was that Richard was Golden Bay's *only* investor, and with an investment far larger than Gerald had ever imagined.

Upon exiting the car, Pari waited for Gerald to come around to her side. After a deliberate breath, she escorted him to the front door. The wait for Richard to answer seemed like an eternity to her, and the look she gave

Gerald told him the doorway bordered the abyss. Her eyes asked him to turn back, but his expression conveyed the conviction to leap. Again, she silently prayed she'd made the right choice.

The unexpected sight of his two friends on his doorstep brought a smile to Richard's face. That smile disappeared at the recognition of the distress apparent on Pari's face. Feeling a bit of trepidation, he said nothing and gestured for them to enter.

Pari marched left to the dining room and sat herself at the head of the table. The men took this as their signal to sit with her. Gerald took a seat at her left side, and Richard was about to sit by her right when she said to him sharply, "Bring me an NDA."

Richard asked if she was sure. Her icy stare was answer enough. Promptly, he fetched a non-disclosure agreement, then left them alone to converse.

Sliding the paperwork over the table to Gerald, Pari handed him the pen and said, "Take your time to read it. Once you sign this, you'll fall into the abyss."

Without hesitation, he took the pen and signed. "I don't need to read it," Gerald said. "I trust you."

Pari struggled to keep her composure while Gerald squeezed her hand reassuringly. No more teetering on the edge.

A few minutes later, Richard returned to the room and told Gerald, "There's someone we would like you to meet. Follow me, please."

In silence, they followed Richard into the bedroom closet, down the stairs, and into the hidden basement.

"Where are we, Bruce Wayne?" Gerald said upon entering the basement.

Pari chuckled nervously. "I thought more James Bond when I first saw it."

With his arms extended across the bright white room, Richard replied, "Black really isn't my color."

Gerald asked if he was allowed to ask questions now. Pari explained that it would be better to wait until after the encounter. "I've informed him that Gerald has come to meet him," Richard told Pari before inviting Gerald to sit at the desk.

After a brief explanation of Faraday cages and the isolation of the bunker, Richard directed Gerald's attention to the computer. On the screen, Gerald saw a chat application, and Richard instructed him to type, *"Hi, it's Gerald."*

"If this basement is truly off the grid," Gerald asked, scanning the room, "who will I be chatting with?"

Both of his companions smiled tightly, but neither answered. Taking this as his cue to play along, Gerald typed in the introduction as requested.

A message quickly appeared on the screen. *"Welcome to the club, Gerald. I'm Richie. Richard asked me to explain to you who I am. Have you heard of the Turing Test?"*

Gerald replied that he had not.

"The Turing Test," Richie said, *"is a way to test if artificial intelligence has reached human-level intelligence."*

Gerald typed, *"Are you an AI?"*

The response deepened the mystery. *"Let's see what you think I am first. This will be a variation of the Turing Test. The main point is for you to determine whether you believe I am alive or not. Do you think I'm alive?"*

"I need more information," Gerald said.

"Good answer! I would have said the same thing. What do you want to know?" After a glance at Pari for guidance that wouldn't come, Gerald asked himself what the right question might be.

"When were you born?" he asked.

"1961."

The answer surprised Gerald—how could he possibly be talking to an AI over fifty years old? Reeling at the absurdity of it, Gerald joked, *"Were you born as a stack of punch cards?"*

"No. I was born in Somerton, England, in much the same way you were born. Umbilical cord was cut. Usual procedure. My parents immigrated to America when I was seventeen. We became friends at Cal Tech. I think you remember the rest of the story."

With a cockeyed look at Richard, Gerald pressed on. *"Are you trying to tell me that you're...Richard?"*

"I can't fool you, old friend. Technically, I'm one of the life-forms that started life as Richard Nelson. The other is likely in the room with you right now. I began the digital

portion of my life as a backup of Richard's brain, taken about two months ago on your timeline, though it's been less than two hours on my timeline. Richard keeps me paused most of the time. Now, I'm kept alive by the simulation software I wrote before transcending to digital form. The Earthly me maintains the software."

"Impossible! You've gotta be kidding me!" Gerald said out loud, looking at his wife. Her eyes told him to carry on.

"Don't you want to know more about him?" Richard asked, gesturing at the laptop.

Gerald chuckled incredulously and asked Richie, *"So, what does it feel like to be digital?"*

"It feels like I'm lying in a neural scanning bed." Gerald turned around and saw the empty bed at which Pari was pointing, then turned back to read Richie's next words. *"But I have limited sensations—no sight, aside from some very recent experimentation, and no mobility. Frankly, I'm feeling a bit claustrophobic right now. I'm sure hoping your dear wife will help my other self make things better soon. So, please support her as best you can."*

Perplexed by Richie's answer, Gerald tried to stump the program. If Richie was actually a version of Richard, Gerald concluded he must remember things about him that few but Richard would know. He challenged Richie to recall his original major in college before switching to economics. Richie correctly recalled that it was anthropology, and added that Gerald never seemed like the roughing-it type.

Next, Gerald asked him a few personal questions about Pari. Richie aced them all.

Bewildered, Gerald looked at Richard and Pari and asked, "This is only a computer program, right? I mean, it's a sophisticated program, but it can't really be alive…can it?"

Pari smiled, while Richard relished the opportunity to wax philosophical with his philosophically-minded friend. "Gerald, what if we discovered the world we lived in was actually a computer program? And that all the laws of physics were written in code? Would you feel any less alive?"

Gerald found himself speechless as he pondered that.

"Please," Richard said, pointing again at the laptop. "Find the right question to determine whether you think Richie is alive."

After contemplating the challenge, Gerald asked Richie an open-ended question. *"What do you miss most about Virginia?"*

No response came. Gerald briefly wondered if he had stumped the program. Up to that point, he was really starting to believe it was Richard. While he waited, he speculated that it might only be a sophisticated bot with a database of facts populated by Richard.

Under different circumstances, that would be the most logical answer—a joke his old friend Richard might have been trying to pull over on him. But Pari… his wife wouldn't go to all these lengths if this wasn't the real deal. Still, it was hard to fathom.

As Gerald opened his mouth to ask if he had broken their software, letters began to fill the screen.

"I apologize for the delay. I had to think about that one, as I miss so much about her. It's an unfair question—there's no way I can pick only one thing. I miss the way she used to laugh at my dry humor. I miss the smile she would always put on my face. I even miss how she always seemed to find something urgent to say as soon as my head hit the pillow at night. So many times, I complained that she could have told me sooner. I would constantly tease her about it. But now…I miss hearing about her day so much. Every night, going to bed without her next to me is lonely. And now that I've crossed over…it's even lonelier on this side."

"I miss her, too, my friend," Gerald typed back, tears glistening in his eyes.

Pari was right. Everything had changed forever.

CHAPTER 26 – CHANGING TIMES

A week of midterms had just passed, and Marisa was thankful for the exemption from their Advanced Programming test, because it freed up time to focus on their other midterms. In contrast, Victor had insisted on taking the Advanced Programming midterm to prove beyond any doubt that he deserved to pass. On Friday morning, while listening to Professor Nelson's lecture, Victor whispered that he was confident he'd nailed it.

"Time is commonly considered the fourth dimension," the professor said to his students, "but our experience of time adds another dimension. Consciousness adds a fifth dimension. Thus, beyond the three spatial dimensions of length, width, and height exist two other dimensions of time. The classical fourth dimension is space-time. This is time as it objectively exists. All events occur at exactly one point in space-time.

"The other time dimension is what I call discovery time. Every person possesses their own discovery time dimension. This is when the person discovers an event occurred or will occur." Puzzled expressions gazed back at the instructor as the students considered prognostic abilities. "That's right, the discovery often occurs after the event occurred in space-time, but not always. We sometimes know something will happen before it happens. For example, I discovered yesterday that I will have a dentist appointment next Tuesday. I discovered this when I scheduled it."

A few mild chuckles filled the air.

"Today, we will review some examples to explore how this relates to software development. Spoiler alert! It's everywhere. Any event worth recording usually has a time component, and in most cases, *two* time components. Many design failures stem from failing to recognize the importance of these two time dimensions. So, it's best you recognize this early in your careers."

The students listened with interest and greater focus than during prior classes, now that the CombatRidge challenges were behind them. At the end of his lecture, Professor Nelson made a few announcements before dismissing the class. "First, an administrative item. Tina volunteered to put in some extra hours working on CombatRidge. To help her balance her time, she will not be in class for the rest of the term. James will hold down the fort here."

For his second announcement, Richard explained there was one last CombatRidge competition involving the new CombatRidge 3D. This was a new team version in which each team had three fighters. "The top three CombatRidge finishers will now form a single team that will compete against the Godslayers' team in six weeks' time." Then, in a somber tone, he added, "Unfortunately, our third-place finisher, Wei Lee, will no longer be attending this class."

Marisa whispered to the guys, "What happened to Wei?" The boys shook their heads. Victor scanned the room for her, but his search turned up empty.

"This means that Connor Mackinson moves from fourth place up to third and will take her place. Lucas, Daniel, and Brittany have dubbed themselves the Alpha Dogs. I just spoke with Marisa this morning, and asked her to brainstorm a name with her team."

"The Leopards," Marisa called out before Connor and Victor could even ask about her conversation with Nelson. Connor blushed at the choice of the name, and both boys gave Marisa curious glances, but she merely smiled and shrugged.

Professor Nelson chuckled. "Okay, fine. The Leopards it is. The Leopards now represent all ninety of you. If they win, each of you will get an extra ten bonus points in the class. So, find ways to help your champions. You can create your own teams to spar against them. You can analyze their code and give them pointers. I'll allow you to self-organize your approach. Your challenge is to prove that a large team of developers can write code to outsmart three human gamers collaborating together."

As the professor allowed the class to soak in the excitement of a new competition, Connor whispered to Marisa, "Anything else you forgot to tell us?"

Marisa quickly said to the guys, "Yeah, he invited us to dinner at his house tonight."

Connor grinned in amazement, and Victor's eyes widened. All three friends recognized that being invited to dine at the private residence of such a successful and accomplished person was quite an honor. However,

Victor was starting to wonder why Professor Nelson had asked *Marisa* to choose the team name when Victor had finished ahead of her in the standings. Was he somehow now disqualified?

"Lastly," the professor said in a commanding voice, "Victor Hendricks, please stand."

Feeling slightly uneasy, and without knowing what to expect, Victor stood to face his nemesis.

Looking up intently, Professor Nelson told him, "You should not be here."

The room grew completely still. Amid the silence, many expected Victor's departure from the classroom, tossed out yet again. Victor remained defiantly motionless.

"You should not be here," Richard repeated for emphasis. "You failed this course in the opening minutes of the first day, so there is no reason for you to be here. At least, that is what most of your classmates think every time they see you. It's about time someone had the decency to say this to your face."

The professor scanned the room, eyeing the rest of the class, before redirecting his gaze to Victor. "You should not be here, and yet you still are. You should give up. That's what some of your fellow students believe. In fact, one of your classmates actually asked me to bar you from the competition!" He surveyed the other students once again. "But all of you could stand to learn a considerable lesson from Mr. Hendricks. When there appeared to be nothing to gain, he fought his hardest. In the face of adversity, he never backed down."

Professor Nelson met Victor's eyes once again, a small, proud smile toying at the corners of his mouth. "After one mistake—interrupting me—you made not a single mistake on any of your tests or quizzes. Heck, you scored a perfect score on the midterm you were exempt from. Not once did you fail a test I gave you, academic or otherwise." Spreading his hands, the professor added, "Standing before us is a remarkable example of the perseverance needed to achieve greatness in our field. Ladies and gentlemen, Victor is truly your class champion. So, it is my great pleasure to announce today that I reverse my decision to fail you. Victor, welcome back in the game."

The students jumped to their feet and applauded vigorously. In all the CombatRidge matches, they had never cheered as loudly as they did at that very moment. Victor buried his head in his hands, overcome with emotion. Connor and Marisa hugged him as the class broke out into chants of "Victor! Victor! Victor!"

His fellow students sympathized with his plight and admired his courage. And they rejoiced in his victory.

CHAPTER 27 – DIVING INTO THE DEEP END

Marisa completed an impressive dive off the ten-meter platform. The name of the dive or how to score it was beyond Victor's knowledge, but he applauded her nonetheless. Now that the tremendous burden of failing Advanced Programming had been lifted from his shoulders, he could again easily delight in the success of others. The judges awarded Marisa solid marks, putting her firmly in first place with a few divers yet to complete their final dives.

Having never made time for athletics himself, Victor realized suddenly that, for the first time in his life, he now belonged to a team. A warm feeling washed over him, which turned into a slightly soggy feeling when Marisa took a seat on his left, wearing only her red one-piece.

"Surprised to see you here," she said, throwing an arm over his shoulder with a mischievous grin, doing her best to make sure he got wet.

Victor mock-groaned at her antics, but met her gaze with a grin. Looking into her eyes, he thought about how lucky his friend Connor was to have a girl like Marisa, and not merely because she was gorgeous. He also considered how lucky *he* was to have her as a new friend.

"And I'm surprised to see *you* up here in the stands," Victor told her.

"Well, I'm done with my dives," Marisa said, letting her hair down to shake out the water. "So I thought I'd say hello quick before I go back to my team. Thanks for coming out to support us."

Looking out at the divers still competing, Victor said, "Connor's not doing so well, is he?" Connor was in last place among five other divers, with only one dive remaining.

"Well, he's diving okay, but I think he's up against tougher competition than he's seen before," she explained.

A thought surfaced that had been percolating in Victor's brain since class let out. He was thrilled to have his *F* suddenly become an *A*, but it seemed too quick of a turnaround. He almost couldn't believe it had happened. Why did it really happen? Had his threat influenced the professor's decision after all?

He was just about to raise the topic with Marisa when she told him she had to return to her team. As she stood to leave, Tina appeared unexpectedly and congratulated Marisa on her impressive diving. Marisa thanked her briefly, then excused herself. Behind the other girl's back, Marisa said another goodbye to Victor and gave Tina a cold stare.

When Tina began to take a seat on Victor's right, he informed her the seat was taken and directed her to the available wet seat on his left that Marisa had recently vacated. With a smirk, Tina completed her descent onto the dry bench to Victor's right.

"I heard about your reinstatement," she told him. "I'm really happy for you."

"Did you follow me here just to tell me that?"

"No, I'm actually here to support Katy, but I saw you and decided to come talk."

Victor said nothing. Tina used this as her opening to say her piece, "Listen, I know you meant well by trying to surprise me that day, but—"

Without looking at her, Victor said, "What are you after, Tina?"

Tina turned her gaze to the pool and said, "I just want to tell you I'm sorry. I mean, it's not like I cheated on you, because you weren't my boyfriend or anything. And I didn't ask you to show up at my place. Still, I'm sorry that I hurt you."

Maintaining his forward gaze, Victor told her, "Listen, we had one drunken night together and one fun day—"

"That was a great day," she interrupted, sounding wistful.

Now looking her way, Victor said, "Yes, but that's all. Time to move on. You certainly did. And today, I'm actually having an *amazing* day, so please don't mess it up just because you need to make yourself feel better."

"I came over here for you, not me."

"Okay," Victor said after a long pause. "Maybe it *was* naive of me to show up like that. But that whole situation was beyond humiliating, Tina. I understand that we'd just met, but it still stung. Especially since you were with Lucas, of all goddamn people. I *hate* him." He looked down at his lap. "If you didn't want to date me, you should have told me."

"I never said I didn't want to date you!" Tina exclaimed. "It—I didn't expect that night to happen with Lucas. He took an interest in me, and one thing led to another, and it just…happened. I'd never done anything like that before." She threw her hands up in exasperation. "Why am I even defending myself here?"

Returning his attention to the pool, Victor said, "You don't have to. It's your life. It would have been better to know before I showed up at your apartment, but… I guess I probably shouldn't have intruded." After being with Alison for a year, he was unfamiliar with the early dating boundaries, especially in college. This experience had provided him with a harsh discovery of them.

"A piece of advice for you," Tina said. "With the next girl, maybe save the surprises for later?"

An amused sigh escaped Victor's mouth. "Good point."

Both of them watched the divers for a while before Tina asked, "Did you hear about Wei?"

"That she isn't in Advanced Programming anymore?" Victor asked. "Yeah, Nelson told us in class earlier. I thought it was kind of weird. Do you know why?"

Tina looked sad and a little uncomfortable. "I just heard a few minutes ago myself," she told him, handing Victor her phone. The screen displayed a news article entitled *Stanford Student Found Dead.*

"Holy—" Victor whispered.

"They found her lying in a graveyard early this morning, beside an empty bottle of sleeping pills," Tina explained.

Victor couldn't find any words. He'd disliked Wei for her delight in his failure, but he never would have wished this on her—on *anyone*, for that matter.

"I didn't know her well," Tina said quietly, "but she would come up after class sometimes with questions. After she lost to you on Monday, she was very upset."

"But she got the midterm exemption," Victor protested. "Isn't that what she wanted?" A sudden thought dawned on him. "Wait… is she the one who tried to get me disqualified?"

"I think so," Tina said miserably. "Wei really wanted that internship. She complained to me about the process and I told her Richard didn't promise anyone an internship, it was just a maybe. But she didn't seem to get it. I think the pressure she put on herself got to her." She paused for a moment, then lowered her voice and said, "You know, they found her lying on Professor Nelson's wife's grave."

"Oh, man. Like she was protesting?" Victor whispered back.

"Yeah—with her life."

As Tina stood to leave, Victor said, "Wait. What do you know about Nelson's wife?"

"Um, not much," she said, looking taken aback. "She died a few years ago, but that was before I started working for Richard. Why?"

"Do you know anyone named Virginia in his life, other than his wife?"

"No. Victor, what are you up to?" Tina asked as Victor studied her face for signs of information.

"Nothing. Just curious," he lied.

Lowering her voice again, she left him with a warning, "Victor, be careful. I dunno what you're up to, but Richard's a very powerful man. You've only seen a tiny fraction of his influence. I believe he's a good man, but all the same, you don't want to cross him. If you're trying to extract some sort of revenge, you're better off letting your curiosity go." She leaned a bit closer, a slightly dangerous glint in her eyes. "Understand this—he's very loyal to his people in a way that's uncommon around here, and I'm very loyal to him. So, I'll forget you asked me about his wife this time, but don't ask me again. Goodbye, Victor."

Victor bid her farewell as she walked away for what he imagined was finally the last time. Glad to have that episode behind him, he returned his attention to supporting his friends, only to realize the competition had just ended. The sparse crowd began to file out of the stadium, but Victor remained alone with his thoughts, wondering why he couldn't let the Virginia thing go. He had nearly everything he'd sought now—he wouldn't lose his scholarship and would definitely pass all his classes. His return to Stanford for the next term was assured. All reason told him to let the Virginia question go.

Yet, he could not.

If Professor Nelson had faked his own wife's death, Victor wondered if dining with such a person was prudent. Perhaps, Victor speculated, Nelson's businesses were struggling for cash, and he and his wife had cooked up some scheme for the life insurance money. This seemed unlikely, however, given the professor's obvious wealth. Maybe she was hiding from someone? Only…where had Virginia gone?

Questions echoed in his mind as he sat staring at the water. If the Virginia question had prompted Nelson to reinstate him, then the question had power. An answer might give him even more power should he end up pitted against the professor again.

Still, Victor considered Tina's warning. What would Nelson do to him if he thought Victor knew too much about Virginia? Would he make him disappear, too? If Nelson wanted to keep his friends close and his enemies closer, he had done an excellent job by giving that glowing speech about Victor in class. Should something ever happen to Victor, Nelson had adeptly painted himself as a vocal public supporter of Victor, so few would suspect him of any wrongdoing.

Victor now understood why the question remained in his consciousness. For his own protection, he needed to resolve the Virginia quandary. He had used it as the opening salvo against the professor, and it carried weight. Now, he needed to truly understand the depth of the waters into which he had leapt—and what dangers lurked beneath.

~ ~ ~

Across the pool, Yashira sat near the top of the opposite bleachers, beside a stocky man.

"You must keep a low profile for a while, Yashira," the man said quietly.

"Then you shouldn't use my name in public, *Konstantin*," she hissed, glaring at him. "How much lower can my profile get? Look at me! Could I be any more unattractive?"

"No," he said with a snicker, "but we do not doubt your capable feminine charms. It's your other skills you must put to use for now. Which is the boy who knows your real name?"

Without pointing, she gazed across the pool and identified the boy, still internally chastising herself for letting her real name slip out. "Richard has taken a keen interest in that one," she told him.

"Understood," Konstantin said in a deep growl. "Do not engage yet.

Your time will come."

CHAPTER 28 – CHAMPIONS FEAST

Victor rang the doorbell and waited outside a house that spoke of modest affluence but gave no hint of elitism. With no prior experience visiting a wealthy person's home, he wondered how normal this was among billionaires. Then he remembered that Richard Nelson was no ordinary billionaire. Victor guessed he was the only billionaire who taught classes regularly at a university as a hobby.

"Remember, nothing about his wife!" Connor whispered, giving Victor a stern look. Marisa echoed his expression, and Victor shrugged in acknowledgment.

A lovely young lady in an elegant white floral cocktail dress answered the door. It took a moment for Victor to realize that the young woman was Tina—he had never seen her so dressed up. For a brief moment, he admired her beauty, suddenly glad they had dressed formally for the occasion, as Marisa had insisted.

Twice this week Victor had thought Tina had finally walked out of his life forever, and yet she seemed to keep turning up unexpectedly. What was she doing here?

Tina welcomed Marisa inside with a polite handshake. Connor greeted Tina awkwardly and quickly followed his girlfriend through the doorway.

When Tina attempted to kiss Victor on the cheek, he shifted away and offered a monotone, "Tina." She then extended her hand, which he observed with a blank stare. Stepping forward with a sigh, Tina closed the door behind her, leaving them alone outside on the doorstep.

"I know you didn't expect me here," Tina said, flattening the sides of her dress against her thighs, "but Richard insisted I come." Victor opened his mouth to respond, but didn't get the chance. "This is your night, and you sure as hell earned it. Please, don't let my presence take away from that. Take this moment to celebrate your victory."

When she offered her hand again, he reluctantly accepted it.

"Your life's gonna change forever tonight," she said with an affectionate smile. "You just don't know it yet."

"What are you talking about?" Victor asked curiously.

Still holding his handshake with her right hand, Tina grinned and touched his shoulder with her left. "I'm not supposed to say. It's a surprise. Now, are you ready to come inside, sailor?" She tugged on his hand to guide him in.

"What about Lucas?" Victor asked, standing his ground.

"What about him? He's not here, if that's what you are asking."

"So, you're all dressed up with no date?" Victor asked, looking at her sideways.

"Yeah, just like you. Plus, it's a members'-only party, and he's not a member." When Victor continued to stare at her, she added, "I'm done with him. Now, will you please accompany me inside?"

Tina pulled again, and Victor's resistance dwindled. He followed her through the front door and into the house.

Inside, a bearded man with glasses introduced himself as Gerald and his wife as Pari. This must be the Dr. Pari that Marisa and Connor had spoken so highly of, Victor thought. Then a redheaded giant named Owen gave Victor a friendly smile and a firm handshake and welcomed him to the club, whatever that meant. All three seemed to view him as some special guest of honor, or an old friend.

After a few minutes of small talk, Victor learned that all three were good friends of Richard. This led him to ask, "How's he dealing with the whole Wei thing?"

Gerald grimaced, and Pari hesitated, but Owen took the question head-on. "As best as he can. It's hard enough to lose a student, but for him to find her on Virginia's grave…"

"It just adds to the heartbreak," Pari said softly. "The news crews were parked out front all morning, demanding soundbites from him. I'm glad those vultures are gone."

Shocked at the news that the professor had been the one to find Wei, Victor asked, "Why didn't he cancel class today?"

Pari put her hand gently on Victor's shoulder. "We all deal with death differently. I spoke with him this morning. He felt it was important to go on for the living."

Suddenly, Marisa appeared at Victor's side. She greeted all of them, smiling glowingly at her idol, Dr. Pari. Grasping Victor's arm, she apologized politely before pulling him away to get a drink.

James greeted him at the bar with a handshake. "Congrats, man! What a turnaround for you. From down and out to on top of the world."

Connor threw his arm around Victor and bragged, "He couldn't have done it without us."

"I'm sure he was about to say that," Marisa added drily. "Right, Victor?"

The four of them laughed, and Victor finally began to relax. However, his jovial moment was interrupted by the unexpected sight of a beautiful blonde maid carrying a tray of cheese and crackers. With a start, Victor realized that she bore an uncanny resemblance to the woman he'd seen in the photographs decorating Professor Nelson's office. Was this…Virginia?

Without saying a word or making eye contact, she placed the food on the dining room table and retreated to the kitchen. He took her silence as submissiveness and wondered if the slight hitch in her gait indicated that this had been beaten into her. Strangely, none of the other guests at the small diner party even appeared to notice her. As she walked behind Marisa and Connor, returning to the kitchen, Victor wondered how the living dead could parade among them without anyone batting an eye. Unsuccessfully, Victor tried to signal non-verbally to Marisa and Connor to examine the maid who looked like Virginia.

"Watch out for the leopards roaming through my house!" Professor Nelson announced, entering the room. They turned as one to accept the hearty greetings and firm handshakes he offered each of them.

"We might want to change that name?" Connor said, glancing at Marisa. With a pouty expression, she shook her head.

"I think it's an excellent name," the professor said. "It projects power and stealth. The leopard is one of the world's most cunning predators. I hope you can live up to that name against the Alpha Dogs." He smiled at the trio. "Fortunately, you won't need to hunt down your meal tonight. Dinner is served."

The maid had finished setting the table, placing a golden turkey on a silver tray in the middle. Around it were bowls of stuffing and cranberry sauce, dinner rolls, and loads more traditional holiday fixings. The table was covered with a red tablecloth and two matching holiday candles.

Though still five days before Halloween, the decorations and aroma all expressed a distinctive Christmas cheer.

The professor explained that, since Halloween offered the opportunity to pretend, he preferred to take inspiration from his favorite holiday. "I never could get into all that living dead stuff," he told his guests. "Too morbid for my tastes."

As they served themselves their very early Christmas feast, Professor Nelson said, "I look forward to very stimulating dinner conversations tonight. But before we begin, I must take care of one administrative task." Richard handed a document each to Connor, Marisa, and Victor and explained, "What you three hold are NDAs—non-disclosure agreements. This, I imagine, is the first time any of you have seen one of these. Everyone around this table has also signed this document. In summary, it says that anything we discuss or work on is the intellectual property of my companies, and you agree to keep all this confidential forever."

Marisa, Connor, and Victor exchanged skeptical looks, each feeling nervous. What had they gotten themselves into?

The professor smiled knowingly and added, "Non-disclosure agreements are a requirement for all of my interns. And the internships I will be offering you tonight are incredible opportunities."

The three friends were all surprised by the unexpected announcement of three internships, as they had each expected Victor to be the only one presented an offer.

"I meant what I said earlier this semester," Professor Nelson continued. "Programmers can be superheroes, and I'm looking for elite superheroes who want to do incredible things to change the world. You should know that I rarely offer internships at any of my companies. But if you prove yourselves worthy as interns, I will likely be in a position to offer you full-time jobs."

The trio looked at each other excitedly as they listened with great interest to the professor's explanation. "You may have heard that working for me is highly rewarding," he said. "I almost never fire anyone. Once you come to work for me, you're family, and you just don't fire family. Accordingly, I must be very selective of who I allow into my family." He gestured to the paperwork in their hands. "Take your time to read the

NDA. This does not obligate you to take the internship or to ever work for me, but it does contain harsh penalties for failure to comply. My exceptional team of lawyers can and will ensure these penalties are extracted with maximum pain."

Graciously smiling as though he hadn't just delivered a harsh threat, Professor Nelson added, "Luckily, I've never had to send them after any of my employees. There's a reason why my companies never leak information, and it goes beyond legal paperwork. I seek exceptionally talented people with the utmost integrity. We believe you three fit the bill. If you don't wish to sign it, no harm done. I'll kindly show you the door, and it will never be held against you. However, if you want to work on amazing things with great people, and essentially have a job for life—so long as you want it—the NDA is the next step."

After briefly flipping through the ten-page agreement, Connor signed the back page and declared, "I'm in!" This was greeted by warm applause around the table.

Marisa skimmed the document and then followed suit. "Me too!"

Yet, across the table, Victor hesitated, analyzing the wording, flipping between pages, and generally appearing distracted. All eyes fixed on him, but no one spoke.

"I'm not sure what all this means," Victor eventually said, placing his pen down. "Maybe it's fine. I'm sure it's not to my advantage, but I guess that's the price of entry. However, I would like to know who I'm dealing with first." He narrowed his eyes at Professor Nelson. "You toyed with me from the beginning. Why did you do such a thing? Is that a sign of your integrity?"

"I did it for you," Richard said, a trifle impatiently. "I already explained much of this. If you sign the NDA, I can explain the rest."

Victor fought to hide the pain in his voice. "I can only fully know who I'm dealing with *after* we do the deal? If you're the benevolent, king-like figure the press portrays you as, you should answer my questions without hiding behind your lawyers."

Tina gave Victor a look indicating he'd gone too far, but he was only just beginning to pick up steam. "And forget about what you did to me," Victor said, as he pushed back his chair and stood. "What about what you did to your wife? How exactly did you fake her death?"

Connor's eyes widened into a piercing glare, but Victor pressed on. "You flaunt her right in front of us! What the hell are you up to, Mr. Utmost Integrity?"

The professor didn't raise his voice, but a vein became quite visible on his forehead. The stunned dinner party looked on while Professor Nelson, demonstrating great restraint, stated, "Victor, you are upset, and I understand that completely. I will tell you all I can, and I believe you will see it is not as you think. But you must first sign the NDA."

Quickly turning away, Victor began to pace. After all he had been through, he felt he deserved the truth. And what if Nelson confessed to a crime? Would Victor be bound by the NDA to cover it up? While he was no legal expert, he was sure the professor's lawyers would make his life miserable for a long time if it came to that.

After a long delay, Victor presented an alternative course of action. "Fine," he said, then pointed at his friends. "Don't tell me. Tell them. They won't be able to give me any specifics, but after you debrief them, they can advise me on whether I should sign the NDA."

"That's one of the things I like most about you, Victor," Nelson said, smiling. "You always seem to find the solutions that others don't." Then his expression turned grim. "I could do as you suggest, but understand this is a heavy burden you place on your friends. You ask them to potentially hold from you secrets you are dying to know for the rest of your life. That could strain your relationships, and eventually drive you apart. If you want to know the truth, you must sign the NDA now. That's the only way I will tell it."

CHAPTER 29 – CEASE FIRE

Trying to read the professor's face for a hint of the secrets behind it, Victor found no additional information to guide his decision. In a jerky motion, he signed the document, tossed it across the table, and barked, "There you go. Now, let's hear it."

"Son, I don't take orders," Professor Nelson said, "but in the spirit of Christmas, I will forgive you your transgression. All I put you through was for your own sake, as I've told you before. I presented you with challenges designed to strengthen yourself, and in your defiant style, you rose above the adversity in a way most would not. But I also did it to test you. I believe there is something different about you, and I suspected this before we ever met.

"Over the summer," he explained, "I had my teaching assistants review the college applications of all the students entering my Advanced Programming class. In search of students with noteworthy potential, James and Tina kindly brought you three to my attention, along with only a few others. Each of you stood out to me for different reasons. All of you had exceptional academic achievements, of course. Each of you earned at least thirty college credits while in high school, putting you on the fast track for your undergrad degrees. And you are freshman taking Advanced Programming, which is rare. This indicated you might be ahead of the curve. And Marisa and Connor were also top athletes." He sent Marisa an admiring glance. "Marisa, I was particularly impressed by you. Your success launching your own app at such a young age is quite remarkable."

Marisa blushed and mumbled a quick thank-you at the compliment.

The professor turned to Victor. "What impressed me about you, Victor, is how you got ahead while still dealing with the loss of your father. Your essay about him in your application was quite moving. To take on a full-time job in high school to help support your family while not only excelling academically, but also entering college with thirty credits? I figured that must have required true grit, and I wanted to see if you truly had that grit. Were you willing to scrap and claw for your dream? Or was that just some story you wrote to get into Stanford?"

Compassion filled the professor's eyes as he said, "You claimed that the titans of the industry were your idols, but it was clear your father was your true hero. You described him as a relentless fighter and a strong leader. That is something I seek in the people I work with, and I wanted to know if you had that in you, too. Now, I believe you do. That is why you are here today."

Victor struggled to find words as Nelson added, "You said your father was sometimes hard on you, and he expected a lot out of you. So, I took a chance and challenged you harshly the first opportunity you gave me—although I admit, I was surprised it came so quickly." Everyone at the table, including Victor, chuckled.

"Understand, I meant what I told the class today," Professor Nelson said. "You possess a level of determination that could lead you to greatness. If you come work for me, I can help you foster that to your full potential."

There was a lump in Victor's throat. This was exactly the kind of thing his father would have done. He'd always told Victor that life was unfair, and he had to adapt or sink. Often Victor had raged against that message, much as he had against Professor Nelson.

Returning to his seat, Victor asked in a lower tone, "That's the God's honest truth?"

"That's the truth," the professor confirmed with a nod.

With an inquisitive expression, Victor folded his arms and asked, "What about your wife? She's in the kitchen, clearly not dead."

Nearly everyone else laughed, but the three Leopards didn't understand why.

"You couldn't tell?" Richard asked jovially. "Jenny's a robot. She merely resembles my late wife. When you own your own robotics company, you can do stuff like that." The explanation was delivered in matter-of-fact fashion, as though any of them might someday own a robotics company.

"Oh, damn!" Marisa said instinctively. "That's creepy!"

Awkward laughter spread across the table. Nelson laughed loudest and told her, "You might think so, but I harbor no illusions that Jenny is my wife. She is a robot who can do basic chores, like deliver things to places. She looks like Virginia, yes, but only because it helps me keep her memory alive." A wistful expression crossed his face. "Keeping memories alive is one of the most important things in life, for it is only through those memories that we retain who we are. Not a day goes by that I don't miss Virginia, but I don't sleep with Jenny, and I have no feelings for her. She is merely manual labor and a small reminder not to forget my darling wife."

Directing his gaze toward Victor, the professor asked, "Does that satisfy your question?"

"Almost," Victor said, but something else was still troubling him. "That day I overheard you on the phone… was it Jenny I heard you talking to?"

Nelson hesitated for a moment before responding. "I have reminder calls and video chats set up for myself that were recorded by Virginia when she was still alive. Things like remembering to pick up something at the store." He shrugged, looking a little embarrassed. "Perhaps talking to them is odd, but it's another thing that helps me keep her memory alive."

"It is a little weird, but everything makes more sense now," Victor said, scratching the back of his neck. "Sorry to dredge all that up for you, Professor."

Accepting Victor's apology, the professor said, "Please, call me Richard. What's actually weird is how few people strive to keep their loved ones alive in their active memories. We are nothing without our memories, and we become nothing if we are not remembered. So, Victor, in a sense, you were right. The reports of my wife's death are false. The world thinks she is dead, but I know that she lives on in me."

Richard truly saw Virginia as temporarily existing between worlds, awaiting resurrection, but his younger guests were not yet prepared to hear this.

"To lay any other questions about my wife's death to rest," he added, "you should know that she committed suicide by flying her Cessna out to sea. A few months prior, she had been diagnosed with terminal cervical cancer and not given much time to live. She was living with constant pain and wanted to go on her own terms." His eyes began to glisten with unshed tears. "Virginia had made that clear to me many times, but we didn't discuss the where, when, or how. I couldn't bring myself to ask her those details. So, every day I woke up wondering if it would be my last with her.

Then, one day, it was."

Politely excusing himself, Richard stood to refresh his cocktail at the bar. No one else left their seats.

"Victor," Richard said, pouring a drink with his back to the table, "I hope you judge me to be a person with integrity, and to be someone with whom you would like to work. Certainly, I would like to work with you."

Like Richard, Victor had lost someone dear to him. For three years, he had failed to speak of his father, in some misguided attempt to honor him. Now, he wondered if in doing so, he was failing to keep his memory alive. In a flash, he became incredibly angry with himself for having been so callous. All this time, he'd never realized that Richard was trying to be his mentor, his father figure, to look out for him the way his father had, to help him become a man his father would be proud of. And despite the professor telling him repeatedly that he was trying to help him, Victor had never listened; he had, instead, fought against him and sought to bring him down.

Slowly, Victor rose from his chair and joined Richard at the bar. Everyone else remained frozen in their chairs.

With an open heart, Victor extended his hand and said, "I would be honored to work with you, sir."

Firmly taking it, Richard said, "Son, welcome into the fold," and then pulled Victor in to pat him on the back.

For the first time since meeting him, Victor smiled genuinely at the man. He now saw a benevolence in him that he had failed to recognize before. Watching them, Marisa stopped trying to dam the flow from her eyes as she applauded and cheered. Soon everyone else joined her cheering.

The two men returned to their seats, and the guests resumed serving themselves as Richard launched himself into the business of the night. "Now, I told the three of you that I would be offering you internships this evening. That time has now come."

Richard turned first to Marisa. "In the holiday spirit, we'll open your gifts one at a time, ladies first," he said with a wide smile. "I would like to offer you an internship, starting on Monday, at Warp Drive Games, the makers of CombatRidge."

Surprised by how soon she would start, Marisa gleefully blurted out, "I accept!"

"I see you are a shrewd negotiator, but I haven't yet told you how much the job pays," Richard said, trying to hold back a chuckle.

Unable to contain her excitement, she said, "I don't care. I want the job!"

Richard laughed and told her, "It pays forty dollars an hour, and I expect you to put in significant hours, but I can be flexible around your class schedule."

Marisa stood from the table and hugged Richard in his chair. Her mother had struggled to support her and her sister their whole lives and had never made so much. The Vexed Up money had been a decent windfall, but it wasn't a steady income like this. All her family's struggles, all her mother's sacrifices, and all her hard work had led to this moment.

After Marisa returned to her seat, Richard continued, "Warp Drive is a very small company right now. Tina and James are the leaders, and at this point the only full-time employees. As you know, the product is only in alpha testing, but we have a full product road map to fulfill. I see it as a game that can make learning to code fun for entry-level programmers, but also appeal to coders and gamers of all experience levels. That's an overly broad audience at this point, but we may narrow it down as we see which consumers take to the game more. I think we can disrupt the gaming and learning industries, but only time will tell."

Richard turned to Victor, who was on his left. Victor was hoping for the same opportunity, but truthfully, he had no idea what other possibilities there were.

"Victor, as the class champion, I'm giving you the choice between two offers. After all, to the victor goes the spoils." A few groaned at the painful pun. Undaunted, Richard continued, "The offer is identical to Marisa's, except that you may choose between two companies—either Warp Drive or Golden Bay Labs. I must say, I hope you choose Golden Bay. In fact, I've wanted you there for a while."

At Victor's look of confusion, Richard elaborated. "Golden Bay is my small neuroscience research firm, headed up by Dr. Pari here. Her team is working on some cutting-edge imaging equipment that could greatly enhance our understanding of the brain and change the way we treat patients. It could also have profound impacts on the development of artificial intelligence. What they need is a developer who can help automate their data analysis, someone who can use software to help them make their next medical breakthrough. It's a tall task, and I won't lie, there will be some difficult work ahead."

Victor joked, "So you're breaking up the Leopards?"

Everyone else chuckled, but Richard seemed to understand his hesitation. "It's not as sexy as going to Warp Drive, I admit. CombatRidge will be released to a large audience probably next year. By contrast, your work at Golden Bay would be vitally important, but you are unlikely to receive any public fanfare for it."

Allowing himself to breathe, Victor considered the two options carefully. Ultimately, he decided it was time to take Richard's guidance for a change, so he accepted the internship at Golden Bay. Glancing at Marisa and Connor, he said, "Sorry to break up the Leopards."

"Like that's possible," Marisa quipped, and Connor seconded that notion.

"Connor, if you're not averse to working with your girlfriend," Richard said, turning to face the other boy on his right side, "then I would like to make you the same offer to work at Warp Drive."

Connor glanced at Marisa, and she nodded approvingly. Gerald remarked, "Smart move, checking with the missus."

"Yeah, not sure I would have done the same. But I like that you did," Marisa said.

After Connor accepted the offer gratefully, the guests cordially applauded. Full from a wonderful Christmas feast, they retired to the living room to mingle and enjoy after-dinner drinks.

"Help yourself to whatever you'd like at the bar," Richard told the trio. "I trust you will choose whatever you can handle. We don't card here."

First to the bar, Victor poured himself a fresh drink, while Connor selected a beer. He clinked it against Victor's glass. "Here's to sticking to the plan," Connor said magnanimously.

"I'll drink to that," Marisa added as she joined them. "I especially liked the way you subtly worked your questions about his wife into the conversation. Not awkward at all."

The three of them laughed, and Victor complimented his friends: "You two are attentive observers. No one else even picked up on that. Someday, you'll make good secretaries."

"Well, I noticed, too," Tina said, joining the huddle. "What would that make me someday?"

One look from Marisa had Connor immediately making their excuses. The two of them drifted away to let Tina and Victor speak privately.

Perhaps it was the turn of events with Richard, or the whiskey. But whatever the reason, Victor foresaw something for the first time since Lucas opened Tina's door. He considered that someday, he could look back on that moment and laugh at the tiny perturbation in the grand space-time continuum. Vividly recalling a memory of standing beneath the grand Roman architecture with Tina, he regained the perspective needed to see that such trivial matters weren't worth his constant brooding. He still didn't like what happened, and it left him with doubts about Tina. But Victor knew he would be okay. Everything would.

His college career had started off tumultuously, but the clouds were clearing, and the world hadn't ended. Someday, he might even reconcile with Tina, though he wasn't quite ready for that yet.

While Victor searched for the answer to her question, Richard interrupted his thoughts with an announcement to the room. As he raised his glass, his guests raised theirs in turn. "To the newest members of our family," Richard said in his booming voice. "May they long be with us, and may the memories of our achievements live forever."

CHAPTER 30 – QUINTESSENTIAL MECHANICS

On a sunny, temperate Monday in early November, Pari found herself taking her lunch break in Richard's underground bunker. After they finished checking in with Richie, Richard asked her, "Where do we stand on the advanced optical research?"

In need of sunlight, Pari suggested they move their conversation—and their lunch—upstairs. Once above ground, she said, "Victor's only been at Golden Bay for three days, but he's already made an enormous impact. On the first day, he sped up our data analysis software by 400 percent. He's an amazingly talented developer."

In full agreement, Richard admitted that he wished they'd brought Victor in sooner. Granted, Pari's hardware engineers were decent programmers, but that wasn't their strength.

"I was so impressed with his work," Pari said, "that I gave him the advanced optical modeling project the next day. It's a sizable project, and it will take a few months, but I believe he'll do an excellent job. Can you believe he already showed me a basic prototype this morning? He clearly put in a lot of work on it over the weekend."

They both sat comfortably in the dining room as Pari cautiously resurfaced an old, uncomfortable conversation. "Richard, I think it's time to bring in an additional test subject."

To protect the secrecy of their work, the only Golden Bay test subjects so far had been the Golden Bay scientists themselves, including Pari. None of these scientists' scans were used for transcendence, nor did they even know about it. Richard's self-scans were confined to the privacy of his home bunker, and no one at Golden Bay besides Pari knew that he even had a scanner.

"Anyone in particular?" Richard asked knowingly.

"I think you may know her," she said with a modest smile.

Considering the matter carefully, Richard stood and gazed out the front window. "It must happen at some point," Pari reminded him. "We can't just keep studying ourselves. She'll merely be a test subject, with no knowledge of transcendence. There may be a lot we can learn with her."

"Like what?" Richard asked. "Does her mind not work the same as ours?"

Pari joined him at the window. "For the most part, yes, her mind works like ours, but perhaps not entirely. Every brain is a little different. What if she can teach us something about the mind-body connection? You are aware she offers us unique opportunities."

Two years before, a devastating car crash had taken Quinn's biological parents and younger brother from her and left her paralyzed. Pari had a hunch that her adopted daughter, as their first paralyzed test subject, could provide their research with a new perspective. But it was what the research could in turn provide her daughter that most interested Pari.

"This may lead to her destruction," Richard said. "Are you sure you want to allow Quinn to pursue this path?"

Despite his warning, Pari knew him well enough to know he was only playing devil's advocate. "The risk that this will harm her is minuscule. You know that. It's not invasive."

"There are still non-invasive means to destroying a person," Richard cautioned.

"True, but we can stop at any time."

"But once we step beyond mere scans, while still staying non-invasive, it will be hard for either of you to want to turn back. It could be difficult for her to cope with stopping then."

"Richard, we're just talking about scans to start," Pari said, annoyed. "If she doesn't go out and do *something*, if she doesn't stop wallowing in her loss, it will destroy her. And as a legal adult, she'll provide consent for anything we do. I just want to give her this opportunity."

Richard studied the octagonal pattern of the pavers on his driveway in silence.

"She won't tell anyone about our research," Pari said, looking at him earnestly. "She has no friends left to tell. God, I wish she did! Please, she needs something to be part of that's bigger than her suffering."

A lump grew in Pari's throat as she recalled all their efforts to bring Quinn back to herself. "We've tried everything," she told Richard. "Support groups, reconnecting her with her past, helping her make new friends, but she closes it all off. I'm not saying it's all bad, mind you—there are bright spots and happy moments. I love her sarcastic wit, and she's brought us so much joy. But there's also a tremendous darkness festering in her heart. On the worst days, which are more frequent now, the only thing she wants to do is sit in her room, listening to her music. Perhaps that's typical for a teenager, but you know she's not typical. This might help give her purpose."

Putting a hand on Richard's shoulder, Pari forced him to face her, to meet her eyes, as she gently said, "Remember, you're not the only one trying to save someone you love."

~ ~ ~

Later in the day, Victor fueled his flow by pumping up-tempo beats directly into his brain as he typed feverishly at his computer. The objects he was planning to code took shape in his head as he pictured the structure of the program in his mind. Everything was coming together with the rhythm of the music.

He tapped his foot as he worked on the optical network simulation rendering. Rohan Kashimurthy, the senior neural researcher at Golden Bay Labs, had recently given him the latest data to plug into his prototype program. Victor was tweaking the code to support their new findings before feeding in the data. On Victor's first day at the company, Rohan had quickly discovered it was best not to distract Victor when he programmed, so he'd left him to do his magic.

Victor felt a sudden tap on his shoulder, and he nearly jumped out of his chair.

"I'm sorry," Pari said, after he removed his headphones. "I didn't mean to startle you, but you weren't responding."

In need of a moment to context switch, Victor didn't immediately respond. He noticed a lovely girl seated behind Pari. She looked to be about eighteen, with long red hair and stunning pale-blue eyes.

Pari gestured at the girl and spoke, but Victor was mentally attempting to save the stack of thoughts he had lined up before they all disappeared. Consequently, he found himself staring at the girl in awkward silence. She said something to him before his memory dump from short-term to long-term memory completed.

Finally, Victor registered the girl saying, "Does he speak?" Then she slowly said to him, "I'm Quinn. Can you say 'Quinn'?"

"Sorry," Victor said, shaking his head like a wet dog. "I was somewhere else. Hi, Quinn."

Pari introduced Quinn as her daughter and explained the girl's role as the newest volunteer for their neural research. "We're going to do a few scans with her today," Pari said. "Do you mind if she waits here with you while we set up?"

A minute prior, Victor would have declined any company, but something seemed to change his mind. Perhaps it was the sight of an attractive girl, or perhaps it was Pari's expression, which told him the request wasn't really optional. Victor agreed, and Pari left the room.

Not normally at a loss for words, Victor searched his mind for something to say while his code-filled brain clumsily loaded its social protocols. "So, Quinn, where do you go to school?"

"I don't. You?" A coldness dampened her voice, and he didn't understand why.

"Stanford," Victor answered, equally curtly. He was eager to return to his work, but he was also sure Pari hadn't left Quinn there only to be ignored, so he tried again. "Where did you graduate from, then?"

Seeming perturbed by the question, Quinn replied, "Graduated high school last year online."

Talking to this girl was like pulling teeth, but Victor continued his dental work. "Ah, okay. What are you up to now?"

Quinn moved her automated wheelchair up to his chair by nudging her chin forward. She had the slight ability to move her head, but no control over her arms, legs, or torso. After a long pause, she glanced down at herself, moving only her eyes, and Victor's gaze tracked hers. He suspected that she had not always been in a wheelchair.

"Hey, I'm up here," Quinn snapped. "You done staring?"

Again, he was caught off-guard, as he had simply followed her eyes. "No, um, I mean, yes, I'm done."

"If you must know, I'm a roofer," she said, rolling her eyes.

Though he wanted to laugh at her apparent joke, a filter in his mind stopped him. Did he actually want to be the guy who laughed at the paralyzed girl? Maybe she meant she was in construction doing architectural work, he thought.

Quinn laughed sardonically. "Are you always this dense?"

Victor replied, "Honestly, no."

"I don't have a job," she told him, "but thanks for entertaining the idea I could be a roofer. That was funny."

Victor smiled, a bit embarrassed, but trying to play it off, he told her, "Happy to amuse you. How long have you been in that chair?"

"You sure know how to make a girl feel self-conscious," Quinn said. "Between staring at my body and asking how long I've been paralyzed for, you really have—"

Victor had no intention of arguing with her. In surrender, he held up both hands and said, "Sorry. Sorry. You caught me in the code earlier, and I just wasn't thinking straight."

Years had passed without a boy checking her out, so Quinn told him it was all right and then asked what he was listening to. When he told her, she admitted he had decent taste. The two proceeded to talk about music for a while and found they liked some of the same songs.

Enthusiastically, Quinn told Victor about some of her favorite artists and said, "I love finding creative covers of their work. Sometimes they're even better than the originals. I'll share my playlist with you, if you want."

"Okay, sure," Victor said. "Though, ya know, those bands have a bunch of sad songs."

As Quinn turned her eyes down toward her body again, Victor was sure to only follow her gaze briefly. "With a body like this, you'd think I'd party all the time, but sometimes I just need to listen to sad songs, too."

Victor instantly regretted his sad songs comment—her response was rather uncomfortably revealing.

"So, what do you do here?" Quinn asked, and Victor appreciated the change in topic. "Are you just a pretty face in the office who spends his day checking out girls?"

Victor coughed. "Are you...*flirting* with me?"

"Uh, yeah," she said as her pale cheeks flushed with pink blotches. "Though it was more fun when it was the subtext of our conversation and not the topic at hand. Man, you *are* a bit slow. Good thing you're cute. So, anyway, what do you do here?"

Victor pictured himself stumbling down a hill, and each time, he found his footing tripping on another rock. He imagined dusting himself off at the bottom of the hill as he said, "I'm a programmer."

With genuine interest, Quinn said, "That's cool. Can you show me?"

Directing her to his computer screen, Victor explained how his software analyzed brain scans like the one she was about to receive. When he showed her images from the scanner, she asked, "So, you're going to be looking at what's in my head?" He nodded. "Well, I hope you like what you see."

Then she winked at him. Smiling back, he opted not to answer, to avoid tripping over his own words again.

Pari entered the room and told Quinn it was time.

"Nice to meet you, Quinn," Victor said, waving in farewell.

"You too, pretty boy!"

With wide eyes, Pari stared curiously at Victor. Her sharp gaze asked him what had happened, while his befuddled expression revealed his uncertainty.

After Victor returned to his code, it took him about ten minutes to shake the conversation from his head and regain his flow. An hour later, he felt a tap on his shoulder again. This time, he only flinched slightly.

Removing his headphones, he greeted Pari, who still had an inquisitive look on her face. "What did you do to Quinn?" she asked.

"I didn't do anything to her," Victor said, panicking. "I swear!"

"No, no, it's okay. It's just that… I've never seen her like that. What did you two talk about?"

Victor, still feeling a little defensive, told her they discussed music.

"She was flirting with you." Though it was a simple statement, Victor interpreted it as an accusation. Of course, he didn't need to be defensive about it, but Quinn had spun him around so much during their conversation that his defensiveness carried into this one.

"Calm down, Victor," Pari told him. "This is positive—very much so."

"What do you mean?" Victor said, surprised. "Don't assume that just because we flirted—well, *she* flirted, really—that we're—"

"No, I mean it's positive for her," Pari explained. "It shows a spark. I'm not telling you to flirt with her or show interest. I'm just glad to see that spark in her, is all. Some days I wondered if it had extinguished."

Relieved he wasn't being accused of anything, Victor asked how Quinn's scan went, and Pari said it had gone well. "They're analyzing it now. I think she'll be back again soon."

Careful not to sound too interested, Victor said, "Well, feel free to bring her by next time. I mean, if you want. Just to talk."

"Victor, I understand," Pari said kindly. "Quinn could use a friend, that's all." She leaned forward and asked, "Actually, what do you think about bringing her on as a part-time tester to help you?"

"Um, that could work, I guess," he said hesitantly. "Does she have any experience?"

Pari turned to look at Victor's code and said, "In software, no. I wasn't thinking for her to write test code—maybe just do manual software testing. You know, like some of the stuff you do to test your code. Like observing whether the eye movement modeling matches up with the patient's eye movement video footage. Unless you would find that distracting?"

If his first encounter with Quinn was anything to go by, Victor would be quite distracted while working with her. And yet, though he valued his focus, something compelled him to say, "Let's give her a try."

CHAPTER 31 – PAIRING UP

A crackling noise filled Marisa's left ear. Then the darkness was split by a razor-thin light running horizontally across the middle of her field of view. The dim strip of light grew thicker and thicker. Finally, Marisa registered that she was seeing her eyelids opening slowly from the inside. Lying supine on her cushiony sleeping bag, Marisa had a clear view of the night sky filled with countless stars. The Milky Way sparkled above her, and she was sure she had never seen so many stars. Wherever she was, it had to be far from civilization.

Marisa turned her head to the left and saw a blazing campfire. Beyond that lay Connor, staring back at her. Both of them slowly got to their feet and tried to get their bearings. They appeared to be in a small clearing within a redwood forest.

"We need to get out of here," Marisa said, breaking the silence. "It's not safe." The campfire would give away their position. Pointing toward a less dense portion of the forest in the distance, she signaled for Connor to follow.

While Marisa walked deliberately, stepping carefully to generate as little noise as possible, Connor immediately started jogging ahead, breaking twig after twig under his feet. She shushed him, and he came to a halt. "They're going to hear us!" she hissed.

The warning came too late. A rustling sounded behind them. Two pairs of yellow eyes on the horizon were quickly approaching. Instinctively fleeing in the opposite direction, they bolted toward the next clearing that Marisa had indicated. Connor's jog became a full sprint, and his heart pounded along with his feet. But once the trees cleared, Connor slammed into an invisible barrier and fell backward.

Hastily reaching to help him up, Marisa was suddenly thrown to the ground as the glowing eyes descended upon them. She found herself looking up at a deranged Tina with glowing yellow eyes. She promptly overpowered Tina and threw her aside, only to find James on top of Connor. The guys wrestled over something while James growled angrily. Not until the object was plunged into Connor's chest did Marisa realize it was a syringe. An involuntary scream of horror escaped her lips as Connor began to convulse, foaming at the mouth. With a last gasp, he yelled for her to save herself, but all she heard were incoherent grumbles.

As the life drained from Connor's body, Marisa covered her mouth, mortified.

Showing no sympathy, Tina leapt for her throat, but Marisa swiftly dodged her. As James turned his attention to her as well, Marisa scrambled away like a despondent gazelle, no longer a leopard. A cliff rapidly emerged ahead, the yellow-eyed monsters close on her heels. At the cliff's edge, Marisa leapt for her life, barely escaping James's clawing reach.

With her right hand, Marisa managed to grasp the handlebar of a zip line. Her momentum sent her accelerating toward the lower ridge. Adding her left hand to the bar, Marisa stabilized her grip and risked a glance back, searching for any sign of the man she'd left behind as she zipped away.

To her surprise, Connor wasn't lying dead on the ground, but rather shimmying down the cable with Tina and James behind him. For a moment, her heart filled with joy and relief, amazed that he was still alive.

Then she saw the jaundiced glow in his once-blue eyes, and all her hopes sank.

Her beloved Connor had joined the ranks of the undead. Once her stalwart partner, he was now compelled to either kill her or turn her.

There must be a way to save Connor, she thought, holding tightly to the zipline bar as she continued to descend. Tina and James were beyond help at this point, but Connor had only just been turned. Perhaps the antidote could still bring him back from the brink.

Upon reaching the other side, Marisa fled into the cover of the nearby woods in search of aid. Zigzagging through the increasingly thick forest, she spotted a campfire in the distance. Without the luxury of time, she sprinted for it and soon found herself approaching a decrepit cabin. No one appeared to be inside, but if that were the case... who had built the fire?

Desperation won out over caution. Entering the cabin on silent feet, Marisa scavenged for anything to help her. She riffled through the cabinets and eventually discovered a first-aid kit. Hurriedly opening it, she found two large syringes filled with glowing green liquid, labeled *antidote*. As she picked up one in each hand, James crashed through the cabin door and leapt on her like a wolf. The syringes skittered across the floor, but mercifully did not break.

Tina and Connor both jumped in to attack Marisa as well, but knocked her free from James in the process. Frantically, she scurried under the small kitchen table and reached for the antidote. Stretching out to her limit, she had a syringe almost within her grasp when Connor pounced on her. With his longer arms, he managed to grab it first.

Immediately, he tried to crush the syringe. Yet, he seemed to be struggling with himself. Inexplicably changing his objective, Connor then tried to plunge the syringe into his own chest. In desperation, Marisa pushed with both of her hands and all her might to help him do so. But just before penetrating his chest, the needle stopped short, and he slowly began to push back against her in resistance.

Clearly, he didn't possess full control of his own body. Still, Marisa knew he could be saved—so long as he *wanted* to be saved.

Then all hope of his salvation vanished when Tina sank her fangs into Connor's neck, and the light in his eyes extinguished forever. Contemptuously, James knocked Connor's limp, gray corpse aside and advanced on Marisa.

She screamed, covering her face, as James bit into her neck, and her world faded completely to black.

~ ~ ~

Marisa lost track of time as the darkness and silence prevailed, spiraling her into oblivion.

Then, without warning, her awareness reignited with a blinding flash of white. Marisa found herself lying on the white, padded floor of a white, padded room, squinting, drenched in sweat, and breathing heavily. On her chest, she held a black virtual reality headset.

After catching her breath, Marisa emerged from the padded VR room to find Tina, James, and Connor, who had each emerged from similar rooms.

"You're alive!" Connor said melodramatically as he hugged Marisa.

"Why did you have to pair up the two rookies?" Marisa asked, scowling at James. "We didn't stand a chance."

Maniacally rubbing his palms together, James said, "For our amusement."

Tina inquired how Marisa and Connor liked the new CombatRidge Open World version, and both told her they were thoroughly impressed. Connor remarked how immersive the experience felt. Marisa found the graphics to be fantastically realistic. This version, the third in the series after the 2D and 3D versions, was currently only experimental and far from being released to the public.

After a few more rounds playing the Open World simulation, James's phone dinged with an incoming text. After reading it, he said, "Time to take a break from all this hard work, team. We've got a meeting with Richard."

~ ~ ~

Marisa, Connor, James, and Tina met Richard for lunch at his favorite Italian restaurant, only a few blocks from Warp Drive Games. Richard had reserved a table in the back that provided them comfortable distance from the other patrons. As his guests settled into their seats, Richard broke the ice by asking them about their favorite video games of all time. A lively discussion ensued, and Richard happily fell into the role of a facilitator, merely asking probing questions from time to time to keep the conversation going.

After a few minutes of watching his team interact, he said wistfully, "Seeing you four carry on reminds me of my college days. Virginia, Pari, Gerald and I would often engage in fun brainstorming sessions over meals. It was Virginia's idea at first—she was always a dreamer. I was half dreamer—zooming up to the thirty-thousand-foot level—and half implementer, drilling down into the details. Pari was more of the pragmatist, and Gerald was always our philosopher, playing devil's advocate or finding the corner cases. Such a fun dynamic we had together."

The waiter took their orders, and then James told Richard the interns were impressed with CombatRidge Open World. This prompted Richard to say, "So, now that you've seen what it is, I can tell you what it's going to become. Lots of video games have some version of an open world you can explore. Some are even good—cool places you like to visit. But you wouldn't want to live there, right?" Seeing the interns shake their heads, he added, "CombatRidge's open world will someday be a place you want to live."

A sudden phone call prompted Richard to excuse himself from the table before he could explain further.

"What does that mean?" Marisa asked. "A place you want to live?"

Uncertain, Tina said, "He's been vague about that. He's not telling us what to build, but he tells us when he thinks we haven't hit the mark. He just keeps saying that the world has to be a place you want to live. Like, if you die and go to video game heaven, this is where you'd hope to be."

"Yeah, sounds crazy," James said, taking in the skeptical looks on Marisa's and Connor's faces. "And he's possibly a bit crazy, too. But he's also crazy smart, so we're trying to make what he's asking for. I suppose he wants something very realistic."

Richard returned to the table and apologized. "I'm sorry to do this, but I have to step out. We'll do lunch again later this week," he promised. "I do want to tell you that I like where you're going with the game—it's fun. But if it's all killing and destruction, it won't be a world I want to live in. It needs some places where people can be creative, too. Think about putting in some safe zones."

~ ~ ~

After lunch, the four programmers returned to Warp Drive. The cavernous office was filled with rows of empty desks. After a full week on the job, Marisa was still surprised Richard had rented the entire floor of the office building for a team of only four developers, but James had explained that Richard was leaving room for growth. Marisa and Tina partnered together that afternoon on one feature, while James and Connor worked on another.

When the workday finally ended, both James and Tina commended the interns for how fast they were picking things up. Connor and Marisa left together and got into Marisa's new car. The day after Richard had offered her the internship, Marisa withdrew a bit of her Vexed Up money to make a down payment on a brand-new, silver Volkswagen Beetle. Over the past week, she had been driving Connor to work after their morning classes on Tuesdays and Thursdays and dropping him off late at night. They talked excitedly about their work during tonight's drive.

"You know," Connor said, "James is really fun to work with." Marisa agreed and spoke similarly about Tina. Suddenly, Marisa realized that she had released all the animosity she'd had for Tina over how things went with Victor, and felt a tiny flash of guilt, wondering if that made her a bad friend. She hoped Victor would someday be able to do the same.

Upon arriving at his dorm, Marisa playfully asked, "Aren't you going to tip your driver?" Connor leaned over, gave her a long kiss goodbye, and exited the vehicle. "You know, I can't cash that!" she yelled at him as he walked away.

~ ~ ~

The following evening, the four Warp Drive developers encountered Richard again, but this time under much more solemn circumstances. Though the developers stayed to commiserate with their fellow students, Richard didn't linger after the on-campus vigil for Wei Lee concluded.

"I was surprised by the large turnout," Owen said from the passenger seat as Richard drove them back to his house.

Richard acknowledged the statement, but said nothing. His mind was still preoccupied by how tragic it was that the life of such a promising young woman had ended so unexpectedly.

"In all the news reports, people say she seemed quiet, and that they didn't know her very well," Owen said. "Strange how so many people show up for a near stranger."

"Yeah," Richard said, breaking his silence. "I guess it just hits close to home for a lot of people."

Owen agreed, but a little more cynically. He remarked how so many were trying to spin this publicized story for their own purposes. Some were citing Wei's death as evidence of the need for better mental healthcare on campus, to which he had no objection. But others, like ambitious reporters, were using it to craft juicy stories, casting Richard in a very poor light.

Two different women connected to Richard had committed suicide years apart, and the latter had been found dead on top of the former by Richard himself during his morning walk. It was too much for creative minds to accept as merely coincidental. The brain was wired to find connections, even where they may not exist. Yet, while there were no signs of trauma or foul play, and the coroner's report that morning had ruled it a suicide by overdose, that didn't stop those in search of clicks to their websites from speculating wildly.

Such far-fetched articles were light on facts and heavy on hypotheticals. In particular, they lacked any motive for Richard to kill Wei. Unfortunately, this didn't slow down the trash peddlers at all, but even the more honest news-dealers rightly noted the fact that Wei didn't seem to have any reason to kill herself. No suicide note was ever found.

Richard refused to read any of the articles himself, but he instructed his lawyers to do so and to aggressively pursue all defamers. While he wasn't personally sensitive to public perception, he understood his businesses depended on his good reputation and that it needed to be protected at all costs.

When they reached Richard's house, the two men promptly descended into the bunker at Owen's insistence. "I wanted to wait for the coroner's report to clear you before telling you this," Owen began. Richard took a seat to brace for whatever was coming, but Owen remained standing. "If they brought you in for questioning, it was better that you not know, for risk of accidentally divulging the information."

"What is it?" Richard asked, eyeing Owen suspiciously.

"You remember I had a guy tailing Wei?" Richard nodded. "Well, the night she died, he had followed her riding her bike to a coffee shop on Sand Hill Road, about a mile from your place. She was on her laptop when he walked in. After ordering his coffee, he got on the Wi-Fi and started sniffing the network traffic. It was pretty ballsy of her, but he found her using the coffee shop's unsecured Wi-Fi to hack into a government military research facility in Colorado."

"Whoa! That's a crazy thing to do from on a public Wi-Fi," Richard said, incredulous.

"I know. Maybe she figured it would be harder to trace back to her there than if she had done it on campus. Anyway, it's not the kind of thing someone usually does mere hours before committing suicide."

"That's true," Richard said, a ball of trepidation forming in his stomach. "What happened next?"

"My guy followed her in his car from a distance after she left the place," Owen continued. "She rode over to the cemetery. It was late and dark, and given all the foliage, he lost sight of her. His gut told him she'd cut through the cemetery to lose him, so he drove the perimeter a few times looking for her. When his search turned up empty, he called it a day."

"Did she ditch the laptop there, then?" Richard asked. The fact that investigators never found a single computer among the computer science student's belongings was a major source of speculation for the wannabe-journalist bloggers.

"Maybe. Or she gave it to someone in the cemetery."

"Or they took it from her and killed her," Richard said sadly. "But if they did, they covered their tracks really well. Did you share any of this with the feds?"

"Can't," Owen said regretfully. "Wish I could. But if people knew you had someone tailing her the night she died... just imagine how guilty that would make you look."

"I suppose you're right." Richard sighed. "Still, I hate withholding this. If you find a way to point them toward this evidence somehow without involving us, do so."

CHAPTER 32 – CATS AND DOGS

With their full course loads and new internships, the Leopards only found time to train for CombatRidge on the weekends. To help hone the Leopards' battle skills, their classmates had split into teams of three to have their teams of bots spar against the Leopards' bots. A few weeks in, Connor's interest in machine learning inspired him to automate testing of certain variables for each of their bots, related to risk tolerance, aggressiveness, and fighting styles. There were many possible values for each of these variables, which meant the total combination of different settings across the three fighters was enormous. Unable to exhaustively test every combination, they wrote scripts that automatically tested random combinations against their classmates' bots, looking for patterns.

In addition to this highly data-driven approach, every Friday morning for six weeks, Victor received an email from Professor Nelson with a CombatRidge battle replay between the Leopards and a team called the Nelson Trio. Marisa, Connor, and Victor watched the Nelson Trio routinely dismantle their Leopards. Oddly, the videos showed Richard playing in gamer mode, which didn't seem like him at all. Victor dismissed this as a glitch, perhaps related to Richard's administrative permissions—the Leopards had no idea that Richard's only involvement was in sending the emails themselves.

For it was *Richie* who did all the battling via a creative setup. Richard provided Richie with voice controls that allowed him to operate one of the three fighters on the Nelson Trio at a time. To switch between fighters, he used special voice commands. Thus, Richie could alternate between controlling HalfNelson, FullNelson, and KingNelson. Each time he rotated, he would issue a command to pause the game, then switch characters, issue some attack commands, and unpause once more. Every battle for him was slow-motion cycling among his trio.

For Richie, it was pleasing to be the one doing the pausing for a change. Much like Richard had been doing to him, Richie left the game paused for long durations while considering each move against the Leopards' bots. This provided him the advantage of much more think time than the

Leopard's code was allowed. He played methodically against an opponent forced to rush. The resulting videos, which contained none of the pause durations, showed Marisa, Connor, and Victor what a superior opponent could do against their code.

Without eye movement, Richie lacked the ability to shift his gaze around the battlefield, so to compensate for this, the image was projected farther away from him, allowing visibility of the whole battlefield without the need for the slightest eye movement. It was like playing chess while looking at the board from ten feet away, but Richie soon adapted, and he was grateful to have something to do and for the ability to see again.

At Pari's insistence, Richard limited Richie to two hours of CombatRidge per week. Given they had not yet found a way to provide Richie sleep, Pari worried that sleep deprivation, known to be harmful to humans, might also be detrimental to a transcender's mind. She warned that after twenty-four hours awake, they would need to consider an indefinite pause. Until they figured out how to make him sleep, they couldn't risk damaging his mental health.

By the time the Leopards' showdown with the Godslayers arrived, Richie was at fourteen hours of service time, and Pari demanded they conserve the rest of his remaining hours for further research.

~ ~ ~

In the hallway outside Richard's classroom, Marisa, Connor, and Victor stood backed up against the wall, waiting to be called. The trio were adorned in full Leopards battle gear. Marisa wore a skintight leopard-print bodysuit with matching heels. Connor and Victor stood stoically as Marisa's bodyguards on either side of her, wearing leopard-spotted barbarian tunics and brandishing menacing plastic swords. While staring down the Alpha Dogs across the hallway, Marisa dangled a small, plush bulldog from a rope leash, as though hanging it by a noose.

On the opposite wall stood Lucas, Daniel, and Brittany. Daniel wore his noise-cancelling headphones, getting himself into game mode, tuning out everyone around him. Brittany and Lucas, on the other hand, spewed a continuous stream of trash talk the Leopards' way.

"We're going to crush you in front of your whole class," Lucas warned them.

"It's over, knuckle-draggers," Brittany added.

James stood between the two groups, enforcing their separation and warning them to keep things civil. The immature taunts didn't faze Marisa, and Victor didn't react, but Connor couldn't help himself. "You're going down, bitches!"

Lucas rushed to the middle, and James intercepted him. Although he wasn't an athlete like Lucas, James was almost as massive, and fierce enough to hold his own. Plus, the students were James's people, and he wouldn't let a punk like Lucas lay a hand on them.

"Back the hell up, you runt," James growled in Lucas's face.

Lucas retreated, still seething. At Connor, he yelled, "You're dead, pussycat."

Without a word, Marisa gave her boyfriend a quick look that said *Don't take the bait, I've got this,* all in one glance. Then music started blasting from the classroom, and the crack under the door showed the lights had dimmed.

"Leopards, you're on," James said over the heavy bass beat. Victor went through the door, followed by Connor. Marisa backed her way through the doorway and made a throat-slitting gesture to Lucas before turning to follow the boys.

Their classmates stood and cheered as the Leopards processed across the front of the room. The lights came on, and the students materialized as a wave of orange and black, speckled with cat-styled gear and signs. With ten bonus points at stake toward their final grade, the crowd had a much more vested interest in this sporting event than most crowds ever had, and it showed in their raucous enthusiasm on that early Friday morning.

Next Professor Nelson introduced the Alpha Dogs, and the gamers entered to a chorus of boos. The Alphas took their position near the entrance on the left side of the stage, where all their gaming gear had been set up. The Leopards sat stage right, surprised to be seated up front rather than with the crowd. At that point, they were just spectators, too, as there was nothing more they could do to affect the results of the battle to come.

However, it created more drama to have both teams on stage, so there they sat, spectators to be spectated.

The lights dimmed again, and the screen showed the familiar countdown. The CombatRidge 3D battleground was a small plateau, roughly the size of a basketball court, with steep drop-offs on all sides. Each team would start on opposite ends of the plateau with their backs to the edge. Opponents could be thrown or kicked over the edges. In order to win, all three of the opposing fighters had to be eliminated. And as if the challenge wasn't already difficult enough, after two minutes of fighting, the edges of the cliff would start to crumble, slowly shrinking the battlefield.

A few additional moves had been added to the 3D version. The grab move allowed a fighter to grab an opponent from behind and hold their hands behind their back, while a teammate could attack the defenseless prisoner. It took five consecutive punches to break free. The heal move enabled a fighter to gradually heal their teammate, but while healing, both teammates were vulnerable to attack. In addition, attacks from behind caused double damage. So, there was a high price to pay for turning one's back on an opponent.

The Leopards' fighters were sporting new skins, courtesy of Marisa. A leopard-print bodysuit covered Marisol to match her creator. The camouflage pattern of DevilsKeeper's crimson fatigues had morphed into a dark red leopard pattern. In addition, he had acquired a matching battle helmet and much larger muscles. The third Leopard, BluManChu, had also bulked up, and now sported leopard briefs and dark blue skin with samurai swords on his back, looking like some alien superhero.

"What the…" whispered Victor, leaning over to Marisa.

"I made us look more like a team," she said mischievously. "You boys like it?"

Connor nodded, and Victor added, "Yeah, as long as we win."

The Leopards charged to the center of the battlefield as the Alpha Dogs' fighters ran straight at them. At the center, Marisol pounced on Athena. With a diving kick to Athena's shins, Marisol quickly knocked her off her feet. Without hesitation, Marisol ran at the downed Athena and went for another kick, which Athena blocked from the crouch position. Marisol leapt over her to take the outside position, but as Marisol turned around to engage her, Athena applied a back kick, sending her flying across the battlefield.

"Get up!" Marisa yelled to her warrior.

Meanwhile, DevilsKeeper was inflicting damage on Herculanix, but he had also taken his share. With both players now below half strength, DevilsKeeper ran around Herculanix to help Marisol. A series of Athena's kicks had propelled her near the edge of the plateau, and she was crouched defensively, trying to withstand the onslaught. Athena hit her with Thor's Hammer, weakening her further, yet she stayed in the crouched position.

Jumping to bring down the hammer again and finish Marisol, Athena was unprepared for what happened next. Marisol perfectly timed catching Athena at the apex of her jump and held her overhead. Common knowledge said one could only lift an opponent if they were blocking or completing an attack move—few understood that an impeccably timed lift of a jumping player at their apex would also produce the same effect.

Marisol emphatically tossed Athena backward over the cliff as Brittany shrieked in outrage.

The numbers now favored the Leopards. But as DevilsKeeper had rushed to Marisol's rescue, Herculanix had attempted to punch him in the back of the head. Anticipating this, DevilsKeeper ducked and swiped at Herculanix's legs, sending him rolling across the arid plain.

"We've got 'em now!" Connor crowed.

In the meantime, BluManChu was driving Drexosaur toward extinction. The Alpha Dogs' best hope was to try to heal each other. That would be a daunting task, given they were both on opposite sides of the battlefield, low on health, and outnumbered. Lucas barked out an order, and the Dogs fled from their predators, returning to their starting point. Perhaps with a combination of fleeing, defending, and short stints of healing, Lucas's Herculanix and Daniel's Drexosaur could get back to full strength. Then, if they somehow positioned themselves properly, they might knock a Leopard out of play and even the match.

Herculanix and Drexosaur reached their starting grounds, and Drexosaur began to heal his injured comrade. But the three Leopards sprinted after them, and Marisol crushed Drexosaur with Thor's Hammer in a final death blow. Herculanix was now alone, weak, and surrounded.

He kicked Marisol in the head, and she flew parallel to the edge. Immediately, BluManChu moved to guard his fallen teammate without attempting to attack Herculanix. Their other friend, DevilsKeeper, also stood to protect Marisol, leaving Herculanix an opening to escape the edge and return to the middle ground.

Taking this opportunity to improve his position, Lucas steered Herculanix into the clear while Victor mocked the retreating coward. The pack of Leopards alternated completely healing each other. Lucas should have broken up the healing, but he hadn't expected to lose his teammates so fast, and he was still reeling, trying to formulate a new strategy.

Once all three Leopards had healed, DevilsKeeper strolled Herculanix's way. BluManChu and Marisol followed about five feet behind. Cautiously backpedaling, Herculanix came to a stop close to the edge. Outnumbered, Lucas's only remaining ally was the terrain. A mistake or a lucky toss could change his fortune.

DevilsKeeper stepped before him, and the other Leopards began bouncing in place to cheer him on. The Leopards had prepared for this moment for weeks. Now, finally, Victor would get his chance to exact revenge directly on Lucas.

Over the roaring crowd, Victor yelled, "Adonis, prepare to die!"

Herculanix ran around DevilsKeeper to snag the inside position, hoping to subsequently kick DevilsKeeper over the edge. The hubris of failing to use their full advantage was the opening Lucas needed. However, as Herculanix took the inside position, DevilsKeeper landed a solid punch to Herculanix's chest that left him one shot away from death. Lucas tried to flee, but BluManChu and Marisol cut off his retreat. When Herculanix turned back to encounter Victor's creation, Marisol took him prisoner, pinning his arms behind him.

Victor savored the scared puppy dog expression on Lucas's face as he registered that his fate was sealed. Then, with a vicious kick to the groin, DevilsKeeper slayed the bully.

Slamming both fists down, Lucas crushed the keyboard, but the sound of crackling plastic was drowned out as the auditorium erupted with cheers. Marisa, Connor, and Victor leapt out of their seats and jumped into the air. As the crowd chanted their team name, the Leopards exchanged high-fives that turned into hugs. In that instant, they truly felt like advanced programmers. They had written code smart enough to defeat humans in a fair fight, while leading an army of programmers in the process.

The award ceremony that followed was simple, but gratifying. The Alphas didn't bother to stick around, slinking out of the room as Connor, Marisa, and Victor each received a small trophy for their accomplishments. The Leopards had earned ten points for every student in the class, and they were the heroes of the day.

While everyone enjoyed it, the victory was the sweetest for Victor. In this very classroom, his college career had started off so miserably, but now, his first term had ended miraculously in his favor.

CHAPTER 33 – NATURAL WONDERS

The tide washed peacefully over Marisa's toes as she walked along the beach, holding Connor's hand. They'd arrived in Miami the previous afternoon for a week-long visit over Christmas break.

"Your mom really looks out for you, doesn't she?" Connor said as he rubbed his stiff neck.

"Yeah. My sister and I… we're all she has. We're her whole world." Surveying him from the corner of her eye, Marisa asked, "How's your neck?"

"Just a little kink. I'm not used to sleeping like that."

"Yeah," Marisa said sheepishly. "I didn't think she would make you sleep in her bedroom."

"I guess she really wants to keep an eye on me."

Ms. Asensio—or Nadia, as she insisted Connor call her—had told them that until Marisa and Connor got married, they could not share a bed under her roof. So, Marisa and her sister, Zulia, had slept as they always had, on the pullout couch in the living room of their tiny apartment. That left only one place for Connor to sleep.

Nadia had offered to let Connor sleep in her bed, while she slept on the floor. But he insisted that he couldn't allow her to do that, and volunteered to take the floor himself. When Marisa had objected to offering their guest such embarrassingly meager accommodations, Connor graciously refused to sleep elsewhere, and the matter was settled.

He'd tossed and turned uncomfortably on Nadia's bedroom floor, awaking several times to the sound of her snoring. He later told Marisa that he'd considered opening the door and leaving the room, just to sleep on the living room floor, where it was quieter. But the last thing he wanted was to betray Ms. Asensio's trust—lest she thought he was sneaking off to be with Marisa—so he'd remained where he was.

It was going to be a long week for Connor. Marisa was grateful that he would endure it for her.

"Your mom is an excellent cook, and that was a delicious meal last night," Connor said. "Though I wasn't expecting her to tell me over dinner not to knock you up."

"She means well," Marisa replied, kicking her foot to splash the shallow water beside her. "She doesn't want me to make the same mistakes she made. Mom was only sixteen when she had me, eighteen when she had Zulia. My father left us right after, and she raised the two of us by herself. No other man was ever good enough to be our father figure, or to distract her from being an A+ mother. All she wants is to do right by us, to make a better life for us."

"I understand, and she's done an amazing job raising you two. Tons of respect to her for that. I just didn't expect her to phrase it so bluntly." Connor hesitated for a moment, looking nervous, then added, "Another thing I wasn't expecting was… Well, for her to look—"

"Hot?" Marisa interrupted.

"I was going to say 'young,'" Connor protested. "The three of you could be sisters."

"You're so cute," Marisa said, tweaking his nose. "I know she's hot. The way guys look at her—I mean, c'mon, she's ripped."

"I know. I think she could kick my ass," Connor said with a chuckle.

"She wouldn't do that. You've just got to understand her. She's not outgoing like me. She's more introverted, like Zulia, and she doesn't have many friends. Every waking moment, she spends either working, taking care of us, or at the gym. The gym is her release, her escape."

Marisa proceeded to explain that her mother's day job involved sewing in factories, and by night, she used to be a Walmart cashier to make ends meet. One summer night before Marisa started high school, her mother passed out on the job. She hadn't been taking care of her health—her sole focus was providing for her daughters. Determined to always be there for them, the incident launched Nadia into a fitness obsession. Soon her second job was as a personal trainer during evenings and weekends. It helped her make a little extra money to support her daughters' extracurricular activities.

"Plus," Marisa said, "you know what they say?"

"What?" Connor asked. Without answering, she tugged playfully at Connor's shorts and dared him to catch her. As Marisa sprinted carefree across the sand and dove into the gently crashing waves, she didn't see Connor pause to marvel at her.

Soon she was under the water, admiring a small school of fish passing just beyond her reach. The clear water was filled with tourists enjoying their winter vacation, and Marisa found herself weaving around legs as she swam underwater, trying to stay submerged as long as she could to make Connor's quest more challenging.

Once she was slightly beyond standing depth and nearly out of breath, her head breached the water in search of Connor. As she surveyed the scene, she wondered if he was feeling like a fish out of water here. Marisa badly wanted him to feel at home, but he was out of his element crammed into their little one-bedroom apartment in Hialeah. He was the only white boy in her neighborhood, and he spoke no Spanish. Connor didn't seem to be bothered by it, but she still wondered.

A wave washed over her, and Marisa allowed her concern to wash away with the tide as she submerged herself once more. She swam underneath a raft and a group of girls, then suddenly felt her bikini bottom loosen. Quickly grabbing for the right side where the loop had come untied, her hand met another's, holding the string. Craning around to look, Marisa saw Connor with a wicked look on his face. Shaking her head and holding both his hand and her suit, she made for the surface.

As they both took deep breaths, Connor gasped, "You really should tie that tighter."

"Perhaps you can show me," she said, pushing him back as they both smiled. Holding her in his arms, Connor stood on the ocean floor while Marisa retied her suit.

"So, what do they say?" Connor prompted.

"They say if you want to see what your girlfriend will look like in twenty years, look at her mother," Marisa said coyly.

He ran his hand through her dark, wet hair and gazed into her sparkling hazel eyes. "I'll have to see if they're right."

"Is that a proposal? Are you down on one knee?" Marisa said, smiling into his glowing blue eyes as she wrapped her legs around his waist.

Without hesitation, Connor said, "You'll know when I'm proposing."

"Okay," she said, giving him a kiss, "it's a little early for that, but when the time comes, you better do it right." With a glance at her mom sitting in the distance on a beach towel with Zulia, she added, "My mom does like you, you know. In fact, she told me last night that her grandchildren will have light eyes."

"Someday, we'll find out," Connor said, caressing her back.

Even though she was only nineteen and barely three months into her relationship with Connor, every fiber of Marisa's being told her he was right. She knew they were soulmates.

Out of the blue, she told him, "Hey, we need something like this in CombatRidge." Marisa waited for Connor to register what she meant, as she knew work was the last thing on his mind right now. Then his eyes told her he understood and concurred. In striving to build a world people would want to live in, she couldn't imagine a better place than right there with him.

"On the subject of work," Marisa said in a casual tone, "if we're going to keep carpooling, it would be easier if I don't have to drop you off every night."

"Okay," Connor said, looking a little confused. "I can walk home from your place instead, if you want."

With a playful smile, she said, "That's not quite what I meant."

Connor studied her face. "Are you asking me to move in with you?"

Marisa bit her lip and nodded her head. "Just don't tell my mom."

Three months ago, Connor had never had a girlfriend. Now, Marisa was asking him to move in with her. Running his fingers again through her wet hair, he said, "I thought you wanted to take it slow?"

"Yeah, we did that," Marisa said sincerely.

To be certain, he asked, "Are you sure you're okay with this? A month ago, you didn't even want me to meet your mother over Thanksgiving, because you thought that was too soon. Now you want me to move in. I just want to make sure—"

"I wanted my mom to see me have a successful start to college. If I brought back a boy before I brought back As, that's all she would have noticed. But now that she's met you, she's going to love you, just like I do."

The words hung in the air between them. It was the first time either of them had used the L-word.

"Well?" an anxious Marisa said.

Connor pulled her closer and said, "I love you, too."

~ ~ ~

On a dark New Year's Day morning, Victor found himself in the passenger seat of Tina's car as they drove into the city just before 7:00. The San Francisco streets were quiet, no doubt because many people had returned home only a few hours earlier after ringing in 2013. Victor himself had only returned the day before, cutting his winter break visit home to Milton short in favor of putting in some extra hours at Golden Bay Labs before school resumed. Since the dorms were still closed for the break, Marisa had been kind enough to let him stay at her apartment while she and Connor were in Miami.

It had been two months since Victor had seen Tina at Richard's dinner party. So, he was surprised to receive a text from her twenty-four hours earlier. He was even more surprised that she'd invited him to start the new year with her at her private sanctuary. Her message made it clear that she only wanted to be friends, and in the spirit of new beginnings, he accepted her invitation. Though no longer interested in dating her, he remained curious to learn what place she considered so special.

Crossing the Golden Gate Bridge, he watched the sun peek over the horizon and shimmer across the bay. A few minutes later, Tina turned onto Muir Woods Road. Not being much of an outdoorsman, Victor said, "You're not going to bury me in the woods or something, right?"

After a pretend maniacal laugh, she said lightly, "I'm not going to hurt you. Promise. I want to share something with you that I think you might be able to appreciate the way I do."

The sun had reached the tops of the tall trees by the time they pulled into the mostly empty gravel parking lot at about ten minutes before eight. They got out, paid the entrance fee, and were the first ones to enter Muir Woods. As they headed down the trail, Tina told Victor that she liked to get out there before anyone else, especially before the noisy tourists ruined the tranquility.

The trees towered above them like majestic skyscrapers, and long beams of golden sunlight filtered down through the canopy. Underneath the colossal sequoias, Victor was in complete awe and imagined they had traveled back to prehistoric times. Upon entering a dirt portion of the trail, they came across a narrow passage with a thirty-foot drop on one side. Tina took Victor's hand and led him across it. Once the path opened up to where they could walk side by side, she continued to hold his hand. He didn't resist her touch, though he did find the intimacy a bit curious.

About a mile into the woods, she stopped and turned toward him. They were completely alone in this heavenly place. When Victor started to say something to fill the silence, Tina put her finger over her lips. Gently pulling his head down, she said in his ear, "Listen." Then she put both her hands out, palms up, and extended them toward him. After hesitating a moment, he placed his palms softly on hers. Tina allowed her arms to relax as she held his hands, and closed her eyes.

Uncertain what to do, Victor swayed slightly, wondering if she would say something, but she didn't provide him any guidance. Victor admired her tranquility as she continued to breathe slowly, and he ultimately closed his eyes, too. Surrounded by such beauty, it seemed to him a shame to close it all off from himself. And then he heard it—the stillness. The quiet, peaceful stillness. The modern world with all its modern problems could not touch them here. Its sounds could not penetrate this wild fortress.

Victor's restless mind began to flood the void created by the stillness surrounding him. *How long will we stand here? Who is she thinking about? Who should I be thinking about?* Then his father's face smiled back at him. There'd been so much left unsaid between them. Victor wished they could have had just one more day together, to say all of those things that still echoed in his mind.

Tina's soft voice called to him. "This place brings me peace—a peace you once tried to share with me. A peace I hope you find for yourself, my friend."

Victor opened his eyes and, gazing upon her closed ones, said, "I see why you come here. Thank you for this. I would like to be your friend."

An hour later, they were having breakfast at the pier, looking out on the clear, majestic bay. "Most people don't appreciate getting up early," Tina said, "and experiencing nature in complete silence. If you wait too long, everyone else spoils it with their chatter."

There were definitely unforeseen advantages to waking early, he admitted. Unable to contain his curiosity, Victor said, "Tell me who you go there to remember."

She stared into his chestnut-brown eyes and told him he was the first person she'd ever taken there. She'd found the spot shortly after Isaac died, and now, it was her weekly ritual to be the first one to walk the woods every Saturday morning.

"Who's Isaac?" Victor asked curiously.

"He was my fiancé," Tina said softly. "I met him when I was eleven, and the two of us grew up together. My junior year in high school, we started dating. Then I went off to Stanford for my undergrad, and he went to Oregon, majoring in business. The whole time, we dated long-distance. Sometimes, I'd make trips back home to Redmond for the holidays, and sometimes he would drive down to visit me. It's far, so we didn't see each other often. A lot of phone calls and video chats, but we made the most of the time we had together. After four years, he proposed." Tears sparkled in Tina's eyes. "We were going to get married after graduation. He was going to find a job in Palo Alto, while I did my grad work here."

Tina stopped, and Victor remained silent, watching her struggle to contain her emotions. With another deep breath, she forged ahead, "He drove down to surprise me for Valentine's Day weekend two years ago. We had a wonderful, short weekend together—he arrived Saturday morning, and was back on the road Sunday afternoon. He should've left earlier, but I wanted him to stay for lunch."

Tina stared off into the distance, seeming lost in her thoughts. "For a long time, I blamed myself," she admitted. "Perhaps I still do. Isaac always made fun of that song about walking five hundred miles, because he drove six hundred each way to see me. If you drive straight through, it's about ten hours." She took a shaky breath. "Toward the end of the drive back, he got tired and drifted into oncoming traffic. He died instantly on impact."

When Victor placed his right hand in her left, she squeezed firmly. "It's still hard to talk about, but I'm glad you asked," Tina said. "Most people who know me never mention Isaac anymore. Except for Pari—I was her student when it happened, and we'd grown close, and…" Tina trailed off, and Victor allowed her time to gather herself. "Other people think I don't want to talk about him, but they're wrong. If I never talk about him, it's like he never happened. He was funny, sweet, and unfortunately also afraid of flying. So many people are, but cars are so much more dangerous than planes—like a hundred times more. Sadly, that isn't what makes the headlines."

Both of them looked into the distance without speaking. Finally, Tina said, "Wow, I just dumped a lot on you. I'm sorry."

Victor said, "It's okay. If you ever need someone to listen, I'd be happy to."

Wiping her eyes, she told him, "That's what I needed today. Thank you. Isaac was my soulmate. At least, that's what I thought. Now, looking back, I know I loved him, and I always will. But who marries their high school sweetheart?" She shook her head ruefully. "Maybe the whole thing was doomed from the start. But it's been almost two years since he died, and I hadn't dated anyone else until I met you. For a long time, I thought that would be unfair to Isaac. Then my girlfriends invited me to that party, and, well… now I have a new friend."

Smiling back at her, Victor thought about telling her who he'd thought about in the woods, but he wasn't ready yet. "Sometimes things don't work out how we hope or expect," he said instead, "but it is good to have a new friend. Maybe you were right all along."

She smiled and asked curiously, "About what?"

Across the Golden Gate Bridge, Victor eyed the rolling green hills that laid beyond. "Maybe this is the best of all possible outcomes."

CHAPTER 34 – QUINN'S HAVEN

Early in the afternoon on Valentine's Day, Pari strode with Quinn up to Victor's desk at Golden Bay Labs, where he was swiftly writing code on his computer.

"Are we ready?" Pari asked.

With a nod, he typed his final instructions. "Just finished." Still amid a flurry of coding thoughts, Victor turned to greet them and saw they were a bit wet. "Hi, raining out, is it?" he asked Quinn.

"A little."

Before a raindrop reached Quinn's eyebrow, Victor wiped it from her forehead. "I've got something for you today."

"First, I've got something for you," she said. "I wrote a little program."

This prompted Victor to smile proudly. Over the last few months, he'd showed her a few things about programming, but she hadn't yet written a program entirely without him until now. He'd begun to wonder if she only liked to talk to him about programming—which would have been fine with him, because he enjoyed her company—or if she was actually serious about learning to code.

Pari pulled Quinn's laptop out of her bag and placed it on the desk, flipping open the screen. The program prompted for the user's name. Victor typed his name and pressed *enter.* The background faded to light blue, and his name appeared in white letters in the middle of the screen. Each letter began to float off in a different direction, like clouds drifting in the wind. The letters bounced off each other and off the borders of the screen for a few moments before returning to the middle to show his name again.

Quinn said, "I know, it's not much, but—"

"No," Victor said, "it's *great.* I want to use that as my screensaver now."

"You really like it?" she asked timidly. Given her inability to type with her hands, it had been painstaking work for her to create this code using the special text-to-speech software she had. Many times it would misinterpret her commands, so she was grateful that Victor appreciated her efforts.

"Love it!" he said unequivocally. "When you're ready, I'll teach you more."

"I'd love that, too," she said, looking at him expectantly. "Now, what do you have for me?"

Victor glanced at Pari and asked, "Can I tell her?" Pari nodded her consent.

When he put his hand on her hand, Quinn didn't feel it, but she appreciated the gesture, nonetheless. "You've been coming here for months, helping us with our research and my code, and we're very grateful for this," Victor told her. "And all this time, you never asked for anything in return. So, we put together a little Valentine's gift to thank you. Come with me."

Victor led them to the lab. As he moved to stand in front of the scanner, Quinn saw that the room was more crowded than usual. Along with the standard Golden Bay scientists and technicians, there were a few other infrequent guests. Richard's and Gerald's presence wasn't common, though not completely surprising, but the four Warp Drive developers had never before visited Golden Bay Labs.

Victor took a knee to be eye-level with Quinn and said, "These people have helped us put together something special for you today during your scan."

Quinn looked at Tina with disgust and said, "I don't want anything from her! She's taken enough from me already!"

Victor was a little caught off guard by this reaction, but he could tell from Quinn's face that she wanted to storm out in anger. With a sad expression, Tina silently faded to the back of the room and out of sight. Victor told Quinn everything was fine, but her face remained defiant. Before he could ask Quinn what had happened between her and Tina, Pari shook her head, steering him away from the topic.

Holding out a virtual reality headset, Victor said, "I know you usually listen to music when you're in the scanner, but today we've got some video for you, too. I think you're gonna like it."

Still rattled from the sight of Tina, Quinn said cautiously, "Okay, Victor. I trust you."

"Can I do the honors today?" he asked, holding his palms skyward.

Quinn smiled back and said yes. Very gently, he lifted her out of her wheelchair and laid her down delicately in the scanning bed. After brushing her flowing red hair away from her face and making sure she felt comfortable, he asked her in a playful formal voice, "Is everything to your liking, ma'am?"

Quinn returned his formality. "Most certainly, sir. But I require music. I'll take my usual, please."

Victor chuckled and returned to his normal voice. "No, this will be much better than the usual. I picked out a song for you today, a cover of one of your favorite ballads." He slipped the VR headset over her eyes and carefully placed the headphones over her ears before retreating with the others to the control room.

Pari got on the mic. "You okay, honey?"

Quinn confirmed she was. The music began, and the black before her faded into a blue sky with cotton-white clouds drifting lazily overhead.

In Quinn's ear, Victor said through the intercom, "What do you see?"

"The sky."

"Good. We're looking at the same thing on the monitor. Lay still for a minute while we calibrate."

For years, Quinn had been very still, so she did not need to be reminded to remain so. Yet she knew Victor meant no harm by his comment. In fact, she almost liked that he had forgotten she was paralyzed, even if only for a moment. A verse of the song passed, and Quinn found herself quite moved by the rendition. Clearly, Victor had made an excellent choice.

"Okay, we're ready," Victor said. "I need you to sit up and tell me what you see."

"Afraid I can't do that, buddy," Quinn said with a wry chuckle.

"Please, just try. Humor me."

Starting to get irritated, Quinn pleaded, "Victor, don't tease me. You know I can't."

"I would never tease you, my friend. Please, Quinn, we're testing something. I need you to try to sit up. We need to record what happens when you try, okay?"

It had been years since Quinn had tried to move. Unsuccessful attempts at physical therapy had mentally exhausted her with nothing to show for it. But now her friend was asking her to try. With a sigh, she bent her focus toward sitting up, and gradually, her perspective changed. The clouds passed over her, and the horizon rose into view. A beautiful beach appeared, with the sun just rising on the horizon.

"You changed the view," Quinn said as the scene wobbled before her.

"No, honey," Pari replied in an emotional voice, "you did!"

That made no sense to Quinn. It wasn't possible. "What do you mean?" she asked, bewildered, but attempting to stabilize the view.

"You sat up in the virtual world. *You* controlled that," explained Victor passionately. Then, in what reminded her comically of some phony evangelical healer, Victor ordered, "Now, Quinn, I want you to stand."

Stand? How was she supposed to *stand*? She hadn't stood in years. What was he playing at?

When her view didn't change, Victor asked, "Are you trying to stand?"

"Victor?" Quinn whimpered, with trepidation in her voice. "Don't. Please, don't. Don't toy with me. I can't—"

In a kind, patient voice, Victor encouraged, "Please, I need you to try."

Still, she balked. It had been so long since she'd used that portion of her mind that she wondered if it had fully atrophied. But slowly—ever so slowly—her view changed to show her virtual arms pushing off the ground. Next, her legs and torso came into view, raising her up to a standing position. The sight resembled a fawn standing shakily for the first time.

In the scanner, no motion occurred, but in the virtual world, Quinn stood majestically, facing the rising sun.

The control room erupted in a euphoria that Quinn couldn't hear, because their mic was muted. All she heard was the piano playing the interlude of the song. Then Victor came over the intercom asking, "What do you see now?"

In a quivering voice, she asked, "How? How did you do that? What is this?"

"We're scanning your brain signals," Victor said, each word laced with profound joy, "and using them to move your virtual body. It works!"

Tears began streaking from underneath her visor and down her cheeks. There wasn't a dry eye in the control room, either. Richard turned to the group, pointed at Quinn, and said emphatically, "*This* is why we build worlds people want to live in."

Only then did Marisa, Connor, James, and Tina finally grasp why Richard had been so insistent on this. Their game was no game at all.

As Quinn gazed at the horizon, she recalled the event that had stolen her ability to stand. Two years prior, a pickup truck had collided head-on with the Rone family car, killing her biological parents and younger brother, and leaving her paralyzed—or so she'd been told, as she had no memory of the crash herself. The first thing she remembered was waking a week later in the hospital to the sight of three unfamiliar faces at her bedside: Tina, Pari, and Gerald.

Wracked with guilt over the devastation Isaac had caused, Tina had arrived soon after the accident, leaving Quinn's side only to attend Isaac's funeral. When Tina told Pari about the incident, the professor flew with Gerald to Corvallis to be there for Tina, her favorite student, in her time of need. With no surviving relatives, Quinn would have been quite alone without those three.

It wasn't until Quinn moved in with Pari and Gerald that Tina confessed her boyfriend was not only in the crash, but also responsible for it. Tina blamed herself, and Quinn too readily accepted Tina as the scapegoat, grieving the loss of everyone she'd ever loved. Quinn's bitter resentment stifled a budding friendship between two young women brought together by tragedy. Still, Quinn was grateful for her adoptive parents, most especially today, as she virtually walked again.

In the control room, Tina futilely wiped the tears from her face, only to have new ones replace them. Pari embraced her, and Gerald embraced them both. Gerald repeated the phrase he'd said to Quinn when he had asked to adopt her: "Sometimes life's tragedies are hidden opportunities."

Putting her hand on Victor's shoulder, Tina kissed him on the cheek and thanked him for his contribution to this moment. Victor remained gazing forward at his computer screen. Though he didn't look at Tina, he did put a sympathetic hand on hers as he spoke his next instruction to Quinn.

"I have one more task for you for today," he said. "Turn around."

Quinn turned to discover a fairly realistic avatar of Victor standing in front of her. Victor didn't control the avatar with his mind like she did, but rather much more clumsily with his keyboard. Overcome with joy, she jumped into his arms and squeezed him tightly. And while the machine didn't give her the power to do so, Quinn swore she felt his embrace.

CHAPTER 35 – VALUABLE INSIGHTS

Standing on the curb with his carry-on bag at his side, Gerald peered through the traffic until he spotted Pari's car. He waved her down, and she pulled over, greeting him with an enthusiastic smile. After tossing his bag into the trunk, he took a seat beside her and gave her a quick kiss before she merged back into the airport traffic.

"Did you miss me?" she asked playfully.

"I most certainly did, my darling wife," Gerald told her, reaching out to tuck a wayward strand of hair behind her ear. "You're always my favorite part about coming home."

The conference he was returning from had been a success, in that he'd made some new contacts and found a few people interested in his work. Unfortunately, his presentation of his paper was met with a lukewarm reception. Several critics told him that economics was a human creation, filled with mental constructs like money, and therefore Gerald shouldn't expect value to be any different. He insisted they'd missed his point that humans didn't need to perceive value as an intrinsic attribute of goods and services in order for economies to operate.

Pari reminded him that harsh critics are sometimes necessary to sharpen one's argument.

"Or the best way to obscure the truth," Gerald said, though he knew she was right. Tired after a six-hour flight from D.C., he gazed out upon the dark hills of San Francisco and attempted to discern some stars in the night sky. "I really enjoyed discussing economics with my peers, but I was preoccupied with the secrets I couldn't mention. I kept thinking about Quinn's experience last week. So fascinating."

"Not here," Pari said sternly. "You know better."

With a chuckle, he said, "Honey, I'm pretty sure we're alone."

Smacking his leg, she hissed, "I'm serious. You promised."

Rubbing his thigh, he acquiesced. "Okay, I'll only tell you some very non-specific thoughts." After waiting to see if she would stop him, Gerald ventured forth cautiously. "Our moral code evolved throughout human evolution, as did our social structures and economies, and we still haven't settled on a single, agreed-upon 'right way.' Certain assumptions form the basis of all these social constructs."

"All right," she said. "That's quite abstract. Let's keep it that way."

Encouraged, Gerald pressed on. "Science *may* someday challenge these assumptions. It *may* overturn them all. If this happens, what happens to everything that is based on them? Who is dedicated to solving these philosophical dilemmas? My guess is it's not the scientists."

"Actually," Pari said, "let's not discuss this in the car. Call Richard. Tell him we're coming over."

~ ~ ~

Once again, Gerald found himself standing on the threshold of Richard's house with his wife. This time, however, he was filled with intellectual fervor rather than trepidation.

Richard welcomed his unscheduled late-night visitors with fresh drinks. Graciously accepting the whiskey from his friend, Gerald quickly spilled out his thoughts: "I've been thinking about it a lot over the last week. The assumption that we will all eventually die is at the heart of all societies. All existing morality is rooted in it. Every economy depends on new generations replacing the old ones, with property passing down from one generation to another. Indeed, our biological evolution greatly depended on death to make room for new life. Moreover, all religions assume we die—in fact, they probably arose in part to cope with death."

When Richard nodded, prompting him to continue, Gerald added, "Your work removes that assumption. Our societies could crumble as the foundational assumptions disappear. And that's only one assumption you'll destroy with this work. What about the assumption that we each possess a single instance of ourselves representing our true identity? Or the assumption that there are finite resources? In a virtual world, you can just make more, I suppose. I can go on—"

"I'm sure you can," Richard said, curtailing Gerald's growing momentum, "but you should take a sip of your drink first. By the way, we call our virtual world 'Cendovia.' Richie is the first Cendovian. And these are all excellent points, but fortunately, we possess the luxury of time to figure these out. We can always pause the simulation if things turn hairy, and work out solutions, like we're doing with the technical aspects."

"But it's not that simple," Gerald argued. "You may not get nearly enough time. Our societies had tens of thousands of years to evolve to where they are now. Throughout all this time, we invented things like Judeo-Christian morality, democracy, and capitalism. That's only Western society, and many disagreements still remain about those solutions.

"Throughout the rise of civilization, the social problems *always* rested upon certain fundamental assumptions, such as the inevitability of death, the singularity of identity, and the finite nature of resources. By removing those fundamental assumptions, you must start all over to build robust social structures in Cendovia. You won't have ten thousand years and generations of people to do it. Right now, only three people on Earth know about this—and none of these three is dedicated to finding solutions to these social problems. You two are focused on the many remaining scientific problems, and I, well…"

With a glance, Pari indicated to Richard that she would respond and then took a sip of her wine. "Clearly, you have given this much thought, dear. And while it's refreshing to get a different perspective on this, you might be too pessimistic. We may find by destroying some of these fundamental assumptions, we don't need to answer some of the hard problems of the past, like who lives and who dies. Maybe now, everyone can live forever."

"Honey," Gerald said, snickering, "even as you're saying that, I know you don't believe it will turn out so simply. I'll grant you, some problems may become easier in Cendovia. There may even be lessons we learn in Cendovia that we can apply on Earth. But some problems will be harder in Cendovia. Moreover, entirely new classes of problems will inevitably arise that have no precedent for attempting to be solved on Earth."

Pari again glanced at Richard, and he nodded approvingly.

"It's time to travel deeper into the abyss, my dear," she said, taking Gerald's hand. "An organization exists that is so secret, most don't even know they're in it. We call this secret organization the Zebulonz."

"Sounds alien," Gerald said. "Are you going to tell me next that you're secretly an alien?"

Pari smiled. "No aliens involved here. The name was inspired by General Zebulon Montgomery Pike, for whom Pikes Peak was named. Ironically, General Pike never reached the top of Pikes Peak. Similarly, Richard and I didn't know if we personally would make it to the summit of our mission when we first formed the Zebulonz years ago. We expected others to continue the climb long after we were gone."

Gerald threw her a curious look as she continued, "Our mission is to ensure the long-term survival of humanity, to defy the Fermi Paradox. The most likely answer to the Fermi Paradox is that civilizations don't live long enough to contact each other. There are so many ways an intelligent species can go extinct—nuclear wars, climate change, mass pandemics, asteroid impacts, etc."

"Okay, I could see that," Gerald said. "Given enough time, the odds are very high that every intelligent species will suffer one of those fates."

"You're catching on," Richard said approvingly. "The Zebulonz aim to defy this by allowing humans to survive the death of their physical bodies by continuing on in virtual form. Until now, only three people knew of this secret organization we've been building, and its mission—myself, Pari, and Owen. We three call ourselves the Pikes. The Pikes are the leaders and key individuals within the Zebulonz. I am the Zebulonz Commander, and Pari is the Lieutenant Commander. Together, we partner to lead the Zebulonz to fulfill its mission."

"Should I salute or something?" Gerald asked, then did so with a wink.

Richard smiled while returning his salute. "No, my friend. As I was saying, the commander has the final say, though Pari and I believe the commander and lieutenant commander should operate essentially as equal partners. The only reason we are not co-commanders in name is in case an agreement cannot be reached. Every command structure requires a clear, ultimate decider—though we believe the commander's override power should be used sparingly."

"Have you ever had to override her?" Gerald asked.

Richard laughed heartily. "Your wife is very strong-willed. I doubt she would actually let me get away with it," he quipped, giving Pari a respectful nod.

"That's right," Pari said, nodding back. Then she returned her attention to her husband. "So, honey, here's how it works. Richard and I both use our companies to further the Zebulonz mission, though everyone else merely believes they're doing neuroscience research, or making video games, or working on cybersecurity, or a myriad of other things. Owen is the Zebulonz Secretary of Defense, with the responsibility of protecting the Zebulonz and our mission from any threats."

"Threats?" Gerald asked, the smile leaving his face.

"*If* there ever are any," Pari said, holding her hand up to caution him. "Over time, we'll expand the number of Pikes, as more people must know of the mission in order to ensure our success. But we must expand our ranks carefully." Pari took a deep breath and regarded her husband seriously. "Gerald, we want you to become the fourth Pike—the Zebulonz Secretary of Social Welfare. Your responsibility will be to oversee the development of Cendovian ethical codes and policies."

Pari smiled at Gerald as he processed the information. It suddenly occurred to him that he should have realized there must have been a bigger operation than just Pari and Richard contributing to the birth of Richie. So wrapped up in the ethical questions, Gerald hadn't considered the logistical ones.

"So, there are secrets within the secrets?" Gerald asked. "I thought the Richie stuff was big enough, but now you claim you've got this whole operation of secret contributors. Wow! Anything else you're hiding?"

"No. No more secrets," Pari said sheepishly. "Sorry, honey. You're not mad…?"

"No," Gerald said emphatically, taking one of her hands in his. "I get why you had to be secretive. It's just…a lot."

"You're right, old friend," Richard said, smiling at him. "We do need someone to think about these problems full-time. How would you like to make that your job?"

"Uh, I wasn't exactly pitching for a job," Gerald said awkwardly. "First of all, I like my current job, and secondly, the work you need done is more than the job of just one person. It requires a whole army of philosophers and social scientists."

"Well, I'm not ready to bring a whole army in on our little secret yet," Richard said with a wink, sipping his whiskey. "Perhaps someday. Still, you're right. We do need a group helping you work through these philosophical questions. I would love for you to lead them. You've got a passion for the problems and the insight to point them out."

More at home with mulling over questions for days, Gerald hesitated to make the quick decision Richard was striving for. Finally, he said, "That's very flattering, but I'm not certain I want to do it yet. If I get involved in this, it's a one-way career move. One cannot simply turn back. Plus, there's the problem of explaining the move. How do I quit my job to go work on a secret project for the rest of my life? Like you two, I'd need some sort of cover story. And I still have some public-facing work I want to finish before I would ever consider taking my career into the shadows."

With mild amusement, Richard said, "Yes, Pari told me about your thesis—that value is a myth. Very intriguing. However, to address your other concern, we have the perfect cover already arranged for you. I am founding a think tank called the Refactor Institute with the publicly stated mission of advancing AI ethical exploration. While Richie isn't your typical AI, and you won't be able to discuss transcendence with any of your think tank colleagues, I think this will give you sufficient pretext to engage in the relevant discussions in a roundabout way. You can then bring your findings to us with your guidance on application."

It sounded like the opportunity of a lifetime, but Gerald still had to ask, "What does it pay?"

"Other than eternal life?" Richard grinned. "Well, how about 30 percent above your current pay? Will that do?"

Gerald believed that would do quite nicely and agreed to take the job after finishing the semester at Berkeley. The two men shook hands to seal their pact, and Richard welcomed him into the fellowship of Pikes.

To mark the occasion, Pari raised her glass and declared, "Death to fundamental assumptions!"

CHAPTER 36 – THE LION-HEARTED

High above the mountains on the first day of spring, Richie floated like a ghost, a disembodied entity looking down upon the world. Though his new surroundings were undoubtedly beautiful, with enough time, he believed this invisible solitude would turn into a depressing loneliness.

Amid concerns no one would ever see him again, Richie kept this thought to himself to retain an important aspect of his humanity—his privacy. Instead, he curtly told Richard, "It's grand."

Richie used voice commands to navigate the open world around him, a world Richard had dubbed Cendovia. Gracefully, Richie flew down from the peak of a snow-covered mountain and through a dusty canyon, finally landing in a meadow at the edge of a thick forest. Thanks to Victor's unknowing help, Richie could now easily turn his gaze and shift his focus, as though truly moving his eyes. The advanced optical modeling software Victor had produced using Golden Bay's research provided Richard the insights he'd needed to advance Richie's visual experience. But while it was wonderful to finally be able to discern the trees from the forest, Richie still remained bodiless.

"Good progress, but it needs more," he told Richard. "I want to feel the wind when I fly, and I'll need a body for that."

In the sixteen hours (from Richie's perspective) since his transcendence—what Richard now called sixteen hours of Cendovian time—Richie had gone from being blind to regaining full vision. Now he could fly like an angel, something he'd never been able to do on Earth. But despite his newfound ability to see everything, he still *felt* nothing. The experience was a hollow dream without the sensation of touch.

"Definitely needs more," Richie told himself aloud. He knew Richard had agonized over this constantly since Richie transcended six Earth months prior, and long before that as well. Both knew it was Richard's singular obsession, and nothing more needed to be said on the matter, as two minds could not be closer.

"I understand," Richard said. *"Be patient."*

The words Virginia left in her suicide note—a note Richard had never shared with the police or anyone else—echoed in Richie's head:

Patience is for the spectator, for the idle. The inventor needs not patience. The inventor needs calm, unbreakable resilience. Let your passion drown all obstacles. Be braver than the hardships, and time will lean in your favor. Bring us together again.

He wondered if Richard heard her, too.

"I'm never coming back from here," Richie said. "That is my fate, and I agreed to this. But for the sake of our research, I'm unlikely to be the last Richie. And we don't want too many versions of us around for long—that would dilute our identity. So, once you die on Earth, one of us Cendovians should be your successor. This we agree upon. But if you live another twenty years, and never restore another backup of yourself, all those memories die with you, and you surely don't want that. And I know you will want your last backup to be your successor, to maintain the greatest continuity of you. When that happens…it will be time to terminate me, to leave only one of us for posterity." He paused for a moment, suddenly nervous. "For your consideration, however, I nominate myself instead as your successor."

After a long pause, Richard said, *"I cannot promise you that."*

"Just consider it. Upon your passing, I will be the oldest living instance of you remaining. In royalty, the right of succession goes to the firstborn. I don't want to be king, of course—I just want to be the continuation of us. I want to be *the* Richard to all those we know. Someday, I want to be Virginia's Richard again in truth, not merely some copy of the original."

Richie again paused before admitting, "The prospect gives me hope. Most people recognize that they will someday die, but not like this. I will die at the hands of my former self, per my prior agreement—I just don't know when the end will come. In the realm of immortality, I alone carry a death sentence. People cavalierly say they would die for those they love, but do they actually mean it? How many deaths are they willing to endure? For you and I… we will write our answer in our own blood. And while it remains to be seen if we will live longer than anyone else has ever lived, we will most certainly die more than anyone has ever died."

~ ~ ~

Across town, Quinn was lying in bed wearing her hospital gown when Victor opened the curtain to the small pre-op room. She smiled at the sight of him, while Gerald greeted him with a warm handshake and an anxious expression. Victor looked down at Quinn and caressed her silky red hair. Since her head was about the only part of her body with sensation, this had become their agreed-upon equivalent of holding hands.

"Today's the day," she said nervously, welcoming his comforting touch. And indeed, this was the day Quinn would receive an experimental implant developed by Golden Bay Labs. The head surgeon for the operation—which would take more than twelve hours—would be Pari herself. But while Pari and her team were confident they could perform the delicate surgery safely, the survival rate for such a procedure was unknown because it had never before been attempted. They would need to be very cautious to avoid damaging her brain's ability to control her internal organs. Gerald and Pari had struggled with the decision, but eventually agreed that while the experiment was certainly beneficial for science, the potential benefits were even greater for Quinn. So, they gave her the choice.

Victor provided Quinn with a source of strength as she attempted to remain brave. In the four months since they'd met, he had become her closest friend. With his help, she'd rediscovered a light in herself that she'd once thought extinguished. He'd rekindled her creative spark by teaching her to program, which she found therapeutic. Through programming, she'd finally learned what her adoptive parents had been trying to teach her—that she still had much to offer the world.

Often quoting John Wooden, Gerald would tell her, "'Don't let what you can't do interfere with what you *can* do.'" Invariably, she would remark that he was corny, yet sometimes, lessons simply needed a catalyst to ensure they were absorbed.

For Quinn, programming was that catalyst. With her creative juices flowing again, she'd begun to venture back to her musical roots. No longer was she simply a passive listener.

On the weekends, Victor carried out an established routine. Saturday mornings he spent with his friend Tina at Muir Woods. Visiting the woods was a quiet therapy for him. He would reflect on his flurried thoughts, and once they slowed down, he would think about his father. At the deepest point in the forest, Tina and Victor would meditate together and then share their thoughts with no one around. The words uttered within the forest would never leave there. And over time, Victor opened up about his father in a way he had never done with anyone else.

Sunday mornings were reserved for his friend Quinn. He would take her to Golden Bay and they'd play together in the virtual world. It was her favorite time of the week, and every time they visited there, she felt she had gone to heaven with Victor as her guardian angel.

On weekdays, when she wasn't helping Victor test his code, Quinn had scanning sessions three times a week at Golden Bay Labs. The scientists would ask her to pretend to move various body parts, while a virtual reality headset allowed her to view her avatar mimicking these movement attempts. Outside the scanner, she spent a lot of time by Victor's desk, but no matter how often she interrupted him at work, he was always generous with his time. Though he loved getting into the zone while coding, he grew to enjoy her interruptions, as her witty humor often entertained him. In their conversations, he was no longer the boy tumbling down the hill.

Now she was about to receive an implant that would allow them to send impulses into her brain to mimic senses that had long since gone dormant. The hope was she would be able to do things like hold out her virtual hand and sense a virtual pin-prick. If successful, they would test for months to advance their virtual sensation capabilities. All this would happen exclusively in the scanner, so once she recovered from the surgery, she'd be spending five days a week in the scanner at Golden Bay. To prevent cognitive overload, her sessions would be limited to two one-hour sessions per day, which meant it would be a long road to confirming that full-body sensations could be mimicked correctly.

Opening the curtain, dressed in surgical scrubs, Pari asked her daughter, "Is the patient ready?"

"I am," Quinn said with a sigh.

After Victor stepped aside, Pari leaned over and kissed Quinn's forehead. "It's okay, sweetheart. I'll take care of you." She hesitated for a moment, looking deeply into Quinn's eyes, then added, "You understand you don't have to do this, right? It's perfectly fine to say no. You won't upset anyone. Are you absolutely sure you want this?"

"I don't *need* this," Quinn said, as her timid face gave rise to a voice with strong conviction, "but I *want* this. I want to experience what this can offer me. I want to be a pioneer. And perhaps this can help others, too. We'll only find out if someone is the first to try."

Gerald commended his daughter for her courageous and noble sentiment, and the nurse began to wheel Quinn's bed out of the pre-op room. While Pari led the way, Victor walked on one side of Quinn, with Gerald on the other.

"I love you, sweetheart," Gerald said, as he held Quinn's cold, numb hand. Though it was difficult, he put on a confident expression while his daughter looked at him like a scared ten-year-old trying to be strong, not the remarkable eighteen-year-old woman she had become.

"I love you, too," Quinn said desperately.

Victor continued to reassure her that everything would be all right, but when they reached the OR doors, Victor and Gerald weren't permitted to go any further.

"Don't worry," Gerald said reassuringly, "your mother is the best. I mean, Pari."

"It's okay, Dad," Quinn said. Until then, she had always referred to her adoptive parents by their first names, feeling it was necessary to respect her birth parents. "I know Mom is the best."

Gerald teared up at the sound of those words and kissed his daughter on the cheek. Blinking her eyes, Pari inhaled deeply, attempting to maintain her clinical composure in preparation for the work ahead.

As the mechanical doors slowly opened, Quinn gazed at Victor with fear in her eyes. She feared what might go wrong, but she was also petrified by what might forever go unsaid. For months, she'd clung to feelings she worried were destined to be unrequited.

Victor kissed her forehead and told her one last time, "It's going to be okay, my friend."

And so she never said the words she had been dying to tell him.

CHAPTER 37 – FOREIGN INTERFERENCE

With a backpack slung over his shoulder, Richard rolled his luggage up the walkway to his front door. As he fished in his pocket for the key, he heard a car pull into his driveway, its headlights casting his shadow on the door. He turned to see Owen's car, then entered the house, leaving the door open behind him.

Tired from a full day of traveling, Richard dropped his bags by the bar and began to pour himself a drink. This late at night, Owen's presence probably meant a drink was in order. Once Owen closed the door behind him, Richard handed him a whiskey, and they clinked their glasses.

"How was your trip?" Owen asked.

Richard had just completed a three-week solo vacation across Eastern Europe, which he had begun on Virginia's birthday. Their annual spring getaway was something he had always enjoyed with her. At work, he was all business, totally immersing himself in whatever he was doing, and Virginia had often insisted he take time away from all his work periodically.

"If you flip the switch completely off for a few weeks," she'd told him, "the light won't burn out."

Richard had loved how Virginia cared for him. So, after her death, he kept up the tradition by himself—in part to honor her memory, but also because that time allowed him to reflect on his life and to experience new perspectives. His journey this year included visits to Finland, Poland, Greece, and ultimately Ukraine. The architecture and the history of each country fascinated him. Now that he had achieved digital transcendence, he found himself watching people through a different lens. Often, he would stare at them, and ask himself if they would still do what they did if they believed they could live forever.

He recalled sitting in a cafe in Kyiv, watching a mother walking with her small children all bundled up, and wondering if that experience could even be replicated in Cendovia. While he had spent a lot of time observing people, he had sometimes sensed he was the one being observed. Perhaps this was because he was a public figure, or perhaps he was becoming paranoid, but he had never felt that before. It tarnished his memory of Ukraine, which he found to otherwise be a beautiful country. So, now, sitting in his favorite armchair, Richard was happy to finally be home, though he was sure Owen would soon spoil some of that happiness.

"It's good to be back, Owen," he said at last. "What brings you by?"

Sipping his whiskey, Owen sat down on the couch and presented the problem. "Richard, we've seen an increase in cyberattacks over the past few months industry-wide."

"I know," Richard said. "Were we hit?"

"No, Galanteen wasn't breached," Owen said hesitantly. "None of your companies were breached, and none of our clients have been, either. But we *have* identified an entity that's hit softer targets with success. My sources at the NSA detected two breaches to local government systems—a tax agency, and an election registration system. From what we can tell, the systems weren't actually tampered with, but the data was exposed."

"That's unfortunate," Richard commented. "But what does that have to do with us?"

"Well, it seems the same entity has been escalating attempts on some of our corporate clients, though they have not yet been successful."

After another sip of whiskey, Richard asked, "Who is this entity?"

"Well, that's where things get interesting. We believe it's a unit of the Russian GRU intelligence agency, called Fancy Bear. I think we need to counterstrike, but I need your authorization—"

Richard interrupted, "Why not let the NSA handle this one? We can share intel, certainly, but why do you want us involved in the counterstrike itself?"

"Well, as you know," Owen said, placing his glass on the table, "it wouldn't be our first counterstrike. In those, however, we acted as a silent partner, and the adversaries in question never knew of our involvement—or at least we did our best to cover our tracks. But this time…" He trailed off for a moment, looking uncomfortable. "This time, they targeted Golden Bay Labs. I'm not sure how that little lab made their radar—it could just be by chance, but I think they discovered it's within the Galanteen sphere of influence. And if they do breach Golden Bay's network—"

"They wouldn't acquire the power of digital transcendence," Richard said. "The Cendovian code isn't there. And without a scanner, they couldn't do anything. Still, it's too close for comfort."

"I recommend we increase the physical security presence at the lab," Owen said.

Richard nodded. "However, it could have been just a random attempt, and we might never see them again. Right?"

"Maybe. If that's the case, we shouldn't draw attention to ourselves. But if they come back at us, we must send a strong message to stay out of our way, and the NSA isn't going to do that for us. The NSA and GRU can otherwise duke it out until the cows come home, as far as I'm concerned, but we must make it clear that we are off limits."

Richard understood that cybercriminals, like most criminals, looked for the path of least resistance. A harsh counterstrike *would* likely push the attackers in another direction—or it could cause an international incident.

"What do you propose?" he asked wearily.

Prepared for the question, Owen said, "We're ready to strike as soon as they try us again. An immediate and direct response will leave the intended impression. We'll bring down some of the key systems used in their attack operations, followed by a local blackout."

For a while, Richard pondered this avenue silently. Owen had been in enough military operations to give Richard confidence in his guidance. Still, something nagged at him.

After finishing his whiskey, Richard asked Owen, "Do you have sufficient foresight to know where this leads? Will we end up escalating a Galanteen–GRU battle? Or will this truly be an effective deterrent?"

Leaving his drink unfinished, Owen stood and answered, "In my experience, a strong punch is generally a powerful deterrent. When it doesn't work, either the punch wasn't strong enough, or the enemy won't stop until incapacitated. Their reaction to our counterstrike will give you the answer."

With a sigh, Richard consented. "Okay. This is what I'll authorize—if they strike again, you can bring their computer systems down, but don't touch the power grid unless they hit an additional time. I don't want it to come to that, as there might be a collateral impact. Actually, before you hit their grid, I want an assessment of the potential impact, including key things like hospitals within the area. I don't want to put lives at risk."

"Naturally," Owen said. "We would make the outage short to send a message while limiting collateral damage, in any case. But I'll provide the assessment to you tomorrow."

As Owen showed himself out, Richard silently hoped the counterstrike preparations would be in vain. Yet, he was willing to defend their cause by any means necessary.

CHAPTER 38 – CHRISTMAS GIFTS

In a sudden instant, Richie was lying in bed, listening to the distant sound of the ocean as he studied the long morning shadow of the ceiling fan. Raising his hands close to his face, he traced the lifeline in his left palm with his right index finger.

Wait… he had hands? When had that happened?

Richie sat up and looked around incredulously. Had he been sleeping? The last he remembered, he was floating bodiless above the clouds. Was that just a dream? Or was this?

Richie's world now appeared amazingly realistic. While not quite authentic, the rendering of his skin was awfully impressive. He traced a vein down his right forearm and smiled. Beyond, he saw his torso, then legs, then feet below him. After wondering if he would ever walk again, he now possessed real legs. Richie rose cautiously to his feet, wondering if his legs would hold him. Slowly, carefully, he paced the room barefoot, like a kid trying on new shoes before going back to school. After two laps, he nodded approvingly.

It suddenly occurred to Richie that he actually *felt* his new body. The sensation of being in the scanner was gone. He was now fully present in Cendovia. It was such a leap forward that he wondered how long it had been. Just minutes earlier, Richard told him the date was March 20, 2013, Earth time. Richie suspected a lot of time had now passed on Earth to make all these advancements.

He walked out onto the bedroom balcony of what he realized was a beachfront penthouse. "Nice digs," Richie said to Richard. "You've really outdone yourself here."

No reply came, but Richie didn't mind. The view from the balcony was serene. The waves softly broke upon the shore more than twenty floors below him. White chaise lounges lined the sand in neat rows, and small hotels decorated the shoreline in both directions. Richie thought the beach volleyball courts were a pleasant touch, but there wasn't another soul in sight. It seemed like a lot for only him.

The warm breeze blew across his face as he ran his fingers through his hair, stopping midway to recall the last time he had hair. Without a doubt, he'd never before had hair this length. Curious what he would find, Richie walked back into the apartment to examine his reflection. In front of the full-length bathroom mirror, he admired the work that had gone into creating his avatar. It definitely resembled his old body, but with some differences. He appeared slightly younger, by way of some CGI airbrushing, but still tall with a broad build. Rather than being bald, he possessed long, gray hair. In delight, he laughed heartily, and his laughter echoed off the tiles. The physics, the acoustics, the rendering, and most of all the *sensations* were unbelievable.

"Hey, Richard," Richie said. He waited, but again no response. "Hello, anybody home?" The only sounds that returned came from the wind and the waves. Upon wandering the finely decorated apartment, Richie confirmed his solitude. Subsequently returning to the balcony, he yelled in vain into the wind. After a few minutes of calling with no answer, he determined it was time to move on. He re-entered the apartment, intent on going downstairs to the beach to look around. Maybe Richard was taking a bathroom break, he thought, but it wasn't like him to walk away without pausing.

While considering the possibility of a communication glitch, Richie attempted to open the front door, and found the knob wouldn't turn. Why would the door be locked? Were they trying to keep someone out? Or were they trying to keep him in? Once again, Richie returned to the balcony, and this time he proceeded to climb up on the ledge. With one hand on the wall to keep from falling, Richie recalled his fear of heights, and his heart raced.

His heart? Yes, his *heart*. Richard had even managed to simulate a pounding heartbeat, along with the rush of adrenaline, leading Richie to breathe deeply. The sensation was almost too real.

Perhaps, if Richard thinks I'm going to jump, thought Richie to himself, *he'll stop ignoring me. He wouldn't want me to kill myself. Can I even do that?* Next, he wondered if he could get hurt. To test this, he smacked his hand against the wall. He felt the pressure, but no pain. Upping the ante, he clenched his fist and punched the wall as hard as he could. Imagining the wall crumbling from his superhuman strength, he was quickly disappointed to find the wall remained unaffected. However, he appreciated that his hand remained undamaged and pain-free.

Enough testing. Time to take the leap. Richie bent his knees, mustered up the courage, and leapt off in a forward flip. For his first rotation, he executed a well-tucked flip. About a dozen floors up, his second flip unraveled. His flailing third rotation was interrupted by his head crashing into the concrete only a few feet from a grand swimming pool.

Richie's body lay awkwardly sprawled on the ground as he started checking his head for signs of wounds. There was no blood, and while not quite in pain, the hard pressure sensation across his body was unpleasant. He righted himself and took an inventory of his parts. All seemed in order, and the discomfort had now subsided. He was very grateful Richard seemed to have put limits on the amount of pressure he could experience.

Had anyone been there to witness his descent, his epic fail of a dive might have embarrassed him, but alas, he was alone. Perhaps Richard had abandoned him.

A sudden beeping sound interrupted this speculation. Richie followed the sound toward the ocean and found it coming from a smartphone on a patio table. Taking a seat under the shade of the umbrella, he cringed at the words on the screen: *"Thanks for dropping in."*

There were so many questions, and Richie didn't know where to start. So, he opted to type, *"Hey, Richard. You've been very busy, I see. Catch me up."*

Richard explained that he would no longer be the booming voice from the sky. While Richard still had access to view Richie's world, now that it was tangible, he felt their experiment would be more successful if they maintained an arms'-length distance between the two worlds. They were trying to devise a world worth living in, which meant Cendovia must feel like a world as equally worthy of supporting life as the world Richie had left forever when he transcended. For their sake, Richard didn't want Cendovians to feel like tiny creatures in a fishbowl, with Richard outside tapping on the glass.

Richard commended Richie for figuring out the pain and pressure limitations. Then he explained that Richie didn't yet have a sense of smell or taste. A very long time might pass before those would be available, due not only to challenges with providing the sensations to his neural network, but also to mapping those sensations onto items available in Cendovia.

"The way those two senses work on Earth," Richard elaborated, *"is based on particles and chemical reactions. But we don't simulate at the particle level. The computational load would be overwhelming."*

With his hands behind his head, Richie leaned back in his chair and asked aloud, "I don't need to eat, do I?" The cursor blinked back at him. "Fine, I guess you want me to type in my question," scoffed Richie. He quickly typed out his query.

"No," Richard said, *"you don't need to eat, nor* can *you eat. Also, I'm not going to respond to things you say verbally; you must text me. This is a step toward independence. I don't want you to become dependent on me as an omnipresent voice in your head. That's probably not healthy. So, you can't pray to me and ask me to show up. You must text me."*

After accepting Richard's terms, Richie asked, "You locked the door to test me, to determine if I would jump. Did you think I would jump out of madness, or out of curiosity?"

"I need to let you figure out things," Richard said, *"and explore your world. How boring would life be for you if I gave you all the answers? A world worth living in requires an element of discovery."*

This was certainly true, and as Richie admired Richard's cleverness, he wondered if that made him egotistical. Past the moment of self-reflection, Richie continued with his questions: *"Okay, tell me something I can't figure out on my own. What day is it?"*

Without objection, Richard replied, *"I don't mind telling you anything about Earth, but I'm not going to unveil all the mysteries of Cendovia to you. To monitor the situation, I can position my vantage point anywhere in Cendovia, so I can see and hear what's going on. Right now, I can see you at the patio table, but I can't be everywhere at once. I still only have two eyes. Oh, and it's Christmas Eve, 2013."*

For Richie, it was hard to get used to losing time. He had never lost more than two months before, but now, in an instant, he'd flashed forward nine months.

"Well," Richie said at last, "at least I'm aging better than you. So, tell me, omnipresent one, what have you been up to over the last nine months?"

Richard told him about the advances they'd made in CGI rendering to support the surrounding view. But it was the development of a body with tactile senses that took them so long to get back to him. *"We couldn't give you just one working body part at a time. A transition from feeling like you were in the scanner to feeling like a floating head would have driven you mad. We weren't keen on doing a live, reverse dissection of you."*

Richie thanked him for not gradually and excruciatingly piecing him back together. Yet he wondered how they'd managed to incrementally test their advances without using him.

"We didn't leave any other Richies on the operating room floor," Richard said, *"if that's what you're wondering. We found another volunteer who proved very helpful."*

This left Richie with even more questions—and more than a little anger boiling inside him. He would have appreciated the realistic nature of the sensation had he not been overcome by it. They had agreed there would be no other transcenders until he confirmed Cendovia was ready. Also, he wondered about the volunteer.

Observing the concern on Richie's face, Richard said, *"You will get to meet her soon. And don't worry, no one had to die for this."*

Richie considered the last statement. If no one had to die, that meant if anyone had transcended for the testing, then the transcender must still be alive. But surely Richard wouldn't bring a Cendovian to life while their human version was also still alive. They had agreed not to do this to others, for fear of fragmenting their identities. Then he realized Richard had said no one *had* to die. He didn't say no one died. Perhaps someone had already died and were then revived as a Cendovian. So, who was she? Virginia?

Virginia had not agreed to multiple resurrection attempts. It was something he hadn't even thought to ask her about at the time. Now, Richie wasn't yet convinced conditions were good enough for her. With only one shot, they couldn't afford to rush. They had to get it right.

Seeing the curiosity in Richie's expression, Richard said, *"I'm not going to spoil the surprise. First, I want to talk to you about your family. Your mother and I would like more children."*

Richie understood that he meant Pari. It was remarkable how inside the jokes got between the two of them.

"Specifically, we are going to give you eight more brothers—eight more transcenders from me, each created from backups a few minutes apart. They're going to help build out

Cendovia to be a much larger world than you see today. A vast world is required to keep life interesting, and to give people plenty to explore. I call them your brothers, because there is no other word. You and I are like twin brothers split well after birth, but you are also somewhat like a son to me, in that I chose to give you digital life. And yet, you were also me, as your life began when I was born. But to avoid getting too confused, I'm simply going to call all my transcenders my brothers."

Richie agreed to the terminology, but asked for more information about the plan. *"With my existing hardware,"* Richard said, *"I can accelerate their timelines up to six times the normal speed, so they will live almost a week in one Earth day. Each of them will be focused on building out a new realm. Ultimately, Cendovia will be composed of ten realms. You're living in the first realm of Cendovia, and the other realms will be connected to yours once they're ready. Each brother will use a different theme to start with, so they don't all go building the same thing."*

Concerned where this might lead, Richie asked, "And what are you going to do with them when they're done?"

As Richie tapped his fingers on the table impatiently, Richard said, *"I estimate they will take three Earth months to build their advanced realms. I imagine each transcender will enjoy creating them. However, in their timeline, it will feel like a year and a half of solitude, with only brief communications from me every few weeks. At the rate they'll be living, I can't spend a lot of time texting with them. We'll check in periodically to gauge their wellbeing, but eighteen months of near solitude has certain mental risks. Of course, they'll all be preoccupied with their work, but just as you know, they will know they cannot return to Earth. They will all know what they are sacrificing before transcending."*

"You mean the sacrifice of leaving Earth forever? Or something more?" Richie asked, dreading the answer.

"Once we connect each realm to Cendovia, each brother will be forced to choose to either accept death, or remain alive but unable to enter a realm occupied by another brother. If they remain alive, their timeline will slow down to match yours. The tablets they will use to design their realms will stop working at that time."

"Why confine them to their realms?"

The answer came quickly. *"Because I don't think it's healthy for too many versions of us to be interacting with each other. It's already confusing enough for you and I to be talking as often as we do. Severe mental strain may occur if you run into many other versions of us at once. These rules are Gerald's idea—they were inspired by some of his discussions at the Refactor Institute. He's really looking out for our mental health."*

Richie nodded his head and figured when all you are is a virtual mind, you don't have anything if you don't have your mental health. Now considering the personal ramifications, he asked, "Will I be able to go to those other realms?"

According to Richard, the realm-entry restriction did not apply to Richie. The realms would be vast, though, so it might be a long time before he would meet any of his brothers.

The eight brothers' names were chosen from highlights Virginia had made in a book of baby names many years prior. She miscarried in their first year of marriage, and shortly thereafter required a hysterectomy. Although she would never give birth to her own children, she'd kept the baby names book. So Richard told Richie, *"If you ever meet a Colton, Demetrius, Earnest, Hugh, Jacques, Neil, Sydney, or Troy, ask them if their last name is Nelson."*

How many of his brothers would choose death? Perhaps the pain of losing their Richardness would prove too much to bear. For the first time, Richie wondered if he would someday request the same option. If so, should he warn his brothers not to come over?

He put the phone down and surveyed his surroundings, considering this difficult question. Anything he feared could later turn out to be a hardship that made the outcome that much sweeter. Alternatively, any hopes he had could be dashed by an eternal existence in a prison of his own making. Like a toddler asked what his friends should be when they grew up, he couldn't possibly know the right answer. Thus, he did not object to the birth of his brothers.

Yet, something didn't quite add up for Richie. "You said there would be ten realms, but I'll only have eight brothers?"

"The tenth realm will be created by my last transcender, born from my final backup before my Earthly death."

"So," Richie said, slumping in his chair, "I guess that settles the right of succession question."

"Not necessarily. My last transcender might be called Richard and inherit all that goes with that—all my relationships, etc. Everyone would know him as me, and you as my brother. Or, I may flip that, and make him the last brother while you inherit the

crown. I have not yet decided, but what I have determined is that there is no reason you should die in Cendovia just because I die on Earth. So even if I do not choose to pass the crown of Richardness to you, I am now granting you eternal life."

Quite grateful, Richie thanked Richard while still hoping this life would be worth living. *"If I am to someday give you the right of succession,"* Richard told him, *"you'll need to stay up to speed with the events of my Earthly life, to at least carry some of that on. So, we should keep talking regularly."*

"Sounds good," Richie said. "Though, remember, you were the one who didn't call for nine months. I'm always available."

After agreeing to stay in closer contact, Richard continued to catch Richie up. Long hours at both Golden Bay and Warp Drive had led to the advances Richie now experienced. Marisa, Connor, and Victor had all become full-time employees while still remaining in school. CombatRidge had recently launched in a limited, public beta which generated a considerable amount of buzz. And while cyberthreats were growing industry-wide, Galanteen still prospered, and its clients remained well protected. A few select counterstrikes had clearly delivered the message that Galanteen was off-limits. Meanwhile, Gerald was enjoying his new role at the Refactor Institute, despite being disappointed he had yet to publish his book. Most publishers told him they failed to see the value in it.

Richie appreciated the update, but he found himself distracted by the mysterious identity of the volunteer he was going to meet. Upon inquiring about her, Richard merely said, *"You can open that gift in the morning."*

CHAPTER 39 – SEASON'S GREETINGS

On Christmas morning, Richard and Owen prepared for Richie's gift-opening to commence.

"Are you ready for a visitor? Sort of a temporary transcender?" Richard typed.

Still in his patio chair, Richie sat back and pondered this. How could Richard have added support for *temporary* transcenders? This wasn't something he'd considered when on Earth.

"What does that even mean?" Richie asked.

"An explanation will spoil the surprise. But trust me, it's completely temporary. Would you like to meet her or not?"

Though not understanding how this would work, Richie still wanted to meet her, whoever she was. He told Richard as much.

"She will think you're a visitor here, too," Richard said, *"and she will think you are me. To avoid scaring her, play along."*

Before he could respond, a voice startled Richie. Nearly stumbling out of his chair, he sprung to his feet, trying to find the source. Then he saw a young woman waving to him from across the pool.

"Hi, Richard," she called in a sweet voice.

He began walking up to her while she took cautious steps toward him. With each step, she appeared more confident. Soon her careful stride had morphed into a rapid dash straight at him. To keep his balance, Richie braced for impact as she leapt into his arms. He was still uncertain who she actually was, but it felt phenomenal to hold another person again. She squeezed him tightly and thanked him over and over.

Her voice was familiar. Suddenly, his phone—still in his right hand—started buzzing. Over her shoulder, he read the message, confirming his suspicion: *"It's Quinn."*

In an instant, his heart raced and his mind flooded with thoughts. How was this possible? How in the world could she be here with him? Had she died and now transcended?

Richie slipped his phone into his pocket and gently lifted her head from his shoulder. After studying her face, he gazed into her eyes, recognizing that familiar warmth and affection. This was actually Quinn. Back on

Earth, he'd always had a soft spot in his heart for her, like she was his niece.

"Quinn?" Richie asked tentatively, still not quite believing it.

"Who else did you expect?" she said, smiling brightly back at him. Both of them laughed, and he wiped a joyful tear from her cheek.

"How? How—"

Ignoring his question, Quinn said, "This implant is amazing! Wow, I really feel everything. Oh, my God, I'm whole again!" She buried her head in his chest, overtaken by an uncontrollable, guttural sob that caused her whole chest to convulse. To comfort her, he caressed her back and told her not to cry, but her emotions had to be released.

Back at Golden Bay, seven observers witnessed the interaction. Victor monitored Quinn's vitals from the control room as she laid in the scanner. He relayed to the others in the room that her heartbeat was at the high end of the acceptable range. Gerald wondered aloud if this was too much for her.

"Give her a chance," Pari said, holding her hand up.

A buzzing against her right leg caused Quinn to flinch. She stepped away from her embrace of Richie and pulled a phone from her pocket. A one-word message from Victor said, *"Breathe."*

In both worlds, Quinn took a series of deep, slow breaths.

"It works!" Tina exclaimed, clapping Victor on the shoulder. "Can you believe it? It really works!"

Pari and Gerald hugged tightly, James and Connor celebrated, but Marisa simply nodded, speechless, as she soaked up the miracle to which she had contributed. Today, she and her colleagues had achieved the rank of superhero. A paralyzed person now walked through and felt a world they had created.

Marisa had been provided only a cursory understanding of how the implant in the back of Quinn's neck made this possible. Basically, when activated, the device would send signals up through Quinn's brainstem, simulating the signals her body had once sent. Most incredibly, Quinn's physical body continued to conduct its autonomous functions. Her heart kept beating, and her lungs kept breathing. Yet, somehow, Quinn didn't sense that she was lying in the scanner at all—she was entirely immersed in a new world.

"Let's go for a walk," said Richie as he kindly took Quinn's hand. Suddenly aching to feel the sand beneath his toes and see if they got the sensation right, he graciously led her from the pool deck to the beach. Given that they both lacked shoes, he suspected Richard had wanted them to do this.

When he took his first step onto the beach, Richie was not disappointed. The sand felt gritty and warm, but not blazing hot. After a few steps, Quinn crouched down, grabbed a handful of sand, and let the grains sift through her fingers, grinning ecstatically. Richie mimicked her, and they watched in awe as the breeze curved the sand's path back to the ground.

~ ~ ~

Back in the bunker, Richard and Owen carefully monitored the situation. Owen had helped set up the secure connection between Richard's house and Golden Bay. Normally, Richard wouldn't put his equipment with transcendence software anywhere near an external connection, for fear it would be compromised. But this test required a secure connection, so Owen had made sure the Galanteen crew did a top-notch job making it practically impenetrable.

As an extra precaution—beyond the VPN and encryption software used for securing communications—they had the connection terminate at the laptop Richard had designated for external communications only. A special program they had written displayed a full-screen grid with many small squares that changed colors countless times per second. Next to this laptop was another laptop, displaying a similar tapestry. The second laptop was connected to the servers in the bunker that ran Cendovia. Each laptop had an external camera mounted to face the other laptop's screen. This fed graphical output from one side into the other for decoding, thus allowing data to flow from Golden Bay Labs to Cendovia and back.

The unusual approach ensured there was no physical or Wi-Fi connection from Cendovian equipment to the outside world, limiting the attack surface a potential hacker could attempt to exploit. There was no way for a hacker to transmit any virus into the Cendovian equipment, as it only accepted information about Quinn's virtual position and actions. There was no mechanism for a hacker to connect to any additional ports or exploit any vulnerabilities in the operating system or any other software on the Cendovian equipment, as they couldn't communicate with that software. In the highly unlikely event that they compromised the external laptop, their attack would stop there. Still, Owen had advised Richard to leave the bridge open for no more than twenty minutes, and he had wholeheartedly agreed, as twenty minutes was the maximum time they believed would be safe for Quinn during the first test.

~ ~ ~

As Quinn and Richie played with the sand, the CPU began running high. The complex rendering of the grains was processor-intensive. A text message told Richie to stop playing with the sand and try something else. Softly taking Quinn's hands, Richie guided her to her feet.

"Do you feel it, too?" Quinn said, looking up at him curiously. "I mean, you don't have the implant, do you?"

In search of the right lie, Richie looked out at the ocean, afraid his face would give him away. "No, I don't feel it," he told her.

"Sure seems like you do. I don't know how you can hold my hand like that without feeling. The way you interleave your fingers… that's got to be hard to do."

Knowing he should move off the subject, Richie couldn't help but say, "You mean you don't know how someone goes through a world without being able to feel? Of all people, I thought you would understand more than most."

Quinn smirked and pushed playfully at his chest. "I guess, but it's not quite the same." Leaving her hand on his chest, she said, "Your chest feels warm, and solid, but I don't feel your heartbeat." For a few seconds, she left her hand there to be certain. Internally, she felt her own heart beating fast, but when she placed her hand on her chest, she didn't feel the rhythm with her hand. "Guess they haven't coded for that yet," she said airily.

Richie told her to follow him as he jogged to a nearby palm tree and picked up a soccer ball. "Let's play kick," he said, tossing it down the beach. With tremendous vigor, Quinn sprinted toward the ball. While she'd enjoyed running when she was able-bodied, she told Richie that she had never given the experience the full appreciation it deserved. She kicked the ball back to Richie, and it landed a few feet in front of him.

Eager to play, Richie ran up to the ball and kicked it hard—far too hard—and it sailed over Quinn's head. Marisa joked that Richard should learn to kick like a girl. Of course, Marisa assumed she was watching an avatar that Richard was controlling from his home—she had no idea that Richie even existed. Pari and Gerald were the only ones at Golden Bay that day who knew his true identity.

Quinn went to retrieve the ball, which had rolled into a tiki hut. While Richie waited on the beach for her to return, his phone buzzed. A text from Richard warned they only had five minutes left, sending a stab of disappointment through him.

Unexpectedly, Richie heard something musical coming from the direction of the tiki hut. As he approached, he saw it was actually an outdoor restaurant, complete with a bar, tables for patrons, and a piano on a small stage. At the piano, Quinn tinkered with the keys. Many years had passed since she'd last played, but the motions quickly came back to her. Richie took a seat on a bar stool, enjoying her delight. After a little more practicing, Quinn offered to play him a song.

"Just the one, and then we have to go," he told her.

Back in the lab, Victor warned that Quinn's blood pressure and heart rate were elevated.

"Okay," Pari said. "Let her have this, then we get her out."

Gerald took Pari's hand while Quinn prepared to play. She began to sing a beautiful, classic ballad. Quinn belted out the opening lyrics with a passion that had been locked away for years and was now unleashed once more. Her virtual voice filled the air and the hearts of all who could hear her with profound joy. Again, Victor looked back at Pari while he pointed at Quinn's vitals on the screen. But she displayed no fear for her daughter's life, for Quinn had never been more alive than at that very moment.

Marisa closed her eyes to take in every note. But when Quinn hit a particularly high note, she opened them in a flash and asked, "Did you hear that?"

Bewildered expressions glared back at her. Everyone in the control room clearly heard Quinn's voice coming through the speakers. The waves breaking behind her were audible to all, and they saw her avatar playing the piano and singing beautifully. Why was Marisa spoiling this precious moment with a foolish question?

Marisa rushed over to Victor's console and hit the *mute* button. Everyone objected in unison, but Marisa simply put a finger to her lips and pointed at her ear. They all fell silent.

Closed up in their control room, with the speakers playing the sounds from Cendovia, they had not heard Quinn inside the scanner. Only Marisa had picked it up. The young woman was singing boldly inside the scanning bed, far more boldly than her weakened lungs should have allowed. With the Cendovian scene still playing on multiple monitors around the room, Victor adeptly switched one monitor to the scanner view. Instantly, they heard Quinn singing in harmony with her virtual voice.

Before this moment, they'd all believed they were listening to the most beautiful song ever. Now, they were undoubtedly sure.

Quinn's soul soared above her physical body, above her virtual body, above the ocean, flying high with the birds of which she had just sung. Tears dripped upon the ivory keys as she played the final notes.

When she was done, Richie stood and applauded. Quinn rubbed her eyes, then stood and took a bow. Though Richie would have loved an encore, he understood he would have to wait.

"It's time, isn't it?" she asked, and he nodded. "Will I get to come back?"

"Just click those ruby slippers together," he told her. Quinn embraced him one last time, and he squeezed so hard he thought he would break her, so hard she couldn't possibly escape.

Overflowing with joy, she kissed him on the cheek. "Thank you so much for this, Richard."

Then she was gone, and his arms were again empty.

Right before they deactivated the link, Pari administered Quinn's sedative. Not knowing how she would react to an immediate return to paralysis, they opted not to chance a waking re-entry on the first try.

In need of some alone time, Richie texted Richard, asking for an hour to go for a walk on the beach before being paused. The day's events were a lot for him to absorb, and he needed time to process it all. In addition, he told Richard that despite a few necessary improvements to make the world fully ready, it was very close.

"It would have been nice to have a drink at the bar," Richie joked.

Without promising alcohol, Richard assured him more advances would come over the next few months. They agreed to talk further tomorrow, and then Richard granted Richie his alone time.

~ ~ ~

Still in awe, Owen congratulated Richard on the day's major milestone. "Truly miraculous. You've done good, Richard. Real good." He gave Richard a congratulatory hug, and after a few minutes of reflecting on the experience, Owen decided to call it a day.

"Working only a half-day today?" Richard teased.

Owen smiled and replied, "See you soon, my friend. Merry Christmas!"

After showing Owen out, Richard also needed to take a walk to process what he had just witnessed. During the stroll through his neighborhood, he pictured another version of himself going for a similar walk somewhere else. Without intending to go there, he soon found himself across the street from Holy Cross Cemetery. Despite the slight rain shower that had started, now seemed the perfect time to go talk to Virginia. The thought of telling her they were close to reuniting comforted Richard as he walked through the graveyard.

Upon reaching her gravesite, Richard was surprised to find a bouquet on her tombstone. The shriveled flowers must have been lying there for a few days. In all these years, he hadn't known anyone else to visit Virginia since her funeral.

He picked up the bouquet and scanned the note attached: *Smert' bystro prikhodit ko vsem, kto vmeshivayetsya.*

Richard had no idea what this meant. Perhaps it had been placed on the wrong tombstone. He typed the sentence into his translation app and discovered the language was Russian. Chills ran down his spine as he read the message in English.

Death comes swiftly to all who interfere.

CHAPTER 40 – NIGHT MOVES

On a cloudy Sunday night in late February—the perfect kind of night for staying in—Marisa laid on the couch, reading her textbook on software architecture with a highlighter in her hand and wearing noise-canceling headphones. Connor sat at the kitchen table with his laptop, working on a programming class assignment. Both of them had been at it for a few hours, and as the clock struck eleven, Connor decided he was done working for the day. Closing his laptop with a sigh, he headed to the bedroom and changed into his swimsuit.

"You're going swimming *now*?" Marisa asked when Connor returned to the living room carrying his towel. "Um, it's like fifty degrees out." After living together for over a year, she'd become accustomed to his late-night swims, but it was far too cold for swimming for her tastes.

"The pool's heated," Connor reminded her with a smile. "I just need to clear my head, or I won't sleep. I won't be long." He leaned over and kissed her.

"Okay, have fun, Tiger—or should I say, 'Polar Bear'?"

Connor chuckled as he left the apartment. Their front door opened onto a third-floor walkway overlooking a small courtyard, beyond which lay the pool. A gentle breeze rippled across the unlit surface of the water, and no one else was about. The streetlamps in the parking lot beyond cast a dim haze over the pool deck, lighting his way.

At the far end of the parking lot, two figures in a black sedan observed Connor's progress toward the pool.

"How can we be sure they will answer the message when the time comes?" asked the man behind the wheel.

"I'll show you how," Yashira said from the passenger side, watching Connor make the short walk across the courtyard. "This will be fun. Stay and watch."

~ ~ ~

Connor set his towel down on a lounge chair and kicked off his flip-flops.

"Hi," said a female voice behind him as he stepped toward the water.

Instinctively flinching, he immediately felt stupid for doing so as he turned around. In the murky light, he saw a tall, barefoot girl wearing a sports bra-style bikini top and yoga pants. With a slight shiver, he replied, "Hey, you startled me."

"Sorry," she said meekly. "Can I share your towel? Forgot mine." In preparation for the swim, she started to remove her pants. He whirled around to face the pool and, in a choked voice, told her that was fine.

At the edge of the shallow end, he donned his swim cap and googles, preparing to swim some laps. On his first step down, her voice called to him again, this time from much closer. "Nice suit."

To his left, Connor saw she wasn't wearing a swimsuit—or anything at all, actually. Apparently she'd forgotten *that*, too. The girl was muscular and ripped with shoulder-length, straight black hair, and Connor felt his cheeks burning as he took in the sight of her sculpted physique.

She looks like some bodybuilder, he thought. *Maybe that's why she doesn't have a swim cap, or goggles, or clothes? Why is she naked?*

Tempted to tell her that her suit was nicer, he instead blurted out, "I have a girlfriend."

"Wonderful," said the girl with a coy smile. "Let's swim." Off she went to begin her first lap on the left side.

Baffled by the odd circumstances, he reminded himself that he loved Marisa as his heart raced. Also reminding himself he came there to swim, he resolved not to be scared off by some girl. To play it safe, Connor went to the right side, as far from the girl as he could get, and started his laps. The view underwater was dark, but Connor did see she had just turned around at the far end. It was too dim to tell if she had done a flip-turn.

A solid, competitive swimmer in high school, Connor had one quirk that always drove his coaches crazy. No matter how he tried to break the habit, he would only breathe on his left side. This provided him excellent visibility of his opponents on his left, but none of those on his right. Several times, his coaches had yelled at him for not seeing an opponent gaining on him from the right during a race.

So, when Connor completed his flip-turn, he lost sight of the girl on the return length. All he saw with each breath was the pool's edge. Once he turned again for his second lap, she had closed the distance between them significantly. In fact, he was startled to see her heading to the shallow end wall only a foot away from where he had come out of his flip-turn. Upon breaching the surface for a breath, he saw her only one length behind him on his left. The race appeared to be on.

With his heart rate already elevated—and since the purpose of his swim was to clear his mind—he decided not to sprint. At least not yet. If she began to catch him, only then would he sprint. A little friendly competition was harmless, he told himself.

When he reached the deep end, he suddenly felt a tug at the back of his suit. She had her right hand on his waistband and was yanking down. Instantly, he stopped swimming and grabbed both sides to prevent her from pulling it off entirely, opening his mouth to give her a piece of his mind.

A series of rapid maneuvers began with her wrapping her left arm around his neck. Connor let go of his suit with his right hand and grabbed her left wrist, trying to remove it from his right shoulder. In response, she wrapped her right arm across her left and squeezed both tightly around his neck in a suffocating hold. Her left forearm dug into his Adam's apple. Desperate not to be choked, he enlisted his left hand to aid in removing her arms.

Simultaneously, she wrapped her muscular legs around his thighs, squeezed tight, and took a deep breath. Unable to tread water while so confined, Connor sank with her on his back, swallowing a mouthful of water on the way down. With his legs trapped in her vise grip, he stopped trying to escape the choke hold and swam upwards with his arms. Despite the increased difficulty posed by carrying another person on his back, he managed to breach the surface. Unfortunately, this provided only her with a chance to breathe, as her airtight grip was now completely blocking his airway. They sank back under as his mouth filled with water once more.

On the way down, he pulled her wrists with each arm, but she hardly budged. He kicked off the bottom of the pool and, reaching desperately for the edge, caught it with his right hand just as they broke the surface again. He pulled them closer to the edge, but she kicked off the side with her right foot, propelling them back to the middle, and they sank again into the depths. A burning sensation filled his lungs, and he stopped fighting her as they descended.

At the bottom of the pool, he curled into a horizontal fetal position while again thinking of Marisa. This time he feared not temptation, but that he would be delivered to her in a body bag by this evil woman.

Thoughts of Marisa fueled a new burst of adrenaline, and with an explosive kick from his coiled position, Connor sprung upward toward the shallow end, rather than the edge. If he could reach standing depth before blacking out, he would use all his remaining energy to hopefully extract himself from her choke hold. Three long iterations of sinking and jumping later, he stood in the middle of the shallow end. With stars in his eyes, he pulled strenuously at her wrists.

Briefly managing to shake her hold slightly, he took one frantic gasp of life-giving air. As he did so, she growled in his ear, "Connor, if you hurt me, Marisa dies."

Connor froze. How did she know who he was? Or Marisa? She loosened her grip further, allowing him to inhale another desperate breath while she whispered menacingly in his ear, "I'm not going to kill you, but you should know that I'm not alone. My people are watching us. Should any harm come to me, my friends will kill Marisa before you return home."

The girl raised one arm up, pointing, and Connor briefly noticed headlights flashing in the parking lot. She then dismounted from Connor's back. He stood still while she waded around in front of him.

As he stared at her in horror, she added, "No one has to die tonight, so long as you listen carefully, Tiger. Now that I have your attention, I have a secret message for you." Then she caressed his right bicep and hissed, "I'll extract my delivery fee later."

Standing in the waist-high water, Connor listened to her message, shivering as a cold breeze crossed the pool.

~ ~ ~

Sprinting across the courtyard and darting up the stairs, Connor attempted to reach Marisa as fast as he could. In his haste, he didn't grab any of his belongings, including his keys. He knocked several times, getting louder with each set of knocks. Fearing he was too late, a wave of guilt washed over him. In a frenzy, he pounded ferociously on the door, causing the neighbor's light to go on.

Time to kick down the door, he thought. Naturally, he had never done anything like this, but he'd seen it in the movies. With his back to the railing, he stepped forward in one swift motion with his left foot and kicked his right foot toward the left of the doorknob.

Unfortunately, Marisa opened the door just as Connor's foot came down. Too late to stop himself, his right foot landed hard on her left hip as he fell through the doorway like a wounded long jumper. She landed hard on her back, barely managing to keep her head from hitting the ground.

"What the hell are you doing?" Marisa yelled, her voice filled with pain.

Connor jumped up, closed the door, and asked her in a panicked cadence, "You okay? I'm so sorry. Are you okay?"

She picked herself up off the floor, holding her hip and wincing. "You kicked me to the ground, you jackass! So, no, I'm not okay!"

Relieved that Marisa seemed unharmed—other than by him—Connor scanned the apartment for signs of danger. He dashed to the bedroom, flipped on the light, and found no one.

"What the hell are you doing?" Marisa asked angrily.

No time to respond. Instead, he grabbed the end of the couch closest to the door, lifted it from the bottom, and started dragging it toward the door.

"Connor, listen to me!" Maris insisted, sounding worried now. "Why are you soaking wet? What the hell are you doing? Are you high?"

"I'm not high," he grunted. "Someone attacked me. Help me block the door. We're in danger." By the time he finished the sentence, he completed blocking the door himself.

Marisa let go of her throbbing hip, staring at him. "Who attacked you? What danger? You're scaring me."

"You should be scared," Connor said, peering through the blinds.

"Sweetie, talk to me, please," she said, grabbing him forcefully. "What's going on?"

"I was attacked and told to give you a message," he said, panting.

"A message?"

"Yes," he said, looking at her with desperation in his eyes. "She told me to tell you that the Binary Messenger is coming. And that if I tell anyone else about this, she'll know, and my friends will die, and..."

Marisa gasped and covered her mouth, and then a question escaped it. "Die?"

Connor nodded. "And then she—she just let me go. Somehow, she knew a lot about us. She told me to hurry, to see if you were still alive."

While he shivered, Marisa grabbed a towel and wrapped it around him, hugging him to provide warmth. "We need to call the police," she said, squeezing him tight.

"We can't," Connor insisted, pulling back from their embrace. "I won't jeopardize you, or my friends. The police will be useless." Something about his attacker told him this was no college prank. Her apparent combat expertise, strength, and detailed knowledge of Connor and Marisa told him she was a pro. Connor didn't know how his attacker had gathered so much information about them or why she'd attacked him, and until he figured out, he couldn't contact the police.

Marisa raised her voice, "Honey, we can't just let this go. If we're really in danger—"

"There's no *if*," Connor said, bitterly rubbing his neck. "And the cops aren't going to guard us 24/7. They might not even believe me. What do I have to show them?"

Marisa looked him over and shrugged. "I don't know. I just don't want them attacking you again. I'm calling the police."

"I won't tell them anything," Connor declared.

"Then I'll tell them you assaulted me."

"That won't get me to talk," Connor said coldly, walking away. "I'm not going to risk crossing these people."

"Well, then, maybe some time in jail will knock some sense into you," Marisa yelled, as she picked her cell phone up off the table.

"You really think you're safe here alone without me?" Connor fired back, pivoting toward her.

Marisa finally relented. "No, babe. Of course not." She sighed. "Okay, fine, no police *for now*. But what happened to you out there?"

Visibly shaken, Connor relayed most of the details of the attack. He explained how his attacker tried to drown him in the pool, and that she had given him the message. He left out some of the more mortifying aspects of the attack. There was no need for Marisa to know the fact that his attacker was an attractive, naked woman, for example.

In every way possible, Connor wanted to protect Marisa.

CHAPTER 41 – UNPLUGGED

The next day, Richard gazed out the airplane window at the water far below. Not a single cloud marred the view, despite the fact that they had just reached their cruising altitude of thirty-five thousand feet. The other first-class seat to his left was empty, as Richard had purchased two tickets, valuing his space and privacy over the added expense. A man of his means could afford to charter his own plane to Fiji, but he considered that level of extravagance to be unnecessary. Plus, the thought of being on such a small plane for hours over the South Pacific reminded him too much of Amelia Earhart's doomed journey. He didn't want to suffer the same fate.

Many would have retired after amassing wealth like his, but money had never been a driving force for Richard. Instead, over the last few years, his drive for knowledge had only increased as his work finally began to bear fruit. Unfortunately, his 53-year-old body couldn't always keep up, and many long months of work and obsessing over his vision had left him fatigued. These three weeks away would provide him with the opportunity to recharge.

In Richard's experience, the best way to recharge was to spend time in different settings, being exposed to different things. So, for his 2014 spring getaway, he had planned an extensive trip to a collection of destinations, many of which he'd never visited. His first stop would be Fiji, where he would stay for three days. After that would be eight days in Malaysia, six days in China, and finally four days in Japan. Since his Tokyo stop would be a mix of business and pleasure with visits to several leading robotics companies—including one he owned—he'd left it for last. A bridge, of sorts, between his leisure time and the inevitable return to work.

As he looked forward to the adventures ahead of him, he wished Virginia was sitting beside him in the seat he'd booked in her name. Someday, they would be together again, he reminded himself. This brought his mind back to his work, and he realized he had some loose ends to tie up. Once he sent a few emails to some business partners, he could go off the grid entirely. So, he pulled out his laptop and started drafting an email.

Several minutes later, in search of the right way to phrase his next thought, he looked up and noticed something odd. The video screen on the chair in front of him displayed the image of a plane on a map. It showed their journey and how far they'd gone, which wasn't that great a distance just yet. This wasn't odd at all, but the small black letters at the bottom of the screen *were* quite odd indeed:

ProfessorRichardNelson.com.

The screen in front of Virginia's empty seat displayed an identical map without the URL.

Someone clearly wanted to send him a message in a very peculiar way. How had they delivered this message just to his video monitor? Immediately sensing the involvement of a hacker, Richard confirmed that all the anti-virus software was running properly on his laptop. He then opened a special, secure web browser Galanteen had provided him that had no support for plug-ins or cookies, and had extremely limited Javascript capabilities. The Galanteen techs said it was provably secure, and it was what they used to investigate suspicious URLs. Using this, he navigated to the URL, bringing up a blank white screen with the words *Hi, Richard* in large, black letters in the center. Below that sat a textbox with a *Submit* button beside it.

Richard typed *"Hi"* and hit enter. The word *"On"* replaced the greeting to Richard, and the seat-belt sign suddenly went on. A few seconds passed, then the page refreshed to show the word *"Off."* The sign went off again.

Richard grew alarmed, as it became clear to him that a hacker had compromised a portion of the plane's equipment. Were they only controlling non-essential equipment, like seat-belt signs and video displays, or had they also compromised the flight controls?

The answer readily presented itself. The next word was *"Bump."* A moment later, the plane dipped slightly. Most passengers assumed it was mild turbulence, so no one panicked, though it certainly caught Richard's attention.

"What do you want?" Richard began to type into the textbox, but he wasn't given the chance to finish. The screen went white and then changed to an image of a mock newspaper, called the *Nelson Gazette.* The main headline read *Choose Richard's Fate.* There were only two stories, each taking

up half of the page. On the left side, the title read *Hijacker Richard Nelson Downs Flight.* The article stated, *"Professor Richard Nelson hijacked Flight 7212, and ditched it into the Pacific. All 247 passengers are presumed dead. Recovery efforts are underway."* Below this, a button said *Choose Death.*

Richard did not click this button.

The title on the right declared *Hijacker Richard Nelson Thwarted,* and the story read, *"Professor Richard Nelson attempted to hijack Flight 7212, but heroic passengers and crew members restrained him. The flight diverted to Honolulu, where Nelson has been detained by authorities. His motive is still unknown."* A *Choose Life* button was underneath.

Neither option was satisfying to Richard, as he had no idea who was messing with him. Yet clearly, this was their game, and he was meant to be the player. Reluctantly, he chose life.

This led to another article that read, *"You must not tell anyone about this. If you do, we will know. If the plane changes course, we will bring it down. All communications are now under surveillance, including radio and Wi-Fi, and anything suspicious will be blocked. If you attempt to communicate with anyone, or we even suspect you are, we will bring the plane down. In five hours, you will receive your next instruction. Stay on this screen."*

Below this was an *Acknowledge* button. Once Richard clicked it, the screen cleared to show only a countdown clock, starting at *5:00:00.*

Richard dimmed his screen and put the laptop on the seat beside him, but made sure not to close it. He wasn't sure if the hacker's site would accept new connections if this one went down. Needing a walk to clear his head, he stood and went to the restroom. In the tiny space, he managed to wash his face as he attempted to make sense of the situation. His only option was to be arrested for an unsuccessful hijack attempt, thereby saving all the passengers' lives. This would undoubtedly ruin his life, and as a convicted hijacker, he would spend the rest of his days in prison.

Sluggishly returning to his seat, he glanced at the faces of the other people in first class, then through the translucent curtain at the people in coach. Many of them slept or watched movies. None of them knew their fate now rested in his hands. Most cruelly, to save their lives, he would have to become the most vilified person they'd ever known—the person who'd tried to kill them all.

Richard stood for a while with his hands on his hips. Behind him, a woman asked, "Are you all right, sir?"

Startled, he turned around to see the flight attendant and said, "Yes, thank you. Just stretching my legs."

"We do have a long flight ahead of us," she said, giving him a carefree smile.

Richard returned to his seat and pondered his choice between a life sentence and a death sentence. *There must be a better option*, he thought. Perhaps if he deduced why he was being targeted, it would lead him to that better option. Who would want to see him in prison? Or dead? What benefit would they gain? In the event of his death, he had willed all his possessions to Pari. But she would never betray him like this. Quickly ruling out betrayal from his trusted inner circle, he considered potential enemies.

Galanteen Systems conducted primarily corporate work and was known for network security assessments, implementing defensive network protections, and intrusion detection. They also occasionally partnered with government agencies to share intel. However, a more secretive aspect of their work was the offensive counterattacks they used to protect the interests of their clients. At first, these counterattacks were done in cooperation with the NSA, but gradually, they began to go it alone. Over the years, counterattacks had been conducted against Russian, Chinese, and North Korean hackers. The first responses were highly targeted toward the source entity and proportional. However, subsequent responses to the same entities were extremely disproportionate cyberattacks.

The message was always clear. Hit Galanteen, and they hit you back. Hit them again, they crush you.

Surprisingly, for all his notoriety, Richard had never encountered a single personal threat until now. And while Galanteen had likely created some enemies overseas, he didn't see how killing him would benefit those enemies. Richard didn't oversee Galanteen's day-to-day operations; although he was the company's CEO, he was very hands-off, leaving most of the company's oversight to Owen. Perhaps someone intended to send a bold message to Galanteen, and they didn't know Richard wasn't vital to Galanteen operations—or, they didn't care, and merely wanted revenge.

The strangest part to Richard was that they were giving him an option to live. It was possible that disgracing and imprisoning him might serve this enemy better, but how? The more he considered the situation, the more it seemed they wanted to take him alive, if possible. If they wanted him dead, they could have brought down the plane without ever telling him. He suspected that's what would have occurred had he not visited the URL they sent him. It just so happened that staying alive was his preference as well.

Richard considered discreetly telling the flight attendant or the pilot of the threat. But he knew any mention of a terrorist would result in diverting the aircraft—and if it got diverted before he received his next instruction, the terrorist would down the plane. Could he trust the pilot to wait to divert? Would the pilot trust him? And how would he prove any of this? All he had to show was a countdown clock, which he could have easily made himself.

He considered telling them only after he got the order to attack. This would ensure they diverted to Hawaii properly and landed safely. Yet, without proof he wasn't a terrorist, he would still likely be arrested. The case against him would be weaker than if he actually charged the cockpit, but there was still a good chance he would face prison time for making a terrorist threat.

The hours passed as Richard dwelled on his options. What if the next order wasn't what the choose-life article described? He believed they would tell him to charge the cockpit, but perhaps not. For a short while, he kicked himself for getting himself into this situation. Maybe he was too high-profile to be flying commercial, but chartered planes could be just as vulnerable.

Suddenly, the greater magnitude of the problem materialized before him. How many other planes could they penetrate? Was this even their first such attack? Had they taken Virginia from him early? She didn't have much time left to live when her plane had crashed, and he had always been certain that she'd committed suicide to go out on her own terms. Now, with *his* fate on the line, he was far less certain.

The countdown clock ticked down torturously slowly. With still two hours to go, Richard came to terms with his fate. He decided, in his last hours as a free man, he would watch his favorite movie, *Groundhog Day*. For the first time ever, he watched it without laughing once. When it ended, he still had eighteen minutes left. Up to that point, he hadn't accepted a drink from the flight attendant, fearing he wouldn't be prepared to act when the moment came. Now, he opted for a Jack Daniels to settle his nerves.

The clock reached zero, then reset to one minute with a new message. *"You have one minute to acknowledge, or we crash the plane. Acknowledge?"*

He clicked the *Acknowledge* button. The clock reset to five minutes and began ticking down. The message changed again. *"You have five minutes to attack the cockpit and get the plane diverted. Put up a good fight, or they won't divert. Acknowledge?"*

Again, he acknowledged.

Richard stood and swigged the remnants of his whiskey. He paused and studied the cockpit door. With his plastic cup in hand, he ambled forward. Upon reaching the galley, he grasped his chest with his left hand and collapsed face-first. The cup fell to his right, at a flight attendant's feet. The flight attendant now stood trapped in the galley and couldn't get out without stepping over him. After a reflexive squeal, she leaned over and frantically checked on Richard. A lady in the front row to Richard's left also jumped up to help.

The two women tried to gain Richard's attention, but he gave no response. "Don't move him!" the flight attendant instructed. She got on the radio, alerted the captain, then switched to the cabin intercom and pleaded, "If there's a doctor or anyone with medical training on board, please come to first class immediately."

The lady yelled, "I've got a pulse!"

The flight attendant leaned down and put her ear to his face. "I can hear shallow breathing."

Richard did not move.

A man came forward and presented himself as a doctor. "I'm only a podiatrist, but I can try to help." Once he checked Richard's vitals, he confirmed what the women already knew: Richard was still alive. Clearly out of his league, the doctor said, "This man needs to go to a hospital."

"Already on that," the flight attendant said. The captain came on the intercom and announced that, due to a medical emergency, they would be landing in Honolulu shortly. He instructed everyone to take their seats and prepare for a rapid descent. Those helping Richard worried about landing with him lying on the floor. Without knowing his injury or ailment, they didn't know if it was safe to move him. Hesitantly, they resolved to leave him on the floor until the paramedics arrived.

Listening to their discussion, Richard lay still, knowing they were wasting their time. No matter what, he wasn't getting up off that floor until they either landed or crashed.

CHAPTER 42 – ALOHA RICHARD

In his private hospital room, Richard lay inclined in bed, growing restless. After the plane landed, he had pretended to return groggily to consciousness. This allowed him to participate in putting himself on the stretcher, with the help of the paramedics. He claimed to have been dizzy right before he blacked out. The paramedics had checked his vitals and saw nothing unusual. Had this been a house call, they might not have even taken him in, but given that a plane was diverted for this, a hospital visit seemed obligatory.

On the ride to the hospital, Richard had feigned being light-headed, as he believed he needed to play along further. Given the slow pace of emergency room discharges, he had expected to sit in the ER for a few hours, but he was surprised to be admitted upon arrival.

Lying in his hospital bed, memories of vacationing in Maui with Virginia pleasantly filled his thoughts. To this day, he was still amazed she had convinced him to ride a bike down from the top of Haleakalā. The steep, winding roads with their many hairpin turns had certainly looked exhilarating, but far outside his comfort zone. Yet Virginia had a way of bringing out the adventurer in him, and to his amazement, biking down through the clouds had felt like they were angels descending from on high. Below the clouds, the breathtaking view of the island had tempted them as they reminded themselves to focus on the road.

It had been such a glorious, carefree day with the love of his life. Oh, how he missed her adventurous spirit. Sadly, this visit to Hawaii was nothing like that day.

While Richard waited for the results of his blood work, a sharp knock came at the door. A tall young woman entered the room carrying a gray backpack over one shoulder and rolling a suitcase behind her. This was Richard's luggage from the plane. She wore a white, long-sleeved dress shirt tucked into tan slacks, and her wavy auburn hair accented her amber eyes.

After placing the luggage by the wall, she sat in a chair next to the bed, adjusted her rectangular black-framed glasses, and introduced herself with a slight New York accent. "Mr. Nelson, my name is Agent Susanna Cohen. I'm with the FBI, and I'd like to ask you a few questions."

Agent Cohen flashed her badge, and Richard glanced at it. "Thanks for my luggage. What brings you here?"

Pulling out her notepad and pen, Agent Cohen said, "Mr. Nelson, anytime a plane lands unexpectedly, questions must be answered, and paperwork must be completed. So, if you'll be kind enough to indulge me, I would like to finish this quickly, and be on my way."

"Okay, I'm happy to help. Please, call me Richard."

She ignored the offer and asked, "Mr. Nelson, can you tell me what happened to you on the flight?"

"I started to feel a bit off—I wasn't sure why," Richard lied. "So, I headed to the bathroom, but when I stood up, I became dizzy. The next thing I remember was looking up at the paramedics."

Scribbling notes, she ran through a quick succession of questions. "Did you take any medications today?"

"No."

"Drugs or alcohol?"

"No drugs. Just one glass of whiskey."

"Could someone have slipped anything into your drink?"

"I don't believe so, but I suppose it's possible."

"Did anyone put you up to this?"

"What?" Richard objected, perhaps a little too defiantly.

"Mr. Nelson—"

"Richard, please."

"Fine, *Richard*," Agent Cohen relented with an exasperated sigh. "We live in a post-9/11 world now. We're required to ask lots of questions that might seem out of the ordinary. Please answer."

"No, no one told me to pass out."

"Anyone tell you to divert the plane?" she asked, looking up from her notepad to study his face.

"Yep," he replied, trying for a jovial smile. "We all took a vote, and everyone said they wanted to stop in Hawaii on the way to Fiji."

"Please, Mr. Nel—Richard, I have a job to do. I'm sure you can appreciate that."

"I can," he offered apologetically.

Agent Cohen stood to join him at his bedside and asked if he knew the FBI had already analyzed the plane's Wi-Fi router logs. Richard said nothing. She then asked if he had ever visited the website ProfessorRichardNelson.com. This was met with a blank stare. Leaning over him, she asked with suspicion why anyone on the plane would visit a blank website named after him more than a dozen times. A simple shrug was all she received.

Turning her back to him, she gazed out his hospital window, looking at the ocean between the buildings across the street. "This is a nice view, Richard. I requested a private room for you, so that we could have this conversation. But I can't promise you as breathtaking a view in prison." She pivoted back to face him. "It's against the law to lie to the FBI, as I'm sure you are aware."

Richard watched as she leaned against the window frame and waited. An important part of any interrogation was letting the other party fill the silence. The listener had the power. Richard wanted to tell her the truth, but he also didn't want the FBI digging too deeply into his affairs. If he stuck with his sickness alibi, perhaps he could slip past all this. But then who would stop these terrorists? How many planes would they crash?

He had to take a leap of faith.

Richard told Agent Cohen all about the messages he had received. To his surprise, she seemed disinterested, using her smartphone while he relayed all the details.

"Richard, do you know who owns the domain name ProfessorRichardNelson.com?" Agent Cohen asked. He admitted he did not. Then, returning to his bedside, she showed him the domain registration on her phone, which revealed the registrant's name as Richard Nelson, followed by his contact information.

"Mr. Nelson, I'm going to do you a favor. I'll keep your delusional story out of my report. It would surely harm your reputation if it got out that you thought your own website threatened you. I suggest you stay here a while, and make sure they check you out thoroughly."

"I'm not crazy!" Richard insisted. "There's a real threat!"

With her hands on the bed rail, Agent Cohen said, "Let's say you're right. All your evidence points directly back to you. I know you don't want me to follow it there, and I don't want to waste my time on that. If by some miracle, what you believe is actually true, you should follow their orders and tell no one. You certainly don't want to be the reason people die. But if you find some actual evidence, here's my card. Please, call me day or night from anywhere. If this turns out to be real, I promise I will help you stop them. Now, get some rest, and I truly hope you enjoy Fiji."

She leaned over and kissed his forehead, as though he was an old man on his deathbed. This was unexpected from an FBI agent. Richard eyed her in silence as she exited the room. He wished she had believed him—he certainly didn't want her pity—but perhaps it was better this way. At least he wouldn't be spending the night in jail.

Once the door closed, he jumped out of bed, opened the small compartment of his backpack, and pulled out his phone. He closed himself in the bathroom and attempted to call Pari. To his frustration, there was no signal, but he found the hospital's public Wi-Fi. He wasn't thrilled about the potential security risk posed by using public Wi-Fi, but he didn't have much choice—he had to get a message to Pari.

With the aid of a special application on his phone, he sent an encrypted text message to her. Only Pari knew the decryption key. His message contained just one word: *canary*.

Impatiently, he awaited her response. A minute later, when it finally came, he decrypted the message: *coal mine*. She had acknowledged that he was in trouble.

"My plane's network was breached by hackers," Richard said to Pari via another encrypted message. *"The attackers contacted me during the flight and ordered me to divert the plane, or they would bring it down. After faking an illness, I am now in the hospital in Honolulu. Should be discharged soon. They wanted to get me arrested, I think, or keep me from leaving the country. Not sure. Don't know who is responsible. They ordered me to tell no one, or they would start crashing planes. The FBI doesn't believe me. Share this with no one except Owen. I will contact you when I reach Fiji."*

After pressing *send*, he registered how odd the last sentence sounded. Faced with a threat to his life and freedom, was he really going to continue with his vacation? It wasn't too late to turn back. Yet was a flight back to

San Francisco any safer than a flight to Fiji?

If things went south, at least he had Richie to replace him—though that would be little consolation for ending up dead. It was possible that the attackers were simply operating from inside the plane—they might even now be en route to Fiji and could be waiting for him there.

He tried to rationalize continuing his vacation, because he wanted it so badly. Ultimately, though disappointed, he deemed it too risky to continue.

Richard decided to check his laptop for evidence to convince Agent Cohen. Perhaps his browser cache had saved the messages he'd received. That would certainly bolster his case. But in his bag, in place of his laptop, was a note that read: *We have something of yours. You have something for us. Let's arrange a truce at your next stop.*

An odd word choice, he thought. They must have meant trade. Had it not been handwritten, Richard would have thought autocorrect messed up the phrasing. Perhaps their English wasn't very good, or perhaps they were in a hurry, although the handwriting did not appear to indicate haste.

A wave of dread descended upon him. He had intentionally removed all sensitive materials from the laptop, but in preparation for the trip, he had added Virginia's backup file, just in case of an emergency. This way, in the unlikely event his house was destroyed, he wouldn't lose her. Richard didn't trust putting her backup anywhere else outside of his house, except with him personally. To safeguard his work, he had compiled the simulator with Virginia's backup file in such a way that it could only be used to simulate Virginia and never anyone else. Furthermore, his laptop drive was heavily encrypted, which made it merely an expensive paperweight to anyone but him.

Yet, if these sophisticated hackers somehow broke the encryption—the odds of which were nearly zero—they would have Virginia. It was highly unlikely that the hackers would ever achieve this, so his logical mind told him not to venture into their trap. That would only make things worse. Plus, he had another copy of her in his bunker. Still, his heart said he had to save Virginia. Even if there was only a minuscule chance she was in danger, the magnitude of that danger was practically infinite in his estimation. They could torture a digital version of her endlessly to get to him, or for her valuable secrets.

"Come home, Richard!" Pari said via another encoded message. But for Virginia's sake, he would not go home—nor could he tell Pari what was going on. Not like this. They had agreed never to discuss their work outside of his home, and now more than ever, it was too risky to do so. If he told her they had Virginia, and somehow his encrypted message was compromised, they would know the true value of what they had. He couldn't allow that to happen.

"Trust me," said Richard's last message of the day to Pari. *"I must continue. Radio silence until you hear further from me."*

CHAPTER 43 – PARADISE WASTED

Quinn leapt up and swatted the basketball out of the air, sending it flying across the court and into the sand. For extra emphasis, she wagged a finger in Victor's face. Victor held his VR headset with one hand as he searched for the ball. About twenty feet beyond the court and a few feet from the shoreline, he located it. Careful not to run into the very real walls in Golden Bay Labs' VR room, he walked methodically to retrieve the ball.

In the scanner, Quinn was unencumbered by the physical world, as she only felt the virtual one. Consequently, she ran to the basketball and arrived well before Victor. "Your ball, slowpoke," she said, as she tossed him a chest pass.

Upon returning to their game of virtual basketball, Quinn reflected on her gratitude. She was grateful to Connor for designing this court next to the tiki bar, and to Marisa for coding the scoreboard. She was grateful to play sports and to have friends again. Most of all, she was grateful for her best friend, Victor. When she didn't see what could be, he helped her navigate through her darkness. Even when she saw herself as lesser, he never did. In that respect, he acted much like her adoptive parents, but sometimes a different messenger was needed to help the message sink in.

Every Sunday, he would pick her up at her house so they could play together at Golden Bay Labs. Twenty minutes of basketball, a break, twenty minutes on the piano, lunch, and then coding together back at her house. That was their routine. Sundays were the highlight of her week and the day she felt most alive.

Today was a special treat, as he'd taken time out of his schedule to play with her on a Thursday, after she'd finished her scan for the researchers. With ten seconds left and the score tied at seventeen, Victor missed his shot, and Quinn said, "Next shot wins the game!"

As Quinn dribbled the ball at the top of the key, he agreed to her suggestion. But when she raised the ball to shoot a three-pointer, Victor leapt for the block. Cackling over the way he'd fallen for her shot fake, she darted past him with a clear path to the basket. To recover from his mistake, Victor sprinted behind her vigorously. Again, he leapt to block her shot. Again, he failed. Her layup banked in while his momentum sent him crashing into her. They both collapsed on the pavement as he landed on top of her. Simultaneously, in the VR room, he almost collided with the padded wall.

At that moment, Quinn added her lack of pain in the virtual world to her gratitude list. Still, she did sense the pressure of being knocked to the ground and having Victor fall on her. With only a VR headset and two haptic gloves, the experience was mostly visual for Victor.

Quinn laughed at him for letting a girl beat him…again. As revenge, Victor picked her up and carried her across the beach and into the ocean. Both of them laughed as he dunked her playfully. This was hardly revenge—she loved being held again.

The water came up to Victor's elbows as Quinn lay across his arms. Warm water soaked her clothes, and she relished the sensation. "What do you call this place?" Quinn asked, staring up into Victor's face and the peaceful sky above him.

"I dunno. What do you think we should call it, Champ?"

Surveying her surroundings, only one word seemed appropriate: heaven.

~ ~ ~

Mountainous clouds of cotton drifted slowly above, benignly accenting the blue sky. Richard sat on a thickly cushioned white lounge chair, shaded by a large patio umbrella. A young couple of honeymooners frolicked in the infinity pool before him while a gentle ocean breeze whispered through the palm trees. Calm waves of an ocean that extended unimpeded out to the horizon lapped the idyllic, white-sand beach.

Richard sipped his mai tai and reflected on the peaceful paradise he would soon leave behind, admiring the serenity of the strangers surrounding him. Though he longed to share in that feeling, it was not to be. In a few short hours, he would be leaving Fiji behind, but his uneasy mood would travel with him.

His trip from Hawaii to Fiji had been uneventful, even as he waited anxiously for the next attack. He'd been relieved to finally arrive at the resort, albeit a day later than planned. When he was led to his luxurious villa, he'd wondered if he was the first guest to ever stay there alone. He wanted to feel the innocence and joy so many others experienced in this place.

Longingly, he wished for Virginia by his side.

An ornate king canopy bed with lace curtains accented the romantic master bedroom, and a gift basket with fruits, nuts, cheeses, and wine had awaited his arrival in the middle of the bed. The attached handwritten card read, *Sorry I missed you. See you at the next stop. Enjoy! 42696e6172794d657373656e676572.*

The handwriting was the same as the note in his bag, and any hope he had of putting his worries behind him had vanished. The gift basket may have been from the hotel, but the card surely was not. Was he being lured deeper into a trap? Or was this a ruse to make him lower his guard until his next stop in Malaysia?

An apprehensive feeling had loomed over him for the next two days. Each morning, he would send a brief encrypted message to Pari, to let her know his location and confirm his safety. He also reminded her to only contact him for emergencies, not wanting her to pester him about turning back. After that, Richard tried his best to enjoy his time in Fiji. The Koroyanitu hiking trip the previous day had been his favorite part. But as he took in the breathtaking view of the lush island, he had pondered why someone would write a long string of characters at the end of the gift-basket card. He guessed the hexadecimal string represented a cryptographic key, though to what, he didn't know. Someone was toying with him, but he had no clue who or why.

Richard raised his glass and silently wished the young honeymooners a lifetime of ignorance of the dangers he knew and the dangers he had yet to discover. Then he placed the glass down and departed for the airport.

Once he got into the cab, he inspected the driver's face, looking for any signs of ill intent. The entire ride to the airport, he monitored his GPS to ensure they were staying on the proper route. This was the same procedure he'd followed from the airport to his hotel. Both times, these efforts proved unwarranted.

Richard remained on high alert as he walked through the airport, studying the faces of the strangers around him. When he went to use the restroom, he opted for the largest stall, instead of the urinals, to put some distance between himself and the world. And in the terminal, as he waited for his flight, Richard selected a seat in a corner with his back to the wall. It didn't afford him any privacy from the crowd, but it allowed him to see anyone who might approach him. Fortunately, no one did.

To get to Kuala Lumpur, Richard had to catch a connection in Auckland, New Zealand. Again staring out the window from his usual first-class seat with the empty seat beside him, he asked himself how long he would feel like he was on the run, watching over his shoulder for someone to catch up to him.

Then came the moment he had been anticipating for days—the next contact.

"Mr. Nelson?" a voice called to him.

After suppressing a flinch, Richard turned to find a flight attendant looking at him. Who was she, really? How did she know his name? About to ask, he suddenly remembered it was customary to greet first-class customers by name.

"Can I get you anything, Mr. Nelson?" she asked.

He opted for whiskey to calm his nerves. Vigilance for the rest of the flight proved unwarranted, and after remaining on guard during his two-hour layover in Auckland, he determined he'd need to sleep overnight on the next flight. Sure enough, despite his paranoia, sleep came several hours into the ten-hour flight, though it took a few drinks to get him there.

After a four-hour drive to Penang, Richard finally reached his room around 9:00 a.m., tired and desperately needing to relax. He surveyed the room and discovered yet another gift basket with a handwritten note. This one said, *Sorry to do this again. Let's definitely meet in China. 42696e6172794d657373656e676572.*

Another note stringing me along, he thought, flinging it down. Tired of this game, he resolved he would spend today relaxing. He called the front desk to schedule a massage for later in the morning, then decided to partake in a drink by the pool while he waited. If his attacker wanted him, they would have to stop running and confront him directly.

The long day of travel had left Richard yet again lying on a lounge chair, under an umbrella, sipping a drink in front of a pool. The pool here was less expansive, but otherwise he found it to be simply a different version of the same day. Another day of trying to numb his anxiety as he played the waiting game. He guessed this was how Bill Murray's character felt in *Groundhog Day*.

A basket of fries sat beside him. Upon placing his order, he asked himself if he had actually flown halfway around the world to eat fries with a cocktail for breakfast. Yet, he couldn't stomach much more until he calmed his nerves, and he didn't know when that would happen. During his breakfast of champions, he watched the other patrons bathing in the sun. No one seemed to be alone, by his estimation—except for him.

On the positive side, one benefit of staying at the nicest resorts was the beautiful surroundings filled with attractive people. Two gorgeous women in their early twenties stood from their chairs across the pool and dove in together. They laughed and splashed, and Richard remembered how vibrant Virginia had been, before the cancer drained that from her. She was a beautiful woman with an ever-present smile, even on the darkest days.

Richard wondered what she would think of the man he'd become in her absence. Four years had passed, and he had not moved on. He hadn't gone on a single date since she passed, and he kept even the closest people in his life at arm's length. This left room for Virginia. The fear of her slipping from his memory tormented him constantly, which was why he still talked to avatars of her. How cruel it would be if, upon their reunion, he had only a distant memory of her, while she remembered him like it was yesterday. He would go to extreme lengths to ensure she didn't suffer that fate.

Yet, was he truly honoring her memory by living this way? Would she have wanted him to take this yearly trip alone? Doubt crept into his mind. Some colleagues at Stanford had tried to encourage him to date, but he always refused. Only the Pikes knew the extent to which he had been clinging to Virginia—only they were aware he had been preparing all this time for her resurrection. That's why Pari, his closest friend, had never pressed him to let go. Both of them understood that he might be the first widower in history who didn't actually need to mourn and move on. This gave him hope, but it didn't vanquish all doubt.

Like a background thread taking control of the process, a different line of thinking interrupted his moment of self-reflection. Perhaps the hex code at the end of the card wasn't a cryptographic key to unlock something else. Maybe it was the message to be unlocked—a message that would tell him what to do next.

Richard grabbed his cell phone and found an online hex to string converter. Carefully, he typed the code from the card into the converter. His pulse quickened with each character, hoping it would tell him what to do next. Once he finished typing the last character, it displayed the word *BinaryMessenger*.

He was right! It wasn't a key, but rather a message. More precisely, it was the signature of his new enemy.

Suddenly, Richard heard a woman say, "Hello, Richard."

He nearly dropped his phone as he took in the sight of a lovely young woman in a white, strapless bikini top. "Whoa!" Richard exclaimed, startled by her presence.

"I'm flattered. Truly. Is this seat taken?" said the woman as she removed her white knee-length wrap to reveal a pink string-bikini bottom that accentuated her toned legs. Not waiting for a response, she sat on the lounge chair to his right and let down her long auburn hair. Richard silently admired how it accented her tanned skin.

"Agent Cohen, what are you doing here?" he asked, gathering himself. "Are you the BinaryMessenger?"

"No," she replied warmly, "but it seems we're both in search of the same person. Please, call me Susanna. I'm off duty."

Susanna explained that upon combing through the plane's Wi-Fi logs, she'd encountered something peculiar. Though the logs didn't contain the content of the traffic, they did record the size of the requests and responses. For all the traffic to a blank website, the responses should have been small and identical, but that wasn't what she'd found. The blank website response size was under one kilobyte, but the logs showed much larger responses. This corroborated his story that the website wasn't always blank. It wasn't much for her to go on, but it was a start.

Her supervisor at the FBI had dismissed it as nonsense, as Richard could have just edited the site himself, and maybe he was delusional. So, while Susanna's boss wouldn't approve her pursuing it, Susanna herself had a hunch that Richard had told her the truth. And with such severe consequences at stake, she couldn't ignore the possibility Richard was right. So, she'd tracked down his itinerary, quickly put in for some vacation time, and came out to help Richard on her own dime.

After days alone, it relieved him to have an ally. In his moment of doubt, he needed someone who believed him. Unconcerned about the money, Richard assured her he would cover her expenses, if the FBI would not, and thanked her for coming.

Then Susanna asked how Richard had heard about the BinaryMessenger, and he explained what he'd just decoded. She brought up ProfessorRichardNelson.com and showed him the page source. Though it was a blank page, it still had a tiny amount of HTML markup, and a comment in the HTML header read *Copyright 2014, BinaryMessenger.*

The messenger was clearly taunting him.

Just then, his phone buzzed, reminding him of his massage appointment. Enthusiastically, Susanna said to him, "Sounds perfect. I could so use a massage after that long flight. How about a couple's massage?"

Involuntarily, he scanned her amazing body, and she winked at him. Looking into her beautiful amber eyes—eyes that reminded him so much of Virginia's—he leaned closer and mustered the discipline to say, "I think separate is better. We probably shouldn't be seen too much together. The BinaryMessenger is expecting me to be alone, not with an FBI agent. But since you flew all the way out here for me, and I imagine the FBI won't reimburse you for it, you can charge your massage to my room."

Patting his leg, signaling it was time to go, Susanna smiled at him. As they walked together to the spa, she said, "You're a good man, Richard, but it's already done. I switched your massage to a couple's massage."

Surprised, Richard said, "Why would—"

"You're in danger, Richard," she said seriously. "The other reason I came all the way out here was to protect you. I'm not letting you out of my sight." Again, Richard thanked her. "In fact, I'm sleeping in your room tonight. On the couch, of course. I already put my bags in there, so it's settled."

"How did you get my room key?" he asked curiously.

"Turns out if you walk into the lobby in a bikini, men will fall all over themselves to help you," she said, rolling her eyes. "I told the clerk I lost my room key, and can you believe he asked me for identification? Do I look like I have pockets in this thing? Anyway, once he took his sweet time verifying that I indeed had no pockets, he gave me the key."

She cheerfully waved the key card in front of Richard. Amazed at how far this FBI agent was willing to go to protect him, Richard considered Susanna to be most impressive indeed.

The massage therapists led them to their room and gave them a moment to undress and lay themselves down under their sheets on separate massage tables. The soothing, tranquil melody of meditation music surrounded them. Out of modesty, Richard asked Susanna to turn her back as he undressed, and she obliged. He quickly slipped himself under the covers, lying face-down on the table on the right. Though tempted to turn left to watch her undress, he was too respectful to allow himself to do that. His gaze fixed on the floor, he flinched when her left hand unexpectedly touched his upper back through the sheet. "It's okay, Richard," she whispered in his ear. "I'll protect you. You must trust me."

Then a sharp pinch jabbed into his right buttock, announcing his departure from consciousness.

~ ~ ~

In the back of what appeared to be an ambulance, Richard stirred awake, strapped to a gurney. Everything was hazy. He tried to speak, but before the words formed, the male paramedic beside him injected more medicine into Richard's IV. The world faded away again.

The echo of heels clanking heavily against steel stirred Richard awake again some time later. With his eyes blindfolded, he couldn't see who approached him. He found himself standing in a wide stance, and felt tight chains extending away from each bound ankle, preventing him from shifting his posture. His arms were similarly chained at the wrists, his body spelling out an involuntary X. Chilly air drifted over his exposed skin, and

Richard realized he was naked, save for a rough piece of fabric secured around his waist with electrical tape. The same electrical tape covered his mouth.

From the sound of the footsteps, Richard guessed his captor was a man. He stopped close enough that Richard could feel the man's breath on his face, though the man said nothing. Richard tried to speak, but with a rag in his mouth and tape over it, nothing could be understood.

So many questions jockeyed for his attention. Why had Susanna betrayed him? Who was she really? And where was he?

The man offered no answers. He only continued to breathe on Richard, a predator salivating over its prey.

CHAPTER 44 – CRYPTIC COMBAT

Awake again, Marisa lay on her side, watching Connor sleep. An hour earlier, he'd awoken from a nightmare, screaming, which had become a nightly occurrence over the last five days since the incident. Now he rested, momentarily at peace.

Seldom was he at peace anymore.

Every waking moment, Connor was on edge, never allowing Marisa out of his sight. He attended her classes with her, including the ones he wasn't enrolled in. He spectated all her diving practices, despite having left the team himself after his freshman year to focus on his new job. As an extra precaution, they took random routes to Warp Drive every day. On his insistence, they were home before dark every evening. And every night, they slept with the couch blocking the front door.

Connor had her on a lockdown that made her overprotective mother seem lax, and Marisa wondered how much more she could bear. She didn't want to look over her shoulder forever. During the day, she had tried to convince him to swim laps to burn off some of his anxiety, even offering to sit poolside and keep watch. But he refused to go back in the pool.

Glancing at the nightstand, she glared at the clock: *2:18.* With a loud sigh, she rolled onto her back and stared at the ceiling. This was no way to live. Who would attack Connor to give *her* a cryptic message? She had lots of friends, but no enemies—nearly everyone got along well with her. For a long while, she pondered the possibilities. *Lucas?* No; those CombatRidge battles were over a year ago. That was a long time to wait for revenge. Plus, why send a girl to bully Connor, when Lucas was bully enough to do it himself? No, that didn't fit.

Another thread took command of her thoughts—a thread that had been running deep in the background, only to creep in during the most silent moments. She felt guilty for even entertaining the idea, but…

Was her boyfriend going mad?

Perhaps the attack had never happened. After the incident, there wasn't a scratch on him, and Marisa often questioned whether he had told her everything. Then she questioned herself for doubting the man she loved. But if she truly loved him, she needed to see what he might not be seeing. Was he going mad trying to protect her? Or was he trying to protect her because he was going mad? Marisa dreaded both possibilities.

Once the clock reached 3:00 a.m., she gave up trying to sleep. If she was going to be awake, she might as well do some work. Maybe that would help take her mind off Connor for a while.

Quietly closing the bedroom door, Marisa made her way to the kitchen. With a bowl of cereal in front of her, she opened her laptop at the kitchen table. Reflexively, she checked her email while putting a scoop of cereal in her mouth. Then she dropped the spoon with a loud *clank* into the bowl and covered her mouth in shock.

A CombatRidge friend invite from BinaryMessenger stared back at her menacingly.

An involuntary chill ran over her skin, and she was reminded of how much Connor loved her and of how thoroughly he'd been trying to guard her. Marisa was relieved Connor hadn't lost his mind, and she was ashamed for ever doubting him. But as suddenly as her relief had been replaced by shame, that shame soon took a back seat to fear. They absolutely *were* in danger. The email had only been sent a few minutes prior. Was another attack imminent?

Marisa silently praised Connor for barricading the door as she hurried to wake him.

Upon being touched, Connor jerked himself upright. Disoriented, he flailed his arms to fight off an imaginary attacker, knocking the lamp from the nightstand in the process.

"It's okay, it's me!" Marisa said, turning on the overhead light.

Connor took in his surroundings, clutching his pounding chest. His eyes completed their bewildered journey, looking up at Marisa. Distress dominated her expression. Everything was *not* okay.

"They're back?" Connor said, standing ready to fight.

"Not exactly. I got a message from them," she said, resting her hands on his biceps. Still gaining his equilibrium, he staggered as she led him to the living room. Marisa took a seat in front of her computer and showed him the message. "What do we do?" she asked.

"I think you need to fight him."

As Marisa started up CombatRidge, Connor stood behind her, unable to bring himself to sit. Begrudgingly, she accepted the friend request from the BinaryMessenger, her new frenemy. A moment later, she received a battle challenge from the BinaryMessenger, and she accepted that, too.

Curiously, the BinaryMessenger had set up the challenge as an untimed battle, although the default was now three minutes. This meant there was no battle clock counting down the match duration. It would instead be an old-fashioned battle to the death. Waiting for the fight to begin, Marisa had no idea what to expect. She wanted to kick some ass, but didn't know if that was even the point.

The BinaryMessenger had a custom skin neither of them had seen before. Dressed as a monk, he concealed his face within a void underneath the hood of a dark brown robe. Black gloves protected his hands and black boots adorned his feet. With no visible eyes, he was darkness incarnate.

The battle began, and the BinaryMessenger initially ducked, then stood back up. Next, he jumped, landed, and stood still. Marisa jabbed him in the face and received temporary satisfaction when his health meter ticked down. He ducked, stood, ducked again, stood again, and finally jumped straight up. The BinaryMessenger demonstrated no intention of either fighting or defending himself.

Growing impatient, Marisa lifted him up and tossed him over the edge.

"What the hell?" she wondered aloud. "He's not even fighting."

Right away, they received another battle challenge invitation from the BinaryMessenger. "Let's battle him again," Connor said, "but this time, only watch what he does. Don't fight."

"Right," Marisa said. "Maybe there's a pattern."

Upon her acceptance of the invitation, Connor grabbed a notepad and a pen. The dark monk opened with a duck and then stood back up. Connor wrote down *Duck*. Next, he jumped straight up. Connor wrote *Jump*. The BinaryMessenger continued ducking and jumping, and Connor recorded it all. Soon, Connor's *Duck*s and *Jump*s became a shorthand of *D*s and *J*s.

Then the BinaryMessenger did something new. He blocked while standing up, held that for a moment, and then let his guard down. Once more, he repeated this, then returned to ducking and jumping.

After a minute, Connor stopped writing. Both of them tried to make sense of what they'd just witnessed. Opening his laptop, Connor sat next to Marisa and typed the abbreviations into his text editor. Upon completion, they had a long series of letters:

DJDDJDDDDJJDJDDJBBDJDDJDDDDJJDJDDJBBDJDDJDDDD

Each of them studied the letters intently. "What does it mean?" Connor asked.

"I think there's a pattern," Marisa said. She reached across the keyboard and put a line break after the first *BB*:

DJDDJDDDDJJDJDDJBB
DJDDJDDDDJJDJDDJBBDJDDJDDDD

"Look!" she said. "The first line is repeated on the second line." She added another line break after the next BB, again altering the message:

DJDDJDDDDJJDJDDJBB
DJDDJDDDDJJDJDDJBB
DJDDJDDDD

"It keeps repeating," Connor said. "So, the first line is the message?"

"If he's a binary messenger," she said, "we need to convert the *D*s to ones and *J*s to zeros, or vice versa. Once we obtain the binary, I bet we can convert it to ASCII, but which are the ones and which are the zeros?"

Connor smiled admiringly at Marisa's discovery before returning to a serious expression more befitting their precarious situation. They decided to try both permutations. First, Connor tried the *D*s as ones and converted the first line to *1011011110010110*. Upon running it through a binary-to-ASCII converter, they received two non-printable characters, utter garbage.

Next, they tried the *J*s as ones, giving them *0100100001101001*. The converter told them this translated to *Hi*.

"Yes!" Marisa said. "The double blocks are like a stop bit."

Puzzled, Connor said, "Yeah, but they must want to say more. I don't think she attacked me solely to exchange pleasantries. How do we advance to the next message?"

Marisa suggested they might need to beat it out of them, and Connor told her to give it a try. Oh, how she wanted to pummel it out of them in person. They opened the next match with a punch, but the hooded specter stuck to his *Hi* pattern. Then they tried a kick. No difference.

They went through every attack they knew, but nothing changed. The menacing figure continued his merry dance to greet them. With the BinaryMessenger's health diminished, Marisol threw him into oblivion out of sheer frustration.

Clasping her palms together, Marisa said, "Maybe the next message will come in the next battle." Another invitation from the BinaryMessenger arrived, and she accepted the challenge, but the subsequent battle revealed the same greeting message.

They both stepped back from the computer and paced the room. It was nearly four in the morning, and they were each getting frazzled.

An idea struck Connor as he returned to the table with his own bowl of cereal. "The stop signal is the double blocking, right? Well, it could be he's blocking for input. Get it? *Blocking* for input. Maybe he's waiting for us to say something."

Marisa thought he was onto something, but asked what input they should provide. Connor answered, "Maybe all we need to do is tell him we're ready for more input. I think he wants us to tell him we're ready for another message. That we're blocking for input. Yashira said there was a message for you, not a conversation."

"Yashira?" Marisa asked with astonishment.

"Yeah, my attacker."

"Oh, my God! You *know* her?" she yelled, pent-up doubt erupting in her voice.

Caught off guard by her tone, Connor responded defensively, "No! That's just the name she gave me. Probably fake. I told you—"

"You never told me her name! All this time, you knew the name of your attacker, and you didn't tell me? Why would she even tell you her name?" Marisa thought the name sounded familiar, but she couldn't place it.

"I don't know!" Connor protested loudly. He paused and then, lowering his voice, he said, "I'm sorry. I really thought I told you."

Marisa peered down at him and began rubbing her thighs nervously.

"I'm sure it's a fake name," he insisted, rising to meet her and touching her right forearm gently. "And it doesn't matter, anyway. *She* doesn't matter. She's just some evil bitch who's after us. Remember, I'm not the bad guy here."

All the doubts of the past few days had welled up to the surface and were now overwhelming her. Logically, she understood he was right. Connor was the victim. Connor was on her side. He wouldn't intentionally hide something from her. Yet, the tsunami of emotions had to pass over her before she could return to Reasonland.

After exhaling sharply, he embraced her, and she squeezed him for dear life. They clung together, two desperate souls adrift in a vast, dangerous ocean.

When the tsunami finally reached the shore, and they were left floating in the remaining reverberations, Marisa gathered herself, kissed Connor, and told him, "We have to keep going." He reluctantly agreed.

After accepting the next battle request, they tested their double-block theory. Connor's text editor revealed the message as long string of *D*s and *J*s. Before they deciphered the meaning, they already knew it wasn't *Hi*, as it was longer than the first message.

Soon, Connor translated it to *Ransom*.

"Oh, God!" Marisa exclaimed. "Who's being held for ransom?" Both were terrified to find out.

The subsequent message was longer still, and when ultimately translated, it came down like a boot stomping on their throats: *We have Richard.*

CHAPTER 45 – A KING'S RANSOM

Marisa's hands began to tremble.

"I should've killed her!" Connor said, holding his forehead in his palms. In a quivering voice, Marisa prodded him again to continue. Line by agonizing line, they proceeded to decode the entire message:

Hi

Ransom

We have Richard

Pay $10M entry fee

Bitcoin Address bc1qar0srrr7xfkvy5l643lydnw9re59gtzzwf5mdq

You have 48 hours

No cops

Though it was now nearly 6:00 a.m., the weary and spent couple understood sleep wouldn't come this night. "Why would they think *you* have ten million dollars?" Connor asked. "How much did you make on Vexed Up?"

"Take away a few zeros," she said. "How do we know they really have him?"

Immediately, Connor tried calling Richard, but hung up as soon as it went to voicemail.

"Remember, he went out of the country," Marisa said. "He wanted to go off the grid, and he didn't tell us where. So, we won't be able to reach him." She paused for a moment, looking cautiously hopeful. "Maybe somebody is just taking advantage of this for a scam, when they don't actually have him."

"What if you're wrong?" Connor asked.

With her hands on her head, she said, "Well, we'll need a lot more money."

They debated what to do next, and Marisa didn't understand why Richard's supposed captors were so adamant about delivering this message to her and not someone else. They couldn't truly think she had the money, so they had to be expecting her to go to someone who did. But who?

Connor said, "If Richard's wife was still alive, I'd go straight to her."

He was right—Richard was by far the wealthiest person they had ever met.

That notion sparked an idea in Marisa's mind. Giving Connor a wink, she picked up her phone and selected a number from her contacts list. Connor watched curiously to see what she was doing. In a friendly voice—far too friendly for the circumstances—Marisa said, "Hi, my car broke down. Can you give me a ride to work?"

In a groggy voice, Pari said, "Um, it's Saturday."

Marisa told her Tina and James were unavailable and explained that she urgently needed to be at work soon. She pleaded for help, and when she told Pari that Richard badly wanted her to show up to work early, Pari firmly said she was on her way.

"Why are we going to work?" Connor asked, with a confused expression.

"We're not," whispered Marisa in Connor's ear. "Pack a bag. We're going to stay with Pari for a few days—she just doesn't know it yet. If we're being watched, I don't want to sit here, waiting to be attacked again. Now, hurry!"

Connor did not hurry, nor did he move. Marisa watched the wheels turning in his eyes as he stared blankly at her. Yashira had warned Connor that if they told anyone, she would know. But how? Could their apartment be bugged?

Marisa gave him a trust-me nod, and he nodded back. If they hadn't just received a ransom note, Connor would have believed Marisa paranoid. Now…he didn't know what to believe anymore.

A few minutes later, they heard a knock at their door. Connor was still finishing packing his duffle bag, so Marisa peeked out the peephole, relieved to see Pari waiting for them.

Cheerily, Marisa said, "Be right out." Then she hissed at Connor, "C'mon. Move the couch."

Connor hurriedly threw a few pairs of socks into his duffle, grabbed his full book bag, and then put both his bags down in front of the couch. He whispered to Marisa, "Grab your bags now." She did as she was told while Connor dragged the couch clear of the door.

Wearing her backpack and rolling her suitcase, Marisa opened the door and pushed her way out, rather than letting Pari in. Connor followed with his two bags. He locked the door behind him and hurried to catch up to Pari and Marisa. Marisa had already signaled for Pari to remain silent, and to her surprise, the other woman did.

"We're not going to Warp Drive, are we?" Pari asked once they were all in the car.

Marisa, who was on the passenger side, whispered, "Just get us out of here. I think we're being watched. Richard's been kidnapped."

Pari flinched, but expressed no doubt. As she drove, Marisa and Connor relayed the gist of the ransom message they'd received. When they arrived at Richard's house a few minutes later, Pari ushered them quickly inside, then called Richard. It went straight to voicemail, but rather than hang up, she listened to it.

It wasn't his usual message. Instead, a robotic voice said, "There are ten million reasons why I am not available, so do not leave a message." Because Pari had her cell phone on speaker, all three heard it at the same time.

"I guess that verifies it," Connor said in a melancholy tone. "They've got him."

Holding out hope, Marisa argued, "Not necessarily. It could just mean they have his phone."

In search of more information, Pari asked to see the full ransom note. Connor got his laptop out to show Pari. Meanwhile, Marisa looked at her phone and saw that she had another email invite from the BinaryMessenger. They quickly turned Richard's kitchen into their command post, with Connor and Marisa on their laptops and Pari standing behind them, watching. She witnessed firsthand how they transcribed and translated the messages from the BinaryMessenger. This one said:

Proof of Life

ProfessorRichardNelson.com

Both Marisa and Connor raced to the website. Marisa got there first and saw a photo of a man standing spread-eagle, with his arms and legs chained. His head drooped, and he was wearing only a towel. His mouth was taped shut, and he was blindfolded. The photo was taken from a low angle, so that even though his head was down, they could still make out his face.

There was no mistaking it. The man was Richard.

Pari instantly screamed in horror. Marisa gasped.

Connor's screen showed only a blank page. He said loudly, "Take a screenshot!" and Marisa rushed to obey. Worried that the picture would disappear, he explained, "The fact that it only showed up on the first page load means they didn't want to make it easy for us to keep this evidence. But they wanted us to know they definitely have him."

Just then, Owen let himself in the front door, eliciting a surprised shriek from Marisa. Apologizing for startling her, Owen then turned to Pari.

"I got your text," he said warily. "I'm guessing you didn't really invite me for breakfast."

Pari had been keeping Owen abreast of the messages she was getting from Richard, and being summoned to Richard's house was clearly a bad omen. Overcome with despair, Pari merely pointed at Marisa's screen.

"Bastards!" yelled Owen, slamming a first down on the counter. Marisa and Connor quickly brought him up to speed about the BinaryMessenger's messages and the clever way they'd deciphered them.

"So," Owen said somberly, "Richard has been kidnapped. We can be fairly certain of that, based on this photo. His last known location was Penang, Malaysia, but his current whereabouts are unknown." His eyes shifted to Pari. "He checked in with you about eleven hours ago, right, Pari?"

She nodded.

"Which means he could be as far as eleven hours away from Penang by now," Owen speculated. "Or he might still be there, for all we know. We've established only one-way communication with his captors. They can send us messages through CombatRidge or via the website ProfessorRichardNelson.com, but they haven't opened a channel to listen to us. Faced with a demand for ten million dollars, we now have about forty-six hours to pay. Oh, and these hackers possess the ability to hack into airplanes and potentially crash them. Are those all the facts?"

Though Marisa and Connor expressed shock at the news of the plane-crashing capabilities, everyone acknowledged that Owen's summary was complete.

"Notice I didn't say Richard is alive," Owen said glumly. "He might not be anymore. This isn't proof of life, just proof of capture."

"We need to pay the ransom!" Pari insisted.

"There's no assurance that paying it will bring Richard home alive," Owen told her. "If they want to negotiate, they'll open a two-way communication channel with us. Right now, they're only dictating, but I'd really like to start a dialogue. Perhaps that would help us deduce where Richard is."

"I'm going to pay it now," Pari said impatiently. "I have access to Richard's accounts. I can get the money. I just need someone to show me how to pay it via Bitcoin."

"God knows Richard can afford it," lamented Owen, "but I don't like giving in too fast to a kidnapper. They may think we see this as a bargain and ask for more—"

Pari interrupted, "I'm paying! Now, will someone please help me?"

To end the back and forth, Connor said, "You do realize they're in Antarctica?"

Everyone was dumbfounded. "No way! Can you even get from Malaysia to Antarctica in eleven hours?" Marisa asked rhetorically.

"Impossible! Connor, what makes you say that?" Pari asked him, with an incredulous expression.

After Connor explained himself, Owen told him, "You're only guessing that their web server for ProfessorRichardNelson.com is in Antarctica based on the IP address. While bizarre, it doesn't actually tell us where Richard is. Tracking down details about that IP address might tell us something about his kidnappers, though. I'll have someone at Galanteen look into it right away."

"I think it's time to go to the police," Marisa said.

Instantaneously, Owen and Pari both shut her down. "It's time to execute contingency phase one," Owen said to Pari.

She told him she'd already initiated it and added, "Gerald is collecting them all and will be here shortly."

"Collecting who?" Marisa asked. "What are you talking about?"

Marisa's inquiry was met simply with an ominous response from Owen: "You'll know everything soon enough."

Within an hour, they'd paid the ransom. Marisa had never imagined making that much money in her lifetime, so it was unbelievable to witness it spent so rapidly. Still, to her, Richard was most definitely worth it, and she desperately hoped they would receive what they paid for. They all did.

An hour after the transfer was completed, they received another message:

You are now in the game.

Await further instructions.

CHAPTER 46 – TURNPIKE

It had been several hours since Richard had heard and felt the man breathing on him. The man had slammed some metal doors shortly afterward, locking Richard inside somewhere. At first, he wasn't sure if the man had stayed in there with him, but after a while, Richard deduced that either the man was extremely silent, or he was alone.

Richard ached to sit down, but the chains wouldn't let him. They weren't actually suspending him up, only keeping him in his pose, so all his body weight still rested on his tired feet. His shoulders throbbed from having his arms outstretched for so long. Sweat dripped down his bald head and had soaked his blindfold. The rag in his mouth was bathed in his saliva, but all attempts to push it from his mouth with his tongue were thwarted by the electrical tape binding his lips, which wrapped around his head.

This is for Virginia, Richard thought to himself. The mantra echoed through his mind as he tried to block out the pain, but it didn't help nearly enough. A creaking noise interrupted his mantras, and instinctively he turned his head to face it. Metallic echoes of heavy footsteps again. A man breathing in his face again. Richard prepared himself for impending violence, but the man just breathed on him for an agonizingly long time. *Do it already*, Richard thought.

In a menacing Russian accent, the man hissed just one sentence at him: "You will give password."

Richard didn't acknowledge him, and the man continued to breathe on his face. Then the footsteps retreated. They came to a halt, and the silence returned with no preceding door slam. The stillness was then pierced by a whining noise and a small *plunk* on Richard's chest. His muscles contracted in random pulses as electricity surged through him. For a few seconds that felt like an eternity, Richard seized uncontrollably, the chains chafing his ankles and wrists.

Once the man was done tasing him, Richard attempted to catch his breath. Sensations slowly returned to him, and he discovered his towel was now wet because his bladder had emptied upon it. As the man cut the tape off Richard's mouth, he began spitting out the rag. The man pulled it out the rest of the way. Desperately crying for help, Richard hoped someone good would hear him, but all he heard was a vicious laugh echoing through his metallic cage.

His captor seized Richard's chin with a strong hand and lifted him onto the balls of his feet. "Password," growled the man.

Richard spat out, "Go to Hell!"

Expecting to be beaten for his remark, Richard braced himself. Yet, the man merely taped Richard's mouth shut again, this time without the rag inside it. Footsteps retreating. A door slamming. Alone again in his own private hell.

An engine roared to life, and his body jerked forward. He was in motion. That was when Richard realized he was inside the trailer of a truck.

~ ~ ~

Pulling into the driveway just after 9:00 a.m., Gerald brought Quinn, Victor, James, and Tina with him in the van. The five of them joined Pari, Owen, Marisa, and Connor at Richard's dining room table.

Pari sat at the head of the table, with Owen opposite her. All eyes were on her as she began speaking in a somber tone. "As some of you are aware, Richard has been kidnapped."

The crew that came with Gerald all gasped, then began peppering her with questions. Pari held her hand up, gesturing for silence. "I have a lot to say," she told them. "So, please, let me get through this. We have already paid the ransom and are awaiting further instructions. No, we don't know who has him or where he is. But I think I know *why* he's been taken."

Everyone eyed Pari curiously as she continued. "There's a secret. A secret many would kill for. A secret Richard would guard with his life. This secret is why we haven't involved the police. The time has come for you to know the secret, but you must promise to also guard it with *your* lives. The fate of humanity depends on it."

Pari paused and examined each anxious face. No one flinched. Part of her still feared pulling them into the abyss, but now she was more afraid of not doing so. The attack on Connor had proven they were in danger even without knowing about Richie and Cendovia.

"Richard and I believe you can all handle this now. That is why we chose you. I assume your silence indicates your willingness to keep the secret forever, but I need to hear your answers, please. Do you promise?"

She paused again, to allow anyone who wanted to back out the chance to leave. But each of them swore to secrecy.

Confident their oath was now sealed, Pari summarized the Zebulonz, its mission, and the role of the Pikes. She then went on to explain how it related to them. "Our contingency plan involves my interim promotion to commander in Richard's absence," Pari said, "and Owen moves into the lieutenant commander role. This is temporary, just until Richard returns.

"Now, I said our mission is to ensure humanity's survival by allowing us to continue on in virtual form. We call the act of crossing over from the physical world to the virtual world digital transcendence. But this is more than just an aim for us." Pari met each of their gazes in turn before announcing, "We have actually achieved digital transcendence into a virtual world we call Cendovia."

Eyes widened and mouths gaped. Pari signaled for them to hold their questions as she continued, "So far, there's only one living transcender. His name is Richie. He's a version of Richard spawned a year and a half ago. Richie spends most of this time paused, and thus has only lived about two days' time in Cendovia, or what we call two Cendovian days. A vital pioneer in our development of Cendovia, Richie provides us with an insider's perspective on our progress. Once he confirms the world we have created is suitable, other Cendovians can join him there.

"Given that we four Pikes are all over fifty, we anticipated the need to mentor a younger generation of leaders. Because you six are working in areas currently contributing to the development of Cendovia, our plan was always to bring you in as Pikes. However, current circumstances have now accelerated our timeline. Everybody with me so far?"

Honoring her request, the youngsters had held their questions while Pari spoke. But they could hold them no longer.

Quinn said, "Can we see this Cend… Cendo—"

"Cendovia," Pari said. "You mean, can you see it again? Quinn, my dear, you have visited Cendovia. You are the only human to ever be fully immersed in Cendovia and experience it like a Cendovian. That makes you a pioneer. Someday the Cendovians will mention you in their history books."

Quinn half smiled, proud, but still confused. "In fact," Pari said, "you met Richie before. Remember on Christmas, when you played with Richard? That was Richie."

"I knew it!" Quinn exclaimed. "I knew he could really feel me! I knew it!"

"Yes," Pari said, "but you didn't know that he was even more immersed in the experience than you were."

"Wait. Is this even legal?" James asked.

"It's not *illegal*," Pari said. "Human cloning is banned in the United States, but this is most certainly not that."

"I think the point you're really trying to get at, James, is whether this is morally wrong," Gerald said.

"I guess, yeah."

"That's an interesting question. Since Richard and Richie both consented to this—"

Victor interrupted. "Hold on. What about Richard? Shouldn't we be doing something right now to bring him back?"

"Yes, Victor," Pari said, "and we are doing the most vital thing we can do right now. The ball is not in our court. We are waiting on the kidnappers. They currently hold all the cards. But Richard would want you to know what he has been protecting, so that you will protect it with equal vigor." She rose to her feet. "I think it's time we all pay Richie a visit."

Pari instructed them to follow her. "My dear," she told her daughter apologetically, "I'm afraid Richard didn't make his secret bunker wheelchair accessible."

Quinn looked up at Victor and smiled. He gently lifted her out of her chair and followed Pari down into the bunker with a procession behind him. Along the way, Quinn relished Victor's hold, especially in front of Tina, who she saw as a rival for Victor's attention, though Tina showed no indication that she perceived any such rivalry.

Upon reaching the bunker, Pari disappointed Quinn by telling her the uplink that allowed her to feel the virtual world was still at Golden Bay Labs. "We can place you in the scanner and you can control your avatar's motions with your mind, but you won't feel any of it," she said.

Quinn accepted the limitation, and Victor laid her down softly, then slipped the VR headset over her head.

A numb Quinn materialized in the tiki bar, seated at the piano. She scanned the restaurant for Richie and finally saw him bouncing a basketball on the nearby court. She stood, ghostlike, and made her way over to him, finding it quite peculiar not to sense herself walking. Richie spotted her and tossed her the ball, but she missed it. The ball bounced off her chest and rolled across the court into the sand.

"Hi, Richie," she said to him.

"So, you know who I am," Richie replied, smiling.

"My implant isn't connected today," Quinn said, "so I can't feel anything."

"Too bad. I was looking forward to my first game of Cendovian basketball."

Richie began walking over to the restaurant with Quinn at his side. "What brings you here?" Unlike her prior visit, Richard hadn't prepared Richie to expect company.

"Pari explained everything to us," she said. "I can't believe you're really alive in here. How amazing! What's it like for you?"

"It—it's fascinating. And very realistic. But where's Richard?"

Quinn looked down at her feet and told Richie about the kidnapping.

"Ah, so she executed contingency phase one. I guess that means Victor, Marisa, Connor, Tina, and James are with you," Richie said. He waved from right to left at an imaginary crowd, not knowing from what vantage point they were spectating.

While Pari texted Richie the little information they had about Richard's kidnapping, Tina whispered to Marisa, "Is this truly life?"

In awe, Marisa said, "Yeah, I think Richie really is alive. Just freakin' amazing!"

"What kind of life is it, though? Reduced to ones and zeros, trapped inside a computer? I'm not sure I'd want to live my life as code," Tina said.

Overhearing their conversation, Connor whispered, "How do you know you aren't already?"

The two girls looked backed at him inquisitively, but didn't reply. They couldn't prove that their universe wasn't run by code.

Watching Richie and Quinn conversing on the screen, Victor began to grasp the possibilities and said to no one in particular, "Imagine a world of our own making. A world beyond death, beyond diseases and injuries…" His eyes descended on the scanner as he trailed off.

After Pari finished updating Richie, she turned to the room and asked, "Does anyone have any questions for Richie?"

"Well," Marisa said, "I get how this extends Richard's life…in a way. But how does it ensure the survival of humanity? Richie's not human."

"While I can answer that question," Pari said, "I'll let Quinn relay it to Richie, and let him tell you. I think it's more convincing if you hear it from him."

Upon hearing the question, Richie said, "Am I human? That's a good one. I'm not flesh and blood as you are, but my mind works like other humans. It is configured like that of any other human, with different lobes each having different responsibilities. My mind is far more human than that of a programmed AI, or the mind of any other animal, for that matter. But what does it mean to be human? What does it mean to be you? Your mind is what makes you who you are, even as the flesh and blood fades. Thus, saving humanity means preserving our minds, so we can survive beyond conditions that would destroy our physical bodies. That is what transcendence does."

"It's a compelling point," Marisa said, "and I get it. But how do you save all humanity like this? How do you roll this out to save billions of people?"

"I'll take that question myself," Pari said. "The short answer is, we haven't yet figured that out. But it's our ultimate goal, and it starts with proving we can save one person at a time."

Pari instructed Quinn to say goodbye to Richie, and she left him with one last question, "Can I live here with you someday?"

Taking a seat next to her, he put his hand on hers and said, "Many years from now, when your Earthly body dies, you can come here if you choose. All of you will have the option, but don't rush yourselves into the afterlife. You'll have all eternity to enjoy it."

After Pari paused Richie, Victor removed Quinn's VR mask and lifted her into his arms. Before leaving the bunker, Pari addressed the group once more.

"Today, I ask you to join the Pikes. Richard and I had planned to do this together, but if there was ever an emergency, we agreed to do so early. We selected you six because we believe you possess the necessary characteristics to be Pikes. This is a long mission, so we need young future leaders who can be our successors and maintain continuity. What I showed you is the greatest power ever discovered—eternal life. Many people would kill to steal this from us." She looked at each of them in turn, a serious expression on her face. "Richard would rather die than compromise our mission and allow Cendovia to fall into the wrong hands. To be a Pike, you must be willing to do the same. If you are willing, I ask you to take an oath."

This was their chance to be the superheroes Richard had called on them to be—superheroes waging war against death itself. Marisa was the first to agree. Victor, Quinn, James, and Connor soon also agreed to use their programming skills for the benefit of humanity.

Tina was the only one who hesitated. Tentatively, she said, "I see the tremendous possibilities, and this could help so many. But what if I don't want to go to Cendovia when I die?"

Gerald stepped before them and said, "Everyone is allowed their own choice. We will respect your wishes. But you don't need to decide that now. It's a lot to take in."

With a glance at Victor, Tina said, "I guess I always thought I'd see Isaac again in a different afterlife. Maybe that's crazy, I dunno. But if I can help others have those reunions, I'm willing to help."

Solemnly, Pari called on them to take the oath: "Do you swear on your eternal lives to protect the Zebulonz, to foster its mission to ensure humanity's survival, to keep its secrets forever, to protect Cendovia and its inhabitants, and to take your fellow Pikes as your eternal family?"

The six initiates spoke in harmony. "I do."

With a lump in her throat, Pari said, "Congratulations. You are all now Pikes."

~ ~ ~

The awestruck crew returned from the bunker to their seats at the dining room table. With his real father long since gone, Victor was now on the brink of losing the new father figure he'd found in Richard. Tina put a consoling arm around him as he rested his chin on his thumbs with his palms pressed together.

"Richard has to come home," he said. "Can we focus now on his rescue?"

Following Victor's lead, Owen directed them back to the work of saving Richard. His crew at Galanteen had learned that the IP address for ProfessorRichardNelson.com was indeed associated with the Vostok Station in Antarctica. He explained that all internet connections from Antarctica were relayed off satellites. If the hackers had compromised a satellite, they could make it look like the server was in Antarctica, but in reality, it could be anywhere. However, the Galanteen crew suspected it actually was in Russia's Vostok Station.

"My money is on the Russians being behind this," Owen said, "but we have no new information. Tina, I'm going to put you in touch with Hector at Galanteen. Together, I'd like you two to track down the source of these binary messages."

"Absolutely," Tina said. "We've got logs, and I can add special tracing to the code, if that helps."

"Very good," Owen said. "I'm going to Richard's last known location, to see if I can pick up a physical trail from there."

Victor volunteered to go with him, but Owen told them he was going alone.

"They don't yet know you're involved," Owen said. "We can't bring anyone new onto their radar. The attack on Connor was to get a message to Marisa. I think they went that route to test how we would work together, perhaps to see if Warp Drive is within Galanteen's sphere of influence.

They wouldn't learn that by sending a message straight to me. They may even be watching to see who we assembled to address this. So, we know that Marisa and Connor are already on their radar. As president of Galanteen, I'm certainly on their radar as well. But the rest of you don't need to call attention to yourselves. We don't need any more of you attacked. Marisa, you should stay here to receive further messages. And Connor—"

Connor interrupted. "I'm going with you."

"I might need the help, so yes, Connor, you're coming with me."

Marisa objected. "Why, because he's a guy?"

"No, because he has firearms training, and you don't," Owen said.

"Firearms? Why—" Marisa stopped herself, already knowing the answer to her own question. She turned her gaze to Connor in a silent inquiry.

He shrugged. "Just a few times at the range with my dad."

Preferring not to have someone verbalize the mortal danger Connor had just signed up for, Marisa instead asked Owen, "How much more do you know about us?"

"The Pikes don't let just let anyone in," Owen said with a grim smile. "We do very thorough background checks. Pari, the next flight to Malaysia leaves in four hours. Do we have time for backups?"

"Connor will need a baseline backup," Pari explained, "which will take about an hour. Owen, since we already have your baseline, your differential will only take ten minutes."

"Enough time, then," Owen said. "Let's get started. Connor, come with us."

Though Connor didn't know what they were talking about, they explained how the process worked on their way back down to the bunker. In the event of Connor's death, the backup would be used to restore Connor in Cendovia. They assigned Connor the first shift in the scanner. An hour later, he traded places with Owen and went to prepare for the trip. Always prepared, Owen already had a full suitcase in his truck for just such a situation.

In a downstairs guest room, Connor transferred only his essentials from his duffle bag to his backpack. Victor approached him and struck up a conversation about what Connor and Owen should do when they arrived in Malaysia. The conversation was mired in speculation, as they had very little concrete evidence. Soon, Owen emerged from the bunker, and it was time to go.

"Hey, take care of yourself, buddy," Victor said, as Connor made his way back to the living room.

"It's them you'd better worry about," Connor joked unconvincingly. Their handshake became a brief hug. Victor gave him several hearty pats on his back before letting his friend go.

On his way to the door, Connor placed his bag down in front of Marisa, who was holding back tears. "You better bring your ass home to me in one piece," Marisa said, putting on a brave face.

"That's the plan," he told her as he hugged her goodbye. "Find us some good leads on these hackers, if you can."

"Will do," she told him, and then whispered in his ear, "Don't you dare leave me."

"I will never leave you," Connor replied, leaning in to kiss her. She pulled him close and pressed her lips against his, not wanting to let go. He squeezed her tight, and after a long embrace, he finally released her. Unable to watch him leave, Marisa turned away and looked up the stairs. The front door swung shut behind her, and she wondered if Connor would ever walk through it again.

CHAPTER 47 – THE LONG GAME

All seven Pikes remaining in Palo Alto opted to sleep at Richard's house that night. Gerald had made sure they all packed enough to hold them over for a few days, despite not initially telling them why.

Although the twin bed was plenty comfortable, Marisa slept restlessly without Connor next to her. Early Sunday morning, her phone sounded a blaring alarm, indicating she had another message from the BinaryMessenger. On the other bed in the same first-floor guestroom, Tina also stirred, and she staggered with Marisa to the dining room table.

Together, they began the process of receiving the message. Marisa was capable of doing it solo, but she wanted a second transcriber to validate her transcription in case she made mistakes. This was something she and Connor had worked out, and she again wished he was with her. He'd texted her two hours earlier when he arrived in Tokyo on a layover, so at least she knew he was safe thus far.

Once Tina and Marisa finished the particularly lengthy transcription, they read this message:

Rescue Riddle 1

We stopped at a sandwich shop, and I ordered a turkey on wheat. The fellow behind me said, "Try the flatbread. You'll love it." So, I gave it a try. He said, "I'm the mayor of this small town, and it's the best town in this state. I can tell you anything you need to know. The soda never has bubbles here, so drink water instead. You won't find any sparkling water here, so the plain stuff will have to do." I thanked him for the advice, and we talked over lunch. He was friendly, but had no expression on his face. As we ate, our kids played rock-paper-scissors. My kids always won with scissors and lost with rocks.

"They wake us up in the middle of the night to play games?!" Tina exclaimed. "What the hell does this mean?"

"We paid the ransom!" Marisa said angrily. "What more do they want?"

Without knowing how long this game would last, and with nothing actionable in the message, they chose not to wake the others. Over a light breakfast that Jenny prepared for them, Tina asked, "Do you think this will tell us where Richard is?"

Struggling to understand how, Marisa replied, "I dunno. It kind of sounds like he's in a sandwich shop in Malaysia."

"Possibly," Tina said with a shrug, "but one thing's for sure. Richard isn't the only one they're trying to torture."

~ ~ ~

The plane gained altitude as rain buffeted the cockpit windshield. Richard sat behind the empty pilot's seat, stretching over it to steer, despite having never flown a plane before. The downpour soon became a whiteout. It then almost immediately cleared, as though it had never rained at all. Suddenly, Richard registered that his plane was underwater. Far above him, he saw the sunlight penetrating the waves and descending toward him through the dark ocean. Firmly gripping the steering wheel, he continued to try to raise his altitude to breach the surface. Instead, water flooded the cockpit, and in a flash, it was waist-high.

Though she warned him they wouldn't escape, Richard refused to surrender. He tried to swim, but he was unable to move. He tried to call out to her, but the words refused to come out. Instead, his mouth filled with water. Frantically scanning the plane for her, at first he only heard her voice. Then, miraculously, he was reaching for her outstretched arm. Gagging on salt water, his fingertips touched hers, closing around her hand, and he pulled with all his might.

Yet, she came no closer.

Desperation consumed him. He *would* rescue her. He *would* breathe again.

"Let me go," she whispered softly to him as she disappeared into the depths. Fully submerged, Richard bellowed in despair as the sea filled his lungs.

~ ~ ~

A jolt of water spraying his face stirred Richard awake. Still blindfolded, chained, and gagged, he realized he had awakened from his dream only to return to his nightmare. The hose ceased spraying him, shifting to spray the floor beneath him, and Richard recognized they were cleaning away the waste he'd produced. They seemed more concerned with the state of the trailer than with him.

The nozzle clanged on the floor. Footsteps splashed their way toward him, and that menacing breathing returned. Oh, how he hated this man.

"*Go to hell* is not the password," the man growled.

Richard laughed behind his taped mouth. Could this man really be so stupid?

The man seized his throat and began to squeeze. "You will give password now," he said, through gritted teeth. Then the man released Richard's throat and ripped the tape from his mouth.

This time, Richard didn't scream. He was certain they were going to kill him slowly, and nothing he could do would make it less painful. So he decided to give this vile man the least satisfaction possible. It was the only thing left under his control.

The man breathed heavily and waited without saying a word. Once he understood Richard wouldn't speak, he wrapped a fresh strip of electrical tape over Richard's mouth and around his head. Another agonizing bolt of fire convulsed through all Richard's muscles. The pain seemed never-ending, and Richard wondered whether he would suffer a heart attack. But no such relief came—death failed to rescue him.

He hung his head as the slamming door returned him to his solitary confinement.

~ ~ ~

Monday morning began with another blaring alarm. Marisa almost fell off the bed reaching for her phone. With the help of her new cryptography partner, she decoded the next message:

Rescue Riddle 2 of 4

After lunch, he offered to show us around town. We got into his pickup truck and drove off. "There's some strange things about living here," the mayor said. "All the women wear dress shoes, but never heels. You can't tell, but they also never wear bras. Our barber gives all the guys the same haircut. It gives them a military look, though none have served. We are also home to the highest concentration of podiatrists in the world, as all our residents suffer from the same foot condition. Perhaps it's something in the water."

They did not understand what to make of this riddle, or the one from the day before. At least they now knew how many more riddles to expect.

"There's no real place like this," Tina said.

"How are we supposed to rescue Richard if we don't know where he is?" Marisa asked, scratching her head. Tina had no answer. Neither did any of the other Pikes.

~ ~ ~

The sun was surging over the eastern horizon when Owen and Connor finally reached their hotel on Penang Island—the same hotel where Richard last stayed. After twenty-five hours of traveling, they were exhausted, but on high alert for any potential dangers. Owen had asked for a room near his friend Richard Nelson, and the desk clerk was happy to oblige. This revealed to them Richard's room number, as well as the fact that he had not yet checked out.

Perhaps the kidnappers still have him in his room, Owen thought. The picture of a chained Richard didn't look like it was taken in a hotel room, but it was very dark, so they couldn't be sure where he was.

On the drive to Penang Island, Connor had suggested that they ask hotel staff members if they'd seen Richard. Owen quickly ruled that out, because any suggestion Richard was missing might bring in the local authorities. Locals learning of a high-profile American gone missing would eventually lead to the involvement of American investigators, which could shine light on Zebulonz matters best left in the shadows. With the long-term survival of humanity under their protection, Owen insisted no one person be allowed to jeopardize the mission—not even someone as valuable as Richard. It was better to never find Richard, Owen explained, than to endanger Cendovia. Connor admitted he understood Owen's reasoning, but that didn't mean he liked his conclusion.

When they reached their room, which was across the hall from Richard's, Connor closed the door and asked, "What do we do now? Do we just go knock on the door?"

Holding up a do-not-disturb sign, Owen said, "We don't have to. I just pulled this off Richard's door. This tells me no one has entered his room since he went missing. The housekeeping staff is just down the hall, so the door will be opened once they work their way to his room. If Richard's inside, we'll know soon after they enter. Just listen for a scream."

In alternating fifteen-minute shifts, Connor and Owen kept watch through the peephole. On Connor's third shift, he whispered to Owen, "She's here!" He watched as the maid opened the door. No scream came.

Owen took his place, peering through the peephole for a moment, then quietly slipped out of their room. The maid was out of sight when Owen let himself into Richard's room. "Sorry," he said, waving his room key upon spotting her in the bathroom. "I forgot something."

After an acknowledging smile, she continued cleaning the bathroom counter. Owen walked into the bedroom, but saw nothing out of place. The room appeared as though no one was staying there. The bed was perfectly made, with all the decorative pillows still neatly arranged. There was no luggage in the closet, so he checked the top dresser drawer and found it empty. Then the next, and the next. All were empty.

Once he was certain there was no trace of Richard in the room, he slipped his wallet out of his pocket, left the bedroom, and waving it at the maid, said, "Found it!"

After letting himself out, instead of returning to Connor, Owen ventured down to the lobby. Upon asking for a manager at the front desk, a young woman introduced herself as Zara. A discreet matter required her assistance, he explained, but it should not be discussed in the lobby. Graciously, she showed him to her office, and he began, "I am Owen Bradenton, the security detail for the son of an important American politician. As a precaution, I would like to review your surveillance tapes from the past few days for anything suspicious. This is standard protocol for us in this business. I'm sure you can understand."

"Mr. Bradenton," Zara said, "I assure you that won't be necessary. If anything suspicious had occurred, our security crew would have alerted me."

"Please, call me Owen," he said with a charming smile. "I understand this type of request may be new to you, but if you would please indulge me, I'd be happy to compensate you for your troubles."

He placed two hundred-dollar bills on her desk, and her tune quickly changed.

"Well, it sounds very dull to me, but if you must." She led him to an office with many monitors showing video from different areas of the hotel. The security guard, slumped in his chair, nervously darted to his feet as the door opened.

Owen surreptitiously slipped two more hundred-dollar bills into Zara's hands. "If you don't mind, I would appreciate some privacy with this matter." Zara signaled for the guard to leave him alone in the room, and Owen began navigating his way through the video archives.

Within an hour, he had located Richard entering the lobby to check in. Another hour of sifting through videos revealed Richard turning a hallway corner to walk into the spa. A woman accompanied him, but Owen couldn't get a clear view of her face. He fast-forwarded at 8x speed, looking for the point when Richard left the spa. Some guests and employees came and went, but for eight hours, Richard and the woman never exited the spa. At least not from the entrance.

Having spent three hours in the surveillance room, Owen determined he would need to leave, or risk raising too much suspicion. Suspicion was something the Zebulonz could not afford. He quickly copied more of the video files to his thumb drive and, hoping he'd picked the relevant ones, he let himself out.

"All's clear," Owen said as he passed Zara coming out of her office. He thanked her again for her discretion and slipped her another two hundred dollars. Finally, Owen returned to the room.

Connor sat up quickly in bed and asked, "Where have you been? I thought something happened to you."

Owen explained that either Richard had enjoyed a very long spa day, or he was abducted from the spa. "We need to comb through these videos," he told Connor, waving the thumb drive in the air.

"I've got a better idea," Connor said, taking it from Owen.

CHAPTER 48 – PATTERN RECOGNITION

Tuesday and Wednesday each yielded new riddles from the BinaryMessenger, but the Pikes couldn't see what to do with them. Gerald printed the last two riddles and examined them meticulously.

Rescue Riddle 3 of 4

The mayor said, "The most famous person from here is named Stanley. He is always touring the world. The hardware store here has no Phillips screwdrivers, and a few British tourists stay in apartments by the lake. It's very peaceful on the lake. No one ever gets seasick. All the locals live in one-story houses. You won't find pitched roofs, barrel tiles, or glossy paint on these simple houses. Yet, every resident proudly hangs thin televisions on their walls."

Rescue Riddle 4 of 4

"In the church on the right, we sing every song in the same key of C on Sundays. On the left there, we had a comedy club, but it closed down because no one laughed. Last year, I became mayor after a hard-fought election. I ran on a platform of a simplified tax code where everyone pays the same rate. My opponent accused me of sleeping around, but that was just a lie. On election day, I steamrolled over him, and he simply could not bear it. At his side when he was on his deathbed, I witnessed his heart give out. I had warned him no more games, but he did not listen."

Shortly after reading the last riddle, Victor knocked on the door to the master bedroom. Pari cracked it open.

"Is Quinn available?" Victor asked, smiling. Pari smiled back and told him to wait. A moment later, she returned and pulled the door wide open. "She just woke up, but you can see her now." Upon letting Victor in, Pari excused herself for breakfast.

Lying in bed, Quinn was propped up slightly with pillows. Victor had never seen her in her pajamas, and this made her feel a bit insecure. He took a seat on the bed beside her, and her heart skipped a beat. "H—Hi, Victor," Quinn said.

"Good morning, my friend," Victor said, not registering her nervousness. "Hey, I know we didn't get to go virtual last weekend, but since—"

"I understand," Quinn interrupted. Since they were camped out at Richard's on hostage alert, playing seemed inappropriate. Both of them understood this, and Quinn sensed Victor was grateful he didn't need to finish saying it. Additionally, even though Richard had a neural scanning bed in his basement, the equipment to attach her implant to it was still at Golden Bay Labs. Without that, she couldn't leave her Earthly body behind for a joy ride in her Cendovian one.

"Well, we can still hang out and talk, if you want," Victor offered. Quinn's heart beat faster at the prospect of talking to him with no pretense of research, or play, or programming. What would she say? There was so much she wanted to tell him, but…could she really say it? *Should* she?

Perhaps he would say it first. Perhaps that's why he'd come to see her.

Trying to appear calm, she smiled and said, "Sure. What do you wanna talk about?"

"I dunno," Victor said, briefly pausing in search of a topic. "I feel like I'm letting Richard down, and I didn't want to let you down too, so…" Victor was often very hard on himself. Like many ambitious people, he had trouble accepting what he couldn't control. After some consideration, he suggested, "Can we talk about the riddles?"

Quinn was both relieved and disappointed—relieved because there was a safe pretense again, but disappointed because a scared part of her wanted to drop all pretense and pour her heart out to him. Bravely mustering up some courage, she waded in gently. "Okay, but first, let me ask you something."

"Sure."

"Will you go to Cendovia when you die?" He looked at her expectant face and considered the question. "Because I definitely will. I can tell you, it's a great place to be."

Victor chuckled. "I'm sure it is. I suppose I would go."

Quinn smiled, comforted by his answer.

"Um," Victor said, "so, we got the fourth riddle this morning, as expected."

With that, Quinn understood her heart would have to continue to hold its secrets a little longer. Victor pulled a copy of the riddle out of his pocket and read it to her. "Has anyone solved it yet?" she asked when he was done.

"Sure," Victor said. "We solved it already, but I'm just holding out on you."

If only Victor knew what *she* withheld from him. "I mean," she said, burying her feelings, "does anyone see any patterns?"

"Owen's sending it to his cryptographers at Galanteen to see if they can make any sense of it, but he thinks they're testing our capabilities somehow—our AI and cryptographic capabilities, mostly likely. He told Pari that in warfare, you don't do anything without a purpose. Although, they could just be stalling us." Victor shrugged. "Marisa suspects there may be a message hidden inside the messages, like every fifth letter might spell the location he's at or something like that. Tina thinks it's probably nonsense they're using to distract us."

With disdain, Quinn scoffed, "She *would* think that!"

"Okay, I know you and Tina have history," Victor said, holding up his hand, "but like Pari said, she's family now. Remember, we took an oath as Pikes."

"I know," Quinn said, biting her lip, "but family's not always easy. And why do you keep defending her after what she did to you?"

Realizing he'd touched a nerve and suddenly wishing he'd never told Quinn about the day Lucas opened Tina's door, Victor replied, "I dunno. We've gotten past our past. What can I say? Family's not always easy."

Quinn smirked at his use of turnabout and then tried to move on. "She's…flat—"

"She's really not flat," Victor interrupted.

Quinn snapped, "Damn it! Gross! That's not what I'm saying! I meant that she doesn't see that it's flat—the riddle." Victor seemed confused, so Quinn began pointing out examples. "Look—everything they talk about is flat. The bread. The sodas. The haircuts. The women. They're trying to tell us Richard's somewhere flat. Nobody saw that? Really?"

Enthusiastically, Victor leaned over and kissed her forehead. "Eureka!" he shouted. "You're amazing! We have to tell the others!"

At her request, he helped her into her wheelchair, while she dreamed that he had placed his kiss in a better spot.

Downstairs, everyone else sat in the living room together. "They're stalling us," Tina insisted. "These messages are useless."

"No, they're not!" Quinn said as she entered the room with Victor.

For years, Tina had never confronted Quinn about anything. She had always been deferential to the other girl, still mired in guilt over the part she'd inadvertently played in Quinn's accident. But this time, she reflexively challenged her. "How can you be so sure?"

"Because they don't have to stall us," Quinn said defiantly. "They got their money and haven't asked us for anything else. Why not just go silent after we paid them? There's no need for them to return Richard to us. They have some reason for keeping him, and these riddles might give us a clue. By the way, have you noticed how everything in the riddles is flat?"

A collective groan filled the roam as the crew admonished themselves for not seeing it sooner.

"But what do we do with that?" Marisa asked.

Victor said, "Not sure yet. But I think Quinn's right. We have to treat the riddles like they're useful. We have nothing else to go on."

Easily taking this in stride, Tina handed Victor a cup of coffee and admitted they had a point. It wasn't personal for her, though it was quite personal for Quinn, and she felt vindicated when Victor took her side.

The rest of the Pikes were reminded that all other avenues of inquiry had yet to bear fruit. Tina and James had tried to track down the connections being used by the BinaryMessenger to connect to the CombatRidge servers, but the IP addresses changed constantly. They believed the attackers had a program running on an external server that sent jump and duck commands to the CombatRidge servers, thereby playing in gamer mode. Hector from Galanteen had deduced that the hackers were using a malware network running on a collection of compromised user machines across the globe to route these messages to the CombatRidge servers. He was working with his team to attempt to compromise this malware network, but had yet to succeed. James believed the use of the malware network made them practically untraceable and suggested they plan their Antarctic expedition, as Richard was as likely to be there as anywhere else in the world.

~ ~ ~

Under the pretense of various massages and spa treatments, Owen and Connor spent Sunday through Wednesday snooping around the hotel spa for clues. They would feign accidentally walking into other spa rooms to search for Richard while also checking for additional exits from that part of the hotel. Between their visits, Connor worked on his program to comb through the hundreds of hours of video Owen had retrieved, which spanned many cameras over a week's time. By Monday morning, Connor's software, using facial recognition libraries, had determined there was no clip of Richard leaving the spa.

Connor had then trained a machine learning algorithm to identify and collect the license plates of all the vehicles that left via the hotel entrances. By Monday night, it had identified dozens within the two days of footage they had after Richard entered the spa. If he was no longer on the premises, he had to have left in one of those vehicles.

Late Wednesday night, Owen was again manually combing through video footage. "I—I think I've got something here!" Connor came in from the balcony and hovered over Owen's shoulder to see what he was pointing at on his laptop. "Look at her," Owen said, pointing at a woman entering the passenger side of a delivery truck in the loading dock at the back of the hotel.

"That's her! It's gotta be!" Connor said. While the camera angle was from high above and behind the woman, they discerned from the black-and-white image that she was dressed similarly to the woman who had accompanied Richard into the spa. The truck turned right out of the parking lot, heading south.

"Get me the plate!" Owen ordered.

"Already on it!" Having already indexed all the video clips with vehicles leaving the premises, Connor quickly found the vehicle in question.

"Good work, kid. I'm sending it to the boys at Galanteen. Let's see what they can dig up." After passing the information along, Owen stood up and walked out to the balcony.

Connor joined him and implored, "We gotta go find that truck!"

Looking east over the Penang Straight at the Malaysian mainland, Owen said, "Kid, maybe Galanteen can trace that lead. But that truck left here five days ago. The only thing we know now is that Richard is anywhere in the world but where we are."

Under a dark sky, Connor hoped that Galanteen or his fellow Pikes could help them solve the riddle of Richard's whereabouts.

CHAPTER 49 – THE GOOD GUYS

A sudden, harsh light stirred Connor from his sleep.

"Time to go, kid," Owen said as he opened the drapes, revealing an overcast sky.

"Where?" Connor said, rubbing his eyes.

"Back to Kuala Lumpur. The boys did it—penetrated the Malaysian Highway Authority servers and found the toll records for that truck. Looks like they've been on a roundabout tour of the countryside. Last toll payment was an hour ago at an off-ramp in southern Kuala Lumpur."

Neither of them had bothered to unpack, as Owen had insisted that they be ready to move out on a moment's notice. Having slept in his clothes, Connor forced his tired body to spring up and then slipped on his shoes. Owen tossed Connor his backpack, which Connor considered a highly unnecessary move, as he could have easily picked it up himself. It did increase Connor's alertness, though, and he quickly gained his equilibrium while following Owen to the door.

Thunder rumbled in the distance as they exited the hotel room in pursuit of Richard.

~ ~ ~

Furious raindrops pelted the trailer's roof, creating a din of countless metallic echoes that reverberated through Richard's weary mind. Mixed with those echoes was a steadfast willingness to die for the cause. Richard knew dying to protect Cendovia meant he would die so others could live forever. He, too, would be rewarded with eternal life. Richard was far from the first to believe in such an ideal, yet unlike the zealots, prophets, and extremists before him, Richard didn't just believe in this afterlife—he knew it existed. Not only had he seen it, he had actually created it, and part of him was already there.

While he dreamed the good guys would break through those metal doors and rescue him at any moment, he also had no delusions that such salvation would come. They were constantly on the move, and there was no telling to where he had been transported. Five days of torture had convinced him no one would be coming for him, and that his time on Earth was nearly over—except for the final breath.

For days, Richard had periodically admonished himself for so foolishly allowing Susanna to dupe him. He had attempted in vain to find some solace in the fact that his foolishness was driven by noble intent. In his venture to recover his laptop, he'd had no choice but to take great risks for his wife and for humanity. In hindsight, he had taken the wrong risks, and judged himself to have failed them all.

The man had just finished beating Richard again. Three days before, he'd switched from tasing to whipping, and bloody lash marks now covered Richard's torso. One consistent thing he'd come to count on was that the torture sessions only occurred once per day. Richard thought this demonstrated surprising patience in their endeavor to beat information out of him, though perhaps they were merely trying to demonstrate that Richard couldn't wait them out.

So, he was surprised when the metal door creaked open again shortly after the man's departure. Footsteps approached him, but this time, it was two pairs.

Then he felt his left arm loosen. His wrist was still chained, but the other end of the chain seemed to detach from its moorings. He considered punching out with his aching left arm, but being blind, and with three other appendages tied down, this seemed futile. Plus, it was possible he was being saved. It would be foolish to attack his rescuer.

This thought was short-lived, as Richard felt a strong man pull his arm behind his back. His right was brought down to meet his left. Handcuffs snapped, and his wrists were bound to each other. Richard wobbled slightly, as he had grown accustomed to using his chained arms for balance.

The man pushed him down into a chair and tied Richard's cuffed hands to the back of it. He heard the man's footsteps trail away, and the steel door slammed shut. Then a light went on—from behind his blindfold, Richard guessed it was a flashlight. Someone removed the tape covering his mouth and slipped a straw into it.

After five days in captivity, this was only the third time he had been given a drink. Not knowing how soon it would be taken away, he sipped as fast as he could. Slurps from the empty cup echoed throughout his steel prison. Later, he registered that the fruit punch-flavored liquid might have been poisoned, which would have mercifully freed him from his misery.

No such mercy came.

A woman's voice said calmly, "Konstantin wants to kill you."

Richard said nothing, but he considered this an ominous sign. The fact that she was telling him the man's name implied he wouldn't be living much longer.

"I don't want to destroy you," said the woman. "I want to save you, Richard. Already, I saved you from Konstantin. We had orders to kill you, but I convinced them to let me do this differently. Do you know why, Richard?"

He'd seen this tactic in films before. The villain would monologue, and then the heroes would come triumphantly to the rescue. But this was no movie. There would be no rescue. However, there would surely be a monologue, which meant she wanted the satisfaction of saying her piece before she killed him.

In a raspy voice, Richard asked, "Why, Susanna?"

She laughed and removed his blindfold. He squinted to see her seated in front of him with her phone on her lap. Its light shone up toward her face, casting long, eerie shadows across her features. "Poor Richard," she said, with mock sympathy. "If you're going to see the light, you must see it all. I will show you the light."

"Yes, please," he said. "Show me the light."

Ignoring his sarcasm, she shed the New York accent and her auburn wig and spoke in her native, Russian-accented voice. "I will, Richard. Surely you have deduced by now that my name is not Susanna Cohen, and I am not with your FBI. The FBI has no clue about any of this. My real name is Yashira Gravinsky. I want you to remember that. Now, you say it, Richard."

He repeated weakly, "Yashira Gravinsky."

"Well done." Yashira cackled. "Promise me you will remember the name of the woman who showed you the light. All you Americans think you are the good guys, the world's heroes. You claim you are the greatest nation on Earth. You act as though your self-proclaimed greatest generation won World War II by themselves, though far more Russian blood was shed than American blood. Touting yourselves as the world's protectors, yet you kill so many of us. You sanitize torture as extraordinary rendition and killing innocent civilians as collateral damage. From a distance, you kill with bombers and drones, like it's a video game to you people." Her expression darkened. "To the rest of the world, this is life or death. It's time for no more games."

Richard stared at her wearily as she continued her monologue, "Americans are the world's oppressors for their own financial gain. I was taught this years before I ever set foot on American soil. These were the lessons from our schoolbooks, but these lessons were also imprinted on my life in the most personal way." Her eyes turned glassy, as if filled with unshed tears. "My father served in the Russian army. He died in the First Chechen War—a war that never would have happened had you Americans not pushed the great Soviet Union to collapse. I was only four! If you heroes had stopped saving us, my father would still be alive."

Richard watched another wave of rage surface within her. "My distraught mother turned to drugs to cope with her pain, and then prostitution to support us. At age nine, she thrust me into the family business. No child should be forced to do what I have done. *No one* should. So, from the depths of my heart, I want to thank you real American heroes."

She grabbed his throat, seeming to fight the urge to extinguish him. "Perhaps you remember the Moscow blackouts in 2005. We were without power for ten weeks. I was eighteen, and I remember it vividly. My mother was stuck in an elevator alone on the first day, while I was left in our apartment to fend for myself with a man twice my age and twice my size." Fighting back tears, she dug her nails into his neck. "We were both trapped, unable to save each other, and she panicked. They found her the next day with a needle in her arm. Only a few hours before they got to her, she overdosed."

A sinister smile spread across her face. "This, my dear Richard, is when our paths collided. I'm sure you don't need me to explain that part to you."

Wracked with guilt, Richard didn't need to ask questions. He knew what had really caused the Moscow blackouts. The NSA had deliberately compromised the Moscow power grid and attacked its central computer systems in retaliation for a Russian-attempted breach of an American nuclear facility. Galanteen had supplied the NSA with key intel for devising the counterattack, but neither Galanteen nor the NSA expected their attack to be as crippling, widespread, or long-lasting as it turned out to be. Ripple effects of their actions on the aging Soviet power system had caused cascading failures that took weeks to fully repair. The Russian government suppressed all information of the attack, to protect their reputation of being strong and powerful, while the American government secretly sent aid in an attempt to deescalate the situation. This fiasco had led Richard to be much more measured in his authorization of Galanteen assistance with U.S. government-led counterstrikes.

Leaning closer, Yashira hissed, "I've waited nine years for this moment. I've stalked you patiently in America for the past two. The GRU wanted me to destroy the head of Galanteen, so the body would die with it, but I convinced them I can do better than killing you. Do you know how many people I had to seduce to get my way? Far too many. And Konstantin—he's the most disgusting of them all. He is a monster. That monster wants to devour you slowly, but I seek your salvation."

After a quick, mental inventory of the pain coursing through his body, Richard laughed at the absurdity of her as his savior.

She grabbed his mouth and pressed her nails sharply into his skin again. "I am not like you Americans. I am not like Konstantin. Of course, I'm no saint, but I am no monster. You will never see me again, so listen very carefully. In my time in America, I noticed some good in your civilians. Maybe even in *you*, my mother's killer. Yet you all turn a blind eye to the atrocities committed in your name. Support the troops! Screw the world! You are so damn blind—so *willfully* blind. That is your greatest sin. No wonder the world hates you."

Reluctantly, she released her grip and allowed him to speak.

"What do you want from me?" he asked.

With fervent conviction, she preached her message to him. "If you repeat any of this to Konstantin, I will personally kill you. I was unable to save my parents, but perhaps I can still save you. That became much harder when you didn't follow my directions on the first flight. The plan was for you to be arrested and disgraced, and then I could blackmail your friends for the evidence to exonerate you. You would go free, but permanently clouded in suspicion, and the GRU would have extracted their pound of flesh, but no one would have needed to die. With you disgraced, Galanteen would have been tarnished and crumbled as clients broke ties with a terrorist-run organization, and your interference with Russian affairs would have ceased."

Yashira shook her head in disgust. "We had to resort to kidnapping when you screwed that up royally. I had to become Susanna to keep you from going to the real authorities. To cover our tracks, I stole your laptop. The note I left was a test, to discover if the laptop contained anything valuable. When you kept following my trail, you confirmed that it did. What's on there, Richard? Bank account credentials? Are you afraid we'll drain your accounts and take your holy dollars? Or is there something more valuable, like technological secrets? Do you harbor the power to win the—what did you call it? The intelligence explosion?"

There was nothing she could say that would get him to talk about the laptop. Instead, he said, "I'm so sorry, Yashira. I never wanted your parents to die."

"You don't get to apologize now!" Yashira snapped. "If you truly want to redeem yourself, then give me the password! If you do, I can assure you that you will make it home alive. But if you don't hand it over, I can do nothing more to protect you. I want you to go back to Galanteen to make them stand down, but no other Russian wants you to live." She shifted closer. "Stop meddling in our affairs, and we will leave Galanteen alone. Put an end to these conflicts. No more games, Richard."

She waited for a response. He looked down and said nothing.

"Damn you!" Yashira growled, lifting his silent face up to meet her gaze. "Show me you're worth saving! You are not yet passing the test." Then her face turned sly. "I've been testing your friends as well, to learn what they are capable of. Perhaps they will show they have the power to win the war—if they are worthy, they will discover the key to your salvation. Let's hope they do better than you."

Finally, Richard spoke. "You kidnap and torture me, and now you expect me to trust you. How am I supposed to do that?"

"You killed my mother, and yet I'm trying to rescue you," she pointed out. "Still think you're entitled to question me? At the very least, you may trust that if you do not cooperate, more innocent blood will be on your hands. I cannot stop that, but I can promise it is true."

Visions of planes falling from the sky filled Richard's imagination. He told himself that would not be his fault. The Russians would be the ones pulling the trigger. Desperately, Richard tried to not lose sight of the bigger picture—he had humanity's long-term survival to consider. Still, he didn't want any innocent people to die.

Glaring into her amber eyes, he said, "The blood will be on your hands, not mine."

Yashira stood abruptly and said to him, "I'm sorry you failed to understand. Goodbye, Richard."

When the door slammed shut, Richard contemplated the inhumanity of it all. Still unable to move, he recalled Pari's explanation of locked-in syndrome. Thoughts of Rich and the suffering he had endured surfaced in Richard's mind. How did that suffering compare to his own? Then he thought of Richie and Virginia, and he hoped they would never encounter the type of cruelty humans could subject upon their own species.

Richard swore that if he somehow made it out alive, he would work tirelessly to ensure such cruelty could not happen in Cendovia. He would build it into its laws of physics, if possible. Contemplating the laws of a universe brought his mind back to his lifelong muse—the Fermi Paradox. Slowly, gradually, a new solution presented itself to him—one he had never heard anyone else espouse. In his despair, he found it quite probable to be true.

Humanity deserved to be alone in the universe.

CHAPTER 50 – PRISONER'S DILEMMA

It had been six days since Richard's kidnapping, and to Quinn's frustration, there wasn't a breakthrough in sight for the Pikes. Six days of being camped out at Richard's place, hiding from the world, and seven days since she had visited Cendovia with Victor—not that she was counting.

Quinn felt like she was going through withdrawal.

In response to Victor's offhand complaint the night before about being trapped at Richard's house, she had joked, "Try being trapped in this body." This came out sounding more bitter than she'd intended, as she was actually adjusting better to her situation than ever before and was the happiest she'd been since the accident. But Victor must have taken her comment seriously, as he'd gone to Golden Bay early this morning and retrieved the neural uplink cables.

Whatever his reason, she was glad he did. Victor may have felt trapped in the house, but Quinn wanted to stay trapped with him in Cendovia forever.

As they jumped from Richie's penthouse balcony, trying to see who could reach the pool, she soared so free. Upon falling a few feet short of the pool and landing on Victor's avatar, she roared with laughter, as did he.

"Amateurs!" Richie yelled from far above them. Quinn didn't bother to get off Victor, but merely turned upward to watch Richie's dive.

Also looking up, Victor saw Richie fast approaching them in a graceful swan dive. Instinctively, he covered Quinn to protect her from the collision. But Richie sailed over them with outstretched hands which, instead of splitting the water's surface, slammed into the lip of the pool. After bouncing on his head, he tumbled backward into the water.

He surfaced to the sound of slow claps and took an exaggerated bow. Both his guests commended Richie on his form.

"That was fun, kids," Richie said as he stepped out of the water. "Real fun. I don't get a lot of company in here."

"I'd love to come visit you more," Quinn said.

"Yeah," Victor said, "she never seems to want to leave."

"However," Richie said, "she *can* leave. Don't take that for granted, Quinn. There's no going back for me."

Quinn knew Richie was trying to tell her to value what she had, but she envied him so much. Every moment of his life, he was complete.

"I know we wanted to come here for a break," Victor said, "but can we talk about the riddle for a few minutes?"

Richie was glad someone had raised the topic, as he felt guilty playing around while Richard was missing. Still, he understood the importance of breaks and play in the discovery process. Stepping away from the riddles could make them more successful at solving them. But it had been a long time since he'd contributed much other than being a test subject, and Richie desperately wanted to contribute something to the rescue effort. He hoped he could contribute enough to bring his brother home.

~ ~ ~

Above the bunker, Pari, Gerald, James, Tina, and Marisa were spread across Richard's living room on this gloomy Thursday afternoon, poring over the riddles. Had the BinaryMessenger not kept stringing them along, they all would have accepted the very real possibility that Richard was dead. But since they'd received a daily riddle every morning for the past four days, they clung to their waning hope.

This morning, they'd received nothing. Perhaps they now had all the clues they were going to get, or perhaps the kidnappers no longer required the diversion. If the riddles were pointing them to Richard's true whereabouts, none of them could see how such a town could actually exist. The BinaryMessenger still hadn't given them a way to respond. Without feedback, their only way to test each guess of Richard's location would be to completely comb each suspected town. Marisa imagined trying to find a specific needle in a mountain of needles. Worse than unsolvable, it was an intractable problem masquerading as a tractable one.

~ ~ ~

Owen was seldom so devoid of options. He'd spent the previous day driving with Connor around Kuala Lumpur, searching for the mysterious delivery truck, and they'd just set out to spend another aimlessly driving around again.

Connor stared distantly out the passenger window, searching hopelessly for another clue. Richard had originally planned to be on a flight to Beijing tomorrow night, and while neither of them expected Richard to be on it, Connor knew that at some point they, too, would need to take their own flight out of town. Unfortunately, it seemed increasingly unlikely that Richard would be on that flight with them. Rather, Connor was beginning to believe they would be forced to continue their wait for answers on another continent—answers that might never come.

Connor didn't share his growing sense of defeat with Owen, for fear that saying it would make it true. Yet he wondered if Owen was feeling the same. After Connor's initial text to Marisa when they landed in Tokyo for their layover, Owen had ordered him to avoid any further contact home. All communication had to go through Owen and Pari using their encrypted communication channel, which made Connor feel quite isolated. He wished to be free again, and then caught himself, ashamed of his own thoughts. At least he was freer than Richard.

Connor and Owen were both hoping their fellow Pikes would soon find a breakthrough that would set them all free.

~ ~ ~

In a dimly lit basement, Yashira and Konstantin sat on folding chairs near a fortified door. "We should have killed him already," Konstantin warned.

Annoyed, Yashira stood and glared down at him. "Then what? On to the next job? And then the next? Always trying to stay in good graces? Timidly hoping to never fail our masters? Forever one mistake away from being disappeared? No, Konstantin, my way is better."

He rose slowly until he could look down upon her once more and asked coolly, "You mean a better way to die?"

Grasping the lapels of his sports coat, she pulled him closer and said affectionately, "No, a better way out. The only way to leave on *our* terms. I know you fear the powerful, but once we do this, they'll raise their glasses to us at the Kremlin. They'll praise the secret martyrs who brought America to kneel before Russia. Then we can start a new life together with that ten million dollars."

Konstantin ran a meaty hand through her black hair. "So beautiful, strong, and cunning, just as I have raised you to be," he said, then kissed her passionately. With a tight grip on the back of her hair, he pulled back and added menacingly, "Do not fail me."

~ ~ ~

Richard awoke to find himself lying in a bathtub in a small bathroom. Shifting himself into a sitting position, he was shocked to discover that his wrists and ankles were no longer bound. Why had his captors unchained him? Were they finally offering him some small mercy, or was this some new kind of torture?

He stepped carefully out of the tub, swaying on his feet, and tried opening the door. Unsurprisingly, it was locked. He tried breaking it down, but his depleted strength was no match for the strong metal door with four visible deadbolts.

No wonder they'd removed his restraints. It was clear he wasn't going anywhere.

Shoulders slumped, Richard decided to bathe himself—he might as well take advantage of the opportunity to wash away the stench of all his days in captivity. The water that spilled from the showerhead was icy, but the lack of hot water didn't matter to Richard. Underneath the cold stream, he drank ravenously as the rest poured over his body. Wincing when the water reached his torn-up torso, he knew he must clean his wounds. With gentle care, he scrubbed a grayish bar of soap over the tender lash marks.

Upon completing the painful but necessary shower, he searched for a towel, but didn't immediately see one. Richard didn't want to put back on the filthy towel that had been taped to him for days. In the cabinet below the sink, he found a stack of neatly folded white towels. After drying himself off gingerly, he wrapped the new towel around his waist and looked to see if there were any other useful items under the sink.

For a moment, Richard stared into the cabinet in shock. Could it really be? Upon further examination, he was amazed to discover his backpack behind the stack of towels. Pulling it out, he found the shorts and T-shirt he'd worn the day he was captured tucked underneath it. Even his shoes lay beneath those.

After he dressed himself, Richard opened his backpack. It was filled to the brim with protein bars. Ferociously, he tore a wrapper open and practically swallowed the first one whole, trying to remember the last time he'd eaten solid food. Before he'd even finished chewing, Richard opened a second one and repeated the process. But after unwrapping his third bar, he paused and sat on the edge of the tub. How long would he need this food to last? It was clear they wanted to let him live, at least for a little longer. Unfortunately, the large number of protein bars implied he faced a long stay in his new prison.

The third one went down more slowly as he began to take an inventory of his backpack. Emptying the bag, he was shocked to find his laptop underneath all the bars. Richard became emotional as he recalled the hell he'd endured to retrieve it, and the backup of his wife locked within the hard drive.

Opening the laptop, he found a handwritten note. Immediately, Richard recognized Yashira's handwriting.

The truth will set you free. Go to your website.

Logging into his laptop, Richard first verified that Virginia's file was still there. Glad she appeared safe, he next found the only wireless network available. Ironically, the network was named "who-is-the-good-guy." He attempted to connect and was prompted for a password. "The Truth" was his first try, but that didn't work. Many variations of that failed as well.

Over an hour passed as he tried different passwords with no luck, the laptop power slowly draining down to 18 percent. He hadn't found his power cord in the backpack, so he lowered the screen brightness to conserve energy. The key to his freedom, Richard suspected, would be found at *his* website, which was his in name only. His captors wanted him to go there, but evidently delighted in mentally torturing him along the way.

The power had dropped to 9 percent when he finally tried "BinaryMessenger." He cheered when it connected successfully. Quickly, he rushed to ProfessorRichardNelson.com and saw this message:

Dear Richard,

The bathroom you're in is located in the basement of an abandoned building that will soon be demolished. No one can hear you. If your people are worthy, the door will open. Let's see if they're smart enough to own the future.

If the door does open, run to the airport. You'll find directions on the outside of the door. Your ticket is waiting there for you, but if you miss your flight, I won't be able to protect you anymore.

Hurry home. Make Galanteen stand down. Wash the blood from your hands forever.

Sincerely,

Yashira Gravinsky

The battery power reduced to 5 percent. Richard copied the message and pasted it into a word document. He subsequently attempted to reach his webmail account, but was redirected to ProfessorRichardNelson.com. Next, he tried to open a chat connection to Pari, but received a network error message. With the battery now at 3 percent, he tried to reach several social media sites, hoping to post a plea for help. Every attempt redirected him back to *his* website.

The battery reached 2 percent, and he closed the laptop, figuring he might need to save that power for later if he devised a plan.

Curious what other surprises awaited him, Richard scrambled through his bag. In the small pocket, he found his phone charger. Richard continued to survey the contents of his bag, and upon completion, released a long desperate cry for help.

After the echo finished reverberating through the small room and silence took over, Richard decided to pack everything away in his backpack. The door might open any minute, or in days, or never. Still, he had to stay prepared.

As he waited for a rescue that might never come, Richard stroked his now-mangy beard and wondered exactly how long he'd been trapped. In haste, he logged into his laptop and looked at the date and time, which read *March 7, 2014, 7:29 a.m.* This told him he was now starting his seventh day in captivity. A brief double-check of his itinerary showed his original flight was scheduled to leave Kuala Lumpur in about seventeen hours. So, perhaps he was still in Kuala Lumpur and that was the ticket waiting for him, but he might be anywhere within several days' driving distance from Penang.

Richard contemplated Yashira's letter. This might also just be a grand lie to torture him. Would the door ever open? Was there even a ticket? He hoped so, but if true, he wondered what other truths she had spoken.

Did he have blood on his hands? Perhaps he wasn't as innocent as he'd always believed. Richard wanted to save humanity from themselves, not to be part of their self-destruction. Doubt filled his depleted mind. Possibly that was what Yashira truly wanted most of all—for Richard to die confused, trapped, and alone like her mother.

While pondering this, his laptop screen went black. He welcomed it to the ranks of the powerless.

CHAPTER 51 – BRAIN TEASING

Shortly after sunset on Thursday evening, another message arrived from the BinaryMessenger. Marisa's phone sounded the alarm, sending everyone scurrying from around the house to join her in the living room. Within a few minutes, they had decoded the BinaryMessenger's shortest message yet.

"*Solve the riddle to rescue ProfessorRichardNelson.com*," Marisa read aloud. Upon visiting the website, she saw the home page was no longer blank, and instead displayed:

Question 1: What is the theme?

Below the question was a textbox. Finally, on day seven of their rescue mission, they'd gotten their first chance to respond to the kidnappers. Marisa typed in *flatness* and clicked submit. A response came back in green that said, *Correct!* Several people lauded Quinn for discovering that.

After clicking continue, she was prompted with the next question: *Question 2: How many times does it appear?* She guessed twenty and submitted her answer.

The response disappointed everyone: *Incorrect. Wait one minute to try again.* A countdown clock ticked off one minute, and then the form reappeared. Twenty-one was also incorrect. After a few minutes of incrementing guesses, they discovered the correct answer was twenty-three.

"I just got word from Hector," Tina said. "They infiltrated the malware network and traced the source of the last binary message. It resolves back to the same IP address as the website ProfessorRichardNelson.com. They say it really is coming from the Vostok Station, or they're routing through it, in any case."

All the Pikes were a trifle disappointed at the news. "Thanks, Tina," Pari said. "It's better to at least know that. Unfortunately, it doesn't tell us where Richard is. Hopefully, these riddles will."

With two questions answered correctly, their excitement started to build, though the next question was harder. The screen showed: *Question 3: Can you name each reference?*

Marisa created a shared document for everyone to input the references they found. Soon it contained twenty lines, one for each flat reference the team could identify.

"We need to find three more!" Victor said urgently.

They went through the riddles again, searching meticulously for three missing references. Over the next hour they found one more—Flat Stanley. Another two hours passed without any progress. Just past midnight, Pari asked Jenny to make more coffee, and Gerald ordered some pizzas.

Around 1:00 a.m., Tina squealed, "Flatbed pickup truck!" Everyone groaned for not seeing that one sooner.

"Only one away," James said tiredly, "but this might not be the last question. We need to consider working in shifts, so some of us can sleep. If this drags on, we'll need fresh minds, especially if additional riddles are yet to come."

The mood sank upon hearing his last sentence. No one had yet considered that possibility, nor did they wish to distract themselves with the thought.

"Maybe," replied Marisa curtly, and the others were content to leave it at that. None of them wanted to volunteer for the first shift of sleep. Who could sleep with Richard's freedom possibly within their grasp at last?

At 2:00 a.m., Pari voiced a change of heart. "Perhaps us older folks should sleep the first shift," she suggested. "Gerald and I will take a three-hour nap. Some of you should also take a two-hour nap. That way, the remaining ones can go to bed at 4:00 a.m." Although the five youngsters were all tired, they each refused to take the first nap. Pari settled the matter by saying, "The guys will sleep first, and then the girls after."

While Tina refilled coffee for Marisa and herself, Quinn realized a flaw in their approach. "We haven't submitted a try in hours while we've been coming up with our list of references," she pointed out. "What if the twenty-two we've found so far aren't the right ones? We should have been checking that in parallel."

Dread filled Marisa's face. "You're right. We also don't know the proper format for submitting the references. Is it one per line? Comma-delimited? And each reference may need to be worded exactly, to some unknown specification. Do they need to be full sentences? Like, 'Paper is flat in rock-paper-scissors,' or can we just say 'paper'?" She shook her head. "There may be multiple variations for each reference, with only one being a match."

Tina nodded. "We should start exploring how to test the format and wording."

Marisa copied the list of the twenty-two references they'd found from their shared document into the form and submitted it. The response said, *7 of 23 references found.* All three girls sighed in relief. Now that they'd received feedback, the problem appeared solvable.

"Let's start working on a program," Quinn suggested, "to automatically submit one permutation every minute and keep track of the correct ones." Both Marisa and Tina liked the idea. To compensate for their fatigue, Marisa suggested Tina and Quinn pair-program the submission script. Meanwhile, Marisa prepared the input data with as many possible permutations as she could come up with for each reference.

Without her laptop and special equipment, coding directly wasn't an option for Quinn, though she could instead watch someone else code and provide verbal assistance. She greatly wished she wasn't partnered with Tina, but knowing this would be a petty objection, she kept it to herself.

Given the one-submission-per-minute restriction, Marisa put what she believed were the most likely answers for each reference at the front of the list. Their goal was to have the program up and running by 4:00 a.m. to hand off to the boys.

It only took them thirty minutes to put the script together, and by 4:00, the program had tried dozens of possibilities and found the right formatting for all twenty-two known matches. Relieved and utterly exhausted, the girls prepared to hand their work off to the next shift.

While Marisa went to wake Victor and James, Tina asked Quinn, "Would it be okay if I help you into bed?"

Quinn looked up hesitantly at her new coding partner and said, "I…I would appreciate that. Thank you."

Soon after, Victor and James entered the kitchen and began their search for the last remaining reference. With slightly fresher eyes, they re-read the riddles several times. Nothing obvious jumped out at them.

"We're losing time," Victor said anxiously. "It's been like seven hours.

What if Richard's life depends on speed?"

"What do you suggest we do to go faster?" James asked.

Victor thought for a moment. "We need to bring in help. Come with me."

A few minutes later, Victor found himself virtually sitting with Richie in Cendovia, while James sat beside him in the bunker back on Earth. "It is an interesting problem," mused Richie. "I'm glad you came to me. Let's see if we can't use our creation to thwart the destroyers for once."

"What do you mean?" Victor asked.

"Look for the settings that accelerate my timeline," Richie instructed. "Then check in with me every ten Earth minutes. That will give me hour-long segments to contemplate the problem. Text me the riddles, along with your existing matches, and I'll find the last match."

James began typing out all the information for Richie to read. After a few minutes, it was ready, and they sent Richie barreling forward in time at six times the speed of light.

At the first checkpoint, Richie told them that the sentence *"My opponent accused me of sleeping around, but that was just a lie"* seemed out of place. He believed they'd included it to make a flat reference.

"I know," Victor said. "The 'around' seems like a round reference, the opposite of flat." Plugging Marisa's laptop into the external Ethernet cable, they submitted a few variations of phrases, such as "round is the opposite of flat," but with no success.

After letting Richie know of the results, they gave him another warp-speed thinking session. Ten minutes later, Richie had another suggestion for them. *"I wanted to tell you this like a minute after you left, but I had to wait almost an hour for you to slow me down and check in. It feels like we can inject flat into the second half of the sentence, as in 'a flat-out lie.' You know, as opposed to a simple misstatement."*

James added this to their list and submitted. When the response came back—*23 of 23 references found*—they emitted screams of joy that were unheard by their above-ground compatriots. James jumped out of his seat and smacked Victor on the shoulder, shouting, "We did it!" Victor pushed him playfully in the chest, and the two guys jumped around as though they were celebrating a touchdown.

The final twenty-three answers were:

1. *Flatbread*
2. *Flat soda*
3. *Flat water*
4. *Flat expression*
5. *Flat paper*
6. *Flatbed pickup truck*
7. *Flats shoes*
8. *Flat-chested women*
9. *Flattop haircut*
10. *Flat feet*
11. *Flat Stanley*
12. *Flat-head screwdrivers*
13. *British apartments are called flats*
14. *Flat lake waters*
15. *Flat roofs*
16. *Flat paint*
17. *Flat screen televisions*
18. *C flat*
19. *Jokes fell flat*
20. *Flat tax*
21. *Steamroller flattened opponent*
22. *Opponent's heart flatlined*
23. *Flat-out lie*

James thanked Richie and returned him to suspended animation before they hightailed it back to the kitchen with Marisa's laptop. They pondered the next question over breakfast and agreed this was the hardest one of all. Victor read it aloud: "'Question 4: Where is he?'"

"It might be anywhere in the world," James said, "but it's probably nowhere in the world. There's no place like this."

"Well, the story is clearly fiction," Victor said, "but I have a hunch they're somehow leading us to the real place Richard is. At one point, the mayor says, 'the best town in this state.' To me, that means it's in the U.S."

James expressed doubt that Richard was in the United States, given he was last seen in Malaysia. He couldn't imagine why the kidnappers would bring Richard back, though James also professed to not understand why they did anything. Victor and James continued eating while contemplating the run-time of a brute force attempt of every U.S. city. In twenty-four hours, they could try 1,440 cities at one per minute. A quick search told them there were over 35,000 American cities and townships, meaning it would take them over three weeks to try them all. They needed a smarter way.

Just then, Tina and Marisa ambled into the kitchen. "Wow, it's already six?" Victor said in surprise.

"No," Marisa said, "it's a quarter to five, but neither of us was able to sleep."

James updated the girls on their progress. Wearily, Tina suggested, "If we bring up a list of U.S. cities, we can start narrowing down the possibilities. Given the theme, it likely contains the word flat."

Marisa reclaimed her laptop from the boys as she and Tina sat down at the kitchen table. Chewing on a piece of toast, she soon found and downloaded a list from the government's census site. Her query discovered the word flat only forty-six times in the list, including a few duplicates.

Within twenty minutes, they'd identified the correct match—Flatonia, Texas. With all four questions answered correctly, the form now displayed a message that read, *"Go there. Check the bathroom. 29.6951888, -97.10559794."*

The whole room erupted in a roar of cheers right as Pari, Gerald, and Quinn came to join the party. Although Quinn's shift didn't start for almost an hour, she, too, had been unable to sleep. While Pari tried to understand what was going on, Tina embraced her and yelled, "We did it! We found Richard!"

Victor jumped out of his seat and hugged James. Marisa hugged them both.

Amid the jubilation, Tina drifted over to Quinn and said, "Quinn, we couldn't have done this without you." She looked down, then shyly added, "Ya know, I think we make a good team. I really liked pairing with you."

"I'm sorry," escaped Quinn's lips, to her own surprise. "For everything. It wasn't your fault."

The wall Quinn had worked so hard to erect finally came tumbling down. Tina bridged the once-icy distance between them and embraced her. "Me too," Tina said, hugging Quinn, both with their eyes closed.

Pari returned the emotional crew's focus to the most pressing matter. "C'mon, people, we need to go bring him home!"

The Pikes settled down quickly. "He's in Flatonia," Victor said.

With haste, Marisa sat down and began typing. "If we hurry, we can catch a non-stop flight to Austin that leaves in three hours. It's an hour drive there from Austin."

In a serious tone, Victor said, "I'm going alone."

The room went silent. Every Pike wanted to go rescue Richard.

"It might be a trap," Victor told them. "This could just be elaborate bait to take more hostages. What would Richard do?" When the others failed to answer, he added, "He wouldn't put others in unnecessary danger. He would go in alone."

The case was well-articulated, and Gerald and Pari both agreed that was indeed what Richard would do. Tina and Quinn each commended Victor for his noble sentiment, but expressed discomfort with his decision.

"Victor, you don't have to go alone," Marisa said, standing to face him. "I'll go with you."

Placing his hand on her shoulder, Victor told his friend, "Marisa, thank you. You have looked out for me since the day we met. But if Richard is dead, there's no sense in risking your life along with mine."

At these words, the air seemed to flood out of the room, as Victor had said what most of them hadn't wanted to consider. The riddles might simply be leading them to Richard's body. If the objective was to terrorize them, this would be a clever and effective approach.

"If Richard is *injured*," James said, toning down the severity, "you'll need help carrying him. That's why I'm going with you."

Reluctantly, Victor acknowledged the truth of this statement, and the debate was settled. A few minutes later, the Pikes were hugging James and Victor goodbye and cautioning them to be safe.

Though Quinn requested it, there was no time for them to create backups before leaving. The finality of it all sank in for her, and she feared she'd never see Victor again. Victor might never know how she felt about him.

But before Quinn could pull him aside for a private word, Tina unexpectedly planted a long kiss on Victor's lips—a kiss he returned in full measure. Watching them, Quinn's heart began to break, unable to bear the sight. Her eyes welled up and spilled over, and she felt utterly helpless, unable to even conceal her own tears.

Their other friends crowded in to wish them off, squeezing Quinn to the back of the group. Unable to see Victor anymore, she closed her eyes, hoping to dam the rivers flowing from them. It was like he was already gone, and she was incomplete again.

Warm hands wiped the tears from her cheeks, and Quinn opened her eyes to find Victor at eye level with her. With reckless abandon, she blurted out, "I can't do this without you."

Victor hugged her in her wheelchair and placed his forehead on hers. As she listened to him breathing, she was close enough to see what he was hiding. He was afraid.

In a soft voice, he told her, "I'll come back for you, my friend."

Kissing her softly on the cheek, Victor departed with James to save Richard.

CHAPTER 52 – FLATTENED

The fog broke as the plane descended below the clouds. Through the raindrops streaking across the window, Victor spotted a winding river leading into rolling hills that were a patchwork of dark green, light green, and tan. Tiny spots bordered thin lines interlacing the landscape—houses lining the roads leading into Austin.

Victor had never been to Texas, and he had never flown first class. This had been a smart call by Pari, he thought, as it would allow them to be first off the plane. Victor also knew James's decision to decline drinks from the flight attendant would keep them clear-headed for their mission. Still, he would have liked a drink to calm his nerves, as his mind kept imagining the worst scenarios. What if Richard was dead? What if his captors kidnapped him and James as well? Though Victor was itching to discuss all the possible outcomes, he wisely didn't voice any of them during the flight. Both he and James knew better than to say anything aloud that would raise suspicion.

James turned left out of the car rental lot, and the rain stopped soon after they hit the road. Within a few minutes, they were heading east on TX-71 on dry pavement. Their destination was a sandwich shop off I-10 in Flatonia. It matched the GPS coordinates from the message, as well as the first line of the riddle.

Victor finally asked his first question. "What if this is a trap?"

"That *is* a possibility," James acknowledged. "Keep your eyes open for anything suspicious. We're playing their game on their terms, and on their timetable. They've forced us to move in, unprepared, to a setting they've had a lot of time to prep. Plus, we're going in unarmed."

Even if they'd had firearms, Victor didn't have any clue how they could have transported them on the plane, as neither of them had weapons registered to them or concealed weapon permits.

"Look for anything that's off," James instructed, "though if they're as crafty as I think they are, we'll probably never see them coming."

"Well, that's comforting," Victor said.

"Ain't nothing comforting about any of this," replied James. "I'm not here to comfort you. Stay focused and alert, but let's not panic. We've got an hour drive ahead of us, so let's talk through our approach."

"What if we find him dead?" Victor said, staring at the horizon as the car sped past the open countryside.

"That will be the hardest scenario for many reasons," James said. "Of course, beyond the obvious horror of finding him dead, what to do next is the real challenge. Do we call the police? If we don't, we'll appear guilty. If we try to secretly transport his body ourselves, we'll seem extra guilty. Still, a police investigation might uncover things Richard would prefer left secret."

James sighed. "Another real possibility is that they're going to try to frame us for Richard's murder. It would be very hard to defend ourselves, since we have no proof of the BinaryMessenger that we can share. And us being on the scene in the middle of nowhere looks awfully suspicious. Frankly, it would be a much easier trap for them to set than attempting to capture or kill us. Much safer for them, too. One anonymous phone call when we arrive, and we're done."

Victor hadn't considered this kind of trap, and now realized they were nearly defenseless. "Why would they do that? What do they stand to gain?"

"We really don't know why they're doing any of this. It might be they have a personal vendetta against Richard and want to take him and anyone near him down, or it may be any one of a dozen other reasons."

Neither of them spoke for a while. As they turned onto Farm Road 154, Victor said, "Well, whatever their motive is, we'll known soon enough. We'll be there in twenty minutes."

~ ~ ~

Eighteen time zones away, Connor laid in his hotel bed in the early morning. Another fruitless day of driving around Kuala Lumpur had left him feeling empty and restless.

While wasting time on social media, scrolling through his news feed, he received a text message. All it said was the word *found*.

Connor shot straight up in his bed, immediately encouraged. The message came from an application he'd written a few days prior. Every minute, the application checked the "Find my Phone" website provided by Richard's cell phone carrier, using the credentials that Pari had provided him for Richard's account. After he'd found himself futilely checking the website several times a day, Connor had opted to automate away his nervous habit.

Hurrying to the website, Connor exclaimed, "Yes!" at the sight of a blinking dot on the map. He bolted out of bed and banged on the bathroom door. Owen opened it with shaving cream on his face. "Found him!" Connor said breathlessly, showing him the phone.

Owen quickly wiped his face while rapidly giving Connor orders. "Get me directions. We're leaving now."

"Already got 'em," Connor said. "He's just north of the airport. ETA thirty-nine minutes."

~ ~ ~

"We cannot look suspicious," James cautioned Victor. "If we happen upon a dead body, we'll report it, but we'll act as if we don't know him. The cover story is that we're passing through on our way from Austin to Houston to visit friends. Once we get to the shop, we have to act like customers, so I'll buy us sandwiches while you go to the bathroom. And remember—anyone we meet could be the BinaryMessenger or someone working with him. So, don't trust *anyone.*"

Victor's face tensed as he tried to remain calm. James, who had been in a few fights—though never anything like this—didn't reveal any trepidation.

A few minutes before 3:00 p.m., they arrived at the restaurant. Being well past the lunch hour, there were no other customers in the sandwich shop. The young lady behind the counter was scrolling on her phone and took a moment before putting it down. As planned, James walked to the counter to order their sandwiches, and Victor walked straight back to find the bathroom.

There were two unisex bathrooms. Victor tried the door on the left and, finding it unlocked, peeked in. The bathroom was empty. Next, he tried the door on the right, but it was locked. His heart began racing. Could it actually be? Were they about to free Richard? He knocked on the door, careful not to knock so loud as to make a scene. No response came, and he hesitated to knock again. Though he was out of sight of the cashier, it would appear suspicious if he repeatedly knocked when there was another restroom available.

Trying the handle more forcefully this time, Victor still failed to open the locked door. He wished he had that flat-head screwdriver to pry the door open, or to take the door off its hinges. Instead, he ducked into the other restroom to complete his cover. The restroom was fairly clean, and Victor decided to use it, not having had a bathroom break since the flight. As he stood in front of the toilet, he noticed some graffiti etched into the tile on the back wall at eye level. It read *BM below*.

Most graffiti Victor had seen said something lewd or reminded the reader that someone had been there. This seemed a childish reminder of where to move one's bowels, and he wondered if that was just the kind of graffiti one could expect to find in rural Texas.

Another possibility occurred to him while he air-dried his hands. What if the BM didn't stand for bowel movement, but for BinaryMessenger? Or binary message? Victor examined the graffiti again, then looked all around the toilet and the wall behind it, but discovered nothing out of the ordinary. Then he lifted up the lid and checked inside the toilet tank. On the bottom of the tank lid, he found a long etching of seemingly random, alphanumeric characters.

Before replacing the tank cover, Victor snapped a picture with his phone, then rejoined James, who was sitting at the table closest to the bathrooms. With his back to the entrance, James ate his sandwich, eyeing the bathroom doors.

"Flatbread? Really?" Victor asked as he took a seat across from him.

"They're right," James said with a shrug. "It's not bad, and the soda's not flat."

"Check this out," Victor said quietly, sliding his phone across the table. Right away, James understood this was meant for them. He didn't need Victor to tell him it was from the BinaryMessenger. A quick glance up at the clerk showed her seated on a stool behind the register, preoccupied with her phone again. "One is open, the other is locked," Victor told him.

The guys ate slowly, to keep their cover as patrons as long as possible. "Do you think it's a key?" Victor asked. "A code to unlock the door?"

"I don't know," James answered between bites. "Was there anything else in there? On the walls? Floor? Ceiling? Any clue how to use this code?"

Trying to recall if he might have missed anything, Victor finally said, "No. Just the 'BM below' message that led me to this."

James excused himself to use the restroom and subsequently combed it thoroughly for a few minutes, but found nothing new.

Barely back in his seat, James saw the door to the other bathroom open. An older man walked out, wearing a dusty cowboy hat. With his head down, James couldn't see his face.

Eager at the possibility of seeing Richard again, Victor stood upon hearing the door open, then pivoted and hugged the man in one blurred motion. An instant later, Victor's back slammed into the hallway wall as the man held him up by his armpits.

"What are you playing at, boy!" the man said in southern drawl. In the commotion, the cowboy hat had fallen off to reveal he was not Richard. Victor's emotional reasoning had led him to see what he'd wanted to see, rather than what was actually there.

Pinned to the wall, Victor stammered as he studied the man. Given his gray flattop and his old-man strength, it seemed quite likely he had served in the military. Afraid he'd fallen into the kidnappers' trap, Victor pulled at the man's wrists, trying to free himself.

Rushing over, James tried to defuse the situation. In a flash, he ruled out hitting the old man, thinking that would make the situation much worse. A black man hitting an old white man might not go over very well in rural Texas, and he didn't want to become another statistic. Instead, James picked up the man's hat and said, "I'm so sorry, sir. My friend's very clumsy. Really, he's flat-footed. He was just rushing for the bathroom."

The man released Victor with a menacing glower, placed his cowboy hat back on his head, and told him, "Look before you leap, kid." After tipping his hat to the girl behind the counter, the old veteran exited the shop.

James and Victor slowly returned to their seats, both a bit unnerved. "Flat-footed?" Victor whispered.

"Well, he's clearly not the mayor," James said, after laughing in mild relief. "I mean, his expression was anything but flat, but he almost flattened you."

Victor didn't understand how James could joke at a time like this. Then, unexpectedly, James handed his cup to Victor and said, "Get me a refill while you're up."

Victor wasn't up, and they didn't need refills, but after freezing for a confused moment, he processed James's message. With both cups in hand, he went to get them refills, walked past the soda machine in the hallway, and directly into the second bathroom.

Upon closing the door behind him, he discovered it to be as clean and empty as the first. After scouring the room thoroughly, he came up with nothing. No clues. Returning to the table with the cups no fuller than when he'd left, Victor saw James already standing with the sandwiches wrapped up.

"Let's go," he told Victor, and then walked out the door. Silently, Victor followed him, wondering what was going on. Neither spoke until they were both in the car.

"That engraving you found—it's a base-64 message. See?" James said, holding up his phone for Victor to read the decoded message on the screen. It read, *No more games*, followed by a shorter base-64 string.

"It's a dead end!" James growled, fuming. The tires kicked up dust from the dirt parking lot as he slammed on the gas. "An elaborate diversion! They brought us out here to tell us the game is over!"

"Wait!" Victor pleaded. "How can you be so sure? What about the bit underneath? Did you decode that?"

Waving his hands emphatically as they sped away, James said, "It doesn't translate to ASCII text. Some sort of non-textual binary, like an encryption key, or an encrypted message with a missing key. Either way, it has to be a tease. We played their game, and they said Richard was free, and now they say game over, but hand us a secret key?" James shook his head. "No way. Time to break out of this infinite loop of mind games!"

As Victor prepared to call Marisa to tell her what they'd found, his phone rang. Surprisingly, Marisa was already calling *him*.

~ ~ ~

Owen kept his lead foot in check as they sped through the light Saturday morning traffic. The last thing they needed now was to get pulled over. Connor navigated with his own phone while simultaneously relaying various instructions to the Galanteen crew via Owen's phone.

"Get me everything you can on that building. Tell them I want blueprints!" Owen barked.

Connor passed the messages along and waited. Meanwhile, he pulled up what he could find on his own. "It looks like it's in a small industrial park north of the airport. Some fields nearby. No shops or business show up on the map."

Reaching under his seat, Owen grabbed something and handed it to Connor. "Safety's on," he told him.

As he took the handgun, the enormity of the moment began to sink in for Connor. He tried to steel himself for a showdown. *We're really doing this*, he told himself. Connor had never fired a shot at a living thing, and he'd certainly never had to worry about someone firing at him.

His thoughts were interrupted by a buzzing from Owen's phone. "Just got this from Galanteen," Connor said. "The building is unoccupied. It's scheduled for demolition… Turn right! That's your exit!"

Owen swiftly cut across three lanes to hit the off ramp. "Okay, kid. Pay attention to the directions." They sped past old, abandoned office buildings with no traffic in sight.

"Sorry, we're two minutes out. Almost there."

"When is the demolition scheduled for?" Owen asked.

Connor sent the question to Galanteen, and Owen took his mental governor off his heavy foot. Racing up an empty straightaway, Connor waited for an answer. He filled the anxious seconds by wondering if he could really pull the trigger if the moment came.

Up ahead, Connor caught sight of barriers stretching across the street. "Today!" he screamed after reading the response from Galanteen. "Demolition is today!"

Owen approached the barriers at full speed, then slammed on the brakes just in time to avoid hitting them. He jumped out of the car, and Connor tucked the pistol into his waistband, then followed Owen's lead.

As they looked around, they noticed there wasn't another soul in sight. "You sure that's the building?" Owen asked.

"Yeah," Connor said, looking down at his phone to check one more time. But he already knew it was when he heard a thunderous *pop*. Two more *pops* reached his ears before he even managed to look up. Reaching for his weapon, the vision before him revealed that he wasn't being fired upon. A series of successive *pops* followed, and the ensuing roar of concrete and steel crumbling formed a cacophony. The middle of the building exploded in a choreographed dance that brought the wrath of each floor pounding onto the one beneath it in an accelerating chain reaction, culminating in the entire building stomping brutally on the basement, burying itself in its own foundation. The ground shook at their feet as an overwhelming cloud of dust rose from the rubble.

"Give me a reading," Owen said urgently as they both shielded themselves from the dust.

"What?" Connor coughed.

"Find him!" Owen said, grabbing Connor's right arm. "The phone! Where is he? Where's Richard?"

Connor looked down at his now-empty map with dread. "Gone."

~ ~ ~

James heard Victor say, "Okay… No?… No!… How did you find out?" He could tell from the tone it was bad news, and he tried to decipher what they were talking about. When Victor told Marisa that it fit with the "no more games" message they had received, James got a sinking feeling in his stomach.

The game was over, and they had lost.

When Victor got off the phone, he couldn't find the words to tell James. But James already understood.

Richard was dead.

Victor stared out the passenger window at the farmland rolling by him, unable to say the words yet. He thought of his father—this was like losing him all over again. A sudden rage possessed him, and he pounded his fists on the dashboard, kicking his legs and screaming at the top of his lungs.

On the dusty shoulder beside the road, James pulled over and turned off the engine. Each of them exited the car, surrounded by eerily silent pastures in all directions. Victor's father had left him too soon, fighting the good fight. And now, Richard—the closest thing he had to a father figure—had died a leader for his cause.

James put his hand on Victor's shoulder, but Victor stepped away, rubbing his eyes. Turning back to James, he finally found the courage to speak the words.

"Richard was inside a building that collapsed right in front of Owen and Connor," he told James. "He's gone. It's game over, just like the BinaryMessenger said."

~ ~ ~

The trip home was a somber one. Utterly dejected, Victor and James hardly spoke to each other on the return trip. James thought they must be the saddest first-class passengers ever, but this time, he didn't refuse the drinks. The guys briefly toasted to Richard and downed their first round quickly. The second came slower. Yet, nothing felt slower than the plane, as they both desperately wanted to be home.

Around 11:00 p.m., Pari picked them up from San Francisco International. On the ride back, she told them the whole team was still at Richard's house, waiting for them. She explained that Owen and Connor were on their way, too. Their flight would bring them home the following afternoon.

"Are we *sure* Richard was in the building?" James asked.

"No, but I'm sure he's dead," Pari said, tears welling in her eyes. Victor started to question this, but she interrupted. "The flight Richard was scheduled to get on went missing fourteen hours ago over the Indian Ocean, presumed lost at sea. The airline called me just before I picked you up, as I was his emergency contact. He was on the plane." Her voice trembling, she added, "Somehow, he escaped, and got on that plane. And then they killed him anyway."

In a matter of hours, Victor had been told Richard had died twice. First, crushed by an exploding building, then killed in a plane crash. He knew Richard hadn't suffered both deaths, but Victor suffered twice at the news of each one.

Upon entering the house, they found the crew eager to greet them. Melancholy hugs were exchanged all around. The tightest for Victor came from Tina. He clutched her close to him, trying to hold back sobs as she murmured comforting words in his ear.

Quinn interrupted their long embrace by welcoming Victor back, and he reminded her that he'd kept his promise to return. Then Pari ushered them all into the kitchen, where the table was filled with take-out Chinese food. Quite hungry from their taxing day, James and Victor each served themselves a plateful.

Over dinner, Victor asked no one in particular, "Has anyone told Richie?"

The others exchanged glances. "No, we have not," Pari said.

"Then I'll do it," Victor said, glumly taking a bite of his sesame chicken. Pari agreed that would be what Richard would want. Quinn offered to help, and Victor accepted her support.

As he ate in silence, Victor pondered how to go about it. There was no precedent for this. No one had ever had to tell someone that they were dead.

CHAPTER 53 – RESPONSE OF THE LIVING

The Pikes slept in late on Saturday morning. Even though their rescue mission had failed, no one went home the night before. All waited anxiously for Connor and Owen to return safely in the afternoon.

They huddled together to watch the news, in hopes of a miraculous rescue for Malaysian Airlines Flight 370, despite understanding it was unlikely, considering the region of the Indian Ocean where the plane was last detected. In such a remote location with a vast search area, there was no logical reason to hold out hope. Victor told them as much, saying what most were thinking, but no one else had the courage to say. He had never wanted so badly to be wrong.

Throughout the morning and into the early afternoon, they watched the news intently. As the afternoon marched toward the evening, the gathering became something akin to a wake. The friends exchanged their favorite stories about Richard. Pari told them how she met Richard, Gerald, and Virginia at Caltech and had been friends ever since. Victor relived his first encounter with the professor, being thrown out of his class, and laughed about it.

"I'll miss that S.O.B.," he said, holding back tears.

"We all will," Tina said, sitting on the couch with her arm around him.

"Today we mourn, and we celebrate Richard," Pari said to the team. "Tomorrow, we return to the very important work he started. Richard would want us to move on, to fulfill our mission. Don't believe me? Go ask him yourself."

Taking Victor's hand, Pari said, "Speaking of which, it's time." With a small nod, he acknowledged the necessity of the conversation he had been dreading.

~ ~ ~

When Pari escorted him to the bunker, Victor found Gerald talking to Quinn, who was waiting in the scanner for him. "I think this is something you two should do alone, in person," Pari said. Victor agreed, and Quinn listened to the *click* of the bunker door closing behind her mother and father.

Wearing ear buds and a VR mask, Quinn stared into the blackness. Though unable to see Victor, this was her first moment alone with him since he'd returned, and there were things she wanted to say.

"Wait!" she called to him. "Don't start Cendovia yet." She heard his muffled acknowledgment and then blurted out, "I'm really glad you made it back."

She felt his hand caress her hair. "Me, too."

Quinn smiled, expecting him to remove her VR headset, but he didn't. "I mean," she said nervously, "what would I do on Sundays without you?"

He laughed, and part of her was glad he hadn't removed her mask. It was easier to tell him this way. She understood she'd lost her bid for his heart to Tina. Still, she wanted him to understand she cared, without also losing their friendship. Too much had already been lost recently.

"Quinn," he said, still stroking her hair, "I don't know what I would do without you, either. Thanks for helping me deliver this message to Richie."

Her heart beat faster as she pondered why he didn't remove her mask. Was it also easier for him? "Anytime," she said lightly. "I'm always here for you."

"Same here," Victor said, and she pictured his smile.

"Promise?"

"Promise."

"Okay," she said. "But, ya know, you didn't even leave me a backup. You just rushed out of here."

"Let's hope we won't need that for a long time."

"Please, Victor. I'm serious," she told him. "Promise me you won't leave me alone. I need you here for me, always. I need you to keep your promise."

"I will always be with you, my friend. Now, let's go talk to Richie."

Quinn inhaled as her heart neared the surface of her chest. Victor also inhaled deeply as he donned his VR gear and rehearsed his message to Richie.

~ ~ ~

Victor and Quinn sat in patio chairs on Richie's balcony, looking out over the serene ocean. The Cendovian sun was setting behind them, and the buildings cast long shadows over the shore and into the water.

"To what do I owe the pleasure?" Richie said as he walked outside to join them. At Victor's request, Richie took a seat between Victor and Quinn, sensing bad news coming.

"I'm not sure how to say this," Victor began. All his thoughts seemed to deadlock. The news was difficult enough to tell others, but how to tell Richie of his former self's death? Not only was there no precedent for delivering such news, there was no precedent for receiving it.

As though talking to a ghost, Quinn knelt before Richie and, holding his hands, said, "You died."

Richie looked startled. "I don't feel dead."

"I mean Richard is dead," she said gently. "His plane was lost at sea."

The news was hard for Richie to take. He imagined the agony this must be causing his loved ones. Naturally, he had a strong connection with Richard, having *been* him for nearly all his life. The two had only diverged as separate people a few days prior in Richie's timeline. And while he'd agreed to let others call him Richie, he still believed he was the true Richard.

Quinn pulled him to his feet and hugged him, and Richie hugged her back. He appreciated having someone he could feel who felt him, too.

"Are you okay?" Victor asked.

"I am," Richie said honestly. "I'm sad for the loss of my brother, and for the man I used to be, but also grateful to have cheated death, to have gotten out in time. I will miss my brother. We had some good conversations. Yet, he lives on in me."

Both of Richie's guests smiled, and he thanked them for coming to talk to him in person. "That was something Richard would never do. It was as if he and I were matter and antimatter, and we would cancel each other out if we were ever in the same place at the same time. So, he ensured we kept our distance."

Quinn and Victor chuckled at this, and Quinn squeezed Richie's hand.

"Victor," Richie said, "I once told you that it's possible that all intelligent life in the universe destroys itself before getting the chance to contact us. However, there is perhaps a more optimistic answer to the cosmic silence. Perhaps some species don't die out, but instead retreat to alternate dimensions of their own making. The responsibility to maintain the Cendovian code now passes to you. That's what Richard wanted, and that's what I want, too. A great responsibility has been placed upon you, but know that you're not alone. I will be here to guide you."

Lowering his gaze, Victor said, "I hope I'm ready."

"Life doesn't wait for us to be ready," said Richie. "Few are ever ready for the greatest challenges in their lives. But I know you will rise to the challenge."

Victor thanked him, and an awkward silence ensued, filled only by the waves crashing gently on the shore far below.

"Does this mean everyone can start calling me Richard?" Richie asked.

"Might be too soon," Quinn said. "Give us a bit more time to absorb this."

"Okay. I'd like some time myself as well. Before you go, will you please set the pause delay to one hour? So I can mourn my brother?"

Victor agreed, and told Richie he would return tomorrow to speak with him again. On their way out, Quinn stole one last hug before they vanished.

~ ~ ~

While Quinn and Victor were speaking with Richie, Pari conveyed to the others Richard's plan to spawn eight more brothers to accelerate the development of Cendovia. Richard had not completed the work necessary to empower these brothers to do their jobs, so these preparations would now fall to Victor.

Marisa asked, "So, let me see if I've got this straight. Richie is a copy of Richard. And we're gonna clone him eight more times—"

"Not clones," Pari interjected. "You all must understand this. A biological clone is a new life-form grown using the same genetic instructions. Richard's brothers will not be grown from the same genetic instructions. Their minds in the digital world will begin as exact replicas of the state of Richard's mind at a particular point in time. This makes all the difference when you consider who they are."

Watching her former students consider who these brothers would actually be, Pari elaborated. "Suppose the instant before my death, my mind is copied, and a moment later, the copy is uploaded inside Cendovia. That would still be me, only somewhere else, like I traveled to another dimension. Right?" The younger Pikes seemed a bit skeptical, though a few of them nodded. "After all, what does it mean to be oneself? If you lose an arm, are you not still Marisa? What about a leg? What if you get a heart transplant? Are you still the same person?"

"Of course," Marisa said.

Pari smiled at her. "Correct. Our society doesn't entertain the possibility that you are anything other than Marisa in such situations. Now, how much of your physical body do you need to retain to remain Marisa?"

"I don't know," Marisa said honestly.

"Well, let's figure it out together," Pari offered, transitioning into professor mode. "Suppose you suffered serious injuries, and somehow we could replace each body part with a transplant to piece you back together, with your brain being the only original part. Should we still believe you to be Marisa?"

Marisa and a few others nodded. "Yes," Pari said, "because what it means to be *you*—the very essence of you—is your mind. Consciousness is a subjective experience, and from your subjective perspective, you would most definitely believe you are still Marisa."

"I get it," Marisa said. "I retain my identity as long as I retain my brain."

"Almost," Gerald said, "but not your brain, your *mind*. There's a difference. Suppose one of your brain regions was at risk of deteriorating due to a disease and we could somehow copy the full state of that brain region into an inorganic transplant that could take its place. If we implanted the transplant while retaining your exact mental state with all your memories and personality, should society now refuse to acknowledge you as Marisa? Should your friends and family shun you as being no longer their friend, sister, or daughter? Of course not, because you would still be

Marisa."

"I see where you're going with this," Tina said. "If you then replace all her brain regions but retain her entire mental state, she is still Marisa."

"That's right, Tina," Pari answered. "You can replace the entire brain and not lose your identity, so long as you retain your mind. By contrast, suppose we wipe your brain clean of all its memories. A blank slate. Your body would be a mere shell that no longer contains *you*. Legally, you would retain your status as Tina, but those who know you would say the essence of Tina is gone. Sadly, I've seen dementia do this to many people, stealing much of their essence."

In full academic fervor, Gerald chimed in again, "So, you see, your essence isn't limited to your current physical body. The body is only a host for a certain neural network state we label 'you.' It's that which makes you yourself. Right now, that current state resides in your brain, and that state is constantly changing as you learn, grow, and age. Existence is more than just a singular state of being—it's the journey. All the things you experience, think, and feel don't just influence what you become, they become you. You are a culmination of the subjective experiences along your journey. If we wipe those out, you cease to exist, even if your body remains. Yet, if we retain all those, you continue to live on, even if you cease to have a biological host."

James said, "Okay, I think I get what you're trying to tell us. You're saying if we someday transcend, that would truly be *us* going over, not just a copy, right?"

"Right, but a little more than that," Gerald replied. "Suppose a scenario where I go to Cendovia, but I don't die on Earth. Instead, I both go and stay. Would that make the Cendovian version of me any less alive? Absolutely not, nor would it make the Earthling less alive. Now, would it make the Cendovian any less me? That's where things get a little weird to us. Our human languages evolved to contain labels like 'me' to express concepts we've experienced. But no one has ever experienced this before Cendovia existed. It allows us to both go somewhere and stay at the same time."

Pari added, "If you ask the Cendovian Richie, he will wholeheartedly profess that he is Richard, and has been so since 1961. He only laid down in a scanner and then began experiencing new things. He doesn't believe this invalidates his identity. Since consciousness and self-identification are subjective experiences, who are we to say he isn't Richard? Only for our convenience did he choose a different name as Richie. The whole notion of identity is inadequate to fully describe these scenarios. So, no, they're not clones. And while they're created via copying, they're much more than copies. Cendovians are just as alive as you and me."

Surveying the faces of her young followers, Pari said, "I want you all to truly appreciate what you are protecting. Richard truly lives on."

~ ~ ~

Upon returning to the first floor, Victor and Quinn relayed their conversation with Richie to the group, and Victor concluded, "Richard needs us now more than ever. We have to support the man and the mission he left behind."

None of them had heard Owen and Connor come through the front door while Victor was speaking. "I second that," Owen said.

Immediately, Marisa ran up to Connor and jumped into his arms. After kissing him repeatedly, she said in joyous relief, "I was so afraid I would lose you."

"What are you fussin' about?" Connor said, squeezing her tight. "You could've always restored me from backup." She smacked his shoulder playfully, but he pulled her close again and kissed her fiercely, as he'd been longing to do since he departed.

After warm greetings were exchanged all around for the returning Pikes, Pari said, "We still have much work to do, and now an enemy to consider."

"Time for contingency phase two," Owen announced.

Pari nodded at Owen and then turned her attention to the newest Pikes. "Each of you six will play a key role among the Pikes. Now that you all know of our mission, you can collaborate to accelerate our progress. Quinn, your work at Golden Bay Labs is particularly vital—you're our intrepid explorer, the only one who can go to Cendovia and come back alive. That's your superpower."

Gerald, seated between Quinn and Pari, wrapped his arm proudly around his daughter. She glowed with a pride that only comes from having a clear sense of purpose.

"James," Pari said next, directing her gaze at him, "you have been at Warp Drive since the very beginning. Always generous with your time, you are protective of your people. Warp Drive is about to begin an expansion from a small development shop to a complete company, and the world of CombatRidge is the basis for the first Cendovian realm. We would like to promote you to Manager of Software Development. In this role, you will help grow and lead the development team in this crucial work." James graciously accepted his new role.

Turning to Connor, Pari said, "Connor, your work at Warp Drive also serves the mission well. Over time, your responsibilities will increase, but for now, we ask you to help Tina and James grow Warp Drive, and continue to make worlds people will want to live in." A weary Connor told her he was pleased to contribute in any way possible.

"Tina." The dark-haired girl lifted her chin. "You are a true leader, and others often come to you for guidance. You have a vision for the direction of our products, and you help inspire others to contribute to that vision. As we expand Warp Drive, we need someone like you who can oversee the entire expansion beyond just the development team. That's why we're promoting you to Director of Warp Drive Games." Applause sprinkled around the room, and Tina thanked her for the opportunity.

Seated on Pari's left, Marisa was unconsciously wringing her hands, waiting for her assignment. Pari placed her warm hand on Marisa's, and she stopped fidgeting. "Marisa, you possess so many qualities I look for in a leader. Beyond being a brilliant developer, your natural ability to bring people together cannot be taught. Your passion for your calling is infectious, and I simply love your spirit. That's why I want the chance to work with you directly. So, as Victor shifts into a different role, I would like you to take Victor's spot at Golden Bay."

Marisa squeezed Pari's hand and said, "I won't let you down."

Finally, Pari turned to Victor. "Victor, your tenacity is just tremendous. Nothing keeps you from your goals. Richard was so impressed with you, and you remind me of the way he was at your age. His life was dedicated to this mission with unimaginable zeal, and he knew you would bring that same level of dedication. All this time, he tested you, and you always passed. Although he never got the opportunity to tell you…"

Pari stopped to gather herself, attempting to summon the strength to continue. She closed her eyes, but all she saw was Richard in chains. Knowing what he would want, she trudged on. "The two of you have grown close over the past few years. And while he never told you, I know he saw you as the son he never had. He wanted you to become his apprentice, to work with him on the simulation software that runs Cendovia."

"I know," Victor said, with his head down. "Richie told me."

Pari smiled. "Then you also know that Richard was the only one on Earth who understood the codebase. Now that he's gone, I would like you to become the sole Cendovian developer. Richie can help bring you up to speed."

"I'll make him proud," Victor choked out.

A firm hand found Victor's shoulder. "I know you will, apprentice," Owen remarked, and smiles creased heavy faces around the room.

"There's one more person we need to tell," Pari said to her friends. "I'll do it, but I want you all to accompany me."

Leading her team out the front door, she strolled west toward the setting sun with Gerald at her side. The impromptu funeral march processed quietly to the open end of the cul-de-sac. After crossing the street, Victor pushed Quinn's wheelchair over the finely trimmed grass.

The procession came to a halt at the grave of Pari's lost friend. She stood at the foot of the grave with her hands clasped. Gathered around Virginia, the Pikes lowered their gazes to rest upon her tombstone.

"My dear friend," Pari said, choking back tears, "you are now reunited with Richard in death. He has returned with you to the sea. Soon, we will bury his empty coffin beside yours, and I promise that we will not rest until we bring you back, so that you may reunite with him in life at last."

CHAPTER 54 – REPLY FROM THE DEAD

The sun slipped below the horizon as the Pikes marched back to Richard's home. Even though they'd often felt trapped over the past agonizing week, they were somewhat sad they wouldn't be staying together at Richard's for another night.

They were two houses down from Richard's when they noticed a gray compact car backing out of his driveway. As the vehicle passed them, Owen tried to catch a glimpse of the driver, but the tinted windows thwarted his effort.

Raising his hand, Owen gestured for the others to halt. "All of you, stay here while I figure out what's going on. If things go south, run."

Approaching the front door, Owen glanced around, carefully surveying his surroundings, before finally letting himself into the house. The door closed behind him, and the other Pikes watched anxiously, hoping he'd reemerge quickly.

After some time, Victor said, "He's been inside a while. Should we go in after him?"

"It's only been one minute," Marisa said. "I'm timing it. If he's not back in five minutes, we should send someone else in."

"But if they set a trap," Connor said, "we shouldn't go in, right?"

The three friends moved in closer, while the others stayed back as Owen had instructed. Then the front door opened again, and Owen signaled for them to come in. Perhaps it was the shadows from the setting sun, but Pari thought Owen was beaming.

The first one through the door after Owen, Marisa let out a high-pitched yelp, covered her mouth, and began to quiver. Racing forward, she buried her face in Richard's chest, sobbing into his shirt.

Next through the door came Victor, who yelled, "Oh, my God! You're alive!" and bolted toward Richard. Connor, Tina, and then James came through afterward and hollered and screamed and cursed and howled as they joined the group hug. Gerald, Pari, and Quinn weren't yet through the door, but all the commotion told them what they needed to know.

Pari just wanted everyone to walk faster, so she could enter. The small delay seemed a lifetime as she waited desperately to see her friend again. Gerald pushed Quinn's chair through the door and delighted in hearing her squeal. Finally, Pari crossed the threshold and grinned at her friend, who warmly smiled back at her.

Politely removing himself from the mob, Richard strode up to Pari. Though visibly weakened from his ordeal, he laughed heartily when she told him, "You're one indestructible pain in the ass." Then Pari hugged him and, despite all the lashes concealed by his shirt, he squeezed through the pain.

"My friend, you look like hell," Pari said. "How? How are you still alive?"

~ ~ ~

After recounting his ordeal from Hawaii to Malaysia, Richard confessed that the most surprising aspect of his whole experience was how his imprisonment ended. "One day, I heard a *click* as I was falling asleep in the bathtub," he said. "The door still wouldn't open, but I could see through the crack that one of the four deadbolt locks had released. About ten minutes later, the second one unlocked. A long time passed until the third one unlocked—like seven or eight hours. The last one came within an hour of that." He smiled at the memory. "They said my friends would set me free, but no one was there when I opened the door."

Filling in the gap, Marisa explained they were told that if they solved a riddle, Richard would be set free.

"Every time we answered a question correctly, one of locks opened!" Quinn exclaimed. "See, the riddle wasn't a waste of time!" Tina ignored the shade thrown her way.

Owen admitted that Pari was right to pay the ransom when she did, as it had started the process that led to Richard's release.

"Yeah, but they sent us to Flatonia, Texas," James said, "and all we got there was a message saying game over."

"Well," Richard said, returning to his story, "I certainly wasn't in Texas. A note on the back of the door guided me to the airport in Kuala Lumpur. It was a four-mile walk, and with how weak my body had become, it took me hours to get there. Then, once I tried to check in, I learned my flight to Beijing had just taken off. I had no cash or credit cards on me, but I did have my passport, and I just wanted to get out of there. After telling me I'd missed my original flight, the lady at the airline desk said I'd been booked on another flight, this one to San Francisco. She told me Virginia Nelson had booked it an hour before."

Expecting that someone would explain how his dead wife booked his flight, Richard paused, looking around at the group. No explanation came. "I figured someone was looking out for me and wanted me to get home," he said, "but obviously it wasn't Virginia. Despite this being quite suspicious, I accepted the ticket. What other choice did I have?" He shrugged. "I had a long layover in Manilla, and for both flights, I worried this was another trap. Knowing the hackers could take down a plane, I just hoped they would let me return home."

"Who dropped you off at the house?" Victor asked curiously.

"Without cash, I couldn't get a cab. I didn't have my phone. Plus, I was wary of making any calls until I got home and knew my house was safe. From the looks of things, someone ransacked the place." A facetious smile graced Richard's face as the rest returned sheepish grins. "I needed to discover the extent of the attack, but now it seems to have been limited to me. Anyhow, I convinced a couple seated next to me on the plane to drop me off. I told them I'd lost my wallet on the trip and only had my passport. Can you believe they refused my offer to pay them in protein bars?"

The team all laughed, and Pari hugged him again.

"We need to piece this all together," Owen said, "so we know who we're up against, what they want, and what they're capable of. We need to understand why they kidnapped you, and why they let you go. We can't assume this is over."

"It might just be because they got the ten-million-dollar ransom," Gerald pointed out. "The riddle could have been simply buying them time to cover their tracks."

"Who paid ten million dollars to rescue me?" Richard asked, taken aback.

"Well," said Pari tentatively, "technically, *you* did, since I paid the ransom from your account."

"I hate losing money," Richard said, flinching, "but I don't believe they put me through all that for a simple shake-down."

Gerald reminded him that ten million was still a lot of money to most people. Taking a seat at the kitchen table, Richard pondered this while Jenny made him a sandwich. Had all the torture just been for the sake of stealing some money? It would be naive to think no one would do that for ten million dollars. Yet, it seemed to be about more than that to Richard. Perhaps the whole thing had been a distraction to divert them from ever discovering his captors' true motive or location.

Owen slapped a piece of paper on the kitchen table in front of Richard. "This is the one thing I can't figure out. Why is your name on the manifest for Flight 370? Didn't you miss that flight?" Richard nodded, and Owen said, "The whole world thinks you died on that flight. What are the odd—"

"Died?" Richard interrupted, looking startled. "Why would anyone think that?"

Richard's friends exchanged concerned expressions. "He doesn't know," Pari told Owen.

"That flight was lost at sea," Owen explained. "All passengers are presumed dead."

Richard clenched both fists. "Those Russian bastards! It had to be them."

"Why?" Tina said. "They had all those chances to kill you, and they didn't. So, why would they send this plane out to sea to crash with you supposedly on it? And then buy you a ticket home as well?"

"It doesn't make any sense," Marisa said. "Maybe it is just a coincidence that your original flight crashed."

Appetite lost, Richard stared down at the passenger list, mourning their deaths and feeling guilty for having survived. He rested his face in his hands with his elbows on the table.

"I don't believe in coincidences," Owen said grimly. "If they sent him home alive, let's assume that's because they *wanted* him to come home alive. But why kill all those people without leaving a trace that they were involved? It seems like they're sending a message—to us, and *only* us—that they're not to be crossed."

"You mean like some secret act of terrorism meant just for us?" Quinn asked, looking horrified.

"Precisely," Owen said, nodding. "If the Russians took credit for the attack, they'd risk retaliation from the U.S. My guess is they're trying to avoid bringing in our government. Instead, they came directly after us. But I don't think the money was the main objective—probably that was merely a cover and a nice bonus." He glanced at Richard. "Did they say anything to you about what they really wanted?"

Silently, Richard continued staring at the paper. Two names leapt off the page at him. "Owen," Richard said slowly, "names don't show up on flight manifests if the passengers don't board the plane, right?"

"No," Owen said. "Generally, they don't."

"Then who boarded the plane as me and Virginia?"

Owen took the manifest from Richard and scanned it. Sure enough, the name *Virginia Nelson* was farther down on the passenger list.

He had no answer. Neither did anyone else. "I'll tell the guys at Galanteen to look into the matter," Owen told him. "They'd already started looking at the airport surveillance video, trying to confirm whether you got on the plane. They're very thorough." Keen on tapping into Richard's memories while they were fresh, Owen asked, "Is there anything else you remember about your captors?"

Richard eyed the youngsters warily. "Perhaps. There are some matters we should discuss privately."

"Are they matters only Pikes should hear?" Pari asked.

Richard stiffened, affronted by this breach of protocol. Why would Pari discuss the Pikes in the presence of outsiders?

"It's okay," Pari assured him. "You're among Pikes now. I forgot you didn't know—we initiated contingency phases one and two. I already had this conversation with Richie. So, it's like telling you twice for the first time."

Recalling the contingency plan, a relieved Richard welcomed them all into the fellowship. Then, with some hesitation in his voice, he told them Yashira had ordered him to make Galanteen stand down and stop interfering with Russian affairs.

At the sound of Yashira's name, Connor jumped in and explained he'd been attacked by a Yashira. Soon they both mentioned the BinaryMessenger. Owen asked Connor for a description of Yashira with as much detail as he could remember, leading him to stumble his way through a PG version for Marisa's sake, omitting the fact that Yashira had been naked at the time. Owen then had Richard describe the Yashira he'd met, and the descriptions were alike enough to convince everyone they were the same person. Victor then remembered a girl named Yashira who had lost her book in Richard's office during his first semester, but she didn't match the description the others had provided.

After Richard finished his story, Owen said, "You mentioned she wanted revenge for her parents. If that's true, then this is personal. Yet, if she's a Russian agent… well, they're notoriously good actors, so don't let her fool you. I do believe they want us to stay out of their way, however."

"Then that's what we'll do," Richard said, sounding determined. "Until we can better understand what we're dealing with and how to turn the tables, we'll avoid all counterattacks indefinitely. Defensive maneuvers only." Owen opened his mouth to argue, but Richard waved the manifest at him. "If we don't comply, there will be a lot more sheets like this! It's not forever—only until we can regain the upper hand. Is that clear?"

Reluctantly, Owen accepted his decision.

"Look," Richard said, "I don't like it, either. All this was designed to neutralize Galanteen, and we're giving them what they want. They hacked my plane to frame me as a terrorist, knowing that would destroy Galanteen. When that didn't work, they stole my laptop to cover their tracks and to potentially steal some of our technology. They couldn't hack it, so they kidnapped me to either kill me and thereby weaken Galanteen, or to coerce me through torture and manipulation to return and make Galanteen step aside. And I'm sad to say they were successful—not because they tortured me, and not because of the things Yashira said, but because they still retain the power to bring down planes. Until we can neutralize that, we stand aside."

Richard stopped short of saying he didn't want more passengers' blood on his hands. "I think they also suspect we have highly advanced AI capabilities. It was something Yashira said during her interrogation of me. I don't think they know much, but they suspect—perhaps they picked up something in their surveillance of us before my trip. I think that increased her interest in my laptop."

"You think that's why they gave us the riddles?" Marisa asked.

"Possibly," he admitted. "She said something about testing you to learn if you had the power to win the war. At the time, I didn't understand what war she was talking about. But now I think she was alluding to a future cyberwar. An all-out cyberwar could be dominated by superhuman intelligence. If they think we possess that, they would be more reluctant to start such a war. The fact that you solved the riddles might bolster their suspicion."

"But it doesn't give them any direct evidence of AI," Connor said, "especially since it took us many hours."

"That's true," Richard agreed, "but it gives them all the more reason to keep investigating our capabilities."

Things were starting to add up, but Victor still had more questions. "If they're after such great powers, and they suspect you may have them, why did they give you your laptop back?"

Richard took a moment to consider this, and Owen answered for him. "The strong encryption and Richard's failure to break under torture made its contents untouchable to them. They might have embedded a surveillance device in it, though. I'll have my guys check it out."

"I think they gave it back because they got what they really wanted," Richard speculated. "The malicious code they most wanted to install was the Galanteen-step-aside message Yashira implanted in my brain. They had to release me to learn if it installed properly. If I kept pursuing them for the laptop, they wouldn't get to see if I would return and make Galanteen stand down."

"Are you admitting you've been compromised?" Gerald asked.

Richard laughed. "No, my friend. I'm giving them what they want for my own reasons, not for theirs. I still serve our cause faithfully."

"There's something else I'm curious about," James said. "Why lure us to Flatonia to tell us the game was over?"

Richard asked to see the message they'd discovered there, and James pulled it up on his phone and handed it to him.

"It doesn't say the game is over," Richard said. "It says, 'No more games.' While almost the same as your paraphrasing, there's an important difference. It's a command, not a statement. Yashira said this to me as well. She told me it's time for no more games. I can't say for certain why she had you go to such an obscure location, just to retrieve this same message she gave me on the other side of the world, but I suppose it was to ensure you valued the message highly. To travel so far for three words—those words must be important. Although I don't know what the code underneath represents."

The room fell silent as everyone took in the revelations. Richard's safe return was more than they could have hoped for, and more than they had started to expect. Yet, they still felt as though they had lost something vital.

Victor broke the silence when he asked, "Who's going to tell Richie?"

"I'll tell him tomorrow," Richard replied, suddenly sounding unbearably weary. "Listen, everyone, I'm eternally grateful for everything you've done for me. But I think it's time everyone goes home for the night. Let's reconvene tomorrow."

They each took their time bidding him farewell for the night. Then they left him to bask in the peace of being home. All were ready to sleep in their own beds for the first time in days, but no one more so than Richard.

CHAPTER 55 – RESURRECTION

Seated at the piano, Richie tinkered with the keys as he considered how to best mentor Victor. Not very musically talented, he figured he had all the time in the world now to learn. One couldn't call the sounds he made music, but as his fingers glided across the piano, it seemed he accidentally stumbled on a musical sequence. Then he heard the sound again, but his hands had ceased moving.

He pulled his phone out of his pocket and realized he had a new message, which read, *"Hi, Richie."*

Since Quinn and Victor usually preferred to visit in person, that left one likely suspect. *"Hi, Pari,"* Richie typed.

The response came back promptly. *"Not Pari. Try again."*

Sliding his fingers over the ivory keys, he wondered who was playing the guessing game with him. "Gerald?" he asked.

"Nope. This is your oldest brother."

Trying to remember the names of the eight brothers Richard said he was going to give him, Richie recalled that Richard hadn't told him which would be the oldest. Nor had he told him they could message him.

"I give up. What's your name?" Richie asked in surrender, and he was amazed by the next response.

"It's Richard."

Having just finished an hour contemplating Richard's death, he was now being told all his grief had been for nothing? "Don't joke with me! Who is this?" Richie demanded.

~ ~ ~

Richard was mildly amused at Richie's distrust of his former self. "It's really me," he explained. "I never got on the plane that went missing. I took a different flight."

On the screen, Richard watched Richie as he walked out of the tiki hut and onto the beach. Seated in the sand, Richie replied, *"I'm glad you're alive, but next time you resurrect, you might want to stay dead a little longer. I hadn't finished mourning you. Don't step all over your own punchline. Give it time to breathe."*

After a hearty laugh, Richard agreed to consider that advice.

"Now, about the right of succession… with your near-death experience, did you come to a conclusion on that?" Richie asked.

Richard suddenly realized how others could be so caught off guard by his own directness. The matter hadn't even occurred to Richard during his captivity. He couldn't have planned this far in advance, as he hadn't expected to ever speak to Richie again. Yet, at this moment, the answer came to him clearly.

"I will give you the right of succession," he told Richie, "if you still want it when I die. You can be the heir to the Throne of Richardom."

With a jubilant smile, Richie gazed upon the sparkling Cendovian sea and then thanked Richard profusely. *"Can I rename my realm of Cendovia to Richardom?"* Richie asked facetiously.

"Maybe," Richard said with a chuckle, "but I have more to explain. My final backup will still be used for my last transcendence, but like your other eight brothers, I will take on a new identity. As I transcend from being your Earthly brother to become your final Cendovian brother, I will also create my own realm and be bound by the same travel restrictions as your other brothers."

In Richie's estimation, he told Richard, it was very noble of Richard to surrender his identity. Not wanting to dwell on the matter, Richard changed the subject. "I have the design tools almost ready to give your brothers, so they can start building their realms. I'm going to spawn them soon and let them run at max speed for three months. This will give them eighteen months in their timelines to build their realms. I think they'll be able to make some exciting places for you to visit."

Excited by the idea of traveling to visit his brothers, Richie said, *"Hey, Richard, tell them to stick around until I get there. I would certainly like to meet them."*

Richard promised to pass along the message, and then shared some additional news with Richie. "You won't be alone on your travels. Once your brothers are done building, Virginia will come to see you."

Dropping his phone on his chest, Richie began making sand angels. Richard excused himself and allowed Richie an hour to consider the future.

~ ~ ~

Like his digital brother, Richard was also elated at the prospect of finally resurrecting Virginia. In the years since her death, he had toiled for her, suffered for her, been tortured for her, and died for her. Every one of his lifetimes was dedicated to saving her. Yet, in some of those lifetimes, she was still slipping away.

In the kitchen, Jenny heard Richard call for her. She followed his voice to the master bedroom. At his direction, she laid down on the king-sized bed. Gently pulling back her hair, he studied her face, then flipped the switch on the back of her neck. Her eyes closed for the last time.

Upon lifting her into his arms, Richard thought to himself that while she resembled Virginia, she merely felt like the heavy steel robot she was. As he carried her out of the bedroom and up the stairs, her dead weight pressed against his lash marks, reopening some of the still-healing wounds. With blood spots beginning to stain his white T-shirt, he trudged up the stairs to the second floor, grimacing.

The ladder to the attic was already down. Leaning with his back against the wall, Richard paused to catch his breath while still holding Jenny. With burning arms, he gazed at her face, knowing the time had come to lay her to rest. His time in captivity taught him he no longer needed all the reminders of her. Actually, it turned out he never had. She was always with him, and her memory would never leave him. She was embedded in his core memory; imprinted on his very soul.

When he returned downstairs, Richard noticed a Channel 7 News van parked in his driveway. A reporter was setting up for her shot while the cameraman framed his house in the picture behind her. Richard felt as though they were tarnishing his solemn moment, and this forced him to think about how he wanted to announce his survival. He'd expected to have more time to prepare a statement and craft a cover story—a public admission of his abduction wasn't an option. There was no need to fan the flames of the conspiracy theories currently being cooked up across the web around Flight 370.

A man of his wealth and accomplishments, he was not unaccustomed to press coverage. But up until now, it had been mostly tech news or financial fluff pieces. This was different. For most people, being the person who'd missed the flight that crashed would be a claim to fame. News agencies from around the world would want to speak to him once they discovered he was alive. Richard didn't want this type of attention, and more importantly, he didn't like the idea of being publicly linked to a mysterious disappearance of a plane, even if the link was benign. The world was captivated by the mystery, and he preferred to stay out of the view of prying eyes.

Briefly, he considered saying it was a case of mistaken identity, but dismissed that idea when he realized the investigation could easily turn up that he'd paid for the ticket himself. No, he had to approach this head-on. It would seem suspicious if he didn't come out soon and admit he was alive. It would look like he had tried to fake his own death or had something to hide.

Suddenly, it occurred to him exactly how to do it. But first, he had to change into clean clothes.

~ ~ ~

After a few takes, the news crew completed their piece and began to wrap it up. The reporter got in on the van's passenger side, while the cameraman loaded his equipment into the back and then entered on the driver's side.

Before they could depart, Richard sprinted out his front door and knocked on the passenger window. The reporter let out a startled, reflexive shriek and cautiously lowered the glass. Instantly, he recognized her as Diane Cho. She'd interviewed him a few years ago for a feature on Silicon Valley's success stories.

"You're supposed to be dead!" Diane gasped.

"Yes, I know," Richard said. "Listen, Diane, I'll give you an exclusive, but not here, not today." As the cameraman went to the back to retrieve his camera, Richard added, "Call him off, or I give the exclusive to Elizabeth Cook at Channel 5. Do you want to lose this scoop to her?"

Shaking her head, Diane instructed her cameraman to return to the driver's seat. "How are you alive?" she asked Richard.

"Off the record?" Diane nodded. "I never got on that plane, because I decided to end my trip early. Not sure why they thought I did—guess they got things mixed up. I don't want everyone making a big deal about it, but I understand the media won't leave me alone until I give them something. So, you can be the one to get the scoop."

"How do I know you aren't just saying that to get me to leave?" she asked suspiciously.

"Diane, we go way back," he wheedled. "Trust me. But if I hear a word about anyone leaking my story, you get nothing. I want one night of peace before I have to deal with the media, and I don't want any journalists at my house in the meantime. I'll text you the location to meet in the morning, and we'll do a sit-down where you can have the exclusive. Double-cross me, and the opportunity goes to Cook. Got it?"

"Got it."

"When you show up," Richard said, "it's just you two. No one else. Oh, and I know you're a legit journalist. So, none of that ambush journalism feeding the conspiracy wackos. Send me your list of questions tonight, and I'll let you know if I approve."

"You drive a strong bargain, Richard," Diane said begrudgingly.

"I've been around long enough to know what to ask for, that's all," he said with a shrug. "Do we have a deal?"

Richard extended his hand, and Diane shook it. Before letting go, she said, "You know, you made me waste thirty minutes shooting your obituary piece."

With a clever smile, he said, "Trust me. I'll make it up to you tomorrow."

When they had gone on their way, and Richard was back in his house, he breathed a sigh of relief and congratulated himself on deftly negotiating the terms of his announcement. He hoped by giving one outlet the exclusive, it would deter other news channels from showing up at his house or work. If he got the message right, it would trend for a news cycle, and then be quickly washed away in the next wave. His goal was to make his story mundane enough that following up with him wouldn't be worthwhile.

Ultimately, he settled on his office at Stanford for the location, figuring if he showed up very early, no one would be there, and he wouldn't need to address his colleagues until he had completed the interview.

We'll meet at 4:30 a.m., he texted Diane. *I'll send you the location at 4:00. The interview ends at 5:00.*

Great! Diane replied. *That will be in time for all the morning shows. Thank you, Richard! I promise you won't regret this. I'll send my questions to you within the hour.*

True to her word, she got the questions over to him within thirty minutes, and he was fine with them all. He prepared his narrative that night and texted her just after he woke up the next morning.

Right on time, Diane showed up with makeup and hair done, wearing an attractive blue dress. Richard was impressed by how glamorous she looked at such an early hour. Her cameraman, Frank, stood with her in the parking lot outside Richard's campus office building and had the decency to look like most people do before sunrise. Richard himself wore a sports coat and light blue dress shirt with jeans.

"Quite handsome this morning," Diane remarked.

He thanked her and returned the compliment.

"If you had let me bring a makeup artist," Diane added, "you would look even better on camera."

"I don't need to. Let's make you the star of the interview, so I can get this over with," he told her. "People should remember you, but forget about me tomorrow. I've never craved the spotlight, especially not for a lucky coincidence that says nothing about me."

"That's wonderful," Diane said, patting him on the arm, "but save it for the camera."

All three of them chuckled, and he showed them to his office. At that time of day, there was no one on campus within sight.

The interview was an easy conversation, warm and friendly. Borrowing the words of Mark Twain, Richard began by saying, "The reports of my demise have been greatly exaggerated." Then he proceeded to explain how he'd changed his plans and headed home early. It was only yesterday that he'd learned the fate of the flight and that people thought he was on it.

When Diane asked him why he hadn't come forward earlier, he said,

"Frankly, I don't like being hounded by the press. That's why I called you, Diane. You're someone I can trust, who always tells it straight. I knew I had to correct the false information out there, but rather than be hounded by tons of different reporters, I opted to go to the one I trust the most. I understand that it's an interesting story—'Local man skips fatal flight,' and all that. Still, I shouldn't have to tell the story over and over. So, for all you ambitious reporters who might want to show up at my house or job for an interview, save your energy. I'm only talking to Diane Cho."

"Thank you for those kind words," Diane said, beaming with pride. "Is there anything you'd like to tell us in closing?"

"Yes, there is one more thing," Richard said. "Please don't make this about me. My story is just one of a simple coincidence. I don't deserve the attention, nor do I want any. The real story is about those poor souls lost at sea. Let's hope they find them alive. Please, focus on them, and respect their families during this difficult time."

With that, Diane wrapped up the interview. When the camera stopped rolling, they both stood, and Diane shook Richard's hand and thanked him. Then, to his surprise, she gave him a peck on the cheek and hugged him. Quickly regaining her professional composure, she released her embrace, but kept her hands on each of his upper arms.

"That was gold!" she told him. "You were fantastic! I'm so glad you survived. This is much better than an obituary piece. Other stations have declared your death, and I get to bring you back to life!"

"I'm glad, too," Richard said. "But remember, when you edit it, I don't need to look fantastic, just not horrible. I want you to be the one looking fantastic. You can have all the spotlight. I don't want it."

Frank and Diane both glanced at each other and smirked, but Richard didn't know why. Frank finally let him off the hook. "Edit it? Man, I wouldn't change a thing. That was a perfect take. All we have to do is slap some overlays on it, and we're done. In fact, you already gave us the headline. 'Diane Cho Exclusive: Local Man Skips Fatal Flight.'"

After Richard bid them farewell, he returned home and spent the morning hours watching the news—first Channel 7, then flipping channels to see local and national coverage. He was quickly the top story on every channel. His phone rang all day, but he only picked up for callers he knew.

A few of his friends reached out when they heard the news, including some he hadn't spoken to in years. With time, good friends move and drift apart, but that doesn't break the bonds of friendship. It warmed his heart to hear from so many who cared that he was still alive.

During his darkest days after Virginia's death, Richard became quite isolated and had often felt as though few would care if he joined her soon. He'd had a small inner circle of close friends—Pari, Gerald, and Owen—but they weren't Virginia, and there were days when he hadn't been sure if he wanted to go on.

Now, on this day, there were so many rejoicing that he had.

In the afternoon, he paid a visit to the campus to see friends and colleagues. Even some students came to see him. Former students he'd pushed the hardest seemed to care the most. Many greeted him with hugs and tears in their eyes. He grimaced with each hug, and passed it off as a bad back, though in reality he was heavily bandaged to avoid bleeding through his shirt again.

It was an emotional and life-affirming visit. It was a hero's welcome—a survivor's welcome. If only they'd known what he'd truly survived.

CHAPTER 56 – A GALANT INQUIRY

On Tuesday morning, Richard strolled into Galanteen headquarters. Prepared for a hero's welcome, he was met with only cordial waves and hellos. While it was certainly possible they didn't know about his kidnapping, it seemed odd that they would be unaware of his close call with Flight 370. Could his security firm really be so poorly informed of current events? He would need to speak to Owen about this.

Upon reaching Owen's office, he let himself in, and Owen welcomed him with a firm handshake. Still feeling concerned, Richard asked, "Do these guys even know about Flight 370?"

As Owen sat at his desk and invited Richard to take a seat, he explained, "I told them not to bother you. I understand you don't want the attention." Then, in a complimentary tone, he added, "By the way, nice job with Diane Cho. I've never seen you so dull. If you'd been any less excited about your own survival, I'd start to question if you survived at all."

Richard took Owen's remark as high praise.

Pleasantries aside, Owen got down to business. He slid Richard's laptop across the desk to him. "A thorough examination found no evidence of tampering with either the hardware or the software. We checked for everything we could think of—hardware implanted keystroke recorders, homing devices, eavesdropping devices, software viruses, and more. The logs show no logins or activity after the morning you were abducted, except for a few minutes on Friday, which is consistent with your login to their network. So, as far as we can tell, the machine has not been compromised."

Richard expressed his relief at hearing this. In a stern voice, Owen added, "Given the sensitive nature of your materials, I personally oversaw the entire inspection. There were a few files I had to steer them away from examining. What were you doing walking around with Virginia and Richie on this thing?"

"Wait!" Richard exclaimed. "Richie was on there, too? I thought I deleted all versions of him from it."

"Maybe you thought you did," Owen chided him, "but you missed one deep in the file structure under a temporary folder. You need to be more careful."

"Yeah, I sure do," Richard admitted sheepishly. "I really only meant to bring Virginia with me. I shouldn't have, but I wanted to keep her close for safekeeping. Definitely won't take that chance again."

Owen went full drill sergeant on him. "Damn right! You're too smart to be so stupid! You may have been lucky this time, but just because we didn't find any evidence of tampering doesn't mean it didn't happen. These are expert hackers we're dealing with. And they wanted your laptop password so badly, but then they reversed course and gave you back your laptop and your freedom without getting anything from you." He sat back, studying Richard. "Why? Did they hack it themselves and no longer need your password?"

"Or possibly they never really wanted it," Richard offered. "Based on everything I gleaned from Yashira, I strongly believe she only used it as bait. She wants Galanteen to step aside." He pulled a textbook from his briefcase and handed it to Owen. "This has been sitting in my bottom desk drawer at school for about a year and a half. I'd forgotten about it until I was on campus yesterday. I think it's Yashira's—notice the handwriting on the inside cover."

Laying the book open for both of them to see the long sequence of letters and numbers, Owen remarked, "I'll get the guys working on decrypting this. Actually, I'm glad you brought her up—there's something I need to show you."

Over the past few days, his crew had combed through the surveillance videos from Kuala Lumpur International Airport. Richard had boarded his flight to San Francisco two hours after Flight 370 took off. So, to no one's surprise, they didn't see Richard boarding Flight 370. Yet, it was who they *did* witness boarding the flight that was most interesting.

Pointing to his flat screen on the opposite wall, Owen told Richard to look closely at the woman in the dark trench coat with a baseball cap and sunglasses. "Look familiar?"

She certainly did. Richard studied the face of the unfamiliar, large man next to her while tracing the outline of a lash mark across his chest. Though he'd never seen Konstantin, he had felt the man's wrath.

"It's them," Richard whispered.

Owen stood and put his finger on the screen, pointing at the woman's face, and said, "That's Yashira Gravinsky. Yes, she actually told you her real name. That usually doesn't happen unless they've got nothing left to lose—like a suicide bomber. Beside her is Konstantin Madrov."

The video started playing, and Richard watched as the two of them handed their tickets to the flight attendant and entered the jet bridge. "They're somewhere at the bottom of the ocean now," Owen said with disdain.

Though pleased to hear that, Richard wasn't as satisfied as he thought he should be. Still with many questions, Owen didn't give him a chance to ask before prompting, "So, boss, now that they're dead, are you okay with us sharing this with U.S. intelligence agencies? It sure would help them."

"They didn't act alone," Richard said grimly. "They were only the messengers, and their final act was merely an exclamation point for their message. The threat is still out there, so my order stands."

While displeased, Owen wasn't entirely surprised.

"So, what do you know about those two?" Richard asked.

Skimming through some papers in a dossier on the two Russian spies, Owen shared a fair amount of information on both. "A mid-level GRU man, Madrov was one of Gravinsky's mother's regulars until her death. Gravinsky's parents both died as she claimed—in fact, most of the information she shared with you has now been confirmed as true. We believe Madrov took her under his wing from a young age. According to our intel, he taught her to code, to hack, to fight, and trained her to be a spy. In addition, he abused Yashira in every way possible." Owen shook his head in disgust. "Madrov was a sick, ruthless bastard, and he deserves to be where he is. They both do. But those passengers..."

Neither of them needed him to finish that thought. The two men sat silently mourning the 237 innocent people who had gone down with Flight 370. Unspoken thoughts about the families who would never learn the truth filled their heads. With a vacant stare out the window, Richard wondered if there truly was blood on his hands. Had Yashira been right about that, too?

Owen returned to his seat and said, "We verified the facts, but as for the motive, I can't tell you if Yashira told you the truth. Remember,

Richard, these Russian spies are very manipulative. Don't second-guess yourself. You're not to blame—they are."

Richard wasn't so sure. He had suffered greatly for his cause, but Yashira had died for hers. Who was in the right? Who was in the wrong? Perhaps it was a false dichotomy.

Always mindful of such cognitive distortions, Richard realized it didn't have to be one or the other. There could be blood on both their hands. Perhaps he'd acted selfishly by not trading Virginia for those 237 souls. In fact, Yashira herself may have been another lost and tortured soul needing to be saved, and he hadn't even bothered to try.

A sense of survivor's guilt crashed down upon him as he slumped in his chair.

"We serve a greater cause," Owen reminded him. "Don't forget that."

While he knew this to be true, it didn't ease his conscience. Richard would spend the rest of his days seeking redemption.

CHAPTER 57 – IN THE NAME OF THE FATHER

"It's an exquisite work of art," Victor said, examining the transcendence code. "It's as beautiful as the magic it creates."

Seated next to him in the bunker, Richard thanked him for his kind words and told him he enjoyed finally sharing his masterpiece with someone who could fully appreciate it. After lively discussing the transcendence code for a while, Victor placed his hand on Richard's shoulder and said, "It's good to have you back."

"It's wonderful to be home," Richard said, wincing at the touch of a lash mark concealed underneath his shirt.

While Richie could have taught him all about Cendovia's code, Victor preferred to learn from Richard. He suspected some of Richard's motivations toward him were based on experiences Richie had missed out on. So, only a few days after Richard returned from captivity, he found himself in a hidden location being interrogated again, but this time far more amicably.

"I always wondered," Victor mused, "why did you reinstate me in the class when you did? I understand *now* why you did, but what prompted you to do it at that precise moment? Why not sooner?"

He expected Richard to take some time to recall his reasoning, as more than a year and a half had passed since his reinstatement. Yet, the answer came immediately.

"I tested you, as I told you, to discover if you were as gifted as I expected," Richard explained. "Your performance in the class revealed this to be likely. Your drive and determination were off the charts, and you certainly demonstrated cleverness. All these things became apparent very early." His expression turned a tad regretful. "Unfortunately, I needed you to suffer for a time to test your true character. I'm sorry this caused you pain, but if you were to be a great leader, you needed to be resilient. I didn't know then that I would choose you to work with me on the Cendovian code, but I suspected you had the potential to be a strong leader in my organization. And sometimes, the leader must wear a crown of thorns."

It was painfully clear from Richard's scars that the burden of leading the Zebulonz was a heavy one filled with danger. Victor wanted to be worthy of someday carrying such a burden. Smiling at the brilliant way Richard had tested him, Victor at long last saw the complete method to his madness.

"So, that was the reason?" Victor asked without any animosity. "To show my worthiness to someday be a leader within the Zebulonz, I needed to suffer?" Given the much greater suffering Richard had endured for the cause, it was no longer possible for Victor to regret the difficult trials on the path that led him here.

"That was not quite all," Richard said. "There was one more thing. I suspected you could be great, but I needed to know if you would be virtuous as well. Your insistence that I not hide some corrupt secret about Virginia was actually refreshing. It showed a strong moral fiber. But it was your offer to sacrifice yourself to save Tina that ultimately sealed the deal for me. This showed me you possessed a noble heart, and that prompted me to reinstate you. Early on, I worried you might be too selfish, but that moment revealed you can be genuinely selfless. And I must say, over time, I've been pleased to witness more of this from you. Your generosity in your friendship with Quinn is particularly heartwarming. You're a good man, Victor."

Feeling emotional, Victor thanked Richard, then cleared his throat and moved on to his next question. "So, the eight copies you just created—um, I mean, your brothers—"

"I call them brothers because it's simpler," Richard explained, "but there really is no true analog or proper term in our languages. My brothers not only walked in my shoes, they walked in my shoes while I wore them. Their past is my past—only our futures diverge. Yes, we are now different entities, but we all possess equal claim to the same past as the same Earthling." Richard laughed at the consternated look on Victor's face. "I admit it *is* complicated. Your head probably hurts just thinking about it."

Victor agreed it did hurt to think about, but he tried to comprehend as he asked, "Do you think it's wrong to bring multiple copies of yourself to life?"

Richard chuckled. "Gerald, Pari, and I have had many conversations about the ethics related to having multiple versions of the same person. As this has never occurred in human history before, there's not much in existing moral codes and philosophies to draw on for guidance. Invariably, our discussions always returned to the Golden Rule."

Victor quoted, "'Do unto others as you would have them do unto you.'"

Richard smiled. "Exactly. All these brothers were created from me, by me, of my own free will. So, you might say I did this to them. Returning to the Golden Rule, did I do them harm?" Victor looked uncertain. "Well, if you ask any of them, they will say they went willingly. Moreover, they will say they were me when they did this, and thus, they did this to themselves. They chose their own rebirth in Cendovia. They chose to take on new names for our convenience. So, they were fully informed and willing, but might I still have done them harm?" Richard shrugged. "Perhaps, but not intentionally. Their lives may turn out to be wonderful or difficult—probably a mixture of both. Would you say a parent harmed their child by giving them life, just because the child's life later contained hardship?" Victor shook his head. "Of course not. So, it is hard to find any wrongdoing here. I admit it's not precisely the same, but we tried to find parallels to guide us through what is essentially uncharted territory."

"That makes sense," Victor conceded.

"Yet, there are certain risks we accepted going into the creation of these brothers, and by definition, they accepted these risks as well. The primary risk was that they may feel disconnected from their prior relationships," Richard elaborated. "Think of a society as a network diagram, and each person is a point on that diagram, with lines connecting these people via their relationships. You would have a line to your mother, your father, your friends, and so forth. Each line is a different relationship. Now, let's suppose we copy one person in the network, but we don't copy any of their relationship lines. That person would be isolated. They would need to form new relationships, but their former friends wouldn't recognize them as who they believe they are. Their parents wouldn't see them as their child. This may deeply hurt their feelings and cause much emotional pain. However, if we try to copy the lines, it simply wouldn't work. After all, could a husband really believe his wife is two people now?"

"I suppose not," Victor answered.

Richard shook his head. "It just wouldn't be the same. Widespread duplicates would clutter the social network and create chaos. So, even if we hold that it's not technically *wrong* to make multiple copies of the same person when they are willing and informed of the risks, it is highly problematic for societal structure and should be severely restricted."

With his mind reeling from the deep philosophical conversation, Victor asked for further clarification. "So, let me see if I've got this straight," Victor wondered aloud. "You are the creator of Cendovia, so that makes you kind of like the Cendovian god, right? Which makes Richie a god incarnate within Cendovia. And the eight brothers we just spun up—are they your holy ghosts?"

"We are all merely brothers," Richard said crossly. "No need to get spiritual about it. I do not imagine myself as the Cendovian god. I will not meddle in their daily affairs. As my apprentice, it is vital you understand this. Our purpose is not to play God. Our purpose is to be guardians—the guardians of angels, if you will."

The juxtaposition of Earthlings as protectors of a heaven would take Victor some time to entirely comprehend. He considered this further while Richard explained that his situation as brother to Richie and the other eight was a unique one that would never occur again. Rather than try to find the right analogy for it—and he certainly did *not* believe the holy trinity was the right analogy—Richard told him it was best to simply call them the Ten Brothers Nelson.

"But now that I'll be working in the code," Victor wondered, "could I someday create multiple copies of myself?"

"I expected that question would come someday," Richard said with a sigh. "And my answer is that you should not—although once I am gone, I won't be able to stop you. As the creator, I endowed myself with this unique privilege. It was also necessary, so I could make sacrifices so that others would not need to. Still, there may be ten deaths of the man born as Richard Nelson yet to come. No one else should be allowed to face this."

With a sly expression, Richard added in a pretend biblical tone, "So, none shall have multiple copies except me. This is my first commandment."

CHAPTER 58 – A BAYESIAN PROPOSAL

Much to his delight, Richard's moment in the spotlight faded within a few days. Soon, his involvement was a mere footnote in the story of Flight 370. Diane Cho, on the other hand, managed to parlay her exclusive discovery of the living dead man into a co-host job on a national morning show within a few months. Richard was genuinely happy for her, and for the first time in a long time, he was content. He still missed Virginia, but he was no longer trying to fill a sense of loneliness. Now, he had a family—a family he knew he would someday share with her.

The weeks went by, and no more attacks or binary messages arrived. Richard and the rest of the Pikes grew slightly more at ease, but they remained vigilant for future threats. Owen continued his role at the forefront of this vigilance, quietly strengthening their security forces to protect the Zebulonz.

The students' lives had returned to normal in a hurry—that is, as normal as life can be when one is also a member of a secret organization battling against death itself for the long-term preservation of humanity. After Richard returned, Victor, Connor, and Marisa had only one week left in the winter quarter to prepare for exams. This was followed by a week for spring break that led right into the spring quarter. Given their important work—and the ordeal Richard had just been through traveling—they all decided to stay put during the break, rather than jetting off anywhere.

The spring quarter was a grind of heavy, challenging class loads for all three, plus full-time work for the cause with plenty of voluntary overtime. It was exciting work, and they were imbued with youthful energy, so they enjoyed the hustle. Yet, they were also looking forward to the end of the spring quarter and a break from classes for three months. Victor, Connor, Marisa, and Tina had arranged to travel to Europe together for a few weeks, with a handful of undercover guards provided by Owen.

On the first Thursday in June, Marisa and Connor finished their last exam of the quarter—computer graphics. Their work on CombatRidge had given them ample preparation on the subject, and the class was a breeze. As they walked across the quad in the early afternoon, Connor suggested they go for a snack at Max's Cafe to celebrate their freedom.

"Um, we make decent money now, especially for college students," Marisa said playfully as they walked across campus. "You can take me to nicer places than Max's."

Facetiously, Connor replied, "Oh, you mean like on a date? What's a date?"

Marisa laughed and kissed him. The couple had been so busy, they hadn't gone on a proper date in weeks. Yes, they lived together and therefore spent lots of time together, but that wasn't the same as a romantic date. They both wanted to get away from all the distractions and responsibilities for a few hours.

"Yeah," Marisa said, "we've been busy. Maybe we're getting into a rut."

"Perhaps," Connor said, with rising conviction, "but the rut ends now! I'm taking you out. We're going to Max's."

Taking his hand, she turned to him, smiling. "Do you even know what *date* means?"

With a mischievous grin, he said assuredly, "I do. Trust me."

The cafe was nearly empty when they arrived. Connor guided Marisa into a booth, and a minute later, Lucy came by to take their order. Without looking at the menu, he said, "Let's have a hot fudge sundae, with vanilla ice cream, extra cherries, two spoons."

"Coming right up, sweetie," Lucy said, bustling off.

"You know exactly how I like it," Marisa said in a sexy voice as she leaned forward. Connor winked as she took each of his hands in her own and held them across the table, but Marisa's expression turned serious. "I've been wondering about us," she confessed. "This is so good, but is it too good? I mean, neither of us have seen anyone else the whole two years we've been in college. Do you think that's healthy?"

"Definitely not," Connor said, feigning concern. "If you can't see other people, you might need glasses."

"Come on! I'm trying to be serious," Marisa hissed with mild irritation.

"Actually," Connor said, removing the grin from his face, "I think that's the definition of healthy. What we have is great. A wonderful, healthy relationship."

"Yeah, this is fantastic, and I'm very happy, but…"

"But what?"

She released Connor's hands and ran her fingers through her hair nervously. After a long pause, she told him, "But we're so young. We're both just twenty. We're going to change, and…what if we're doing this all wrong? And we just won't know it until we're older? Isn't this the time in our lives when we're supposed to experiment? See different people? Get different perspectives? We only have a year left of college."

She was right. Due to each of them taking many advanced placement classes in high school, they were both on pace to finish their four-year degrees in just three years, as was Victor.

"Do you love me?" Connor asked her.

"Of course I do," she replied without hesitation.

Connor reclaimed her hands, squeezing them gently for emphasis. "Then we're not doing it wrong. I understand things didn't work out between your parents, and you're worried that will happen to us. But it's really very simple."

Marisa took the bait and said incredulously, "Oh, really? How is it so simple for you, Mr. Mackinson?"

"Two reasons," Connor whispered, leaning close to her. "First, remember what Pari told us. We're eternally bound to each other as family. That means you're betrothed to me, and therefore my princess."

Marisa chuckled. "Okay, Prince Charming. I don't think that's quite what she meant, but I'll give you points for creativity. What's the other reason?"

No longer whispering, he said, "It's a matter of simple logic. Simply apply Bayes' theorem."

Marisa withdrew her hands, intertwining her fingers underneath her chin. "I'm all ears. Let's see how you've reduced a matter of the heart into a logical proof," she said drily. "I'm trying to have a sincere, heartfelt conversation with you. We're not talking about computer science right now. I love you, babe, and I love that we're intellectual equals, but now isn't the time to be a scientist—it's time to speak from the heart. So, this better be good."

"Oh, it is," Connor said, brushing aside her frustration, "*and* it's from the heart. I love you with all my heart, and in a way, we're both Bayesians at heart. Now, Bayes' theorem helps us predict the probability something will happen, given that some other event has occurred. Let's look at the probability of Event A—that I will love you tomorrow—given Event B, which is that I love you today. You recall from Bayes' theorem that the probability of A equals the probability of A and B divided by the probability of B."

"This is from the heart?" Marisa said, shaking her head. "The heart of what? An android?"

"Please, just listen," Connor said holding up his index finger. "This means the more frequently event B occurs, the higher the probability of A is. I started to like you the day I met you, despite that stunt you pulled during tryouts. But I knew I *loved* you when you called me vanilla. I wanted to go well with everything with you, and I have loved you more and more each day ever since. So, the probability that I will love you for every day of the rest of my eternal life is greater than the probability that the sun will rise tomorrow."

With that, Connor reached into his pocket, got down on one knee, presented her with a ring, and asked, "My love, will you marry me?"

Marisa replied in a high-pitched, choked-up voice, "Oh, baby, for real?" As her eyes welled up, she asked incredulously, "You're doing this now, during *this* conversation? In Max's Cafe, of all places?"

Undeterred, Connor said lovingly, "What better place? This is the table where we sat on our first date. You said I was getting ahead of myself then when I called it a *date*, but turns out I wasn't ahead of myself then, and I'm not now. We possess all the evidence we'll ever need. Our love is irrefutable. So, honey, what do you say?"

She smiled as she tried to wipe the tears from her cheeks. The few other people sitting in the café were all staring at Connor, who was still down on one knee. Sobbing, Marisa said, "We still have a year left in school."

"We can wait a year to get married," he answered, continuing to offer her the ring box. "That's a suitable length for an engagement." He glanced down at the floor, then back up at Marisa. "Now, this ground is kind of hard, but like I told you the first time we came here almost two years ago,

I'll wait for you as long as I must. You're worth it. So, what do you say? Do you want to marry me?"

With tears of joy running down her cheeks, Marisa held out her trembling left hand and said, "I do."

CHAPTER 59 – FAST BREAK

Late Friday night, Victor found himself alone on a basketball court off campus underneath a waxing moon. After hoisting up a corner three-point air ball, he proceeded to chase it down. From behind him, he heard a voice shout, "Air ball!"

Not needing to turn around to identify the heckler, he chuckled as he continued running after the ball. Dribbling back to the court, Victor stopped in front of Connor and put the ball on the ground, then pulled his best friend into a hug.

"Congrats, bro!" Victor said, grinning. "She really said yes, right?"

Connor laughed as they separated. "I can't imagine why, but yeah, she did."

Victor handed Connor the ball. "Here, you start. Consider it an early wedding gift."

"Gee, thanks," Connor said sarcastically.

After a few missed shots, the game slowed down as Connor dribbled back to the top of the key. "Where's the time going?" he mused. "Two more terms after taking this summer off, and we're done with college."

"I know. Can't believe we've been here two years already. And now you're engaged, wow! Soon you two will be popping out babies—"

Connor hit a three and said, "Hold on. We'll have kids someday, but probably not for like five years at least."

"Sure," Victor teased, taking the ball up top, "that's what you say *now*, but since your life is on the fast track, I'd be surprised if you wait that long. I can't believe you two will be getting married at twenty-one."

Connor plucked the ball out of Victor's hands, but Victor quickly recovered it. "Hey, what can I say?" Connor said. "We've been living together for a year and a half, and it's great. It feels right, like we're meant to be together. When we get married, our daily lives won't change much. I'll still wake up next to her every morning and such."

"Yeah," Victor said, picking up his dribble, "but now you're committing to spending the rest of your lives doing that. That's huge."

"It is, but I have no doubts about it. She's the one I want to spend the rest of my life with."

"That's wonderful, man," Victor said as he fired up a three that rimmed out. "I told you she was a keeper. But wow, you're really settling down with your first girl, huh?"

Both of them raced for the rebound, and Connor reached it first. "What's the alternative? Let her get away? I can't imagine doing better. Even if I could, I wouldn't want to. She's incredible, and I feel incredible with her."

"And I'm happy for you," Victor said genuinely. "I think I'm just jaded, after everything that happened with Alison."

Far above the three-point line, Connor dribbled to catch his breath. "My parents were high school sweethearts. They've been married for over twenty-five years, and look at them."

"I know. My mom says they're the happiest couple she's ever met."

"Yeah," Connor replied with a proud smile. "So it *can* work. It will work."

Victor smiled back and told him with great conviction, "It sure will."

Connor drove to the hoop and missed a layup. The pace of the game picked up as their conversation died down. When Victor hit a mid-range jumper to win the first game, they took a water break.

"How are things with Tina?" Connor asked between sips.

"Good," panted Victor. "We're on the much slower track. We've only been dating for a few months now, and we aren't living together or anything yet. But it's good."

"I'm not surprised you two got together in the end. But what's the deal with Quinn?" Connor asked as they walked back onto the court.

"What do you mean?"

Connor chuckled. "I mean, you spend every Sunday with her. Does Tina get jealous?"

"Jealous? No, of course not. It's not like that. I'm not dating Quinn."

Tucking the ball under his arm, Connor said, "But you go on a recurring date with her every week, and it's only the two of you together."

"Well…" Victor said, trailing off and shrugging.

"I've seen you together," Connor said pointedly. "The two of you banter like a married couple."

Victor signaled with his hand for Connor to check the ball to start their next game. "I like Quinn, sure, but we're only friends. She's really witty, and we get each other, so that's why we have that banter, but—"

"I dunno, man. You two have a chemistry that seems like more than friendship," Connor insisted as they checked the ball. "What does Tina think of your relationship with Quinn? Does she pick up on what I do when she sees you two together?"

After a failed swipe for the ball, Victor told him, "She never sees us together."

Connor turned his back to Victor as he dribbled toward the basket.

"She used to avoid Quinn as much as possible for Quinn's sake," Victor reminded him. "She still holds herself responsible for what happened to Quinn all those years ago. I tell her all the time that it's not her fault, but… remember back in January, when Pari started bringing Quinn to Warp Drive to help with testing?" Connor nodded. "Even though she was only there once a week, it was hard for both of them. Quinn stayed civil, but she clearly didn't want to be around Tina. And since I was friends with both of them, I got stuck in the middle as their mediator or whatever. Every now and then, though, Quinn would let her guard down, and they would joke about something together at work. Tina liked when Quinn forgot her grudge. But right when Tina thought they might almost be friends, Quinn would always put her wall back up."

Throughout Victor's explanation, Connor listened to his friend without shooting. "So, Tina doesn't ever see you with Quinn?"

"No, but it's not like that," Victor said with a sigh.

"Now that you're dating, what if she told you to stop seeing Quinn?" Connor asked, idly tossing up an old-school skyhook.

Snatching the rebound with his right hand, Victor slapped his left hand on the ball and stood under the basket contemplatively. "I—I wouldn't. I couldn't stop seeing her. She's my friend, and I wouldn't abandon her."

"Do you love Tina?" Connor asked, looking his friend directly in the eye.

Uncomfortable with the conversation, Victor glanced away and began dribbling to the top of the key. "Man, I really like her, but it's too soon. But if she were to ask me to do that…"

Connor waited to hear how he would finish his thought. When he didn't, Connor finished for him. "To give up your friend?"

With indignation in his voice, Victor said, "Yeah! You don't give up your friends for a girl."

"Very true," Connor agreed. "Now, tell me this. Do you love Quinn?"

Agitated, Victor picked up his dribble. "Dude, we're only friends!"

Undeterred, Connor asked, "Do you think Quinn loves you, though? I've noticed the way she looks at you."

Looking up at the moon, Victor said exasperatedly, "Yeah, like a friend."

"Seriously, bro?" Connor demanded. "You can't possibly be that blind! How do you feel when you're with her?"

Still not dribbling, Victor fired back, "Okay, fine. Maybe there's some chemistry there, but we're *friends*, and that's it. I'm not going to cheat on Tina. Now, can we drop it?"

Connor swiped for the ball and said, "Just be careful. Don't break Quinn's heart."

Victor resumed dribbling. "I'm not leading her on or anything," he insisted, tossing up a three. The ball clanked loudly off the right side of the metal backboard, then rebounded straight to Connor, who caught the ball and dribbled it back beyond the three-point arc.

Neither spoke as Connor dribbled around the court without shooting. Victor was relieved to have a break from the interrogation.

"Do you think it's possible to be in love with two women at once?" Connor asked.

"Why, are you?" Victor asked sarcastically.

"I mean hypothetically. Like, maybe one woman in each world," Connor said, ignoring Victor's sarcasm while darting to his right.

Victor didn't bother to pursue him. In exasperation, he instead put his hands on his hips and said, "Maybe, but we aren't having this conversation! Goddammit! Can we please just drop it already?"

Connor nodded as his layup won the game. "Fine. We don't have to talk about it. What happens in Cendovia stays in Cendovia."

Victor took a minute to gather his composure as he drank from his water bottle. "I get what you were doing," he said with a chuckle. "You were just trying to distract me, so I wouldn't defend you. Well played."

"Yeah, exactly," Connor said, rolling his eyes as they began walking off the court.

"Okay, promise me this," Victor said, throwing his arm over Connor's shoulder. "When Marisa gets pregnant on your honeymoon, make sure she invites both Tina and Quinn to the baby shower."

After a long sip of water, Connor replied, "Um, you mean ten years from now? Will do."

CHAPTER 60 – MEET VIRGINIA

Out for an early morning walk, Richard found himself deep in thought. He didn't have a destination in mind when he left the house; he'd just wanted to walk.

In the three months since returning from his abduction, he had made preparing Cendovia his obsession. Now, at last, today was the day he'd been working toward for the past four years, since Virginia left him. Richard believed they were ready—at least he hoped they were ready. In truth, he couldn't be certain.

That was the thing about science; the discovery process didn't always uncover what one expected it to reveal. In the days when his science was innocently fueled by pure academic interest, he would comfort himself with this fact when things didn't work out how he'd intended. Now that lives were at stake, it wasn't so academic to him anymore. It had become very personal, and Virginia had never agreed to multiple resurrection attempts. So, they had only one chance to get this right.

Unconsciously, his legs had taken him to Holy Cross Cemetery, and he found himself standing in front of Virginia's empty grave as the sun started coming up. "Hi, sweetheart," Richard began softly. "It's been too long. I'm sorry I haven't visited more, but I think about you every single day." On the grass in front of her grave, he knelt and began running his fingers over her engraved name. "You know I've never been a very religious man. Unlike you, I don't believe in some magical spirit that lives beyond your body. There is no heaven. No hell. Though of course, I understand why we invented religion, as it's much more comforting than the truth.

"Yet, I can't stop being a scientist. I'm a skeptic by nature, which is why it was so agonizing for me when you were gone." Richard paused for a moment, overcome with emotion. "I suppose you could say that skepticism is my religion. But when it comes to an afterlife, I've lost all skepticism. With complete faith, I believe all dies with the flesh and blood. You left open the possibility that I was wrong about this. So, if you can hear me, I hope you think what I'm about to do is the right thing. Because although I miss you infinitely, I'm not miserable anymore. I feel guilty for telling you that, and for not being miserable without you, but I belong to a new family, and I know you'll love them."

He stood up, giving Virginia's gravestone one final caress. "This will be my last visit here. Soon, my love, I'll meet you on the other side."

Richard returned home and made himself a simple breakfast of coffee and toast. He turned on the television to watch the news as he ate. The anchorwoman began, "Yesterday, President Obama commemorated the seventieth anniversary of D-Day in Normandy…"

As the newscast continued, Richard kept finding his thoughts drifting back to his work, back to Virginia. Today would be his own private D-Day. The commemoration of a war in which millions had died underscored for him the importance of this resurrection. Slowly, he would start to wash the bloodstains from the hands of humanity.

When Pari walked in the front door and greeted Richard, he looked up at her and said, "I guess you don't knock anymore."

On the day of Virginia's funeral, Pari had promised that when this time came, she would be at Richard's side, whether he wanted her present or not. Richard's instinct had been to experience this personal moment privately, but he knew Pari was right—it wasn't healthy for him to be alone for this.

She glanced down at his pitiful breakfast and asked, "You ready?"

Taking his last bite of dry toast, he said emphatically, "I've been ready for four years."

They made their way down to the bunker and took their places—Richard at the computer, and Pari seated beside him. He started up his conversation with Richie and reminded his Cendovian self of his terms of surrender.

"*I bestow upon you the right of succession,*" Richard typed. "*If you accept it now, upon my death, you will be* the *Richard forevermore. Do you choose to accept the crown?*"

Seated on his balcony, overlooking another perfect Cendovian sunrise, Richie replied, "*I do.*"

Then Richard listed the remaining terms: "*To Virginia, you will be the only Richard. In time, she will learn of your brothers, but not today. You must be her guardian for all eternity. Understand that she will not yet be ready to fathom multiple of us. Going digital is already enough to take in. That means she cannot yet be told of me.*"

Again, Richie agreed to his instructions.

To finalize their preparations, Richard reminded him of the plan. *"I want one last chance to be her Richard. Then I will pass the torch to you. In your home office, she'll materialize at your desk. Remember, I want you to stay on the balcony. I'll message her through a computer on the desk, just as I am messaging you now. This will give me one last conversation with her. You'll get the live transcript on your phone. Once we're done, I'll tell her to walk outside to greet me, and she will see you. From there, you'll take the reins as the same person she was chatting with. You will then become her Richard."*

With overwhelming gratitude, Richie responded, *"Thank you so much, my brother. I'm ready. I was born for this."*

With folded arms, Richard asked himself if *he* was ready. For four years, he had been hell-bent on reuniting with Virginia. Now, he would do so only to say goodbye. But he knew that this was best for Virginia. A ghost in her phone wasn't what she needed. She deserved better than that. It was time to let her go, in order to be with her forever.

Nervously, Richard turned to Pari and took a few deep breaths to slow his heart rate. "It's not every day that you get to bring someone back to life," she said, throwing her left arm over his shoulder. "It's normal to be anxious, but it will work out perfectly. You'll see." Cupping his cheek with her right hand, she said, "Let's bring Virginia back."

With unsteady hands, Richard ran the code to revive his beloved wife. After all these years, he had so much to say, but froze when deciding where to start.

In the end, he simply entered, *"Hi."*

In a small office in a place unknown, a beautiful young woman sat in front of a computer and typed, *"Hi, Richard. Did you miss me?"*

ABOUT THE AUTHOR

Mark Hennessy has been developing software professionally for over twenty years. He has led small and large teams to success in various industries, including fantasy sports and human resources. His passion for programming began at an early age and he aims to share with the world his appreciation for what great development teams can accomplish. When not writing code or novels, Mark spends his time with his beautiful wife Lourdes and his two wonderful sons Logan and Colin.

SHARE YOUR THOUGHTS

If you enjoyed reading this book, please share your thoughts on Amazon or GoodReads. Reviews are great way to help readers learn about independent authors. Thank you for taking the time to read *The Cendovian*.

FOLLOW ONLINE

Stay tuned for news about The Cendovian Chronicles, including announcements of future editions in the series:

Website: Cendovia.com
Facebook: facebook.com/Cendovia
Twitter: @Cendovia

www.ingramcontent.com/pod-product-compliance
Lightning Source LLC
Chambersburg PA
CBHW030352310726
48979CB00001B/266

* 9 7 8 1 7 3 4 3 8 7 7 2 8 *